the Monster

USA TODAY BESTSELLING AUTHOR
L.J. SHEN

"Maybe we were never meant for each other. But that night at the carnival, when you showed me who you were, I figured out who I wanted to be."

The most important thing I'd ever read was scribbled on the door of a portable restroom, engraved into plastic at a carnival on the outskirts of Boston.

Lust lingers, love stays.

Lust is impatient, love waits.

Lust burns, love warms.

Lust destroys, but love? Love kills.

Maybe it was always my destiny to fall in love with a monster.

When other kids stayed awake at night fearing the pointy-toothed beast hiding in their closet, I longed to see mine.

I wanted to feed it, domesticate it, understand it.

Sam and I were only allowed to love each other in the dark.

Once our story unfolded, and the truth came to light, I was the one to cut the cord.

My name is Aisling Fitzpatrick, and I have a confession to make.

Sam Brennan is not the only monster in this story.

To monsters everywhere, and to sword-yielding Pang and Jan.
Thank you for storming into my life.

Playlist

"You Are in Love with a Psycho"—Kasabian

"Rock & Roll Queen"—The Subways

"I'm Not in Love"—Kelsey Lu

"Good Girls Bad Boys"—Falling in Reverse

"Wow"—Zara Larsson

"Listen Up"—The Gossip

"The End of the World"—Skeeter Davis

"What would an ocean be without a monster lurking in the dark?
It would be like sleep without dreams."
—Werner Herzog

Prologue

Sam

Age 9

THIS IS THE LAST TIME YOU EVER CRY IN YOUR LIFE, SHITHEAD.

That was the only thing that went through my head when the woman who gave birth to me punched the doorbell five times in a row, clutching the back of my shirt like she was disposing of some punk who'd TP'd her house on her neighbor's doorstep.

The door to Uncle Troy's penthouse swung open. She shoved me past the threshold.

"Here. All yours. You win."

I flung myself into the arms of Aunt Sparrow, who staggered backward, pulling me to her chest in a protective hug.

Sparrow and Troy Brennan weren't really my aunt and uncle, but I spent a lot of time with them—and by 'a lot', I mean still not enough.

Cat, AKA the woman who birthed me, was giving me away. She'd made up her mind tonight when she'd passed by me, on her way to her bedroom.

"Why are you so small? Pam's kid is your age, and he is, like, huge."

"Because you never fucking feed me." I flung my joystick to the side, giving her stink eye.

"You're, like, ten or eleven, Samuel! Make yourself a sandwich."

I was a nine-year-old and a malnourished one at that. But she was right. I should make myself a sandwich. I would if we had the ingredients for it. There weren't even condiments in our house, only drug paraphernalia and enough booze to fill the Charles River.

Not that Cat cared. She was blind with rage because I stole her cocaine and sold it to some wiseguys down the street then used the money to buy four McMeals and a Nerf gun, when she left me unattended tonight.

Grandma Maria was the one who did the heavy lifting when it came to raising me. She lived with us, working two jobs to support us. Catalina was in the background, like a piece of furniture. There, but not really. We lived under the same roof, but she moved out whenever her boyfriends were whipped enough to let her stay with them. She went to rehab centers, and dated married men, and somehow had money to buy expensive bags and shoes. Kids at school kept telling me their dads said Cat knew the curve of every mattress at our local Motel 6, and even though I wasn't sure what it meant, I was sure it wasn't good.

I once eavesdropped on Uncle Troy telling her, *"He is not the fucking Hamptons, Cat. You can't visit him periodically, when the weather allows it."*

Catalina had told him to shut his trap. That I was the worst mistake she had ever made while she was high.

That day, I got expelled. Beat the shit out of Neil DeMarco for saying his dad and mom were getting a divorce because of my mom.

"Your mom's a slut, and now I have to move to a smaller house! I hate you!"

I'd given him a different reason to hate me by the time I was done with him, one he would always remember because it changed his face.

When Cat picked me up, she'd yelled at me that she'd fuck up my face like I'd done to Neil, but I wasn't worth breaking her new nails over. I'd barely heard her. Everything inside my head was swollen from the fight and from thoughts that made my head hurt.

But I knew she'd be too cheap to take me to Urgent Care, so I didn't complain.

"All ours?" Aunt Sparrow narrowed her green eyes at Catalina. "What are you talking about? Today is not our day with Sam."

Aunt Sparrow had red hair and freckles and a body like a scarecrow, all bones and skin. She wasn't as pretty as Catalina, but I still loved her more.

Cat rolled her eyes, kicking the duffel bag with my stuff. It hit Uncle Troy's shins.

"Don't pretend like you haven't been gunning for this all along. You take him on your family vacations, he has a room here, and you go to all his soccer games. You'd breastfeed him if you had any tits, which sadly, you don't." Catalina swiped her eyes along Sparrow's body. "You always wanted him. He'll complete your boring little family, with your boring little daughter. Well, it's your lucky day, because the asshole is officially yours."

I swallowed hard and glared straight ahead at the flat screen TV behind Sparrow's shoulder. Their living room was a mess. The good kind of mess. Toys strewn everywhere, pink fluffy blankets, and a purple, glittery toddler scooter. *Brave* was playing on the screen. It was Sailor's favorite movie. She was probably asleep.

She had a bedtime. Rules. A routine.

Sailor was Troy and Sparrow's two-year-old. I loved her like a sister. Whenever she feared a monster was hiding under her bed and I was there, she'd slip out of her toddler bed and pad into my room and slide under my blanket, clutching me like I was a teddy bear.

"Keep me thafe, Sammy."

"Always, Sail."

"Not in front of the kid." Troy stepped toward Cat, putting space between her and me. My stomach growled, reminding me I hadn't eaten since those McMeals I'd shoved down my throat.

"Sam, can you give us a minute?" Sparrow ran her fingers through my dusty hair. "I got you that *Ghost of Tsushima* video game, like you asked. Grab a snack and play while we finish up here."

I took some beef jerky—Uncle Troy told me protein would help me grow taller—and disappeared into the hallway, rounding the corner but not getting into my room. I'd had my own room here since I was in first grade. Grandma Maria said it was because Troy and Sparrow lived in a good school district, and we needed their zip code to register, but even after I got expelled from my first school, I still came here often.

My "real" house was in a bad neighborhood in Southie, where tennis shoes littered every power line, and even if you didn't pick fights, you'd sure as hell need to finish them in order to survive.

Eavesdropping, I heard Troy growl, "What the *fuck*?" from the doorway. I liked how he said the word 'fuck.' The sound of it gave me whiplash, and the skin on my arms turned all funny. "Maria has barely been gone for three weeks, and you're already pulling shady shit."

Grandma Maria passed away in her sleep less than a month ago. I was the one who'd found her. Cat had been out all night, "working." I'd held Grams and cried until I couldn't open my eyes anymore. When Cat finally got home, with whiskey breath and smudged makeup, she told me it was all my fault.

That Grams was too tired of my bullshit and decided to bail.

"Can't blame her for kickin' the bucket, kid. I'd do the same if I could!"

I packed my duffel bag that same morning and hid it under my bed.

I'd known Cat wasn't going to keep me.

"First of all, watch your mouth. I'm still grieving. I lost my mother unexpectedly, you know," Catalina huffed.

"Tough shit. Sam never had *his* mother to begin with." Troy's voice made the walls rattle, even when he spoke calmly.

"The boy is untamable. Dumb as a brick and as aggressive as a stray dog. Me sticking around ain't gonna help. It's only a matter of time before he lands in juvie," my mother spat. "He's a monster."

That was her nickname for me. *Monster*.

The Monster did this.

The Monster did that.

"Look, I don't care what you and your perfect little wife think. It's just too much responsibility. I'm out. I can't send him to therapy and shit like that. I'm not made out of money." Catalina stubbed her heel on the floor. I heard her rummaging through her Chanel bag for her cigarettes. She wasn't gonna find them. I smoked half the pack in the backyard while she was getting high in her bedroom. The rest were in my bag.

"If money is an issue—" Sparrow started.

"*Bitch, please*," Cat cut into her words viciously, spluttering. "Keep your money. And I hope you are not dumb enough to think you're better than me, with all the help you're getting from your husband and harem of nannies and tutors. Sam's the spawn of the Devil. I can't do this alone."

"You're not doing this alone," Troy ground out. "We have shared custody of him, idiot."

Fire blazed in my chest. I didn't know Sparrow and Troy had legal custody over me. I didn't know what it meant, but it sounded important.

"Either you take him or I drop him off at an orphanage," Cat yawned.

In a way, I was relieved. I always knew once Grams died, Catalina would get rid of me. I spent the last few weeks worrying she'd set the house on fire with me in it to get insurance money or something. At least I was still alive.

I knew my mother didn't love me. She never looked at me. When she did, she told me I reminded her of *him*.

"*Same Edward Cullen hair. Same dead, gray eyes.*"

Him was my late father, Brock Greystone. Before he died, he was employed by Troy Brennan. Brock Greystone was weak and pathetic and a weasel. A rat. Everyone said so. Grams, Cat, Troy.

My worst nightmare was becoming like him, which was why Catalina always told me I was so much like him.

Then there was Uncle Troy. I knew he was a bad man, but he was an honorable one, too.

The wiseguys down my block said he had blood on his hands.

That he threatened, tortured, and killed people.

Nobody messed with Troy. Nobody kicked him out of the house or yelled at him or told him he was their worst mistake. And he had that thing about him, like ... like he was made out of marble. Sometimes I looked at his chest and was surprised to see it moved.

I wanted to be him so much that when I thought about it my bones began to hurt.

His existence just seemed louder than anyone else's.

Whenever Uncle Troy disappeared in the middle of the night, he always came back bruised and disheveled. He'd bring dunks and ignore the fact he smelled of gunpowder and blood. He would tell us bad jokes at the table while we ate, and to make sure Sailor wasn't scared anymore, he'd tell her he saw the monster family that lived in her closet move out.

One time he bled all over a donut, and Sailor had eaten it because she thought it was Christmas frosting. Aunt Sparrow was close to nuclear explosion. She'd chased him around the kitchen with a broomstick while Sail and I giggled, swatting it about and actually catching his ear twice. When she finally caught him (only because he let her), he captured both her wrists and lowered her to the floor and kissed her hard on the mouth. I thought I saw some tongue, too, but then she swatted his chest and giggled.

Everyone was so happy and laughed so much, Sailor had an accident, and she never had accidents anymore.

But then I'd felt my chest tighten because I knew they'd send me back to Cat later that afternoon. It reminded me I wasn't really a part of their family.

It was the only good moment I had. I'd play it over and over, lying in my bed, every time I heard Cat's bedsprings whine under the weight of a stranger.

"We'll take him," Sparrow announced coldly. "Off you go. We'll send you the paperwork as soon as our lawyer drafts the documents."

My chest filled with something warm just then. Something I'd never felt before. I couldn't stop it. It felt good. Hope? Opportunity? I couldn't put a name on it.

"*Red*," Troy breathed his wife's nickname.

And just like that, my insides turned cold again. He didn't want to adopt me. Why would he? They already had one perfect daughter. Sailor was cute and funny and *normal*. She didn't get into fights, hadn't been expelled three times, and definitely hadn't broken six bones in her body doing dangerous shit because pain reminded her she was still alive.

I wasn't an idiot. I knew where I was headed—the streets. Kids like me didn't get adopted. They got into trouble.

"No," Sparrow snapped at him. "I've made up my mind."

Nobody spoke for a moment. I got really scared. I wanted to shake Cat and tell her how much I hated her. That she should've died instead of Grandma Maria. That she *deserved* to die. With all her drugs and boyfriends and rehab trips.

I never told anyone how she used to give me shots of rum to make me sleep. Whenever Troy or Sparrow paid us surprise visits, she'd rub white powder on my gums to wake me up. She'd curse under her breath, threatening to burn me if I didn't wake up.

I was seven when I realized I was an addict.

If I didn't get the white powder daily, I shook and sweated and screamed into my pillow until I ran out of energy and passed out.

I was eight when I kicked the habit.

I'd just refused to let her give me rum or powder. Went crazy every time she came near me with that stuff. Once, I bit Cat's arm so bad a part of her skin stayed in my mouth, salty and metallic and hard against my teeth.

She never tried again after that.

"You're fucking lucky my wife is stubborn as hell," Troy hissed. "We'll take Sam, but there will be stipulations—and many of them."

"*Shocker*," Cat bit out. "Let's hear them."

"You'll hand him over and sign all the legal paperwork, no negotiations and without asking for a penny."

"Done," Cat cackled humorlessly.

"You'll fuck off from Boston. Move far away. And when I say far, Catalina, I mean somewhere he can't see you. Where the memory of his deadbeat mother doesn't burn hot. Another planet is preferable, but since we can't risk aliens meeting you and thinking we're all cunts, two states away minimum is my requirement. And if you ever come back—which I *sincerely* recommend against—you'll go through me if you wanna see him. You walk away from him now, you lose all your motherly privileges. If I catch you messing with this kid, *my* kid…" he paused for emphasis "…I *will* give you the slow, painful death you've been begging for almost a decade, and I will make you watch your own death in the mirror, you vain waste of oxygen."

I believed him.

I knew she did, too.

"You'll never see me again." Cat's voice rattled, like her throat was full of coins. "He is rotten to the core, Troy. That's why you love him. You see yourself in him. His darkness calls to you."

That was when I turned into a pillar of salt. Or at least that's how it felt. I was afraid if someone touched me, I would shatter.

I could be like Troy.

I had darkness. And violence. And all the things that made him great.

I had the same hunger and disdain for the world and heart that was just that—a heart—with nothing much inside it.

I could turn a corner.

I could be something else.

I could be *something*, period.

That was a possibility I'd never considered before.

Cat left not long after. Then Troy and Sparrow talked. I heard Troy pour himself a drink. They discussed lawyers and what to tell Sailor. Sparrow suggested they send me to a Montessori school, whatever the heck that was. I tiptoed my way to bed, too tired to care about my own future. My knees knocked together, and I felt the beef jerky crawling up my throat. I made a pit stop in the bathroom and puked my guts out.

Orphan. A mistake. A monster.

I didn't know how much time passed before they walked into my room.

I pretended to be asleep. I didn't want to talk. All I wanted to do was to lie there with my eyes closed, scared that they'd decide they didn't want me after all or that they were going to tell me something I didn't want to hear.

I felt my bed dip as Sparrow sat on its edge. I had Boston Celtics green and white linen, a PlayStation, a TV, and a Bill Russell jersey hanging on my wall. My room was painted green and full of framed pictures of me with Troy, Sparrow, and Sailor at Disney, Universal, and in Hawaii.

My room back in Cat's house was just a bed, a dresser, and a trash can.

No paint. No pictures. No nothing.

I never asked myself why.

Why the Brennans took me in.

Why I was a part of this fucked-up arrangement.

"We know you're awake." Troy's whiskey breath fanned my hair over my eyes, making my nose twitch. "You'd be an idiot to fall asleep on a night like this, and my son is no idiot."

I cracked my eyes open. His silhouette took up most of my room. Sparrow put her hand on my back, rubbing it in circles.

I didn't shatter.

I released a breath.

I'm not a pillar of salt after all.

"Are you my real pops?" I blurted out but wasn't brave enough to look at him when I asked. "Did you knock Cat up?"

I should've asked this long ago. It was the only thing that made sense. "You'd never give me the time of the day otherwise. You can't let me hang out here just because Grandma Maria once scrubbed your toilets. Am I a bastard?"

"You're not a bastard, and you're not mine," Troy said point-blank, averting his gaze to the window. The Boston skyline stretched out in front of him. All the things he owned and ruled. "Not biologically, anyway."

"I'm a Greystone," I insisted.

"*No*," he hissed. "You're a Brennan. Greystones don't have the heart gene."

I'd never heard about that gene. Then again, I skipped school most days in favor of smoking cigarettes outside bars and selling whatever it was I stole that day to help pay for my next meal.

"I ain't perfect," I sat up, glowering. "So if that's what you want, some perfect yes-kid, kick me out now."

"We don't want you to be perfect." Sparrow rubbed my back faster, harder. "We just want you to be ours. You are Samuel. A gift from God. In the Bible, Samuel was gifted to Hannah after years of praying. She thought she was barren. Do you know what barren means?"

"A woman who can't have kids." I shuddered. To have kids, you first had to make them, and I knew exactly how people went about making them—I caught Catalina practicing a bunch of times with her clients—and it was damn gross.

Sparrow nodded. "After Sailor was born, the doctors told me I couldn't conceive again. Turned out, I didn't have to. I have you. Your name means 'The Lord Hears' in Hebrew. *Shma-el.* God heard my prayers and surpassed my every expectation. You're exquisite, Samuel."

Exquisite. Ha. That was a word I'd use for a famous painting or some shit, not a nine-year-old ex cocaine addict, recovering alcoholic, who was an active smoker, and half the size of kids my age.

My childhood was such a bust, my innocence and I no longer shared a zip code, and if she thought a few home-cooked meals and some back rubs were going to change it, well, she was in for an unpleasant surprise.

"Tell me why I'm here. Why I'm not in an orphanage. I'm old enough to know," I demanded, balling my fists really hard, clenching my jaw. "And don't talk to me about the Bible. The Lord may have heard Hannah, but He sure as shit ain't been listening to me."

"You're here because we love you," Sparrow said at the same time Troy answered, "You're here because I killed your father."

Silence descended. Sparrow shot up from my bed, her eyes really wide and really big, staring at her husband. Her mouth hung open like a fish. Troy carried on.

"He said he deserves to know. He's not wrong, Red. The truth, Sam, is that shortly before your father died, he kidnapped Sparrow with every intention of killing her. I had to save my wife and did so without thinking twice. I wanted you to have a father figure. A person to look up to. The plan was to take you to basketball games every now and again. Provide guidance, advice, and a fat college fund to kick-start your life; getting attached was never in my plans, but it happened, anyway." He looked me right in the eye. "Very early on I realized you were not a project. You were family."

"You killed my father," I echoed.

I knew Brock Greystone was dead, but Catalina and Grandma Maria always said it happened in an accident.

"Yes," he said simply.

"Who knows?"

"You. Me. Cat. Aunt Sparrow. *God.*"

"Did God forgive you?"

Troy smirked. "He gave me you."

Depending on who you asked, that could be seen as a punishment.

Now Brock was dead, and Cat was gone. The Brennans were my only shot at survival, whether I liked it or not.

"All right?" Troy asked. With his Southie accent, it came out as "*Aight*?"

I stared at him, not sure what to think or do.

"I'm going to go get some dunks now." He leaned down to grab my shoulder bag, retrieving Cat's pack of cigarettes from it. It was close to midnight. He was definitely going to one of his "businesses."

"Donuts always make everything better," Sparrow pointed out, carrying on with the lie. "Be safe, honey."

He bent down to kiss the top of her head. "Always, Red. And you…" he tousled my hair with his massive palm "…no more cigarettes. This shit could send you to an early grave."

That was the moment I decided I was going to smoke until my lungs collapsed. Not because I wanted to defy Uncle Troy, but because dying young didn't seem like a bad idea.

When he left, I turned to Sparrow. My nerves were shot. I couldn't trust myself not to vomit again, but this time in her lap. And I never vomited, never cried.

"He didn't want to take me," I said.

She ran her fingers through my hair, brushing it back to normal. "No, he didn't. But only because he didn't want your mother to walk out of your life."

"But you didn't give a shit about that. Why?"

"Because I know no mother is better than a bad mother, and every day you were with her made my heart hurt."

"Grams left, too."

"She didn't leave, honey. She died. It wasn't up to her."

"I don't care. I hate women. I hate them."

"One day you'll find someone who changes your mind." Sparrow smiled privately, like she knew something I didn't. She was wrong.

Grams died and left me with Cat.

Cat almost killed me multiple times.

Women weren't reliable. Men weren't either, but men I could at least punch in the nuts, and men never made any promises. I didn't have a father or a grandfather to get mad at.

"I will never change my mind," I muttered, fighting my heavy eyelids that demanded I pass out.

I crashed in Sparrow's arms hours after Troy left.

When I woke up the next morning, I found a golden chain on my nightstand.

I scanned the Saint Anthony charm on it. My initials was engraved around the coin.

S.A.B.

Samuel Austin Brennan.

Years later, I'd learn Troy and Sparrow petitioned to legally changed my name from Greystone to Brennan the same hour they filed for full custody of me.

I knew who Saint Anthony was, the Patron Saint of all lost things.

I was lost, but now I'd been found.

Next to the necklace was a paper plate with a glazed donut and a hot cup of cocoa.

I was a Brennan now.

Boston underworld aristocracy.

Privileged, respected, and feared above all.

A legend in the making.

I intended to live up to my namesake at any price.

I would never be lost again.

My parents failed, but me? I'd prevail.

I would rise from the ashes and make them proud.

Would soar into the sky.

This was the first time I felt this way.

Certain.

Aisling

Age 17.

The heart was a monster.

That's why it was locked behind our ribs, in a cage.

I'd known this all along, from the moment I was born, but tonight I *felt* it, too.

Twenty minutes after taking the Mass Pike out of Boston, I finally came to terms with the fact that I was lost.

I drove with the windows rolled down, the humid summer air whipping at my wet cheeks. The tears kept on coming.

The scent of spring's blossoms lingered in my nostrils, heady and sweet, mixing with the crispness of the night.

She is never going to smell spring blossoms again.

To smile lopsidedly, like she is holding the secrets of the universe between her lips.

To press a dress against my chest and shimmy her shoulders excitedly, exclaiming it's, "Tres you!"

Why'd you have to do this, B?

I hate you, I hate you, I hate you.

In the distance, neon lights flashed from striped yellow and red tents. There was a giant sign in the middle of a glittering Ferris wheel.

Aquila Fair.

Drown.

I needed to drown.

In lights and smells and noises, with simple lives that weren't mine.

I took a sharp turn right.

I parked among the SUVs, beat-up vehicles, and sports cars, stumbling out of the Volvo in my black hoodie, cut-off shorts, and sneakers. The Daisy Dukes were my doing. I took scissors to an old pair of jeans and cut them off so that the curve of my ass was visible even from space. My attire usually resembled that of Kate Middleton. Prim, proper, and princess-like. But tonight, I wanted to piss *her* off for dying on me. To give her the middle finger for not sticking around.

"American girls show skin like men don't know what awaits under their garments. You, mon cheri, will make a man earn every inch of you, and dress appropriately and demurely, you hear?"

My feet carried me forward, the mouthwatering fragrance of cotton candy, buttered popcorn, and candy apple trickling into my system.

She didn't like it when I ate junk food.

Said Americans were in the habit of eating themselves into type 2 diabetes. *She* had a lot of ideas about Americans, all of them bordering on xenophobic, and I used to spend half my time arguing the merits of America with her.

Tents that offered live shows, vendors, and a small arcade surrounded the rides, serving as a border. The *ding-ding-ding* of machines, peppered with the mechanical noises from the rides, reverberated in my empty stomach. The Ferris wheel sitting in the center was bathed in an ocean of lights.

I bought myself pink cotton candy and a Diet Coke and walked around.

There were couples making out, laughing, fighting. Clusters of teenagers yelling and hooting. Parents screaming. Children running. I was irrationally, maddeningly angry with all of them.

For being alive.

For not grieving with me.

For taking for granted the rarity of their precious condition: alive, healthy, and well.

I tossed the remainder of cotton candy into a trash can and looked around, deciding what ride to go on first. From the corner of my eye, I noticed a giant sign.

The Creep Show: A Haunted Mansion Experience.

Haunted mansions were my playground.

I lived in one, after all—my house held the secrets of seven generations of Fitzpatricks—and I'd always been drawn to ghosts and monsters.

I took my place in line, shifting from foot to foot as I checked my phone. My mother and brothers were all looking for me.

Cillian: Where are you, Aisling? Call me back immediately.

Hunter: Yo, sis. You okay? Sounds like you were involved in some heavy shit. Sending hugz from Cali.

Mother: I heard what happened. Quite terrible, dear. Please come home so we can discuss this. So dreadful that you saw this.

Mother: You know how bad my anxiety gets when I can't get hold of you. You need to come back home, Ash.

Mother: Oh, Aisling, what am I to do? You didn't even make my herbal tea before you left. I'm a wreck over here!

That was my mother. Self-centered even when it was my world imploding into miniscule pieces. Always worried for her own well-being before mine.

I tucked my phone back in my pocket and craned my neck to look at the carts as they slid back from the jaws of an evil, laughing clown. Muffled screams bled from the inside of the ride. The people who came out stepped out of the carts with wobbly knees, buzzing with excitement.

When I was finally put in one of the wagons—it looked like a rickety pod with red paint smeared all over it to symbolize blood—I was alone, even though there was enough space for two people.

I knew nothing would happen to me on a fair ride.

Still, I felt lost, fragile, and unbearably lonely tonight. Like someone had peeled away my skin in one go and left me to carry my bones and veins and muscles in a messy heap.

I'd just lost my best friend. The only one that counted.

I grabbed onto the shirtsleeve of the guy manning the ride, tugging.

"I want to get off."

He gave me a slow once-over, his gaze lingering a second too long on my bare thighs.

"Hell, sugar, I'd like to get you off, too. But you'll have to wait till the end of my shift. I need the money," he slurred, sounding stoned.

I clutched onto his Hurley hoodie sleeve, throwing fourteen years of etiquette lessons out the window in one moment of desperation. "No! I want to get off the ride. Unless you can put someone in the cart with me?" Hope trickled into my voice.

"Bro, it's, like, a ride anyone four feet or over can get on." He shook my touch off, frowning. "You'll make it out alive."

"I know. It's not that I'm scared. I just—"

"Look…" he raised a hand to stop my stream of words "…if I don't press that red button over there every three minutes, I lose my job. You getting out or sucking it up?"

I was about to answer that it was fine, that I was just being silly, when someone stepped forward, cutting the entire line behind them.

"She'll suck it up, Sir Smokes-a-Lot."

A curtain of unshed tears blocked my vision, and I knew if I blinked it away, everyone would see I was crying. I was so embarrassed I wanted to die. Blurry Stoner Guy pushed the metal rail open obediently, muttering a quick hello to the stranger approaching us, ducking his head down.

The person slid into my cart, pulling the metal bar against our waists, flicking a cigarette sideways, an umbrella of smoke cocooning us together.

I wiped my eyes, mouthing a mortified *thank you*. When I looked up, our gazes collided, and my insides crushed like a glass ceiling shattered by a supernova.

Him.

I didn't know him, but I dreamed of him.

I'd dreamed of this man every night since I was nine.

Since I'd started reading kissing books under the covers about brave knights and the princesses who loved them.

Beautiful and princely, with eyes that could see through your soul.

He looked to be in his early twenties. With tawny, wind-swept hair tousled in untidy sexiness. His eyes were two silver moons—the kind that change color in different lights. His skin glowed, like he'd been dipped in gold, and he was so tall his knees poked out of the cart. He wore a black V-neck that clung onto his muscular chest and biceps and black jeans ripped at the knees.

A Saint Anthony charm was wrapped around his neck, held by a tattered leather string.

"I—I'm Aisling." I stuck my hand out to him. Our cart jerked forward and whined as two girls my age jumped into the pod behind us, gossiping hotly about a girl named Emmabelle who used to go to school with them and apparently had sex with half the football team then sucked off the other half.

He ignored my outstretched hand. I swallowed, withdrawing my hand and dumping it in my lap.

"Bad night?" His eyes lingered on my puffy eyes.

"The worst." I didn't even have the good manners to smile politely.

"I highly doubt that."

"Oh, I'll bet you anything my night is going worse than anyone else's in this carnival."

He offered me an arched eyebrow, showing me his handsomeness had a devilish quality to it, the kind I suspected very few women could resist.

"I wouldn't bet with me."

"Oh? Why's that?"

"I always win."

"There's a first time for everything," I murmured, starting to think he was a little too confident for my liking. "I bet you anything I'm having the worst night out of all the people in this carnival."

"Is that right? *Anything?*"

"Within reason." I straightened my back, remembering myself. *She* always told me to behave a certain way. If she was a ghost hovering above me right now, she would not appreciate my attire. The least I could do was not lose my virginity to this handsome stranger in a stupid bet.

"I'm guessing you're the sensible one." He twisted his lighter between his long fingers, back and forth, a movement I found oddly soothing.

"One, out of …?"

"Your siblings."

"How do you know I have siblings at all?" I felt my eyebrows rise in surprise.

He stared at me boldly, his eyes saying things no stranger had any business telling me. It was like the world was his, and since I was a part of it, he could have me, too. Suddenly, I realized whatever was happening here was very odd and at least somewhat dangerous.

I wanted to strip for this man, and I'd never wanted to strip for any man, for any reason, especially not romantic reasons—and I didn't mean just my clothes.

I wanted to make him explode like a piñata, clawing into his gut, unearthing every single quality, trait, and bad habit that he had. Who was he? What was his story? Why did he talk to me?

"You think you're nothing special," he said softly.

"Do people think they're special?"

"Those who aren't do."

"I'm guessing you're the troublemaker out of your siblings." I tucked my hair behind my ears. He smirked, and I felt it in my bones. The way the air heated up just because he was content.

"*Bingo.*"

"You must've been a hellion growing up." I cocked my head sideways, as if a different angle would show me a picture of him when he was nine or ten.

"I was such a troublemaker, my mother threw me out when I was nine."

"Oh, I'm sorry," I piped up.

"I'm not. I dodged a bullet."

"And your dad?"

"He didn't." The man retrieved a cigarette pack he kept in his rolled-up shirtsleeve, a-la Jack Nicholson in *One Flew Over the Cuckoo's Nest*. He cupped his palm over his mouth and lit another cancer stick. I noticed Stoner Guy saw and didn't say a word. "He was shot when I was a kid."

"Deservingly?" I heard myself ask.

"Very much so." Hot Stranger sucked on his cigarette, the orange ember flaring like that thing behind my ribcage. "How 'bout your folks?"

"Both alive."

"But someone else isn't. Otherwise, you wouldn't be crying." He exhaled a spiral of smoke skyward. We both watched as the gray mist above us evaporated.

"I lost someone tonight," I admitted.

"Who?"

"No offense, but that's none of your business."

"None taken, but just for the record..." he tilted my chin up with the hand holding his cigarette "...everything in Suffolk County is my fucking business, sweetheart, and right now, you're within county limits, so think again."

An odd feeling washed over me. Fear, desire, and kinship battled inside me. He was direct and aggressive, a fighter. As unlikely as it sounded, I knew he and I were cracked in the same place, even though we'd both been broken in different ways.

Our cart began to move, slicing through a black vinyl curtain. A giant, plastic zombie leaned forward from a veil of green smoke, laughing lowly into my ear.

"The monster's gonna get ya."

There were beasts twirling, screaming zombies that spat water in our faces, and a family of corpses having dinner. A baby's red eyes shot lasers at us.

The train of carts ascended to the top, slow and steady. People all around us squeaked in excitement.

"Do you ever feel lost?" I whispered.

The stranger laced his fingers with mine on the scratched plastic bench beneath us. His hand was warm, dry, and calloused. Mine was cold, soft, and sweaty. I didn't pull away, even when danger began humming around me, thickening the air, depriving me from oxygen.

Play with monsters, but don't be surprised when you get beaten.

"No. I had to find myself at a young age."

"Lucky you."

"I wouldn't use that word to describe me." He chuckled.

"Not Irish, then?" I couldn't help but probe.

He didn't *look* Irish—he was too tall, too broad, too tan—but he had that Southie accent most blue-collar Irish men sported.

"Depends on how you look at it," he answered. "Back to the subject at hand—your being lost."

"Yes, right." I cleared my throat, thinking about *her* again. "I don't think I'll ever find myself. I don't have many friends. In fact, I only had one really true friend, and she died today."

"There is nothing to find. Life is not about finding yourself. It's about creating yourself. There's something liberating about knowing your own bones, all the things you are capable of. Being unapologetically yourself makes you invincible." His voice seeped into me, hitting roots. Our fingers tightened together. Our cart jerked here and there while zombies sent arms flying in our direction, trying to catch us. People around us giggled and screamed.

He hadn't said he was sorry for my loss like everyone else had. "And who are *you*?" I breathed.

"I'm a monster."

"No, really," I protested.

"It's true. I thrive in the dark. My job is to implement fear, and I am some people's nightmare. Like all monsters, I always take what I want."

We reached the highest point. The peak.

"And what I want right now, Aisling, is to kiss you."

The cart jerked back, screeched, then tipped down, falling at an increasing speed.

The stranger muffled my scream with his mouth. His hot, salty lips sealed mine possessively. All my inhibitions, fears, and anxiety evaporated. He tasted of cigarettes, mint gum, and sex. Like a *man*. I let go of the rails, clutching the thin fabric of his black shirt, drawing him close, drowning in what we were in that moment. A monster devouring a princess, with no knight in sight to save her.

He tilted his head and cupped my cheek, his other hand cradling the back of my head. His tongue prodded my mouth open, touching mine—gently at first—before I let our kiss deepen. Our tongues twisted together, dancing, teasing, searching. My stomach dipped, and my anxiety dissolved.

The world felt different. Brighter. Bigger.

Warmth pooled between my legs, and my groin rocked forward on its own accord. I felt achingly empty. I squeezed my thighs together just as I felt a lash of fresh air on my face.

The ride was over.

We were back out.

He broke our kiss, drawing back, his face expressionless. Terrifyingly calm.

The girls in the cart behind us mumbled "holy shit" and "that was hot" and "yeah, it's definitely him, Tiff."

Him who?

"First kiss, huh?" He wiped a smudge of saliva from the corner of my mouth with his thumb, cold amusement dancing in his eyes. Like I was a toy. Something laughable, replaceable. "You'll get the hang of it."

The girls behind us giggled. My soul fired up its imaginary laptop and opened Zillow in search of a suitable place to bury myself from shame.

"Are you seriously not going to tell me your name?" My voice came out hoarse. I cleared my throat. "Imagine if you really were my first kiss. I could be scarred for life. You might traumatize me. I'd never be able to trust another man again."

Stoner Guy flung the metal bar open, striding down the line of carts. "Time's up. Everybody out."

The stranger smoothed my hair away from my face.

"You'll survive," he croaked.

"Don't be so sure."

"Don't underestimate me. I know a whole fucking lot about people. Besides, I already told you, my name is Monster."

"Now, that might be your nickname—" I started.

"Nicknames are more telling than birth names."

I happened to agree. My father called my older brother, Cillian, *Mo Orga*, which meant "my golden" in Irish Gaelic, and my middle brother, Hunter, *Ceann Beag*, which meant "little one."

He never nicknamed me anything.

My name meant vision, a dream. Perhaps that's all I was to my father. Something that wasn't real, tangible, or important. I was meant to be an idea. A pretty vessel for him to parade and exhibit.

A little daughter, pretty, prim, and proper, without the pressure of breeding me for some big role. To take over his company one day. To give him male heirs to continue his legacy. I was my mother's gift from him, and I played my role, doting over her, fulfilling her every whim, and filling the hours he was away on business with shopping trips, doing each other's hair, and more.

Now I was planning to go to med school so when I graduated, I could also take care of her physically. Jane Fitzpatrick always did detest visiting her doctors. She said they were judging her, misunderstanding her.

I couldn't wait for the day I'd be qualified to replace her physician and check another box in the impossible wish list my parents had set out for me.

"I'm not afraid of monsters." I squared my shoulders.

Pleased with my answer, he flicked my chin. "Maybe you're one of us. You just said yourself you don't know who you are."

I tried to go after him. I wasn't too proud to follow him around, ask him what he meant. But he was quicker, sliding out of the cart quickly, and with the feral grace of a tiger, he walked away.

He disappeared in the throng of swirling lights and bodies, evaporating into thin air, as monsters did.

I came here to drown.

Now, I could hardly breathe.

Three hours later, I was still buzzing with adrenaline and pain. I tried all the rides. Ate too much candy. Drank root beer on a bench and people-watched. The distraction did not dull the pain. I continued to play the moment I found out she was dead over and over again in my head like I was trying to punish myself for ... what? Not stopping it? Not getting there sooner?

There was nothing I could have done to prevent it.

Wasn't there? She asked you for help. You never gave it to her.

I looked for Monster all night, even when I didn't mean to. My eyes wandered, scanning the lines and couples and throngs of people.

I wondered if I'd made him up in my head. Everything about our encounter seemed unreal.

When I took a restroom break at the portable toilets, I noticed the back of the door was freshly engraved with words. Words that seemed intimately directed to my eyes.

Lust lingers, love stays.

Lust is impatient, love waits.

Lust burns, love warms.

Lust destroys, but love? Love kills.

S.A.B.

When the clock hit midnight, I gave up. I wasn't going to find him.

My phone was blowing up, and I knew my parents were going to send a search unit if I didn't come back home.

A missing seventeen-year-old girl was a non-issue if it had only been eight hours since you'd last seen her.

A missing seventeen-year-old oil heiress whose daddy was one of the richest men in the world sure was, though, and I had no doubt my family would raise a ruckus.

I was a Fitzpatrick, and Fitzpatricks should always be protected.

I glanced at my phone again.

Mother: I am getting increasingly worried. Just text me, please. I understand that you are upset, but you are upsetting us all by disappearing like this! I cannot get any sleep. You know how much I need my sleep.

Mother: Your father will be blaming me for this entire ordeal. I do hope this pleases you, Aisling. Getting me into trouble.

Oh, *Merde*. Put a lid on it, Mother.

Hunter: Da will have a heart attack, sis. Just sayin' (more hugz from Cali).

Cillian: Stop being so emotional. She was the hired help.

Da: I am sorry for your loss, Ash. Please come home.

Leaves crunched beneath my feet as I made my way to Mom's

Volvo XC90. I was about to swing the door open, get inside, and gun it back to Avebury Court Manor, our house. That was when I heard it. A crunch that had nothing to do with my feet. My head snapped up in the darkness. Toward the edge of the parking lot, about three cars down from my vehicle, was a corner nestled between a thick line of trees leading to the woods by the highway. Secluded and dark.

"No, no, no. Please. I know I fucked up, but I promise, I'll stop." Someone wailed. A man.

I squinted, ducking between my car and an Impala, peeking at the two figures under a thick mass of leaves. One of them was standing, holding a gun. The other was on his knees, in front of the standing figure, like he was praying to a merciless god. Maybe it was the fact I'd already witnessed one death tonight, but even though my adrenaline kicked in, I couldn't muster the hysteria I probably ought to feel right now.

"Lying will get you nowhere," the standing man clipped harshly.

"What makes you think I'm—"

"Your lips are moving," the standing man kicked the man on his knees with the tip of his shoe, eliciting an animalistic wail. "I told you there won't be a third time."

"But I—"

"One last wish, Mason," the man *tsked*, and my blood ran cold because I recognized that voice. I would recognize it anywhere, I realized, from tonight until the very last day of my life.

It was the voice of Monster.

My monster.

The man who gave me my first kiss.

The guy on his knees was trembling, trying to contain his frightened tears. He shook his head then finally, blurted out, "If Nikki asks, tell her it was drug-related. I don't want her to know the truth. She's suffered enough."

"I will. Goodbye."

With that, Monster used the gun pressed to the man's forehead and popped off two bullets. From the dull thuds, I gathered there was a silencer on the gun. I slapped a hand over my mouth, muffling a horrified scream that ripped out of my throat.

He'd killed a man.

He'd killed a man out in the open.

And he hadn't even *blinked*.

My legs shook, and I fell to the ground, the concrete biting into my knees. I scrambled for my keys in my hoodie, my knees hot with fresh blood oozing out of them from my fall.

Run, Merde. Run.

I unlocked the Volvo and glided into the driver's seat, frantically wiping the tears and sweat from my face to clear my vision, biting on my lower lip to suppress a scream.

This night is not happening. It's just a figment of your imagination.

A slam on the window beside me made me jump so high my head hit the car's roof. I twisted my whole body and saw it was Monster. He must've caught sight of me, or worse … heard my scream. With shaking fingers, I started the car, blinded by tears. The Monster jammed something into the side of the door casually, unlocking it with terrifying ease, preventing me from throwing the car into reverse.

He parked his hands on the car's roof, his biceps bulging from his short sleeves, looking blasé and indifferent.

"You're having one hell of a night, aren't you, little Aisling." The deadly calm in his voice made everything so much worse.

"I didn't see anything," I exclaimed, jerking back, like he was going to strike me.

To my surprise, he started laughing. Wholeheartedly. A guttural noise that sounded weird coming from him, like he wasn't used to laughing.

"Now you believe that I'm a monster?" He leaned forward, his lips hovering close to mine. My blood turned to ice, and yet, for the life of me, I couldn't pull away this time. *It must be the shock*, I told myself. This was a fight-or-flight situation, but my traitorous body went for secret option number three: freeze.

No. This wasn't just fear. There was something else thrown into the mix. Something hot and pungent. Something I didn't want to know about myself.

Know your bones.

This beast just put two bullets in someone's head, and yet here I was, my body humming, sizzling, begging to be touched by him.

"Are you actually going to let me kiss you?" He furrowed his brows, his lips practically moving over mine. I was spellbound. Speechless. I had to move.

Move, Merde. Move.

Finally, I managed to shake my head no.

He tugged my lower lip between his teeth, sucking on it teasingly then swiping his tongue over the inside of it.

"You're a beautiful liar, Aisling." His low tenor vibrated in my stomach. "Guess you found yourself, then. You're a monster, too." He kissed me again, with lips and teeth, before finally pulling away.

"Tell anyone about this, and I will find you, and I will kill you, too. Now, I suggest you run. Far and fast. I'm giving you a two-minute head start before coming after your ass."

With that, he turned around and ambled away, the streetlamps catching his silhouette and making him look like the complex villain you secretly root for in a film noir, sliding into a car parked a row from mine.

Slow. Steady. Lethal.

I floored it, never looking back.

Driving so fast, the car whined and died as soon as I got home.

Shortly after the Aquila Fair, my brother Hunter came back from California for good.

Golden, tan, and blonder than ever. He moved into a penthouse downtown with a girl named Sailor, who'd been hired as his babysitter. I'd seen her a few times, when her mother used to cook for us on special occasions.

Da liked to rule all of us with an iron fist, and Hunter was by far the hardest to tame.

A few days after Hunter and Sailor moved in together, I'd visited him at his penthouse. Sailor was out, and he was taking one of his extras long showers, which I suspected involved a lot of self-pleasuring, seeing as he wasn't allowed to date anyone since moving back to Boston.

I gave myself a tour around the living room, which looked like it had been staged by a professional before being put on the market for sale. Everything was too neat, too shiny, too modern to look livable. The only hint that people actually lived here was a row of pictures sitting on the mantel by the floor-to-ceiling window. Even before approaching them, I knew they were put there by Sailor, not Hunter.

Hunter never did consider himself to have a true family, and seeing as he'd lived away from the house since age six, I couldn't exactly blame him.

My curiosity got the better of me, and I walked over to the mantel. The first picture was of the young redheaded woman, which I recognized as Sailor, her face youthful and full of freckles, hugging a middle-aged, dark-haired man and an older replica of herself, whom I recognized as Sparrow.

The second picture was of the redheaded girl at a party with two blonde women her age. They were all laughing, wearing goofy neon sunglasses.

I recognized them as the Penrose sisters. They were on the local news the other day, for shoveling snow outside senior citizens' houses.

The third …

The third was a picture of Sailor and the Monster.

My monster.

The guy from the carnival.

He stared into the camera, looking grim and serious, while she looked at him like he was the moon. Her spot of light in the endless darkness.

"Yup. That's her. My ball-busting roommate," I heard a voice behind me and jumped back with a gasp, slapping a hand over my chest, afraid my heart would accidentally leap out.

I turned around quickly and offered Hunter a polite smile. We were still more acquaintances than siblings.

"She looks beautiful."

He shrugged, sauntering deeper into the living room with a towel wrapped around his waist and nothing else, his blond hair dripping water. "She's okay."

"I'm guessing those are her parents." I pointed at the first picture, playing innocent. He nodded.

"And these two?" I moved to the Penrose sisters, playing dumb. My heart pounded in my chest. I didn't know why, but I had a feeling about these girls. This group. I wanted to be a part of them.

"Persephone and Emmabelle. Her best friends. They're sisters. Another bucket list dream I can't fulfill because Sailor is on my case."

"What do you mean? What do you want to do to them?"

"I want to do *them*." He rolled his eyes, looking at me like I was a complete moron.

"And who is this guy?" I asked nonchalantly, pointing at Monster. This was it. My big moment to find out his name. I didn't know what I was going to do if I found out he was her boyfriend. How could I tell my brother that he was living with a woman who was dating a murderer?

But no. That wasn't the thing that bothered me the most about the idea of Sailor and Monster being together. It was the fact that he had a girlfriend. That he had moved on. Of course he would. All we shared was a kiss and a theme park ride.

I thought I was going to be sick.

"That's Sam Brennan." Hunter ran his fingers through his hair, pushing it back. "Her brother. Well, adoptive brother, I guess. Her parents adopted him when she was barely a toddler. A real piece of work and the current number one mobster in Boston. All the gangs and mafia families on the East Coast have a bounty on his head. His chances of reaching an old age are below zero."

The Monster was a mobster.

No surprises there.

But now he had a name, an identity, a context.

Things were about to become very complicated.

Aisling 18, Sam 26.

"For heaven's sake, Aisling, what are you doing? They're here. Hurry up!" Mother chided me, her heels clicking on the marble floor behind me. My mother's delicate fingers wrapped around my wrist, tugging me.

"Come on, you know I don't do small talk very well. You'll need to save me from mingling. Especially with the matriarch. She works for a living. You know I don't do well with the middle class."

I followed her to the foyer, a boulder the size of Connecticut settling in the pit of my stomach.

Today was the day my parents decided to invite Sailor's family for dinner. Mother wanted to get to know the Brennans. Well, that was her main excuse. Really, she just wanted to force Hunter to visit her.

Even though Hunter was against the arrangement, I'd met Sailor plenty of times since they moved in together. We became fast friends after a peculiar charity ball we'd both attended, in which she introduced me to Persephone and Emmabelle.

She was funny, quick-witted, and loyal. But no matter how much I tried, I couldn't get her to talk about Sam. She was crazy protective of him, and every time I asked about her family, she changed the subject.

The butlers swung the double doors open. The Brennans stood on the other side. Mrs. Brennan, with tangerine hair and sharp emerald eyes, held a steaming dish in her hand.

Sam's eagle eyes snapped to mine. The unpleasant curl of his lips warned me not to act like we'd previously met. Seeing each other wasn't a surprise to either of us. I had no doubt Sam knew his sister lived with my brother.

He never bothered to seek me out.

My father, oblivious to my gigantic internal meltdown, conducted the introductions.

"And this is my daughter, Aisling." *Athair*—father in Gaelic— waved his hand in my direction, like I was a decorative ornament. Gerald Fitzpatrick was a plump man with a face the color of a shrimp, beady eyes, and three chins.

Sam offered me half a nod, barely glancing my way.

"Pleasure to meet you," I said steely. Sam ignored me.

My brother Cillian stood tall and imposing yet still looked small in comparison to Sam.

"Don't even look at her, Mr. Brennan. Aisling is prime rib. Not a hotdog and therefore not on your menu."

"Cillian, for shame." Mother clutched her pearls, like she hadn't shared his opinion. Sam grinned, taking his phone out and checking something, like our presence around him didn't even register.

Cillian walked over to Troy, Sam's dad.

"May I offer you and your wife a tour of Avebury Court Manor?"

The man sized him up. My guess was our mansion interested Troy Brennan just a tad less than the state of the weather in Gambia.

"You may, but I'll pass," Troy drawled, "on the grounds that you're a cun—"

"We'd love a tour!" Sparrow elbowed her husband's side.

Sam tucked his phone back in his pocket, indifferent to the

awkwardness. Judging by the introductions alone, tonight was going to be long and painful.

"Aisling, go with them while I check on the cook. See if they need anything," Mother instructed, and I knew what it meant.

Keep them company so I don't have to. So I can fix myself a drink and hide in my room a little longer.

I fell into step behind Troy, Sparrow, Cillian, and Sam. His casual jeans and tee were replaced with gray slacks and a black button-down shirt. His hair was cropped closer to his scalp. His shoulders were so broad they blocked half the hallway.

We were the only two people who didn't engage in small talk, although both Troy and Cillian seemed painfully bored with Sparrow's sourdough bread recipe, which included letting the dough "rest" in the sun, feeding it, talking to it, and generally treating it like a Tamagotchi.

We ascended the stairs to the second floor. My house was terrible. Soulless and glitzy, like an endless hotel lobby. Limestone and gold accents winked from every direction; dramatic curtains and fountains attacked your eyeballs no matter where you looked. If *nouveau riche* had a face, it would be Avebury Court Manor.

Cillian showed the Brennans the left wing, also known as the family hall, filing through our rooms as he recited our family's history like we were the Kennedys.

Sam slowed his stride gradually. At first, I didn't think it was intentional, but soon, we were walking at the same pace, eight feet away from the rest.

He was the first to speak.

"Suffering from a jock itch?"

I gave an unwavering smile that did nothing to calm my nerves but didn't answer. His presence alone had me feeling disoriented, excited, and manic.

"You're awfully slow," he continued. His husky voice trickled into my system, like sweet venom.

"You're awfully rude."

I stared ahead at our families' backs. Cillian was standing in front of a portrait of Cormac Fitzpatrick, the first-generation Fitzpatrick who arrived in Boston after the Great Famine. Troy and Sparrow looked about ready to fling themselves out the French windows.

"Found yourself yet?" he inquired.

Not even close.

I felt my cheeks reddening under my makeup. "I had a bad night that night."

"That doesn't answer my question." He chuckled.

Cillian shot us a frown. "Hurry up. And remember, Brennan, I'm watching you."

Sam smiled at my brother, who was only a few years older than him. "Like what you see, Fitzpatrick?"

"Not even remotely." Cillian narrowed his eyes.

"A word to the wise: I don't like being told what to do, but for the right price, I can be motivated into doing just about anything."

"And you're proud of that?" Cillian drawled.

"Immensely. You'll be lining up for my services the minute Daddy isn't able to pull you out of whatever bullshit you get yourself into."

"Don't hold your breath," Cillian muttered.

Sam slowed his pace. It didn't surprise me Sam didn't care about Cillian's warnings.

"My brother is a character," I said defensively.

"That's just a nice way of calling someone an asshole. Sailor tells me you're going to med school."

I nodded curtly.

"Why?"

"I want to help people."

"No, you don't."

We officially lost our families. Cillian was too busy showing Sparrow and Troy the library, our family's pride and joy. Sam stepped under a little alcove with a window overlooking our vineyard, snatching my wrist and tugging me with him out of sight.

34

I gasped, digging my nails into my palms, half-crescents of anxiety and anticipation denting my skin.

"You kept your mouth shut." He looked at me like he wanted to touch me.

I knew what he meant. I never went to the police. Never said anything about the man he killed.

"I'm trustworthy."

"Most people aren't," he said.

"I'm not most people."

"I'm starting to see that. Listen carefully now. Your daddy is a very rich and important man, and I'm a very ambitious and a very bad man. I want his business, and nothing is going to stand in my way, least of all you. So stay the fuck away from me and don't give me those puppy eyes, begging to be fucked right there in front of your entire immediate family, like you are doing right now. You have no idea what you're asking for. Men like me eat girls like you for breakfast. And not in a pleasurable way. You got that?"

I did. The game was over before it had even started. Sam was a monster, and I was a princess stuck in an ivory tower, bound to be saved by someone else. His adversary, probably.

I nodded, even though my head hurt and the back of my nose and eyes pinched with tears.

"Yes. But …"

He raised an eyebrow, waiting for more. I didn't know what to say.

"Yes?" he hissed, finally.

"One last kiss," I murmured. "I won't tell. You know I'd never tell."

He seemed to consider this, before tilting his head down toward mine.

"One kiss," he whispered, his body brushing mine. "One last measly, stupid kiss. And don't you dare come back for more again."

My lips fell open.

He gave me a lustful, devastating kiss. It was bold and demanding and sexy, and it created a damp, cold spot in my panties. He sucked my lower lip into his mouth, and I whimpered, biting him desperately in response, not sure what I was doing but doing it anyway. My hands found his hair, tousling it. His tongue stroked mine. I wanted to feel it between my legs, and brushed my breasts against his chest, chasing the friction.

He laughed into my mouth.

"You're feral."

"I know," I grumbled. "I'm sorry."

"Don't be. I fucking love it."

Love. The way he said that word made my toes curl inside my pumps.

He grabbed me by my butt cheeks and hoisted me so that my thighs encircled his leg. His fingers dug into my flesh as he ground me up and down his muscular thigh, giving me much more than the friction I was after. Each movement made my clit scrape against the fabric of my panties. It was like he was rubbing two twigs together to create fire, and the fire was a climax, climbing up my spine from my toes.

"I feel like I'm ... I'm ..." I tried to articulate what it was, but I couldn't. It felt like floating and crashing at the same time. I was quivering. I wanted him to do more of the things he knew how to do that would make me feel this way.

"Empty?" he hissed into my mouth, his tongue wrestling mine.

"Yes. That's it. I feel so empty."

"I wish I could fill you with my fat cock."

"Oh," I cried as he rubbed me against him faster and harder, and everything inside me clenched, my muscles bunching.

"God ... I'm ... I mean, *am* I ...?"

There was nothing I hated more than not knowing. I knew everything there was to learn from textbooks and webminers. But I didn't know this. It made me feel like a kid. Like a cliché.

He laughed when it happened. When a wave of warm pleasure descended on my body, little earthquakes everywhere.

"I think you did." He kissed me deeper, his hands everywhere on me, his thumb sliding up my torso, rubbing at my nipple under the fabric of my dress.

"Huh," I sighed into his mouth, *"La petite mort."*

He tore his lips from mine, frowning at me.

"Say what, now?"

"La petite mort," I repeated. "A brief unconsciousness. *A little death*, in French. That's what they call that beat after an orgasm, sometimes."

My French governess had told me that. Sam's eyes twinkled with so much delight, my chest flared with pride. His smiles were like human handprints. Each one was just different enough to be completely unique.

"You, Aisling Fitzpatrick, are a lovely torture."

He broke our kiss. Everything was blurry, and my panties were really, *really* wet.

I pressed my fingertips to my lips. "Oh gosh, what did we do?"

His lips were swollen and bruised, but otherwise, he looked cool and collected.

"I assume that was rhetorical, so I'll spare you the answer." He was already fishing for the cigarette pack in his back pocket.

"Do you have a girlfriend?" I blurted out.

He chuckled, a cigarette clasped between his straight white teeth. "Don't worry about my having girlfriends. I never will."

"Why not?"

"Because no woman is worth it, least of all one that is the spawn of a man I'd like to bleed dry of his money."

He lit up his cigarette. His gothic, wintry gray eyes felt like ice cubes rolling down my skin.

"You know, I would never tell if we hooked up." I swallowed my pride. Even I didn't know why I wanted him so badly. I just knew I did. He made me feel like I was in a parallel universe whenever we were together.

"I just told you this was our last kiss."

"But why?" I insisted.

"Because I want your father's business."

"I won't tell."

"You're not worth the risk." He shrugged, puffing away on his cigarette.

"There will be no risk," I said. A voice inside me warned me that that was enough. It was *her*.

He doesn't want you, mon cheri. Turn around and walk away.

But I didn't.

So Sam looked down at me, frowning.

"Even without the risk, you're not worth it. You are too young, too innocent, and far too sweet for me. Now do your self-respect a favor and walk away."

But it was too late.

My pride took such a beating, I had to retaliate, even though I had absolutely no tools to do so.

"I feel sorry for you," I said, feeling incredibly *un-sorry* for him, but incredibly sorry for myself.

"You do?" He smirked, humoring me. "Why?"

"Because you're a half-literate, barely educated dropout. You probably don't even know the multiplication table. That's why you do what you do. You don't have a choice."

"You're calling me dumb?" His smile widened, his eyes sparkling with mischief.

"You *are* dumb." I tipped my chin up. "But it's okay. You're hot and ooze that look-at-me-I'm-dangerous vibe, so I'm sure you'll find someone."

"Don't forget rich." He snapped his fingers.

"Not by my standards," I smiled coldly. Holy hell, it was like my mother took over my mouth. "Just try not to make conversation. You're not very good at it."

"Based on you dry humping my leg like a bitch in heat five seconds ago, I'm sure I'll be able to keep them entertained some other way."

His words were crass, but his nonchalant smile dissolved into a grim mask of coldness.

"You ... you ... you ..."

"I'm ... I'm ... I'm ... *what*?" He clapped my mouth shut by tapping his finger to my chin, smirking. "*Right*?"

Before I could answer, Sam vanished.

He ignored me for the rest of the evening.

Four hours later, I crawled back to my room, still in a daze from dinner.

Sam had impressed everyone with his dry wit, sharp mind, and that aura that surrounded him. The one that promised a swift yet painful death if you crossed him.

I found my finite mathematics textbook—the one I'd left open on my Queen Anne desk because I'd been stuck on the same problem for an *infinite* amount of time—glaring back at me.

I groaned and reached for it, about to close it.

"I'll try solving you tomorrow. I have bigger problems to work out now."

Like how I cannot stop obsessing over Boston's most notorious mobster.

My hand stopped over the slick, chrome page. I blinked. The problem was solved, only not in my handwriting.

In fact, *all* the problems on the page were solved. Every single one of them.

How did he ...?

"Are you calling me dumb?"

Yes, I did. But Sam wasn't dumb. Based on this page alone, he was closer to a math genius.

Angry with him, and with myself, and with the world, I slammed the math book shut with a thud. A note floated down to the floor from it. I picked it up.

Was that, like, hard?

He'd quoted *Legally Blonde.*
And served me my own ass in the process.
Ouch.

One

Aisling

Present Day.
Age 27.

I'M IN.

The thought momentarily derailed me from everything else teeming in my head. The noise, the pain, the second guesses.

I descended the stairs to Badlands, the most popular nightclub in Boston.

I'd been categorically banned from Badlands. I'd even been turned away at the door once, as the bouncer drawled, *"Boss showed your picture around, jailbait. Said he'll fire anyone who's dumb enough to let you in."*

I was twenty-six then, but that little fact didn't deter him. From the moment Sam Brennan purchased this club two years ago, using it as a hub for all his bad seedy dealing, he refused to let me set foot in it, even though my brothers had been visiting here on a weekly basis.

"I can't believe they didn't ID you, bitch. Sam's gonna shit so many bricks, he'll be able to build a replica of the Empire State Building!" Emmabelle—Belle for short—hi-fived me, whisper-shouting as we shouldered past hipsters, brushing along psychedelic art deco wallpaper and neon faux taxidermy.

Belle was my only partner in crime when it came to going out on the town, seeing as both our other friends—Sailor, and Emmabelle's baby sister, Persephone—were new mothers, and therefore more interested in catching power naps and exchanging breastfeeding tips than downing drinks at a bar.

Belle was also the owner of Madame Mayhem, a notoriously sordid club downtown, and always enjoyed sniffing around the competition, so convincing her to come here today was no issue.

Badlands was darker and smaller than I'd imagined it. Dripping decadence. We reached the end of the stairway. I noticed that the club was no more than a few velvet couches, a small dance floor and a long bar made out of black wood. Above the bar, small, vintage televisions were lined up, all of them playing the same black-and-white movie: *Dr. Strangelove*.

"Fool's Gold" by The Stone Roses played in the background, shaking the floor beneath my knee-high leather heels.

Partygoers in costumes sniffed cocaine off the bar, and there was a couple at the far corner of the club having full-blown sex on the couch. The girl, dressed as the Queen of Hearts, bounced up and down on the guy while sitting on his lap, her dress covering their dirty deed.

This club was Sam personified. Dark and wretched yet oddly beautiful.

I smoothed a hand over my outfit. It was Halloween. A great excuse to cover my true identity. I went for Julia Roberts in *Pretty Woman* and put on a short, blonde wig, complete with sunglasses, scarlet-red lipstick, and blue miniskirt, and cropped white top.

Belle had covered her blonde hair with a raven wig, a-la Uma Thurman in *Pulp Fiction*. She blew on an e-cigarette theatrically, looking around for her next victim. "Anyway, Sam's an asshole for blacklisting you in the first place."

"Sam's an asshole for many reasons, none of them have anything to do with blacklisting me, but banning me from his club for no apparent reason just shows how much of a tyrant he is," I murmured.

I didn't speak ill of Sam often—or anyone else, for that matter—but when I did, it was to Belle, because I knew she wouldn't judge me.

"Do you think he did it because you are Hunter and Kill's sister?" Belle asked.

"No, I think he did it because I remind him of all the things he wants to forget," I said honestly but didn't elaborate.

The carnival.

That kiss.

Our conversation.

Sam never thought he'd see me again. I wasn't in his plans, and whatever wasn't in his plans had to go. That was why he treated me as he had—with indifference dipped in cruelty. Looking past me whenever we were in the same room. Never acknowledging anything I said or did.

Both Belle and I perched on high stools at the bar. I motioned for the bartender to get us two gin and tonics, doing my absolute best not to slump and/or cry into someone else's drink.

At twenty-seven, I'd only been to bars a handful of times. I'd been too busy with med school until a second ago to really dive into the club scene, and now I had a residency. *Or so people thought.* But tonight, I wanted to do something reckless, dangerous, and stupid. To remind myself I was alive.

Tonight, I wanted to seek Sam Brennan out, even though I knew I shouldn't.

Because tonight, like that *other* night, I watched someone die.

And whenever death was close, so was my need to curl into the soul of a monster and hide from the world.

To make matters complicated, I saw Sam all the time.

At dinners, charity events, and parties.

He had been working for my family for almost a decade now.

Somehow, I'd let the worst happen. I continued loving him from afar, like the sun loved the moon. Coexisting, but distantly. Eternally star-crossed, but never close enough for comfort.

We'd spoken very little to each other since that evening, even though our families had grown close to one another through Hunter and Sailor. Seeing him was always a bittersweet cocktail of elation and pain.

I'd learned to get high on both feelings.

"Forget about Sam tonight." Belle sucked on her straw, inhaling the gin and tonic like getting trashed was an Olympic competition. Under her costume, she was the closest thing to Margot Robbie I'd seen up-close. Feline blue eyes, sunshine blonde hair, delicately arched brows, and a sinfully full bottom lip.

"You haven't gone out once since you started your residency at Brigham and Women's Hospital. That was over six months ago. Find yourself a hookup. Have fun. You earned it, Doc."

"I don't do hookups," I pointed out, crushing the lime with my straw in my drink like it wronged me somehow.

"Time to change that. It makes no sense that an OB-GYN in train-ing—*a woman who literally takes care of everyone else's vagina*—does not care for her own. You can't pine for an unrequited penis. There are plenty of fish in the sea."

"Well, I sincerely hope you don't get mercury poisoning, Belle, because you seem to enjoy sampling said fish a bit too much." I took a generous sip of my drink, knowing I sounded prudish and regretting my remark immediately.

Belle threw her head back and laughed, far from offended.

"Oh, Ash, you are a hoot. That's the thing most people don't know about you. Underneath the polished exterior, the American Princess longs for the monster to steal her, not for the prince to save her. You're kind of a dangerous creature, when you want to be."

The drinks kept on coming, and the indie music was good and loud. Before long, Belle pulled me to the dance floor, where we ground against each other to the sound of The Shins, Two Door Cinema Club, and Interpol.

Tendrils of my blonde wig stuck to my face and lip gloss as I sweated away the memories of today's shift at the clinic, and I belted out the words to "Runnin' with the Devil" by Van Halen with a drunk, elated crowd, once again using noise and lights to drown my sorrows.

Ms. B.

Needles.

Death.

Mother.

Despair.

At some point, Belle zeroed in on a man as she always did.

Emmabelle Penrose was a self-proclaimed non-monogamous woman. While she wasn't predatory, she was definitely not looking for a serious relationship and loved nothing more than indulging in one-night stands. Monogamous relationships were a foreign concept to her, like a bidet or brown sauce. She was aware it was something other people enjoyed, but was never tempted to try it out herself. But in the rare times she'd picked a lover, be it a woman or a man, she was fiercely devoted to them and made them feel like the center of the world.

Which was probably why she broke more hearts than she could count.

Her victim tonight was a tall, dark, and handsome type dressed as Zorro.

They met halfway, striking up a conversation while I self-consciously danced by myself before retreating back to the bar.

She reappeared by my side ten minutes later.

"We're going to the Four Seasons. He's got a friend in management who can hook us up with a presidential suite. Doesn't he give Antonio Banderas a run for his money?" Belle sank her teeth into her lower lip, watching him from across the room as he retrieved both their coats from the cloakroom, sending her nervous glances to make sure she didn't run away or change her mind.

I leaned my forearms against the bar, smiling. "Definitely, but the costume's a bit cheesy, no?"

L.J. SHEN

"Cheesier than Domino's pizza. Luckily, I'm spending one night with him, not a lifetime." Belle winked, smacking a kiss on my forehead.

"Happy Halloween, Doc. Make sure you don't leave here alone and text me if you need anything, yeah?"

She left without waiting for an answer.

I entertained the idea of calling an Uber and going home, but then what was the point? My parents were still out, attending one of their charity dinners, which was the reason I was here in the first place; normally, when my mother was home, she insisted we spend time together. My brothers were with their respective wives and children.

I'd be going back to a pointless and excessively large manor to dwell in my own thoughts, dark memories, and regrets.

I signaled the bartender to get me another gin and tonic, downed it, and got back on the dance floor, dancing by myself.

Ten minutes later, a guy in a Ghostbuster uniform began dancing in my vicinity, drawing closer to me as he did. He looked young. Younger than my own twenty-seven years. College-aged and blond, his face pink from the bite of the Boston cold. We danced around each other for a while before he yelled in my ear, "I'm Chris."

I leaned forward to answer him, even though I knew there was no way Chris and I were going home together. For better or worse, I wasn't the type to go home with a random. I wasn't a nun by any stretch of the imagination, and I wasn't dumb enough to save myself for Sam, but I could also count on two fingers the men I'd slept with in my lifetime and knew their addresses, full names, phone number, and—embarrassingly—college grades.

"Ash," I answered, keeping it vague.

Ash could mean Ashley or Ashlynn.

Aisling wasn't a very common name, and everyone knew the Fitzpatricks in Boston.

"You look hot as fuck, Ash." He licked his lips, undressing me with his eyes.

46

"Thanks." I smiled grimly, mentally putting my clothes back on.

"Can I buy you a drink?"

I was aware I was treading into tipsy territory, but I was still far from drunk. I nodded. "Anything bottled works. I'll open it myself."

"You don't have a bottle opener."

"I have teeth," I replied.

Literally. Figuratively.

He arched a brow, grinning.

"Right on."

Chris brought me a beer. We danced some more. When "Heads Will Roll" by the Yeah Yeah Yeahs started, Chris shifted behind me and began grinding against my ass. He was hard, and I was over it. Over everything, really. Especially today.

I wasn't going to see Sam tonight. He wasn't here. My whole plan was a bust, and it was time to cut my losses and lick my wounds back home, where I could at least drown my sorrows in more alcohol without risking getting raped.

"It's been fun, Chris. Thanks. Have a good night." I grabbed my small clutch and turned toward the stairway, but Chris had other ideas. He snatched me by the arm, pulling me back to the busy dance floor, his rancid vodka breath wafting toward my face.

"Not so quick, Pretty Woman. Where's my thank you for the beer?"

Ah-ha.

He was one of those men that thought buying a girl one drink got them a direct ticket into their panties. I reached into my clutch, plucked a crisp ten-dollar bill and threw it in his direction, smirking as it floated between us, sailing down like a feather all the way to the sticky floor.

"Here. Buy yourself something nice. Maybe the common sense not to sexually harass women."

I swiveled on my heel again. He snatched my arm *again*. This time, he yanked me closer, my body slamming against his. My heart began to strum erratically as his fingers dug into my flesh, leaving rings of bruises.

"Nuh uh. I have something else in mind for payment."

"Then I suggest you rethink it, because I'm not that type of girl."

"Is that why you're dressed like a *whore*?" He raised a challenging brow. "Spare me the speech, Ashley. We both want each other, and it's going to happen."

I looked up, trying to shake him off. He tightened his grip on my arm. I opened my mouth to warn him I was going to scream, when out of nowhere, Chris was jerked backward and picked up by the collar of his Ghostbuster costume like a cub.

I took a step back, knocking over another person on the dance floor, letting out a surprised yelp.

Sam Brennan.

The Monster himself was here, a dark horse holding Chris in the air, with a bouncer on either side of him. The college guy flailed, helplessly clutching to the collar of his costume to prevent himself from choking.

He showed up.

"Get rid of him, but not before breaking a few bones," Sam ordered dryly, dumping Chris on the floor in a pile of limbs and moans, like he was a bag of trash.

"Oh, man," Chris whined as the two burly guys grabbed each of his arms, yanking him toward the stairway. "Sorry. I didn't know she was a VIP. C'mon, Brennan. *Please!*"

"Shut up," Sam quipped.

"Am I banned from the club?" Chris whined.

Sam frowned at him coldly. "By the time my men finish with you, you'll be lucky not to piss blood for the rest of your life. Take him out." He pointed at the door up the stairs, and the bouncers immediately followed his order.

Sam took a step toward me. I took another step back, my knees knocking together in a mixture of fear and desire.

I'd been caught red-handed at his club, dressed like a legendary hooker from the nineties. *Lovely.* He was definitely going to be serving me my own ass. Maybe even tell my brothers and father about this.

I squeezed my eyes shut, getting ready for a verbal beating.

"Follow me," he rasped softly.

"I'm sorry! I ..."

Wait, *what*?

Why wasn't he tossing me out to the street right along with Chris?

I looked around, internally cursing Belle for bailing on me. She was crazy enough to get into a fistfight with Sam. And somehow win.

Sam pressed his hand on the small of my back, ushering me toward the bar then past two bodyguards blocking a narrow, dimly lit hallway. Every cell in my body prickled with alarm. We passed by four doors—two on each side of the corridor—all of them open. *The card rooms.* Underground betting venues Sam operated, masquerading as Badlands nightclub. Everyone knew Badlands was notorious, but only a select few were privy to the true reason it was famous.

Apparently, only the richest and most respected men in New England could secure a membership to Sam's little gentleman club— and only if they were vouched for by one of his few trusted contacts.

I caught a glimpse of the rooms. Brown, oaky, and smoky, the men inside clutched cigars between their teeth, drinking expensive scotch, laughing and placing bets.

Silently, we went up the stairs toward a door that obviously led to his office. He opened the black wooden door and closed it behind us, leaning against his desk.

I looked around, blinking away the harshness coming from the fluorescent light, drinking in more details about his life. Nothing about the room screamed money or power. It looked like just any other office of a nightclub owner. Sam wasn't a flashy man. Meaning, he looked the part when it came to being rich, but he wasn't desperate to show off his wealth.

We were now together—alone—with no one to stop him when

he'd grind my body up and turn me into meatballs for defying his words and showing up here.

My heart beat so fast I thought I was going to puke.

"Look, I—" I tried to explain my presence at the club, but he raised his hand to cut me off.

"What happened to you tonight is not a representation of my club or the people inside it. I know things can get rowdy in here, but sexual harassment is where we draw the line. I'd like to offer you a hundred-dollar voucher for your troubles, Miss ... *Roberts*." His eyes scanned me, though there was no desire or want in his expression.

I bit down on my lip to prevent my mouth from gaping in shock when I figured it out.

Sam didn't recognize me.

He had no idea who I was.

How would he? With my bleach blonde wig, costume, full face of makeup, *and* sunglasses.

My heart lurched, urging me to take advantage of the situation. The opportunity was overwhelming. To have Sam without really having Sam.

I knew Boston's favorite monster was notorious for sleeping with every willing woman. Why not me?

Because it is immoral, corrupt, and unfair, a voice inside me chided, in a slight French accent, *her* accent. *Not to mention, you deserve a man who would beg for you, not vice versa.*

Yeah, she still haunted me. A decade after her death.

But Sam didn't have any morals. Why not play by his rules?

"Who said I didn't want the attention?" I tilted my chin up, adopting a smokier, raspier tone than my own.

Sam arched a thick, dark eyebrow, lazily perched on his desk, strong arms folded across his massive chest.

"Your body language did, for one thing. Some read books, I read people. You tried tugging your arm free, the international signal for get-the-fuck-away. I noticed you on the monitor." He flicked his chin toward the screen on his desk, in which black and white footage of the club from every angle danced across multiple frames.

I let loose a blood-red smile.

"You're right. He wasn't my type. But that doesn't mean I didn't come here to get some action."

"Is that so?" he asked, disinterested.

"Yes." My voice barely shook when those words I found at the carnival on the restroom wall came to mind.

Lust lingers, love stays.

Lust is impatient, love waits.

Lust burns, love warms.

Lust destroys, but love? Love kills.

S.A.B.

Samuel Austin Brennan.

Was I an idiot to think it was him? That these words were once upon a time directed at me?

"Better get out there and try your luck, then." His voice was like a freezing cold shower dousing my advances.

"Or maybe we could help each other." I played with a tendril of bleached hair, careful not to tug too hard on the wig and blow my own cover.

Sam's smile was wry and skeptic. "Who said I'm on the prowl?"

"Your blood type."

"You know my blood type?"

"*Hot-blooded,*" I explained.

"Hot or cold, you can't handle me, sweetheart."

"Try me."

His gaze glided down my body slowly, as if trying to decide if I was worth unzipping his pants. I trembled, aware he could find out who I was any second.

The more we spoke, the more my voice became unsteady. Shrill. Aisling-like. He seemed to be considering this, stroking his chin.

"Turn around," he instructed.

I did, painfully aware he was checking out my ass. It was a good ass. Four yoga classes a week with Mother, despite my busy schedule as a first-year resident. But that was the thing with unrequited love: you always deemed yourself unworthy of the subject of your admiration.

"Lift your skirt for me." His steel voice cut through the air behind me. I did as he asked, even though I knew he would find something unexpected.

My white cotton underwear, sensible and a size too big. Practical for a woman who wore scrubs all day and completely out of character.

I heard him chuckle. My heart sank.

"Get out of here."

I spun my head around, my skirt still bunched up my waist, my ass in his direction.

"I know men like you," I hissed seductively.

"There are no men like me."

"I can make it good for you," I insisted.

"Doubt that." He tilted his head sideways, laughing quietly. "*Out.*"

Brazenly, I pushed my panties aside, to show him most of my behind, while playing with myself. The sound of my arousal meeting my fingers filled the air, making it known that I was very much ready to be taken.

"Please ..." I let my head fall sideways, biting down on my lower lip as I provided him a good angle to watch me masturbate.

He said nothing.

Small mercies. He is giving you another chance. Don't blow it.

I turned around before he changed his mind, swaggering toward him on my thigh-high, high-heeled leather boots, knowing it was now or never. Sam Brennan would never give Aisling Fitzpatrick a chance, but to this stranger he still might. When I was close enough to touch him, I sank down to my knees, looking up at him through my big, dark sunglasses.

"May I?" I asked, placing a hand over his groin.

He looked down at me, his thunderstorm eyes twinkling playfully.

"Make it fucking good, Roberts. I don't fuck rookies."

I lowered the zipper of his slacks. In the decade since the carnival, Sam Brennan had successfully graduated from a guy to a man. He'd ditched the ripped dark jeans and soft tees in favor of Armani slacks and black dress shirts, and now smelled like the decillionaires I knew and brushed shoulders with, wearing a cologne I was pretty sure both my brothers favored, and cost a grand a pop. The only thing to remain of his younger self was the St. Anthony charm engraved with his initials S.A.B. hanging around his neck and those taunting eyes that could look into people's souls.

I lowered his black designer briefs, my fingers brushing through the trimmed dark hair of his groin. His cock sprang out. Hard as a rock. Thick and long—frighteningly big—with a purple vein running along the shaft.

As far as cocks went, it was beautiful. My mouth watered and I licked my lips.

Instead of going straight to business, I tilted my head carefully, keeping my wig intact, and gathered his balls into my mouth, sucking on them gently.

He hissed, dropping his head back, not expecting the move. I ran one finger around his shaft, teasing him as I pumped and sucked on his testicles, inhaling the musky, earthy scent of his privates.

"Motherfucker," he groaned. "That's some move."

Stifling a smile, I sucked, teased, and licked, almost entirely ignoring his cock that kept jerking and growing more swollen and big, demanding my attention. After a few minutes, Sam grabbed the back of my wig, jerking me to the main event—the star of the show. I gasped, slapping his hand away immediately in a bid to keep my wig on.

He frowned down at me, momentarily taken aback.

"Got anything against dicks?"

"Not at all." My voice was breathless, pathetic. "Sorry. It's just that my hair is a mess under the wig, and I don't want you to see it."

A raven, blue-black mess you will recognize immediately.

"Are you under the impression we're about to have our fucking wedding photos taken?" Pleasure twirled in his grey-hued eyes. "Who the fuck cares?"

"No, you're right, of course not."

Silly girl, Ms. B's song tutted in my head. *So submissive and easy.*

"While we're at it, why don't you take off the sunglasses?" He cocked an eyebrow. "Makes me feel like I'm getting head from Stevie Wonder."

Because you'll see my eyes and recognize them, too.

My eyes were the kind of blue you didn't see every day. Father said they were only matched by the ocean in their blueness.

I grabbed his shaft and deep-throated him, making him nearly roar with pleasure.

"Nice diversion, Roberts. Faster."

I began pumping in and out, still amazed that Sam Brennan's cock was in my mouth.

My fascination—no, *obsession*—with him knew no bounds, something even I couldn't deny. But it was harmless, too. We were both single, of age, and constantly in the same vicinity. He changed my life in ways and shaped it into something different and deeper. Giving him good head was the least I could do to pay him back for putting me on the path I was today.

"All right, let's see what your cunt or ass is made of. On your feet, Pretty Woman."

I rose to my full height, euphoria swirling through me like a storm. He grabbed the back of my head and kissed me. A lazy, horny kiss. Full of tongue and teeth and intent. Nothing like the kiss we'd shared on that haunted ride all those years ago. It didn't unfold slowly like a well-crafted book.

Sam pulled away from me suddenly, frowning at me.

"What?" I asked, panting hard, my underwear already soaked. I clutched the collar of his dress shirt, rubbing my covered tits against his chest shamelessly, already on the brink of orgasm. "What, *what?*"

"Ginger," he hissed coolly. "And honey."

"Ginger?" I blinked frantically behind my shades. "What do you mean?"

"There's only one woman I know who smells of ginger and honey."

Me.

It was me.

Me and my stupid French-imported shampoo Ms. B got me addicted to.

Without warning, Sam tore the sunglasses from my face, yanking the wig off at the same time. My long, tar-black hair fell down my shoulders in thick waves, all the way to my butt. My blue eyes widened at him.

So screwed—and not in the way I was hoping for.

I coughed, probably choking on a desperate apology that my body refused to spit out. I knew he wasn't going to hurt me—not physically, anyway—but I had no doubt he was going to punish me.

Revenge was Sam Brennan's favorite language, and he spoke it fluently.

"Fitzpatrick," he growled like a beast.

"Sam, I—" I shook my head. *Merde!* "Please. Just one time."

"Spare me the bullshit. I'll deal with you later. First, I'll give you what you've been begging for for over a decade and remind you why *you...*" he bit my lip hard

"*...do...*" he grabbed my panties through my skirt, tearing them in one practiced movement—I thought it was impressive, especially as they weren't exactly snug "*...not...*" he shoved two fingers into me in one go "*...fuck...*" he fanned his fingers open inside of me, stretching me so I became unbearably full—I shuddered violently with need and pleasure, my knees weak—I pushed toward him, buckling my hips, shamelessly begging for more "*...with me.*"

He bared his teeth, kissing me hard again as he fingered me mercilessly. Hungrily. Violently. Passionately. It was a different kiss. A kiss of pent-up lust. The kind that had built up for years from stolen glances and almosts. I felt the kiss in every bone in my body, in the cells on my skin.

Our mouths moved together, and I pushed my groin forward, signaling him to thrust deeper with his fingers, my nails sinking into his muscled shoulders through his shirt.

He withdrew from inside me and roughly grabbed my ass, hoisting my legs over his waist. He carried me to a nearby pool table, where he perched me on the oak edge, his erect cock poking my belly. Sam reached for his back pocket, pulling a condom and ripping the wrapper open with his straight white teeth.

"Are you a virgin, Aisling?" he asked, his index finger brushing my naked pussy now that my destroyed underwear were discarded somewhere on his office floor.

Even though I knew the question wasn't unwarranted—I'd never dated anyone seriously, never brought a man home for the holidays or to official dinners, and was the shyest, nerdiest person he was probably acquainted with—the question left a hot, stinging sensation on my pride. Like he'd slapped my soul.

"Would it matter?" I snatched the condom from him, rolling it over his cock with shaky fingers. I was going to give this man the fuck of his life if it was the last thing I did. Ruin any other pussy for him.

"Not in the fucking slightest."

"Then I suggest you find out for yourself." My eyes leveled with his, and for a moment, his gray pupils rendered me speechless.

I'd met men. Many beautiful, successful, rich men. But they were all the same. Their posture, mild manners, and soft hands robbed them of the authentic masculinity Sam oozed without even trying.

He was carnal, raw, and dangerous, and there was no one else like him.

He knew it. I knew it.

Sam smiled his crooked, bad guy smile.

"So fucking smug. If you want to be taken, you'll be taken the

Sam Brennan way. No regrets. No repeats. And no fucking telling your parents, kiddo."

With that, he turned me around so my back was to him, dipped his hand between my thighs, and borrowed my wetness, coating my rectum with my juices.

My eyes widened with surprise. I'd never had anal sex before. Sam pushed a finger into my tight hole while thrusting into my pussy at the same time.

With one, deep, fierce thrust, he was inside me.

I felt full, so full with Sam's finger in my ass and his cock in my pussy. I let out a moan. My puckered nipples became so sensitive, the friction from my bra alone tipped me close to the edge. I threw my head back and grunted.

Don't come on the fourth thrust. At least have the good grace to pretend you are not putty in his hands.

"Not a virgin, then." He started moving inside me, holding my waist in place with one hand, playing with my rectum with the other. The friction between me and the pool table he screwed me against caused my clit to tingle. I squeezed around him each thrust, angling my body just right for deeper penetration, while I sneaked my hand between us, kneading his balls.

I'd only been with two men before Sam—both of them I'd met at university—and both were a calculated warm-up in my quest to get ready for the grand event, AKA Sam. Even my sex life was designed and planned to make him mine.

I'd dated the two Harvard prodigies I knew were experts in the sex field and coaxed them into teaching me all their dirty tricks. I took notes, morphing from a shy, fumbling newbie to a nymph in bed.

I'd bit and licked and teased and tickled where necessary.

Sucked and pushed and squeezed.

Not for them—for *him*.

But I hadn't anticipated *him* making me feel this good. It was a total mind-fuck.

When Sam slid another finger into my snug hole, I began moaning more loudly, clutching the pool table desperately, losing control of my legs, almost caving in to the pleasure. He rode me hard, and when I felt the first spasm of an orgasm tingling from inside me, he pulled out, taking his cock in his hand from behind me and placing it between my ass cheeks, my anus coated with my juices.

"Well, well, little Aisling Fitzpatrick is all grown up, and she knows how to fuck like a porn star." Sam laughed callously, trying to minimize this moment, to dismiss what was happening here.

Him.

Me.

Forbidden and wrong and still, against all odds, happening.

He eased into me slowly, mindfully, and even though it hurt more than I was willing to admit, I soldiered through the pain, sliding the rest of him into me by pushing my butt toward him, until he filled me to the brim.

There was intense silence, which I used to familiarize myself with the feeling of being full of him from behind. I felt him shuddering against my back with pleasure.

"Your pussy might be used, but this asshole has never been fucked. I can tell."

I didn't say anything because it was true, and the truth hurt more than him inside of me because it was a painful reminder of how pathetically in love I was with him. He leaned forward, still inside me, and brushed my hair away from my shoulder, his lips finding my ear.

"You had to leave me a first to take, didn't you, Aisling Fitzpatrick? You poor, romantic soul."

With that, he pulled out then thrust into me again in one go. I cried in pain, holding the pool table tighter, but after the first few rolls of his hips, the pain morphed into pleasure. Especially when he repositioned me slightly higher on the table so my clit was again teased by the fuzzy pool table. My fingers were still playing with him, rubbing against the sensitive spot between his balls and ass cheeks.

My whole body was on fire, and I clenched my ass cheeks, all my muscles quivering as my release began to wash over me again in forceful waves.

"I'm coming," I cried out.

Sam groaned, giving a few jerky thrusts. We came together.

My vision was spotty, and everything shifted out of focus. I could feel myself milking the orgasm out of him, how hard he was inside me.

I let my upper body go limp against the pool table, closing my eyes, aware that my skirt was still pushed up around my waist as he carefully slid out of me from behind. Every inch of him coming out was excruciating, and I suspected there were a lot of inches of him.

With my cheek still plastered to the green fur of the pool table, I heard Sam shifting around the room, moving around. Slowly, I shimmied my skirt down my thighs so that at least my bare, bruised butt wasn't on full display.

"Get the fuck up, ice princess. My grand vintage billiard table is not meant for sleep."

I turned around, deliberately climbing on the table and lounging there, my forearms digging to its surface, making myself comfortable. If I was good enough to be screwed against said billiard table, I was also good enough to sit on it.

"Ask nicely," I said, in my cold, upper-crust tone—the one I knew he hated so much. "And I might."

"I never do anything nicely. You should know by now. Where'd you learn all your little bed tricks?" Sam sat behind his desk, buckling his belt, his reptilian air concealing any sign we'd just screwed each other's brains out.

He lit a cigarette, puffing a swirl of smoke in my direction.

"You mean, *fuck*?" I hopped off the pool table, smiling as I picked up my wig and sunglasses. "Don't forget I spent seven years among people whose sole purpose in life was studying the human body. I had some pretty good time exploring all the ways to make a person scream in pleasure … *and* pain. You haven't seen the half of it." I rearranged my skirt and wig, forcing myself to head to the door. Not because I wanted to but because I had to pretend I at least had a shred of dignity still left inside me.

It was a well-known fact that Aisling Fitzpatrick had been head over heels in love with Samuel Brennan since the day we'd met. There was no need to shower Sam with undivided attention and desperate love declarations. We had a great hookup. Now the ball was in his court.

I wanted anything he was willing to give me.

A fling, a relationship, and everything in between, just as long as he'd have me.

Pathetic? Maybe. But I wasn't hurting anyone. No one but myself.

And Sam? As scary as he was, I knew he would never lay a hand on me in ways I didn't want him to. He was dangerous, yes, but not to my life. Only my sanity.

"That's more than I wanted to know about you, kid," Sam said around his lit cigarette, frowning at the monitor on his desk as he watched what was going on at the club.

"What are you doing these days, anyway? Pediatrician, right?" He huffed.

"OB-GYN. Brigham and Women's Hospital," I answered, smoothing my skirt over my thighs, taking another step toward the door.

Stop me. Tell me to stay. Ask for my number.

"You really thought you could seduce me by dressing up?" he asked out of nowhere.

"I did, didn't I?" I said haughtily then rolled my eyes. "Honestly? I dressed like this to get in, not to seduce you."

"Why did you want to get in?" His eyes were still on the screen.

"Because Badlands is the hottest place in Boston."

"You don't care about the hottest places in Boston," he pointed out.

"Of course I do," I said stonily, internally wondering if he'd considered me, my likes and dislikes. "Sometimes even good girls want to be bad."

"Which is why you were banned from this establishment in the first place," he deadpanned.

"That's unfair."

"Fair and I don't even share the same fucking planet. Which part of my character made you think I care about being fair?"

Between extortion, murder, and money laundering, Sam didn't exactly have any spare time to join the League of Justice as Captain Nice Guy. Still, calling him unfair seemed … well, *unfair*. He did throw out a guy who had assaulted me, after all.

"I'm banned from your establishment because you know if I get too close, you'd actually have to pay attention to me, and every time we're together, magic happens," I countered, challenging him.

Leave, mon cheri. You are not doing yourself any favors, Ms. B's voice urged in my head.

Sam sat back, finally ripping his gaze from the screen to look at me.

"The only magic we shared today was that I made your asshole about an inch wider for life. Regardless of that, you pulled a dirty move, Miss Fitzpatrick."

"We monsters do what we have to do. You know that better than I do." I shrugged.

"You're no monster," he hissed.

"You have no idea who or what I am."

"What was your objective? One fuck?" he seethed.

"One? No. A few? Sure, depending on your attitude," I replied noncommittedly, starting for the door.

He could deny me all he wanted, but when we were on that pool table, he'd looked at me like he did at the carnival. With a hunger that told me he was going to devour me and leave nothing for the man who came after him.

"Aisling," he barked when my hand found the door handle, about to push it open and leave.

I stopped but didn't turn around, my heart rioting in my chest.

"If we fuck—and that's an *if*, not a *when*—that's all we'll be doing. Every single thing you were born and bred to achieve—a respectable husband, children, a family, a Labrador to complete your Christmas photo—I rejected before you were even born. It will be just that. Fucking. And no one could ever know about our arrangement, for obvious reasons."

We both knew what the obvious reasons were, and neither of us dared to utter them aloud.

He was offering me something. A start. I knew the rest would be hard-earned. Sam Brennan was a broken man, but not beyond repair. I believed that with my entire heart even and maybe because of the things I'd witnessed him do over the years.

He had gotten my family out of trouble countless times, saved my older brother from losing the family company, and doted on me from afar.

He may not have known it about himself, but he did have a moral code, and rules, and hard limits.

I was going to make him see himself the way I saw him. Then maybe, just maybe, he could see me for who I was. A woman worthy of his attention.

For now, I was willing to take what he was willing to offer, even if it was just carnal, angry sex.

Oui. You officially lost your mind, mon cheri.

"What do you have in mind?" I propped a shoulder on his doorframe, exhibiting the nonchalance of aged goat cheese.

Sam rubbed at his jaw, thoroughly annoyed with the entire situation.

"Well, we can't fuck around in your place since you still live with your parents—what the hell is that all about, anyway?—and I never let anyone into my apartment, so I guess you can meet me here tomorrow. Same time."

"Why not there?" I shot out.

"Huh?" He looked up from his screen, already done with the conversation.

"Why don't you let anyone into your apartment?"

"Because I hate everyone," he said inhumanly slowly, looking at me like the answer was crystal clear and I was a perfect idiot. "Why the fuck else?"

"So no one's ever been in your apartment?"

"My parents visited once or twice. Sailor knows the address but is not allowed to come there. Why do you still live with your parents?" He threw the explosive question at my feet. I hitched one shoulder up, feigning calmness.

"I don't see the point of paying for a place when I basically live at the hospital."

"Don't act like living in your own apartment would require you to wash a mug. You're too rich to do shit yourself, and you and I both know that. Why are you still hiding behind Mommy and Daddy?" he repeated sternly.

The truth was complex, surprising, and worst of all … unbelievable. He would never buy it. Even if I told him. Which I did not consider doing since the truth was embarrassing. I was a puppet. A pawn in my parents' game. Nothing to be proud of.

I shook my head.

"Does that mean I'm no longer banned from Badlands?" I asked.

"Oh, you're still banned, missy. I don't want to see you partying with these losers. One of the bouncers will show you through the back door when you get here tomorrow, but you're not allowed at the bar or any of the card rooms."

"See you tomorrow, Monster."

"Nix," he nodded his goodbye.

I all but made it back home in a tornado and Googled his nickname for me, elated and terrified and pleased and joyous.

Nix: A water being, half-human, half-fish, that lives in a gorgeous underwater palace and mingles with humans by assuming a variety of attractive physical forms (usually as a fair maiden).

Nix was a female monster.

Sam still thought of us as the same.

Dark, unpredictable creatures, lurking in plain sight.

Now that he let me in, I was going to destroy every single one of his walls and finally make him mine.

Two

Sam

TEN HOURS AFTER BEING BALLS DEEP INSIDE AISLING Fitzpatrick, I got a call that Catalina Greystone, AKA Mother Dearest, had finally (and uneventfully) kicked the bucket.

"Just thought y'all should know. What with the fact that they're gonna knock the whole thang down next week. Not that the property's worth a dime, mind you. But I thought, why not let her son know?" Cat's neighbor, Mrs. Masterson, munched on something crunchy in my ear via a particularly annoying phone call.

Because I don't care, I was tempted to reply.

Catalina's death was new to me but not something I was interested in finding out more about.

She caught me at my personal trainer's, flipping a truck tire that weighed almost as much as I did. I put her on speaker, tossing the phone on the foam floor as I continued flipping.

"How'd you get my number?" I grumbled, not mentioning the special code it required to get through to my line.

"Your daddy gave it to me. Troy somethin'."

So Troy knew she was dead, too. I was surprised he didn't show up at my door this morning with a bottle of champagne.

"Well, I appreciate the heads-up, but I can't imagine there's anything in this house of value to me."

Other than my fucking long-lost childhood and memories of drug and alcohol abuse.

Cat had tried reconnecting with me over the years since dropping me off at the Brennans' with nothing but a duffel bag and bad memories, but the truth of the matter was, I'd rather get fucked by a cactus—raw—than exchange a word with her.

Hell, I'd marry the goddamn cactus if it meant never seeing her wretched face.

Fortunately, being the garbage human that she was, Cat hadn't gone through extreme lengths to try to reach out. She sent me letters periodically and tried to call every now and again, especially when she had money troubles, which—cue the surprise act—was fucking always.

As if giving a fuck was on the menu for me. By the address on the letters (that went straight into the trash—unless it was wintertime, in which case straight into the fireplace), I figured she spent the last half decade on the outskirts of Atlanta, sucking soggy cock to fund her drug and designer bag problems.

One especially slow night at Badlands I even Google-mapped her address and wasn't surprised to see she lived in a place I wouldn't even store my shoes. A rickety wooden thing any wolf could blow over and knock down.

If I cared enough for revenge, I'd have gone there to do exactly that. Made her homeless. As it happened, not enough time had passed for me to think of her as an afterthought, let alone an enemy.

"Aren't you gonna ask how she passed away?" The woman on the other line continued nagging. My trainer, Mitchell, a man who looked like a rock (not to be confused with *The* Rock), handed me a fresh towel, offering me a what-the-hell look.

He wasn't used to me giving strangers the time of day.

"Air bike and ropes next. You've got sixty seconds to recover, Monster," he mouthed, offering me a fist pump I refused to reciprocate on the grounds I wasn't fucking five, before scurrying behind a black curtain to allow me some privacy.

"Hello? You still there?" the Southern woman on the other line demanded, her nasal voice grating.

I picked up the phone from the floor.

"Listen, Mrs. Masterson, I appreciate your motherly concern, but to say Cat and I weren't close would be the understatement of the fucking century. There's nothing I need from her place. I'm a busy man. I don't have time to go down to Georgia."

But I had every fucking intention of going down on Aisling tonight, and that was a problem. A pleasant shiver prickled my skin. Who would have thought little Nix had it in her? To con, deceive, and weasel her way into my club—into my *pants*—and give me the fuck of a lifetime?

Not me, that was for sure, but I was happy to give her a replay and finally get her out of my system. See all the tricks she picked up in med school and mar that pale, milky skin of hers with my nails and teeth. She was swan-like. Elegant and aristocratic. And it made fucking her so much more pleasing than my usual flavor of pointy long nails, botoxed lips, and ass implants.

There was something simply not as exciting about being buried in a woman that had already seen more dicks than a urologist. Experienced or not, I could tell by the ice princess' touch she didn't give it out so easily.

She couldn't have.

She was hopelessly fucking obsessed with me.

And fuck, for the first time in a decade, that little fact made me proud rather than annoyed.

"Drugs. She had an overdose. That's how she passed away," Mrs. Masterson continued, unconcerned with my lack of interest in the conversation. "Poor thang. Girl Scouts found her. Came to try to sell her some cookies. Would you believe? They looked through the window. Saw her lying on the floor and called 9-1-1. Poor children. No one ought to see somethin' like that, let alone kiddies. They say she'd been like that for days. Maybe a week. No one came to check on her.

Her phone log said no one even called. She was a lonely woman, your mother."

I was hardly surprised. Cat was about as lovable as an SS soldier and just about as endearing. When she was younger, she had her looks to save her. Once her beauty had faded, she became just another haggard junkie, and life tended to be harder on those people.

"Look, I know you two weren't exactly thick as thieves..." the old woman on the other line sighed "...still, son, you should be here."

"I'm not—"

"Boy, I don't know how to be clearer than I am. There's something of hers you should see," she cut me off briskly. "Let's leave it at that, shall we? She told me you were a rich man. That means you can afford to take the time off work and get your ass down here, mister. I know I'm old, but I ain't stupid. I don't mean you should come here to pick up some Walmart china or family albums. There are some things you need to see."

I started to hate her less despite myself. "Like what?"

"I ain't tellin'."

"You're an infuriating woman, Mrs. Masterson. Has anyone ever told you that?"

"All the damn time." She cackled, and I could tell by her cough she was a heavy smoker like me. "So, is that a yes, little Greystone?"

"*Brennan*," I corrected, clenching my jaw, staring at an invisible spot on the wall. The same wall I looked at day in and day out when I did my hundred chin-ups five times a week.

Should I or shouldn't I entertain my fucked-up, morbid curiosity about Cat's life or whatever was left of it?

The answer was simple. No. She was a complete stranger at this point. Twenty-six years had passed since I'd last seen her. And still, like a fly to a pile of shit, something compelled me to get a closer look at the mess she'd created for herself. That, paired with the idea of relishing Cat's failure at the most basic human thing—survival—was something I wanted a front-row seat to.

"I'll be there by tomorrow morning."

"Smart move, boy."

I hung up and called my travel agent, giving him the details. I heard him typing away on his keyboard.

"There's actually a flight going out of Boston Logan Airport in a few hours. Better catch that one, 'cause there's thunderstorms rolling in tomorrow and there could be delays."

"Book it," I ordered.

I was going to stand Aisling Fitzpatrick up, but that wasn't a problem. If there was one thing I knew for certain, it was that Nix—*little monster*—would never turn me down.

She would be there next week. And the week after that.

To be used, abused, and devoured.

She'd always been mine.

That was what made her so dangerous and why I stayed the fuck away all these years. The fact that she was at my disposal. Just one horny mistake away from calamity. An unconditional woman was nothing foreign to me, but they usually wanted *something*. My money, my power, the glow of being under the dark wings of Boston's underground king.

Aisling, however, I couldn't figure out. She had more money than she knew how to count. She was more of the reforming type than the women who wanted the bad boy, and her motives always seemed disturbingly genuine.

I didn't know what her angle was, and it didn't matter.

Her family was my biggest client, and I wasn't going to fuck up my job for any woman, not even one as sweet as her.

Mitchell sauntered back in. His beefy body in that small gym top gave the appearance of trying to stuff my fat cock into a normal-sized condom.

"Ready?" He raised his fist for another pump.

I ignored it, once again, sauntering toward the ropes.

"Always."

Hours later, I was standing in Cat's living room or whatever the fuck you wanted to call the small, dingy rathole she used to occupy.

Mrs. Masterson gave me the key, but not before feeding me a questionable apple pie and sweetened iced tea that tasted suspiciously like the store-bought Costco brand.

Cat's house was about the size of my spare room back in Boston. Most of her furniture was hand-me-downs and crap you'd drag from a street corner's curb. Her bathroom cabinet had enough prescription drugs to restock a fucking pharmacy. The house exhibited all the usual signs of a shitty life: plastic bags full of useless things strewn everywhere, outstanding bills pinned to a board, half-full beer cans scattered about, and a bunch of used condoms in her bedroom's trash can.

She died a hooker. It probably should have saddened me, but it didn't. She lost all pity privileges when she made me an alcoholic and cocaine user before I knew how to wipe my own ass properly.

I rolled up my sleeves and got to work immediately, peeling wallpaper to see if there was something interesting hiding behind it, sifting through the hoarder-type garbage, and opening every cabinet and drawer in the damn place. I flipped the house upside down, even yanked out the leaking faucet from its place, but for the life of me I couldn't find that thing Mrs. Masterson was talking about that would make it worth my while to visit.

I knew asking the old hag was pointless. She'd just shove more half-frozen apple pie down my throat and tell me Cat wanted me to find it for myself.

You could always count on Cat to make things harder for me, even from the fucking grave.

Usually, I was good at extracting information in not-so-nice ways, but even I had my limits, and I drew them at physically attacking eighty-five-year-old women who were half deaf and possibly fully blind.

I decided to call Sparrow, whom I considered my de facto mother. True, she hadn't pushed me out of her vagina, but she sure as shit was there to get me out of trouble while I was at school. She fed me, fought my battles, and celebrated my wins.

She loved me more fiercely than any mother would her child, but the damage had been done. My soul was broken, my eyes were open, and my heart was frozen.

"What's up, Sam?" Sparrow asked on the other line. I could practically imagine her rolling dough in the kitchen, red hair snaking everywhere like medusa, an apron with a witty phrase wrapped around her waist—which was still boyish and slender.

"Sparrow. I'm at Cat's place in Georgia. She died of an overdose."

"Troy said," she answered quietly, and I could sense she was about to launch into her condolences, so I talked fast.

"I think there's something here I should see, but I'm not sure where to find it."

I was good at raiding places, but I usually found weapons under the mattresses and between cracks. Cat's secrets, wherever they were, weren't anywhere obvious.

The good thing about Sparrow was that she thought like a criminal. Maybe because she married one. So instead of asking nagging questions, she said, "Check the nightstand drawers or the little nooks in her closet. That's where women usually stash their secrets."

"Done, and also duly noted. Nothing."

"Ripped the carpets and floor up?"

"Every inch of them," I answered, flicking books off the shelf by her bedroom window. All four of them. "Any other ideas?"

"Are there any pictures hanging there?"

I looked around, about to say no, when I found one.

Cat always had *one* picture hanging up everywhere she lived.

It was in the bathroom, of all places. A lone sole picture of Troy Brennan, my adoptive father and Cat's ex. Catalina Greystone had never gotten over Troy Brennan, and I couldn't blame her. No one else could measure up to the man so feared and loved his name was whispered on the streets of Boston.

"One," I said distractedly, refraining from adding who was in the picture.

"Rip it. It'll be behind it," Sparrow said with conviction.

"This is why I don't trust women."

"That's okay. We don't trust men right back. Oh and, Sam?" she asked before I hung up.

Here we go.

"Mmm?" I casually flicked the picture to the floor. Sure enough, there was a square-shaped hole in the wall behind it. Just big enough for me to shove my hand into.

"I'm sorry for your loss. And I know you don't see it as a loss, I do, but I cannot find joy in knowing the woman who created you has passed away. Because at the end of the day—she gave me you. And I love you so very much, son."

An unpleasant shudder ran through me. Sparrow wasn't the emotional type, but she sure as shit had her biannual little speeches that made me want to vomit.

I hung up and pulled the shoebox Cat had stashed inside that hole, ripping it open.

The ice around my frozen heart cracked, just an inch.

Letters.

Two hours after finding the letters, I was still sitting on the floor, looking like Gulliver in a Barbie house—the junkie, whore edition— reading through them again and again and a-motherfucking-gain, digesting what I'd just learned.

Apparently, Catalina made Mrs. Masterson promise she'd make sure I'd find these letters, and she had a damn good reason for it.

My estranged mother wanted me to know her life story. At least a part of it. Question was—*why?*

Even as I read the letters for the hundredth time, I still couldn't figure out if she wanted sympathy, revenge, or to give an explanation for her behavior.

All twenty-three letters were addressed to Gerald Fitzpatrick, then CEO of the oil company Royal Pipelines and the man I currently worked for on retainer as a fixer.

Coincidentally, he was also the father of Hunter Fitzpatrick, my sister Sailor's husband, and Aisling Fitzpatrick, the woman I had fucked hours ago. I could still feel her sweet warmth wrapped around my cock whenever I thought about it. I pushed the memory away bitterly.

What I'd read in those letters changed the entire course of my life.

My dearest Gerald,

Thank you for bringing new hope into my life. For making me see that there is more than what I was left with after Brock passed away.

The word 'mistress' rings licentious and cheap, doesn't it? It doesn't do justice to what I am to you, my dear. To how I feel about you.

I know you'll never leave Jane for me. I'm not stupid. I've learned to live with the burden of being the other woman. All I ask is for a part of your heart. It could be small. A fraction of what you gave to her.

Could you offer me a chunk of that organ that beats inside your chest?

Thank you for inspiring me to become a better person, a better mother, a better lover.

Yours forever,

—Cat.

My dearest Gerald,

We are having a baby! Can you believe it? I sure can't.

I'm so excited. I know it wasn't in your plan. Trust me when I say it wasn't in mine, either. Not when Sam is practically a little boy. A pre-teen. Look, Gerald, I know you and I haven't been together for very long, and here I thought the diaper-changing days were behind me, but I really think it's a sign. I guess life has its way of showing us our paths.

I included our pregnancy test. Would you like to come with me to my first OB-GYN appointment? No pressure, but I would love that.

Oh, and by the way, I would absolutely adore it if you could bring me some prenatal vitamins from the store next time we see each other. Gotta keep the little one healthy and strong!

Yours forever,

—Cat.

Dear Gerald,

I did not appreciate it today when you breezed past me when I came to see you at your office. You may be done with me, that much you have made abundantly clear, but you are definitely NOT done with the baby growing inside of me. I am not getting rid of him (YES, HIM) for any price in the world, much less the amount you have offered me to have an abortion.

You can ignore me all you want. For weeks, for months, for eternity. At the end of the day, this baby is coming out of me, and it is yours. You are going to have to face this reality, one day or the other.

Call me back. You know my number.

Yours sometimes,

—Cat.

Gerald,

I want you to know I will never forgive you for what you did to me. To us.

You are a killer. A murderer. I had a son. Jacob. He was inside me. I was pregnant. He kicked and rolled and always moved in pleasure whenever he listened to his big bother's voice.

He was your child.

I understand that this posed a complication to your perfect life. But it was still the one thing I looked forward to and made me push through my bleak life.

I also understand you own an oil company, that you already have heirs, that the battle over your will, when you die, is going to be a vicious one.

BUT HE WAS YOUR SON.

He was your son and you yanked him out of my body cruelly. You hit me. You threw me around. You pried him out of me. You beat me so badly, you left no room for doubt what was going to happen next.

I had a miscarriage after what went down between us yesterday. That was your plan, wasn't it? To beat him out of me? Well, it worked.

I bled and bled and bled until I had to run to the hospital, where they told me I lost him.

I was five months pregnant, Gerald. Which meant I had to go through a still birth. Did you know I was three months sober? Had been since I found out we were pregnant.

I wanted to give this baby a new, fresh start. To raise Jacob and Samuel together, and give them the opportunity to fulfill their potential. To turn over a new leaf.

To atone for all my sins.

Now all of that is gone. I am back to square one, confused and lost as ever.

And you, of course, are still not answering. You got what you wanted. My complete destruction so I won't be a threat to you anymore.

As I'm writing this to you, I've found the bag of crack you left at my doorstep. I know it was you who asked the drugs to be delivered. You always loved me more when I was high, even if it meant I wasn't there for Sam.

Fuck Sam, right? If push comes to shove, we can always give him a little something to subdue him, too. That was your idea. To drug him so he would be quiet. So we could talk on the phone. Well, it stopped working once he was old enough to fight back, and we all know how that turned out. He'd almost bit my skin off the last time I tried to drug him.

Don't worry, Gerald, I'll take the drugs. I'll fall down the rabbit hole. I'll become a useless body, an empty container that's only good for one thing—giving you pleasure.

And again, the cycle goes.

Drugs. Alcohol. Rehab. Rock bottom. Repeat.

This is all your fault, and if they ever take Sam away from me, I hope you know it'll be on your conscience.

Forever not yours,

—Cat.

Gerald,

As I said on our phone call yesterday, I am not going to leave you alone until you pay me for my silence.

You made me miscarry our unborn son. The media is going to know who you really are and what you're capable of unless you pay up.

And no, I am definitely not going to take your measly 50k and move away, especially as you and I both know that'll mean having to leave Sam behind. No way am I going to be able to raise him on my own, and it's not like Troy and Sparrow are going to let me take him away anyway.

300k will allow us a fresh start. A good rehab center. An apartment in a decent school district. Do the right thing, Gerald. I have people I know in California who could help me. Pay up and make this nightmare disappear.

With hate,

—Cat.

Gerald,

Fine. 150k it is.

When I pointed out 300k would mean I could take Sam with me, you laughed in my face and said the boy wasn't your problem. It's on you that I left my son behind, not me.

You have plans for him, don't you? You said so yourself. Broken, impressionable men from the wrong side of the tracks make good soldiers. The rich thrive on the poor. Well, think again, because Troy Brennan took him under his wing, and if there is one person in Boston who is stronger than you, it's Troy. I trust he would protect Sam from you, although I don't entirely trust you not to get your claws on Sam anyway. Use him and drain him of anything good and worthy he possesses, like you did to me.

I don't know how far 150k is going to get me, but I know it's not going to be far enough away from you.

I will never forgive you.

For throwing me back into the arms of drugs.

For making me miscarry Jacob.

For making me leave Sam.

You are a monster, Gerald. And monsters are born to be slayed.

You tore my family apart, and one day, the same will be done to you.

Samuel has Troy now, and Troy is the one man you cannot push around.

For the last time,

—Cat.

I dropped the last of the letters on the floor, raking my fingers through my hair.

Apparently, Cat and Gerald had had an affair. Not only that, but that affair had resulted in a child. An unborn son named Jacob. Gerald objected to Jacob's birth so badly that when he realized Cat was keeping him, he'd decided to beat him out of her.

He got her hooked back on drugs then paid her off to move away and leave me behind.

There were holes the size of the fucking White House in this story.

For one thing, the woman in the letters sounded nothing like Cat. Catalina was cynical, ill-tempered, and about as motherly as a studded dildo. Either she put on one hell of an Oscar-worthy act for Gerry Fitzpatrick or she really had been on the brink of changing. My bet was on the former.

I doubted he was the one who had told her to drug me. The timeline didn't add up. There was no way they'd been lovers for that long.

Other than that, it seemed legit. The details lined up.

Cat did have a spell of sobriety a few months prior to skipping town, followed by a few, erratic weeks of binging on drugs and spiraling downhill.

I also had the misfortune of knowing Gerald personally, so I happened to be privy to the fact he was a notorious adulterer who'd yet to find one pussy he didn't want to stick his cock in.

I didn't know him to be violent, but I didn't know him to be *non*violent either. The circumstantial evidence against him was substantial, and I didn't put it past him to commit a crime of passion if he needed to save his own skin.

He and Jane Fitzpatrick were a match made in upper class hell. They both came from rich families, were of the same cultural background, and had a lot to gain by marrying one another. They also had another thing in common: they were both intolerable—to the point of not being able to stand each other.

Over the years, the old man had cheated on his wife more days than I could count. It wasn't farfetched to believe that Cat, whose favorite flavor of dick was married, had managed to land herself a fat wallet for a lover in Gerald Fitzpatrick.

The letters were all addressed to Gerald's then bachelor pad, another telltale sign that they were genuine. I knew all of the Fitzpatricks' properties like the palm of my hand, and the address Catalina had sent the letters to before they bounced back was the same address Gerald had used to meet his mistresses, before gifting the property to Sailor and Hunter as a wedding gift.

There were also pictures attached to the letters.

Polaroids of Cat perched in Gerald's lap, kissing his cheek.

Pictures of them in exotic locations. On vacations. Birthdays. And a pregnancy test so old the two pink lines were faint and weak.

Not only did all the facts line up immaculately, but I *remembered*.

Remembered her brief period of soberness.

Remembered the day Cat came home looking like a train wreck, bleeding and bruised.

Her brokenness, so pathetic, so whole, even I couldn't hate her in that moment.

How she crawled inside her bed, balling up and crying uncontrollably, shaking like a leaf, and I found myself helpless, torn between helping her and hating her for yet again failing to feed me.

How in the middle of the night she had skulked to my grandmother's bedside—Grandma Maria and I had shared a room the size of a closet—and croaked, *"Call an ambulance. I have to get to the hospital. Now."*

The betrayal was overwhelming.

Gerald knew I was Catalina's biological son all along, and he still used my services.

According to her, he'd been distantly grooming me for the job I was doing today.

He had driven my mother to drugs and alcohol.

Impregnated her then beat her to a point of miscarriage.

Then made her leave me.

I could've had a different life.

A *better* life.

He deprived me of a fair, second chance and wasn't even man enough to come clean about it when our paths crossed again.

Gerald Fitzpatrick robbed me out of a future, my family, my unborn brother.

For that, he was going to pay.

With his blood.

With his tears.

With his goddamn miserable fucking life.

I'd been Boston's fixer my entire adult life. Since Troy had decided to retire from the gig when I turned twenty-two and turned to more lucrative and legal businesses. I'd always viewed it as his birthday gift to me. I took over the family business, tackling each problem the rich and influential people of Boston came to me with, no matter how wildly unorthodox it was.

By twenty-two, I'd broken enough bones and crushed enough skulls to be feared and respected everywhere I went, both by the criminals and the law.

Troy was playing house with Sparrow, running their restaurants and staying away from the heat by the time my name hit the FBI's most wanted list. He knew I was different—a few shades darker with an appetite for blood—and had long given up on taming me.

My whole life, I'd fixed things for other people.

It was time to allow myself the luxury of one, uncalculated destruction.

Kill everything Gerald Fitzpatrick loved and cherished, just as he did to me.

Karma never lost an address.

And I was going to make sure his would arrive in a timely fucking manner.

Catalina Greystone's tombstone was black.

Irony was a bitch, but it sure had a decent sense of humor.

I didn't know how or why Cat had been buried in a cemetery in Atlanta but had an inkling my adoptive mother had everything to do with it.

Sparrow was a practical yet inconveniently sentimental person. Even though she wasn't religious, the vein of Catholic virtue ran thick and full in her body.

She couldn't bear knowing Catalina would get cremated then

thrown into a trash can when no one claimed her ashes. Sparrow couldn't chance the slight unlikely scenario in which I'd ever want to go visit her grave.

I spent the next couple days in my hotel room in Atlanta, ignoring phone calls, taking discreet meetings with local gang leaders and drug lords, and plotting my revenge on Gerald. On day three, I checked out and went to Catalina's tombstone. Mrs. Masterson called to let me know they already put the stone up and asked if I wanted to go see it with her. I declined politely—there was only so much shitty apple pie and idle conversation a man could tolerate—but I still decided to make a pit stop at the cemetery before heading to the airport and back to Boston, mostly to ensure the bitch was six feet under and very much dead.

The mossy earth sank beneath my loafers as I buried my fists inside the pockets of my black pea coat, strolling toward the tombstone—smooth, fresh, and shiny, a memorial to my broken childhood.

I stopped when I reached it, smirking grimly when I noticed Sparrow had omitted the word 'mother' from Cat's short list of titles. Guess it was petty o'clock when she placed the order for it.

The air was bitingly cold, unusually so for Georgia, the wind lashing against my face. I lit a cigarette between numb fingers, smirking around it as I used the tip of my loafer to smear a smudge of mud over the glossy stone, dirtying it up a little.

"Good riddance, sweetheart."

I crouched down, touching the gravestone with the hand that held my cigarette, marveling at how brief human life was. One century at best was hardly enough time to enjoy what this planet had to offer.

"You know, Cat, I thought about killing you often enough. Every other month, maybe. There is something poetic in taking a life from the person who gave you one," I *tsked*, surprised to discover I wasn't as happy as I thought I'd be about her finally being gone. "But then it all boiled down to the same thing: killing a person is taking a risk. You were never worth the risk. That's your life story in a nutshell, isn't it,

Catalina? Never more than an afterthought. So many lovers, and fake friends, and fiancés, and even a husband, yet no one has ever visited your grave. Only an eighty-five-year-old neighbor who would find Stalin lovable. I guess it's goodbye." I stood up, taking one last drag from my cigarette, flicking it over the tombstone then spitting on the lit ember to snuff it out.

I turned around without looking back.

Another one bites the dust.

Three

Sam

"**D**O *NOT LET THIS SPIN OUT OF CONTROL,*" TROY WARNED the following day while we were sitting in my office in Badlands, enjoying a hot toddy—heavy on the whiskey— and the blissful sound of my workers running around in the hallway, fulfilling my orders.

He rifled through the stack of call logs between Catalina and Gerald from decades ago that I handed him a few minutes before. His fingers were still tinted blue from the outdoor cold, his pale face tinged pink by Boston's winter's bite.

"How did you even find this prehistoric piece of evidence?"

"I'm a very resourceful man," I drawled.

"No shit."

The first thing I did when I got to Boston was dig deeper into the Cat/Gerald affair and find out more about their relationship. From the calls they'd made to each other, the two had begun bumping uglies when I was four years old and ended on the cusp of her leaving when I was nine.

It was unbelievable and yet completely logical that the first and only time Catalina had said the truth was also the time she confessed to something as appalling as an affair with the man who paid me thirty million dollars annually to make his problems go away—and to never touch his daughter.

Catalina was a fucking headache, even after her death, but Gerald was the real villain of the story because his drug wasn't crack cocaine. It was pussy, and he should have known better.

"Remember your sister is married to Gerald's son. We're family." Troy smoothed a hand over his blazer, his expression loaded with hostility. Everything about him was cocked and ready to detonate like a loaded pistol.

We sat across from each other, me and my adoptive father, looking like a mirror image of one another. Same black Armani slacks, tailor-made for our gigantic size. Same Sicilian handmade loafers. Same black dress shirt—or navy blue, or dark gray, but never white; pale colors were highly impractical when part of your job description was drawing blood by the gallons.

Even our mannerism was comparable. He had an oral fixation he soothed with a toothpick that he stuck to the side of his mouth, and I used cigarettes.

But what it boiled down to was this: Troy and I weren't blood-related.

He had frosty, alabaster blue eyes. Mine were gray, like Brock Greystone's.

His hair was jet-black, peppered with gray at the temples and his widow's peak. Mine was toffee-brown.

He was pale. I was tan.

He was built like a rugby player. I was built like a rugby *field*.

And he was born into money, while I'd had to adapt to it.

The phrase 'eat the rich' always amused me. I'd learned from a young age that it is the rich who eat you. That was why people hated them so much.

If you can't beat them, join them.

I was never going to be poor again, which was why touching Aisling Fitzpatrick was unwise. The Fitzpatricks made me richer. A whole fucking lot richer than I was when I started out with this gig, breaking legs for congressmen and stashing mistresses on exotic islands.

"This is not going to touch Sailor, Hunter, Rooney, or Xander," I assured him, referring to my sister, her husband, and her children. I flipped my Zippo back and forth between my fingers, losing interest in the conversation.

"Hunter's gonna blow a gasket," Troy noted.

"Hunter's too busy creating his own family to give a fuck about the one who turned their back on him when he was in boarding school," I snapped, baring my teeth.

It wasn't like the Fitzpatricks were winning any Brady Bunch awards anytime soon. If anything, they gave the Lannisters a run for their money.

"I'm not going to spare the feelings of every motherfucker I've ever had a beer with. Hunter'll survive. Gerald has earned my wrath."

"As far as I'm concerned, Gerald can get your wrath, too. I have no dog in this fight, Sam." Troy's nostrils flared, and I could tell he was measuring his words carefully. He'd oftentimes tried to diffuse situations I'd stormed into, mainly because he knew the potential of my exploding was high to almost fucking certain. I liked breaking things and watching them shatter. Call me nostalgic, but chaos reminded me of my childhood. And I was always ready for a bloodbath.

"I just want to make sure you don't do anything too impulsive. I know you, son. You've always been trigger-happy."

"Not as happy as I'd like to be." I dropped the Zippo, fingering my St. Anthony charm tied to my neck by a leather string. "Which brings us to the next topic. I caught the Russians smuggling a hundred and thirty pounds of hashish into one of their delis. Whatever Vasily Mikhailov sold—and it was not fucking pastrami—he didn't hand over a cut from the earnings."

So I cut his face. An eye for an eye and all that.

Perhaps cutting the Bratva boss' face wasn't the most calculated thing I'd ever done, but it sure brought me pleasure to see him screaming in pain as he writhed beneath me.

Troy snarled. "Don't get me started about the Russians. You had no business taking over their territory in the first place. Back to Gerald Fitzpatrick." He spun his index finger in the air, rewinding the topic. "I want you to sit on this information until we confirm it. I know it looks bad—"

"It's airtight," I lashed out. "I have proof. Hard facts." I slapped the papers between us.

Not everything Cat had said was true, but most of it was. Enough to warrant my need to wring Gerald dry. The guy murdered my baby brother. My only biological family in this world. Brock was gone. Cat was gone. I could have had something. I could have had a person to take care of.

"And *still...*" he slammed his fist over the desk between us "... you know something he thinks you don't know. You have the upper hand now. Operate within the scope of your role, but don't turn this into the Red fucking Wedding. I know you, Sam. You enjoy delivering slow deaths much more than fast killings. Torture him, but don't finish him completely."

He had a point. Why go to Gerald with this information and give him the opportunity to defend himself when I could milk it out of him the good old-fashioned way, by making his life a living hell?

If revenge and punishment were forms of art, my work would be all over the Louvre. I could pluck Gerald's soul out with a fucking spoon and feast on it, all without upsetting my sister and her gigolo-looking husband.

"Fine," I drawled, lounging lazily on my leather chair. "I suppose I could torture him a little. But I *will* go for the throat eventually."

"Eventually is still at least a few months away, and I hope I can stumble across some information that will make you change your mind between now and then." Troy stood up, buttoning his blazer, his gaze cold and yet somehow approving.

More than he hated that he'd created a monster, he loathed that he loved it.

My ruthlessness, rough edges, and appetite for blood came from him.

I surpassed him in all of the above.

Troy was an honorable mafia boss in his own backward way. He was well-versed in destruction but only inflicted it on those who had crossed him.

Me, I was corrupt to the bone. Nothing was beneath me. Well, other than rape, pedophilia, beating women and children … you know, the usual subhuman crap.

Any adult man was fair game, and if they wronged me they were done.

It gave me a certain advantage.

"You good?" He stopped by the door, frowning at me.

I lit a cigarette. "Why the fuck wouldn't I be?"

"Cat—"

"Was, like her namesake, just another pussy. I don't consider her death an event worth mentioning. The awful apple pie I had to endure from her nagging neighbor next door caused me more discomfort than knowing she had been left to rot in her apartment for a week before people found out."

"*Arright …*" His eyes flicked to mine, still searching for a flash of emotion. "Don't get too wild with your revenge plot against Gerald, ah? Remember, the matter is still under investigation."

No point in mentioning I'd already dug a grave with his name on it in the forest where Troy killed Brock.

I could've had a brother.

I could've had an unconditional someone.

"Sure." I smiled.

Sure.

Aisling

Flipping through a medical chart, I smiled tightly as my phone danced inside the front pocket of my scrubs. I ignored the vibration against my thigh.

"The tests came back, Mrs. Martinez, and I thought we could go through them together and talk about what they mean for you and what I recommend you do next." I regarded the woman sitting in front of me in my office.

She blinked steadily, back straight, fingers laced together on my desk, bracing herself for more. Outside, snow came down in sideways sheets. You could barely make it out through the narrow, thick-glassed windows lining the walls.

I fell to the seat in front of her. My phone buzzed again.

"Well. Okay. Let's see, shall we?" I started flipping through her charts, my eyes burning with emotion as I took in her blood tests. "What do we have here? It says here that … oh, excuse me. Just one moment." I lifted my forefinger, plucking my phone out of my scrubs' pocket, internally groaning. Someone better had died. My family knew not to interrupt me while I was at work.

I had three missed calls from Hunter.

One from Mother.

Worst of all, a text message from Hunter.

Years ago, when we were all still youngsters, thrown into different academic establishments and internships around the world, my two siblings and I made a pact. Since we had been raised to believe our phones might be tracked because of who we were, we couldn't simply write something as straightforward as "Quick, there was an explosion in one of our refineries, Da's fault." So we decided that if something was truly urgent, we'd text each other a secret code: *Clover*.

An ironic take on the Irish belief that a four-leaf clover brought good luck. Hunter's text was in all capitals.

Hunter: CLOVERCLOVERMOTHERFUCKINGCLOVERRR RRR.

"I have to take this. I'm sorry." I shot up from my seat, hurrying out of the office, hustling onto the main clinic's floor, my phone glued to my ear. Hunter answered before the dial tone started.

"Ash. You have to come home. It's Da."

"Is he okay? Is he hurt?" I sucked in a breath, realizing I was already clutching the key to my sensible Prius in my hand, leaving Mrs. Martinez and my responsibilities behind as I darted out the door.

"Physically? He is fine. For now, anyway. There's no way of knowing what Mom is gonna do to his ass in the next few hours. Listen, Ash, there's a scandal. Someone leaked some photos and text messages of Da with … uh …" He stopped, and I could tell he was trying to find the right words that would inflict as little pain on me as possible.

That was Hunter. Brutally beautiful and heart-shatteringly soft.

"Just spit it out, Hunt. I know Mom and Dad aren't giving Romeo and Juliet a run for their money. I've lived under their roof my whole life, for goodness' sake." I slipped into my car, flooring it on my way to Avebury Court Manor. "What'd he do?"

"It's a sex scandal," he blurted out. "Not shocking, I know, but this time there are some pretty graphic pictures on the internet. Da called me as soon as they surfaced. Devon is working to take them down as we speak."

Devon Whitehall was the family lawyer and one of my father's closest allies. A British aristocrat with a mysterious past. Hunter, the natural-born charmer among us three, was in charge of everything PR and media related at Royal Pipelines, my family's oil company. It made sense he was the first phone call Da made.

"Wow." I tried to disguise the hurt in my voice, mainly because I knew I wasn't the one who should be hurt. Mother was the wronged one. My eyes burned with unshed tears.

Merde, Mother is going to have a heart attack.

"That's ... ironic," I managed to cough out.

"Ya think?" Hunter deadpanned, snorting.

Once upon a very long time, Da or *Athair* (meaning father in Gaelic), as we children referred to him, had dragged Hunter from his school in California all the way back to Boston because a sex tape of Hunter had hit the internet. It made the rounds and provided some very unfavorable headlines for the family. *Athair* went to extreme lengths to punish Hunter for the national embarrassment he'd caused the Fitzpatrick clan. So this was definitely irony at its best ... and worst.

Not that we didn't know my father cheated on my mother, but he always kept it under wraps and never, ever let it leak. He had the reputation of a flawless family man, and whoever managed to bring him down must be gloating right now.

"Where are you? How is Mother?" I took sharp turns and stole yellow lights whenever I could, ignoring the persistent snowflakes falling down from the sky as I zipped my way through the Back Bay.

"I'm just getting into Avebury Court right now. Sail and the kids are with me. Cillian, Persy, and Sam are already there. Mom is ..." Hunter paused, drawing a breath. "I don't know how she is, Ash. She hasn't picked up the phone. Hurry. You're the only one who could ever get through to her."

I'm the only who makes the effort, I thought bitterly.

"All right, love you."

"Love you, too, sis."

With that, he hung up.

My knee bounced against the steering wheel the entire drive home.

Mother. Fragile, vulnerable Jane Fitzpatrick.

Who drowned her sorrow in shopping sprees, cried every time I opted to go out with friends and not stay with her, and always had a ready-made request on the tip of her lips to make me serve her in some way.

Growing up, I'd thought I was just like her.

Meek, shy, and elegant. I'd tried so hard to become what people expected me to be. The fragileness of Jane Fitzpatrick, from her bony structure to her dainty beauty, drew a lot of admirers and the envy and ire of women over the years. But as time passed, I realized I was stronger than my mother, much stronger, and more independent, too.

Which implied I looked like my mom but had the same characteristics as my dad.

That was something I was too grossed out to explore right this moment.

Jane Fitzpatrick slipped in and out of depression like it was her favorite gown, and my father, although he was now retired and dabbled with the family business only a couple hours a day, did very little to try to help her.

Which was why I'd decided to stay at home as long as I could before I'd eventually get married and start my own family.

People always silently judged me for my decision to remain home.

They always assumed I stayed because I wanted to be coddled.

No one had suspected I stayed because I was the one doing the coddling.

But I did just that, flipping the tables and becoming *her* parent. Her first real depression happened when I was eighteen; I hadn't slept, spending all my time filling her baths, brushing her hair, giving her daily pep talks, and taking her to doctors.

Since then, I'd helped nurse her through her ups and downs three more times. So having my father so carelessly ruin all my work felt like a stab in the back.

I parked in front of the house with a screech then threw the double doors to our mansion open, ignoring the pitter-patter of my heart at the sight of Sam's Porsche, which was parked next to Cillian's Aston Martin and Hunter's G-Class Mercedes.

Finding everyone was hardly a task. I followed the shrieks and hysterical cries of my mother, all the way from the foyer to the second dining room. Her wails bounced across the high ceilings, ricocheting against marble statues and family paintings.

I came to a halt when I reached the dining area. Mother and *Athair* were standing at the center, the gardens and heavy burgundy drapes their backdrop as they engaged in a screaming match from Hell.

Mother was so red I thought she was going to explode. Da tried the inconsistent method of apologizing profusely one moment and heatedly defending himself the next. Behind them, I spotted Cillian sneering down at them distastefully, one of his arms draped tenderly over his fair-haired wife, Persephone, who held their son, Astor, close to her chest.

Hunter, Sailor, and their children were there, too. Standing at a safe distance in case Mother started throwing sharp objects, which wasn't unlikely.

Cillian snapped his fingers once, and two maids rushed inside, wordlessly scooping up the toddlers, who had no business seeing their grandparents like this.

Devon, our family lawyer, was not in the room. I could see him behind the French doors leading to the gardens, talking heatedly on the phone, trying to defuse the situation with the media, no doubt. His footsteps dented the otherwise pristine, untouched snow.

Then there was Sam. He lounged against the wall in the corner of the room, his fists shoved into the pockets of his slacks, a slight, cunning smirk on his lips, all devastating beauty and casual destruction.

I squared my shoulders, feeling my nostrils flare with fresh hot anger.

It had been a week since I'd seen Sam. Since we shared a romp. Since I convinced myself I could worm my way into his heart.

The next day, I'd come to his club, just like we'd arranged, only to find out he was out of the state.

"Sorry, love, but Boss is on more important business than a casual fuck. Guess your two minutes of being Brennan's mistress are up," one of his soldiers had said as he laughed in my face when I demanded to go inside.

My ears pinked in shame when I thought about that night. Sam hadn't even bothered to pick up the phone and make a call. Text me. *Anything* to let me know that our plans had changed.

Time had grown thick and sticky since I'd last seen him, each minute lasting forever, like it had moved against a current. Now that he was in front of me, and I couldn't even give him the scolding he deserved because we were in my family's company.

My eyes shifted from Sam back to my parents.

"No one asked you to be faithful, Gerald!" Mother flung her arms in the air, exclaiming loudly. "That would be too much for you, wouldn't it, dear? But why couldn't you be discreet about it? How much do you think I can tolerate? I am a walking, talking joke! Look at these pictures. Just look at them!" My mother tossed a newspaper in the air, slapping it against my father's meaty chest.

From my spot by the door, I could see it was a picture of my father titty-grabbing a busty blonde who was giggling at the camera. It was obvious he was butt naked as was she. She was sitting in his lap, and it was also obvious that they were doing it.

"To make matters worse, she is twenty-five! Younger than your own daughter. What were you thinking? Aisling, there you are!" Mother turned to look at me, momentarily forgetting she was in the middle of publicly humiliating my father. "Be a darling and ask someone to give me my special tea with honey and ginger and see to it that my hot bath will be ready soon."

Everyone's eyes turned in my direction, surprised and puzzled that I'd been asked to do the task of a butler's. They shouldn't be. If they looked closely, they'd see I'd been the help in this house all along.

"Of course, Mother." I smiled tightly, gliding out of the room with as much elegance and nonchalance that I could muster, delivering requests to the maids to ensure she would be taken care of while I was gone. I returned back to the dining hall just in time to see Mother throwing her wedding band at my father.

Deciding he'd had his fair share of dark entertainment for one evening, Cillian stepped between them.

"Enough. Who do you think could've leaked this?" Cillian demanded. "It's not the woman in the pictures. She is married now, with a child on the way, and is horrified by this coming out. Hunter spoke to her earlier. She claims someone hacked into her old phone and stole the images illegally."

"And by her hiccups and hysterical crying, she said the truth, too," Hunter added from the corner of the room.

"I'll bet! I never would've given her the time of the day otherwise! I've been careful. I swear." *Athair* shook his fist in the air, his chin wobbling in unison. "This is a setup. You know I'd never do you wrong, Jane my dear."

My mother took another step back from my father, staring at him like he was a complete stranger. Her striking beauty highlighted how tragically lacking he was in the looks department.

Gerald Fitzpatrick's skin was pasty, splotchy, and marred pink. He was a heavy man with beady black eyes and thinning white hair.

All of us siblings looked like variations of our mother, despite having different coloring, with Hunter being the most aesthetically pleasing out of us.

"Shut up," Cillian barked at Da, scanning the room impatiently. "Any idea who could have done this?"

"If we start counting our enemies, we won't leave here until next year, and we have a vacation booked in the Maldives next summer." Hunter checked his Rolex, cocking a sarcastic brow.

"I'll take care of this." Sam stepped forward to the center of the room.

He clapped a hand over my father's shoulder. "Come on, Gerry. Let's get to the bottom of this mess. Privacy, please." He snapped his fingers in our general direction, signaling all of us to go out. "Jane, you too."

Everyone trickled out of the room slowly. Everyone other than Mother. I had to take her hand and yank her out while she protested with huffs and puffs.

"It's not fair! I want to know what they are saying." She clutched my arm a bit too tightly as I steered her toward the kitchen, where the servants could watch her. "Oh, Aisling, be a darling and go eavesdrop on them. You know I'm no good at not being seen. You can slip in undetected, I am sure."

"*Mother*," I groaned, feeling a looming headache blossoming behind my eyes. "Brennan wanted them to have privacy."

"Brennan is a brute and a beast. Who cares what he wants?"

She had a point, and I was feeling especially inclined to ignore any instructions Sam had given me after the past week.

I took the bait.

After wrapping Mother's bony fingers around a steaming cup of tea in the kitchen and asking one of the housekeepers to keep an eye on her, I discreetly slipped into the adjoined sunroom to investigate what Sam and Da were talking about.

The voices from the dining room could carry to the sunroom easily; years of listening to my brothers and father drinking port and discussing business and women crassly had taught me that.

I pressed my ear to the wall, listening intently.

"Let's take it a step back. Tell me about your former lovers, any potential bastard children who might be lurking around looking for a nice check." Sam's voice was smooth and hard as marble behind the oak doors.

"Jesus Christ, Brennan, talk about a loaded question. Well, in the last decade, I had Bonnie, Sheila, Christie, Ulrika, Ruthie—"

"Start with the first year of your marriage and move your way up," Sam cut him off briskly. "We need to be thorough."

"That could take days!" my father protested.

There was a black hole in the pit of my stomach, and it was full of dark feelings. The extent of the betrayal robbed me off my breath. He was so careless. So selfish …

I heard something snap, and when I looked down, I realized I dug my fingernail so deep into my palm, it broke.

I always knew both of my parents enjoyed the odd affair—but this was too much. I felt dirty sharing my DNA with the man.

"Days," Sam mumbled impatiently, just as disgusted as I was. As if he had a right. As if he wasn't known for his conquests between the sheets. "Fucking charming. Let's try to narrow it down. Think of someone with the potential to seek revenge. Anyone you knocked up? Someone you might have hurt personally? Those would be the people most likely to dig through the dirt and harm you. No one wants to come out as *the* mistress, but people will have no qualms compromising someone else to take you down. It's possible one of your other mistresses hacked into your latest one's cloud to shed light as to what she considers foul play on your end."

"I don't do foul play," Da roared, his face rattling the leaves on the plants in the sunroom. "I take care of my mistresses and provide them with money and jewelry and expensive cars."

I felt lightheaded. No wonder my mother was so messed up. This man was inhumane. He treated women like prized horses. And growing up he was the person I looked to for compassion.

"I'm sure you make them feel like fucking rock stars, Gerry. But accidents happen, and you're a virile man. Any chance you have any bastards lying around? Maybe women who had to get hush-hush abortions?"

Sam always called my dad Gerry. He was the only person to do so. Despite and especially because it drove Da mad.

"No. No bastard children. And I'm not that virile. As you are well aware, not all of my children are biologically mine."

I winced, knowing exactly who he was referring to and blocking this piece of information from my consciousness. To me that person was still my beloved brother. But it was an important reminder Mother, too, dabbled in romancing people outside her marriage—and was less than discreet about it.

"You're not really giving me much to work with here," Sam growled. Something about the way he said that, with a tang of obvious frustration, made the fine hairs on the back of my neck stand on end.

True, Sam was hotheaded, but he was also pragmatic. Detached and cold when it came to business. He was only explosive and unpredictable when it came to his personal life. Like when Sparrow or Sailor was in trouble or he and Troy had disagreements.

"Make me a fucking list, Gerry. Of every single woman you stuck your dick into. If I can't be thorough, I can't be helpful. No use in paying me a small fortune for sitting around and babysitting your two fully grown sons."

"I'm also paying you to keep away from my daughter," my father reminded him. I winced, pressing my ear harder against the door.

"Yeah." Sam chuckled. "Some challenge that is. Make the list." He rapped his knuckles against the dining table.

I knew the conversation was over, so I scurried out of the sunroom as quietly as possible, hurrying toward the kitchen to Mother to fill her in on their conversation.

I crashed headfirst into a wall.

No, not a wall. Worse. Sam's granite chest.

"Ow." I scowled, stumbling back as I rubbed at my forehead.

Turning around to make a beeline in the other direction and avoid Sam, I got snatched right back to his side. Sam, with his killer instincts, caught me by the hem of my blue scrubs and pulled me into an alcove between the dining room and the sunroom, his smoky, minty breath colliding with my face. Hot and fresh and intoxicatingly sexy.

"If it isn't my favorite tight hole. Been eavesdropping, *Nix*?"

His casual sexism would have fazed me had I not known it was a front. I'd seen Sam handling his sister and adoptive mother and knew that for all his crass words, he was capable of adoring women.

There was little point in denying the allegation, especially since we got out of the adjoining rooms at the same time. I tilted my nose up and squeezed my shoulder blades together, like *she* had taught me, her French accent reminding me inwardly, *Better die on your feet than live on your knees. Show courage, mon cheri!*

"It's my house, Brennan. I can do whatever I want, including, but not limited to, spending time in *my* sunroom."

"You are many things, Aisling, including the daughter of two of the most pathetic creatures I've ever encountered and a champagne socialist, but you are no idiot. So don't act like one. What were you doing in there?"

If he wanted me to bring up the fact he stood me up, tell him how much it hurt me, he had another thing coming.

I was in love, not a doormat. There was still a slight distinction between the two.

"Admiring the plants." I smiled sweetly.

"Bullshit."

"Prove it."

He scowled at me. We both knew he couldn't.

"Well, then. Nice talk, Brennan. Are you done now?" I brushed his touch off, sneering at him like my mother would at the help.

"Not quite," he answered, mimicking my upper-class drawl, the one my mother had taught me to use whenever we were in well-bred company. "I'm glad I caught you here. I have an update about our situation."

"Our *situation*?" I arched an eyebrow.

"Our fucking arrangement," he spat out, exposing his white fangs with an unpleasant chilling smile. "It's canceled. I'm not interested anymore. You were a great sport. Five out of five stars. Would highly recommend. Unfortunately, I have some pressing issues right now and no time for complicated pussy."

The crassness of his words almost robbed me of my breath. How dare he? How dare he try to hurt and belittle me every step of the way, when I hadn't done anything remotely unfair to him the entire decade we'd known each other?

All I did was seek his company, be nice to him, and give him myself on his terms. And each time, he found new and creative ways to show me that he wasn't interested, and the one time that he *was* interested, he deemed it a lapse in judgment.

I smiled a chilly, unfriendly smile that made my bones go cold.

"We had plans together? Sorry, I don't recall. Either way, thanks for giving me an update about a date I had no plan attending. Now, don't you have to go do some work for my father?" I tapped my chin. Behind his hard gaze, I could tell he was mildly confused by the brand-new backbone I'd decided to exhibit.

"Chop chop now!" I clapped my hands, my tone a cheery singsong. "As you pointed out earlier, my father pays you a small fortune, and not for your intellectual skills—which, by the way, I find lacking. Let us know when you have more information for us about the leaker." I turned around and walked briskly, leaving him in the foyer without as much as a second glance.

I went to the kitchen, scooped my mother up like she was no more than a child, and took her to her room, where a hot bath had been waiting for her. I washed her hair, telling her all the things she wanted to hear.

That she was pretty, and loved, and powerful. That my father would crawl back with jewelry, vintage bags, and vacations. That if she wanted to, she could push him around with some legal papers that would scare the bejesus out of him.

"Oh, Aisling, I won't be able to sleep at all tonight. Mind stroking my hair until I do?" Mother moaned, when after hours of tending to her, I'd said I needed to hop into the shower.

I smiled tightly, sitting myself back on the edge of her bed. "Yes. Of course."

I stroked her hair for hours. When she finally fell asleep—by that time, my fingers were numb—I retired to my own room, took a quick shower, slipped into my bed, and started crying.

Crying for Mom, for all the suffering she had to endure in her marriage.

Crying for Mrs. Martinez, whom I'd left in the middle of an important meeting to try to extinguish another Fitzpatrick fire created by my selfish, self-centered parents.

And crying for myself, because I wasn't like my brothers or their wives.

I didn't have my happily-ever-after. My destiny was to fall in love with the monster in my story, the character most likely to be slain.

But most of all, I cried because of Sam.

Because he was the only man who could break my heart.

And because he chose to do it. Often.

Four

Sam

THE FIRST BULLET I SHOT PIERCED STRAIGHT THROUGH THE man's chest. A clear shot into his heart.

The second bullet flew to his friend's forehead, making the man snap back like a bowling pin and land on top of his fellow soldier with a cry.

There were very few people who were as good marksmen as I was.

A retired veteran once told me I'd have made a great sniper. Joining the army was never in my cards. I was a selfish man who liked to wage his own wars and didn't have the time or patience for anyone else's.

Silence hung in the air, the echoes of the gunshots still buzzing in my ears. The faint scent of gunpowder and blood hung heavy in my nostrils.

I didn't get into gang fights often, but when I did, I relished the hell out of them. Violence calmed me. Made my blood run cold rather than stir hot and restless.

Calmly, I tugged a cigarette out, lighting it as I sauntered toward the place where the two men were lying. We were in a Brookline attic, just above the deli where a massive drug deal had taken place just a few weeks earlier. Vasily Mikailov's territory, which I'd conquered in recent months.

Back when Troy Brennan ruled the streets of Boston, the gang crime rate was low to nonexistent. Everyone had their own corner of the world to rule, to reign, and to hold. Troy was a fair underboss. He didn't have a severe case of megalomania—something you couldn't say about his predecessors—and had no trouble sticking to Southie, an area which he ruled with an iron fist.

I, however, had different rules, different aspirations, and an entirely different approach to life. You either bent or snapped for me. There was no middle ground, and I wanted it all—every nook and corner of the city and everything inside it.

From the moment I took over, there had been bloodshed. I didn't settle for a finger. I took the whole fucking hand and built an empire on the ruins of bones and blood.

The Italians had been the first to bow down. They did so immediately. The majority of them ran to New York and Chicago after my first round of massacring their top bosses. The event was marked in the local newspapers as Night of The Long Knives, where I killed no less than ten mobsters in their beds.

The latinx had followed suit, scurrying to the edges of illegal betting and drug-dealing after I struck them.

The Russians, however, put up a fight. Brookline belonged to the Bratva, and I had to pry it out of their hands, using a lot of force and raising the body count on the streets. It had been an ongoing, uphill battle with many casualties, many assassination attempts—on both sides—and a hell of a lot of headache.

Bending down on one knee, I drew a black plastic glove from my back pocket, slapped it on, and pried the first bullet from the man's chest. Next, I moved to my other casualty. Thankfully, the bullet wasn't smeared in too much brain matter, which would have been a bitch to clean.

I wiped both bullets with the men's shirts and pocketed them, sighing as I straightened back up and proceeded to deal with the rest of the situation.

"How bad is it?" I clipped, my annoyance loud and apparent.

"Bad," Becker, one of my soldiers, wheezed behind me like a fan, shifting on the floor of the dusty attic. "I think they got my lungs."

"Pretty sure I broke my arm," Angus, beside him, added.

Both assholes didn't even have a high school diploma yet somehow managed to medically assess themselves. I walked over to the two useless oxygen wasters I'd hired to do my dirty work, surveying them coldly.

Unbelievable. Not only had I ended up doing the job myself and wiping the floor with the two Bratva idiots who stole money from me—*fine*, didn't pay me the cut I deserved for the deal—before putting bullets in them, but now I had to usher these two pussies to get medical help.

And don't get me started on falling off the fucking rails and acting like a jealous girlfriend in need of a bloodbath, because I had a long-ass fucking month.

"Get up." I rolled Becker over with the tip of my loafer, taking a long drag from my cigarette, releasing plumes of smoke through my nostrils like I was a dragon. "I ain't carrying your ass to the car honeymoon-style. You too, Fucker Junior," I spat in Angus' direction.

They limped behind me, leaning against each other for support, and stuffed themselves into the back of the van I'd driven to Brookline. Behind the wheel, I made a call to Dr. Holmberg, the man I'd hired on retainer to tend to my soldiers and myself.

For obvious reasons, walking willy-nilly into the hospital with gunshot wounds wasn't exactly an option.

Dr. Holmberg picked up on the third ring, the acoustics surrounding his voice implying he was talking from deep inside someone's asshole.

"'Ello?" He sounded groggy.

"Enjoying an afternoon nap, fucker?" I inquired politely, taking a turn toward the South End, where he was located. "Make yourself a cup of coffee. I have a job for you."

"Sam?" He sobered up instantly, clearing his throat. "Oh, Sam, I'm sorry. I thought your secretary left you the message. I'm not home. I'm in Greece until next week."

That explained why he was asleep when I called him. There was a time difference. It *also* explained why the reception was so bad. The fact his message hadn't been received did not surprise me. I went through secretaries like I went through one-night stands: fast and leaving a pile of angry, mistreated women in my wake. I was currently in between assistants—and also in between fucks, seeing as having sex with Aisling wasn't a possibility anymore. My shit with the Fitzpatricks was complicated enough.

"What the fuck makes you think I talk to my assistants regularly?" I lashed out. "Next time, have the stones to tell me directly when you take an unauthorized vacation. Now give me your cousin's address. I've got two injured soldiers I would very much like to keep alive because they owe me three weeks' pay of work."

Whenever Dr. Holmberg wasn't available, he referred me to his cousin, Raul, who was technically a registered nurse but was still discreet and got the job done. At this point, with Becker and Angus' lackluster performances in the field, they were lucky I didn't let the local mailman tend to their wounds.

A nurse was more than they deserved.

"Raul's out of town, Sam. Visiting his son in college," Dr. Holmberg murmured sheepishly.

"Is anyone in your family familiar with the concept of *work*?" I muttered.

"Yeah, I know, it's unfortunate."

"The state of your face after I'm done with you will be unfortunate," I deadpanned. "What the hell were you thinking, skipping town without having a medical backup for me?"

"It was poor planning on my behalf. I agree," he said mildly, doing anything he could to ensure I didn't actually break his nose upon arrival. "Surely you know someone who works in the medical field who can help you out?" Dr. Holmberg said, knowing damn well ushering the two fuckers in the back of the van to a hospital was out of the question. It was as good as admitting to the crime.

Even though the local DA and police department were in my pocket—I went to the sheriff's son's christening and the DA's father's funeral, I was on such good terms with them—I wasn't dumb enough to rub it in their faces and *make* them ask me hard questions. Even if the DA and the police liked me, there was still the FBI to think about, and they were breathing down my neck recently.

"You'd be surprised, Holmberg, but I don't know many doctors. Or fucking astronauts, for that matter. My line of work is killing people, not nursing them back to health."

That wasn't entirely true, though.

I knew Aisling Fitzpatrick, and she was a doctor.

A good one at that, if I were to believe my sister, Sailor, who wasn't in the habit of handing out unwarranted compliments.

Nix also knew how to keep secrets. Came with the territory of being a Fitzpatrick and belonging to one of the most notoriously corrupt families in North America.

Perhaps standing her up without an apology then throwing what we shared on Halloween in her face the last time we met, proceeding to take a nice, big dump on her pride and lighting the entire situation on fire wasn't the best tactic to handling things with her, seeing as I needed her now.

Normally, I was more calculated than to needlessly poke and humiliate people who didn't deserve it.

Normally, I didn't handle Aisling Fitzpatrick.

She brought out the worst in me. I was borderline allergic to her. So sweet, so innocent, so accommodating. Still living with her fucking parents.

And really, rejecting her was doing her a favor. I was going to have her father's head on a platter in about two seconds, when I exposed him for everything he was and squeezed the truth out of him.

See? Even I had my fucking limits.

They were few and far between and faded, but they were, apparently, in existence.

Then there was the oath part. Even though I was a world-class bastard, I wasn't a dishonorable one. The Fitzpatrick men paid me good money not to touch Aisling, which meant I needed to at least make a half-assed effort to keep my word.

"Perhaps you could—" Dr. Holmberg started, but I'd already hung up the phone and was calling Sailor to ask for Aisling's number.

My sister and Nix were good friends. The wallflower and the lady.

"Does that mean you are finally going to ask her out?" Sailor asked on the other line. I heard her washing something in the background, probably Xander's bottles.

I threw a glance to the back of the van, where Becker was bleeding out—possibly parts of his lungs—and Angus looked like his arm had been screwed into the rest of his body by a blind toddler.

"Are you fucking high?" I scowled at the road, talking to my sister. "She's a child."

A child I'd done some pretty grown-up shit to.

I didn't think eight years were a big deal in terms of an age gap. I slept with women who were in their mid-twenties sometimes, although I naturally gravitated toward women my own age. But Aisling wasn't only eight years my junior. She also had that pure as the driven snow halo of a blue-blooded angel.

A blue-blooded angel who sucked your balls like the future of the country depended on it then proceeded to take it up the ass like a pro.

"High? Oh, I wish. I can't do shit while breastfeeding. Not even drink a glass of wine." Sailor sighed wistfully, reminiscing about times when she didn't have a husband to knock her up as soon as she pushed out a baby.

"If you want sympathy, I suggest you talk to someone with a heart," I grumbled.

"Oh, really? So what's the thing beating in your chest?"

"It's not beating. It's ticking. Probably a bomb."

She laughed heartily. "Don't be too harsh with Ash. You know she is a gentle one. Love you, asshole."

"Bye, shitface."

I hung up and called the number Sailor had given me. Aisling answered on the fifth ring, just as I was about to hang up and make a U-turn, delivering two, sweaty, injured beefcakes straight to her manicured front lawn.

"Hello?" Her sweet voice filled the van, flooding the goddamn place like an overwhelming perfume.

"It's Sam," I hissed in annoyance.

"Oh," was her response. It was a response I was familiar with as she'd often used it when people told her things she did not like. But she'd never used that 'oh' with me before. "How can I help you, Mr. Brennan?"

I was Mr. Brennan now?

Being an asshole certainly had its cons. I trudged forward with my request.

"I have two injured soldiers. I can't drop them at the hospital for obvious reasons. If I bring them over to Badlands, could you get a triage kit and treat them? You'll be paid handsomely."

I hated asking for favors and could count on one hand the number of times I had to do so. Usually, I had some kind of leverage over people, something they wanted back from me, hence the luxury of not ending a demand with a question mark.

"What are their injuries?" she asked, cold and quiet. "Give me the physical description, please, not your medical assessment, unless of course you went to med school without my knowledge."

For the first time in my life, I got the ice princess treatment everyone else received and not her unabashed adoration.

Not that I could blame her, after shoving her pride into a blender and setting it on high that night at Badlands.

"One has a broken arm. The other was shot in the chest."

"Where about in the chest?"

"Lungs. Meet me at Badlands in thirty."

She was going to ask me if she was still banned from the nightclub, and I was not going to lift the ban. Nothing was going to lift the fucking ban, Jesus himself included.

If it were up to me, Aisling Fitzpatrick wouldn't be allowed near a red-blooded man who wasn't a relative until the end of her days. Not to mention a fucking herd of them, drunk and sweaty, in my club. The memory of her being yanked by that asshole in my club scorched through my brain. I'd almost killed the kid. The only thing that stopped me from slashing his throat in a room full of people was I didn't know it was Aisling at the time.

"No," she said flatly. "We'll do things my way. Hold on a sec."

She rummaged through things in the background. Little Nix was just full of surprises, wasn't she? First, she gave me the fuck of my life. Now she was saving my ass, or at least my soldiers' asses. I was half-sad to see the opportunity of ramming into her with my cock again go to waste because of her father.

"You won't have the equipment I need. I'll text you an address in a few minutes. Come alone—just you and your soldiers—and make sure no one sees you."

I was going to ask questions. The most pressing one being *"what the fuck?"* but she hung up on me. Not a minute later, she texted me a Dorchester address. I drove to the address and was surprised to see that it was a residential building. One of those never-ending red-bricked Victorian structures a variety of college students and gang members favored.

I hurled Beavis and Butthead out of the van and dragged them to the black wooden door, punching the doorbell. The door opened on its own accord—unlocked—and when I stepped inside, there was a wordless sign leading to the basement. The apartment itself looked not only residential but occupied. Canned laughter of daytime

TV shows echoed from somewhere inside the apartment, and the welcome rug was damp with melted snow.

What. The. Fuck.

Dragging Becker and Angus like they were sacks of potatoes down the stairway by the hem of their shirts, I dumped them at the foot of the bright, clean, white basement, scanning the place. *Motherfucker.* I knew an underground clinic when I'd been in one, and this was definitely it with an off-white couch, a shelf full of medical books, a fake plant, and cheap paintwork.

Illegal. Operating. And goddamn secretive.

The place looked empty.

Aisling walked out of a white door, dressed in one of her signature dresses that made her look like a sexually oppressed British royal. *No scrubs*, I noted, even though she'd been wearing them last time I saw her at Avebury Court Manor.

Even wearing something Queen Elizabeth would deem too conservative, the pale pink against her snowy skin made me want to tear off her stupid dress and eat her out on the floor. Especially now that I'd decided *not* to.

"What do we have here?" She went straight to Becker and Angus, notably ignoring my existence. She slapped on a pair of elastic gloves, starting with Becker. She flipped him over like he was a fish she considered buying at the market, zeroing in on his wound, frowning. Yet again, I realized that she was delicate looking but could hold her own. She wasn't physically frail and wasn't squeamish.

She pointed at Becker, not even asking for his name. "I'm going to start with this one, since he needs urgent medical attention. Make yourself useful for a change and help me set him up on the table, will you, Sam?"

Was that a dig? I'd bite her head off if I were in a position to do so. As it happened, she was doing me a solid, so I hoisted a mostly unconscious Becker against my shoulder, ignoring her patronizing tone, and followed her into the small room, which had a surgical table, a desk, and a large medicine cabinet.

The room was fully decked out in medical equipment, anesthetics, IV stands, and a blood pressure monitor.

The what-the-fuck questions were piling up, nice and high, as I tried to piece together how this meek, innocent woman, who was doing her residency at Brigham Hospital as an OB-GYN, knew about a place like this, let alone had easy access to it.

"What the hell is this place?" I hissed, not accustomed to being kept in the dark. Especially as I'd always thought I knew everything there was to know about the youngest Fitzpatrick.

"A friend of mine owns it. He treats people without insurance here. People who cannot afford urgent care," she explained primly, signaling me with her chin to the spot where she wanted me to dispose Becker. So I did.

"Are you helping him do this? It's fucking illegal, Aisling. I can't let you do this."

This made her bark out a laugh. "I've seen you shoot someone in the head and you are here so I can patch up your hitmen. Oh, the hypocrisy. Dare I say, Sam, this is so deliciously rich I think your statement alone should be in a higher tax bracket than my family."

"You and I are not the same."

"According to you ..." She shrugged. "You're nothing to me."

"I am your father's right-hand man. My job is to keep his kids out of trouble. I will do whatever the fuck I need to to stop you from getting thrown in jail."

"You will keep well away from me, Brennan, and let me do my job, or I will never help you again."

She went to a nearby sink, dumped her elastic gloves, and scrubbed her hands with soap before putting on a new pair as I glared at her. She had a point. Her access to this place could be beneficial to me. There was no reason why old Gerry needed to know his daughter was being an idiot as long as it worked in my favor.

"Can I see your ticket?" she asked, her back to me.

"What the fuck do you mean?" I frowned.

"To the show you are apparently watching. Get out, Sam. I'm working here."

Concealing my surprise (and delight at discovering this bossy side of her), I leaned against the door, giving zero fucks about Angus, who was still in the reception with his dangling arm and porn star moans.

"I think I'll stay and see you in action, if you don't mind."

"I do mind."

"Allow me to correct my statement—I don't care if you mind. I'm staying."

"I won't treat him," she threatened but was already getting to work cutting his shirt vertically with a pair of scissors.

"Yes, you will. Your need to be helpful overpowers your hatred toward me."

"Don't be so sure," she muttered, working quickly and efficiently, removing the bullet from Becker's lungs without breaking a fucking sweat.

"Your Hippocratic Oath, then."

It was beautiful. Watching Aisling, the girl I knew since she was seventeen, withdrawing a bullet from a man's lungs with the steadiest of hands while he was writhing in pain, twisting underneath her. I could tell the bullet didn't pierce *through* the lung, but it was still damn impressive.

"Any news?" she asked as she began stitching him up.

"About?"

"My father and the media circus around him."

You mean the one I created by hacking into that poor woman's cloud just to satisfy my bloodthirsty tendencies?

It only mildly satisfied me to see Gerald shitting bricks in front of his entire family while he tried to explain that headline. I had much bigger plans for him, and I was going to execute them. Soon.

"Still working on it."

"A bit slow, aren't you?" Her delicate brows pinched together as she wove the needle in and out of Becker, who at this point was passed out. She looked like an English rose working on a quilted dress, not like a doctor stitching up a B-grade mobster.

"You got a problem, speak to my manager."

"You are your own manager," she pointed out.

"That's right…" I paused for effect "…and I don't care what you think about my services, so tough fucking luck, Nix."

"So taciturn," she *tsked*, treating me like I was no more than a boy, like Sparrow would when I had preteen meltdowns and didn't know what to do with my energy. "Almost like you have something to hide."

"Looks to me like you're the one with the juicy secrets. Tell me about this friend of yours who is operating this place." I motioned with my hand around us. Maybe it was time to replace Dr. Holmberg. This place looked legit, and the equipment was much better.

"I will do no such thing. I respect his privacy."

Interesting.

I scanned the back of her head, her raven-blue locks twisted together into a braid, flung over one side of her shoulder. The contrast of her dark hair with her pale everything—eyes, skin, features—made her delectable and forbidden, much younger than her twenty-seven years.

"You know I'll find out either way. Do yourself a favor and give me the information now," I hissed, not used to people talking back to me.

Another first for me, sponsored by the unlikely Aisling Fitzpatrick and her newly found spunk.

She turned around, a hint of a smile on her lips.

"I'd like to see you try. Now please help me return Dumb to the reception, and fetch me Dumber. Go on, now." She waved me off with a huff.

Nix went on to put Angus' arm in a makeshift cast then proceeded to tell him how to tend to his injury, talking to him like she was a teacher and he was a schoolboy who had just crapped his pants in the middle of morning assembly.

As I watched her, I reminded myself that my need to fuck her was really about my desire to fuck Gerald Fitzpatrick over. Nothing more. She was a great fuck, sure, and a fairly harmless girl who'd been chasing me around for a decade. Of course I wanted in her pants. What man wouldn't?

I just wanted to ruin another thing that was precious to Gerald.

Only in Aisling's case, I was going to spare her. Or spite her by not giving her what she wanted. I really wasn't sure which of the two had driven me to not touch her. All I knew was I had healthy instincts, and my instincts told me to stay the fuck away from this woman—far away.

When she was done, and both soldiers were waiting for me at the reception, she sauntered back to the small sink for another vigorous scrub of her hands and arms, still ignoring me like her life depended on it.

"What do I owe you?" I took out my wallet, plucking out a wad of cash.

"Nine grand, plus supplies, so let's round it to eleven. Cash only." She plucked a paper towel off the stand, wiping her hands then slam-dunking the wad of paper into a trash can.

I stared at her, waiting for the punchline. When it didn't arrive, I narrowed my eyes.

"You're kidding me."

"Heavens, Brennan. I'm a highborn woman. I lack anything resembling a good sense of humor. Goes against everything I've been taught in Catholic school," Ash said gravely. "Do you think it would be less pricey if you took them to the hospital?"

"I think if I took them to the hospital, they wouldn't have been treated in some frat boy's fucking basement."

She poked her lip with a finger as she considered my words, unaffected. The only thing reminding me I was the one in control of the situation was her bottomless eyes. They held a promise to always want what I had to offer.

"They're alive and well. Same result as you'd get at the hospital. I'm sorry, I assumed you'd have this kind of money handy. Would you like me to let you know about our payment options, Mr. Brennan?"

The little shi—

I stepped forward, eating up all of the distance between us in one go, baring my teeth as I boxed her in with my arms on either side of her shoulders, against the wall.

"What are you playing at, Nix?"

"Nothing." Her eyes widened innocently. Blue, so terribly blue, and every shade of the color under the sun: ocean, sky, crayon, you name it. "You asked for my services. I assumed you were prepared to pay for them."

"You don't need the money." I was chest-to-chest with her now, and here it was again, that faint ginger smell mixed with flowers and honey that gave me déjà vu of things and places I'd never experienced.

I'll do things to you you will never forget.

"Neither do you. So pay up. I'll be seeing you at Thanksgiving dinner. You can pay me then." Ash smoothed her dress, which was now stained in Becker's blood.

Right.

The world still turned on its axis, and our families continued to play nice with one another, oblivious to my vendetta. Other than Troy, who knew better than to ever let it slip.

The Fitzpatricks were hosting a Thanksgiving dinner next week. I wouldn't miss it for the world, but for all the wrong reasons, and none of them had anything to do with their cook's stuffed turkey.

"Now if you excuse me …" Nix ducked under my shoulder, trying to slip away. I pushed forward, pinning her in place against the wall. If it wasn't for the slight quivering of her chin, I could have sworn she was cool as a cucumber. But that small shake betrayed her, and I seized the opportunity to tilt said chin upward, forcing her to look at me.

"How about a kiss?" I coaxed, my palm sliding from her wrist to her waist, down the curve of her firm ass, squeezing as I pulled her closer to me. I didn't like the power shift between us and wanted to remind her who was the boss. I felt her thighs shaking against my sprawled fingers, ready and wanting, shivered into me as I gathered her close. Her body was soft, smooth, feminine. With hidden curves I had no business thinking about and was paid to ignore.

Her heat radiated between our clothes, and I stifled a groan, yanking her braid, extending her neck and forcing her to look at me.

"Would a kiss be a sufficient form of payment?" I murmured, my lips gliding down the side of her neck.

She said nothing, her heart slamming against mine erratically, begging for more.

Rearing my head back, I crashed my mouth against hers punishingly, resenting her for my need to taste her—and myself for yielding to temptation.

It was a brutal kiss, with teeth and claws and tongue, designed to humiliate her, to remind her which one of us was in control.

Aisling's lips molded over mine immediately, compliant and soft. She moaned gently, her tongue meeting mine thrust for thrust, like we were fucking each other, her fingers curling around the collar of my shirt, drawing me closer. I bit her lower lip until I split it open, her warm, metallic blood trickling into my mouth. She tensed but didn't break the kiss.

Break the fucking kiss, Aisling.

Show me I'm too much for you.

I sucked on her blood, pulling her entire lip into my mouth, and she let me, the little monster that she was.

"You taste like an ashtray," she purred into my mouth. Viper-like, her words dripped venom while she still devoured me hungrily, not letting go.

"Maybe so, but you taste like an easy lay, my least favorite flavor of woman." I chuckled darkly, putting more pressure on her lips, kissing her harder, tasting her blood and her tears and her anguish and enjoying all of them because they were *mine*.

So fucking salty. So fucking sweet.

I was hard. So hard, I knew I was in real danger of taking her on the surgical table she had used just minutes ago to stitch up the two morons on my payroll. I tore my mouth from hers, brushing my thumb over her cheekbone. She stumbled forward, losing balance. I let her fall on my chest but didn't help her right herself.

"Now we're even." I shoved the wallet back into my pocket, surprised to see that despite feeling her tears earlier, her face was dry and calm.

"Oh, you thought a kiss would be your payment as opposed to the eleven grand you owe me? Oh my..." she clutched the pearls on her neck, twisting them exaggeratedly, like her mother would "... my apologies, Mr. Brennan. I don't accept sexual favors as payment. That would be my father's specialty, and I very much doubt he'd be interested in what you have to offer. I would still like the money at Thanksgiving. What's the common interest your loan sharks use? Forty-five percent? That suits me. Now, have a good rest of the day, Mr. Brennan, and do take care."

Five

Aisling

THE ELEVEN THOUSAND DOLLARS WAS WAITING ON THE nightstand in my bedroom the following morning, stacked high and neat, pinned with a golden bullet. There was also one penny right beside them, and a note scribbled messily in bold, long strokes.

Here. Buy yourself something pretty.

It should have terrified me.

The fact that Sam had been in my vicinity—in my *room*—while I was sound asleep. He could've slit my throat if he wanted to. Instead, I felt white-hot thrill washing through my veins as I imagined his imposing, colossal figure casting a shadow over my sleeping body, his hands that could snap my bones like twigs so close to my spine.

He'd been there when I was in my flimsy nightgown, my hair fanned over the white satin pillow, dreaming of his crushing weight above me, making love to me.

I knew he would not send anyone else. No. None of his soldiers would do. He would never allow them to get anywhere near me. He violated my space, yes, but I knew there were limits between us. Unwritten rules that made me feel safe.

I picked up the bullet—cold, metallic, and heavier than I expected—mulling it over as it sat in my hand.

Did he stop and stare? Did he replay the kiss we'd shared at the clinic in his head? We'd almost tore each other's mouths apart.

I could still feel a faint pulse against my lips.

Sometimes I suspected Sam felt it, too. The wild electricity buzzing between us every time we were in the same room. Whenever he looked at me with those silver moon eyes as they slanted just so, zeroing in on me, watching.

Other times he would be in my vicinity, having a meal with my father or a beer with Devon, Cillian, and Hunter, and ignore my existence so thoroughly, so convincingly, I'd forget I was in the room, too.

He was a mystery, and mysteries were meant to be unearthed, uncovered, and unfolded. I'd finally caught his attention—snatched it against his will—grasping onto it with bloodied fingers, and I had every intention of keeping it.

I was going to fight him tooth and nail, go head-to-head with the underworld's king just so I could have him. Prove to him that I was worthy of his attention and his love.

So I did the only thing I could do, knowing that I had an entire week to wait until Thanksgiving dinner, when I'd see him again.

It was crazy, and dangerous, not to mention illegal, and yet, so classically Sam I couldn't resist the temptation. Show him I was Nix through and through. A cunning monster who just happened to look good in a gown.

The night after he put the money on my nightstand, I drove to Badlands, found the back door to the place right behind the building, by an alley and stacked monopoly money—11k of it—and pinned it with the lone penny he'd left for me. Then I drenched it in gasoline and set fire to it.

I knew he would never know the difference. That he would think it was really the money he had given me, but I'd donated that money to my charity of choice. Something Ms. B would have wanted me to do.

I ran back to my car, ducking behind the window as I peeked to see the back door opening as the stench of burned paper seeped through the cracks. Sam appeared, accompanied by Dumb and Dumber. Dumb ran back to the office to bring a fire extinguisher while Dumber desperately tried to defuse the fire by pouring water and handfuls of snow on it, his arm still in a sling.

Sam just stood there and grinned devilishly, watching the money burn.

He didn't need a written note to read the *fuck you* in what I did. *He knew.*

The Fitzpatrick clan had always been huge on Thanksgiving.

I suspected it was because we had so much to be thankful for.

Not only were we one of the richest families in the country, but we were also blessed with nieces and nephews, all rosy-cheeked, healthy, and barely into their toddlerhood.

The day of Thanksgiving butlers fretted about the long table in our dining room, rearranging maple leaf bowls made out of gold, pumpkins, champagne glasses, and ornaments. The centerpieces were bursting with fall and winter fruit, and everything was laced with gold and silver. Warm and inviting candlelight illuminated the room, and the scent of cinnamon and sugared dough traveled from the kitchen, tickling my nostrils.

Pacing back and forth in my off-the-shoulder orange Givenchy dress—I knew wearing it would please Mother, who had recently been quite the pain to serve and dote on—I stopped by the window, watching my brother Cillian unload his family from his car, an imperial frown on his face.

He opened the door for Persephone—Persy, that was what we called her—scooping little Astor into a BabyBjorn he strapped over his shoulders. My breath caught, and my heart squeezed at the sight of my brother doing something so fatherly, so caring, in such a natural manner despite his usual cold and aloof demeanor.

The minute Astor was secured close to his chest, Cillian leaned down and pressed a kiss on his son's head.

I realized I was jealous. Jealous of my good friend Persy, who deserved this life more than anyone else I knew—and still, I wanted what she had for myself.

Not who she had it *with*, obviously—I was crazy, but not the shade of crazy who was okay with incest—but I wanted it with someone I couldn't have. *Sam.*

Turning away from the window, I pretended to busy myself by rearranging perfectly arranged ornaments at the center of the table.

Sam was going to arrive soon, and I needed to gather every dollop of strength to face him with my head held high and my back straight.

"Ash?" I heard a voice wonder behind me and turned around to find Persy tucking a lock of her blonde hair behind her ear. She was wearing a romantic evening dress with a beautiful floral print, holding a wide-awake baby Astor in her arms. His marble-blue eyes glittered at me with delight, a shock of chocolate hair covering his tender head. He threw his chubby arms in my direction, and I scooped him up with a thrilled squeak, pressing him to my chest and inhaling his intoxicating baby scent.

"Hey, Pers…" I rubbed my cheek against Astor's silky strands, marveling yet again at how much he looked like his father "…how are you?"

"I'm great. You looked thoughtful through the window. Which was why I bypassed the usual hugs and kisses routine to see how you were doing. Your mother looks … preoccupied." She took a seat at the table, eyeing me curiously.

Preoccupied was a very nice way of putting it. My mother was working me to the bone these days, asking me to help with her bath, read her books, and drive her around because she didn't want to converse with her usual driver. But I wasn't in the mood to talk about that.

"Where's Cillian?" I walked around the room with Astor, who wanted to reach and touch everything.

"With Gerald in his office. I can't believe he did that to your mom." Persy bit the inside of her cheek. She had always been nice and gentle, and I knew she spared me the more blunt words I was bound to hear from Sailor and Belle.

"I can." I put Astor down on the carpet, allowing him to explore his surroundings.

"Sailor told me Sam asked for your number," Persephone continued, scanning me with eager eyes, as if looking at me would inspire me to spill more information. *Merde.* I knew my friends were invested in my quest to make Sam Brennan notice my existence, but at the same time, I hated how they treated me. Like I was a silly, naïve girl incapable of bagging the man of her dreams.

I felt especially pathetic, considering Persephone was happily married to my brother, the catch of the century according to People Magazine, and Sailor was married to my *other* brother, who treated her like a queen. Emmabelle (who was Persephone's sister) might not have been married—but it was by choice.

I was the odd one out. The doomed girl mourning her unrequited love.

And I definitely didn't want them to know about my current relationship with Sam, which put me in a less than a favorable position.

"It was nothing." I waved a hand around, following Astor to make sure he didn't bump into anything or decided to stick his fingers in outlets. "He just needed some help. Something work-related."

"Huh." Persephone sprawled in her seat, tapping a finger over her chin thoughtfully. "But maybe it's a start? He never contacted you before, and you're hardly the only person he could turn to."

Persephone was such a romantic, anything short of Sam trying to maim me with a machete would register in her mind as a prime example of his undying love for me.

I rolled my eyes. "You're grasping at straws, Pers."

"Weirder pairings have happened. Look at your brother and me," she said eagerly, making her case. "You just need more patience as you pursue him."

"Cillian always had a boner for you. He just hid it like a thirteen-year-old. Sam is not pursuable," I concluded, feeling like a phony since I was definitely waist-deep in this cat and mouse game with Sam.

But I didn't want to jinx things or jump to conclusions. Plus, if nothing came out of it—which was likely; my plan was farfetched—at least I wouldn't have to deal with more pity from my friends.

"If your brothers are pursuable, so is Sam," Persy determined, putting her foot down. "You should go for what you want."

"But what if what I want is everything that's bad for me?" I turned around, finding her gaze. "What if I'm stupid to want Sam Brennan? He is a gangster. A murderer. An underground boss and my father's right hand. So many things can go wrong. If they'll go in any direction at all …"

"You just described love." Persy grinned. "Love is a risk. It's a storm that either disrupts your life or clears your path. Sometimes it does both at the same time. Focus on getting the guy. Everything else will fall into place."

An hour and a half later, the evening was in full swing.

Everyone was at the table, digging into the delicious food Cook had made.

Honey-roasted turkey, buttery mashed potatoes, pumpkin pecan bread pudding, golden baked apples, and savory sausage stuffing.

Candlelight danced around the room, casting playful glows on familiar faces, as chatter rang from all across the table.

Sailor and Persy's au pairs sat in the far corner of the room with the children—Astor, Xander, and Rooney—gossiping and tending to the babies. Sam sat all the way at the other side of the table from me, and even though I could feel his eyes on me every now and again, assessing, daring, challenging, I made it a point to stick to conversations with my mother, Sailor, Persephone, and Emmabelle.

Normally, I would try to talk to him, ask him questions, form some sort of a connection. Not right now and not today. I was no longer the girl who chased him. Or so I wanted him to think.

"The concept of Thanksgiving is still jarring to me," Devon complained from the other end of the table, next to Sam, in his imperial, posh English drawl. He cut his turkey into frighteningly even pieces and looked entirely too good for a man who didn't model for a living. "Who exactly are you lot thanking?"

Devon was what Belle referred to as appallingly gorgeous. All soft blond, sandy curls twisting at the ears and the nape of his neck, piercing blue eyes, and the bone structure of a deity.

"Um, God?" Hunter threw a piece of sweet potato into his mouth, chewing. "You're just bitter because we have stuff to be thankful for. Big-box stores, the First Amendment, Jewish deli food, and, of course, Scarlett Johansson. What do you have to be thankful for?"

"Footie, brown sauce, and being generally intellectually superior to the Yanks," Devon deadpanned, regarding all the food at the table like it was suspicious.

"By footie you mean soccer?" My father frowned. He'd been fairly quiet the entire night.

"No, by football I mean football. The one where you *kick* the ball with your foot…" Devon patted the corners of his mouth unnecessarily with a napkin "…as opposed to *holding* it in your hand while running, crashing into random people like a barbarian trying to sneak the rival village's best-looking maiden."

"Keep trashing football, and the only thing you'll be thankful for this Thanksgiving is getting out of this meal in one piece." Troy offered a stony smile, swirling his whiskey in his hand.

"So, Sam, you're the last single man standing. Up for a quick trip to Sin City to play blackjack at the casino this weekend?" Devon changed the subject.

"You're still doing that?" Sparrow darted poisonous arrows at her son through her jade-green eyes. "It's dangerous, not to mention reckless. You're already blacklisted from three hotels."

Sam smiled, eating and pretending like the conversation didn't swirl around him.

"Not surprised." Hunter chuckled, raising his virgin Bloody Mary to his lips. "Do I want to know what for?"

"Winning too much money." Devon laughed, pouring himself another drink. "Sam is the best blackjack player I've ever seen in my lifetime. A wizard with numbers, really. He makes all the calculations in split seconds."

I thought back to the finite mathematics homework he'd worked out for me when I was still a teenager. Devon wasn't exaggerating.

"What a great way to utilize your analytical talent," Cillian drawled sarcastically.

"Better to waste a talent in the wrong place than not have one in the first place," Sam pointed out.

"Your main talent is to find your way into rich people's inner circle," Cillian countered, his tone easy. "Which you've been doing very well since childhood."

"Anyway, cards at Badland tonight," Hunter said. "Right after dinner."

I wanted to hear more about Sam, but my mother was desperate to draw me into the conversation she was having. She did that often. Lured me into small talk to save her from awkward lulls. She said she found socializing tiring, yet she threw events all the time and counted on me to do all the talking and fundraising on her behalf.

"I'm so lucky to have Aisling…" Mother patted her eyes with her napkin, sighing heavily "…I don't know what I would have done without her. She is my anchor. No wonder she works at bringing life into this planet. She is my perfect angel."

"She sure is saintly, ma'am." Emmabelle flicked up a brow in my direction, giving me the stink eye. I knew Belle would love nothing more than if I showed my devilish side a little more often. "*Too* good to be true. Almost."

"Right now, she is working day and night to help me with a charity event this month," my mother started, and I could see the rest of my friends had already trained their face to stoic politeness, knowing she was going to yap about it for hours.

I felt my phone buzzing under the table, in my lap, and looked down. The number flashing across the screen signaled it came from the clinic. *Merde.*

I ducked my head down, swiped the bar to the green circle, and answered. "Yes?"

It was the call I dreaded. The one I didn't want to receive.

A patient who had been struggling pretty badly.

"Yes. Of course. No, it is not a bad time at all. I'm on my way. Thank you."

I hung up the phone, smiling brightly to everyone at the table, realizing for the first time the phone call drew everyone's attention. Sam's eyes rested on me lazily, swirling the whiskey in his tumbler as he watched me with a mildly entertained look I wanted to wipe off of his face.

The whole night he'd been looking at me like he couldn't decide whether he wanted another round in the sack with me or wanted to kill me. I wished he'd just make up his mind and put me out of my misery.

"My apologies, but I have to run. Something important at work." I stood up abruptly, patting my mother's shoulder. Everyone's attention made my ears hot and my fingers tremble. "Compliments to our chef. I will send her flowers tomorrow morning for her troubles. Thank you, everyone. Have a good evening."

With that, I dashed out, running straight to my Prius, not even bothering to grab a coat on my way. I made a beeline to the address I punched into my phone.

It took me an hour to get to the residential building in Westford. A newly built apartment complex with a tennis court, a pool, and an indoor gym. There wasn't security or anyone manning the reception, though, something I'd asked about in advance, just to be on the safe side.

I went to my patient's house, did what I had to do, and got out of there three hours later. All thoughts about the Thanksgiving dinner I'd left behind were now demolished and gone. All I thought about was my work, my patients, and *her*.

Oui, mon cheri. It's not easy doing what you do.

My knees were wobbly and my breath erratic as I made my way to a gas station across the road, trudging over the half-melted, dirty snow. I pushed the door to the small mini mart open. I bought a Coke for myself and a cake and drink for the old man manning the register, which he thanked me for. I poured myself out into the bone-cold November winter in Massachusetts, pressing the back of my head against the wall and taking a gulp of Coke.

Sometimes I hated what I did.

Most times, really.

But then I remembered Ms. B and how I failed her and convinced myself that I deserved it. My occupation. My choices.

Staring down at the Coke in my hand, listening to the faint hiss of fizz coming from the liquid, I suddenly burst into tears, sobbing uncontrollably as I dragged myself down the length of the wall, crouching to my feet and burying my face in my satin Givenchy dress.

"It's not fair." I shook my head, seeing the black splotches my mascara left on my gown through blurred tears. "Nothing about this is fair."

"Tell me about it," an edgy tone that could cut glass made me snap my head up.

Sam.

Sam wore a pea coat, looking like a dashing eighteenth century earl, and leaning on the wall opposite to the one I was sitting against, an unlit cigarette stuck between his gorgeous lips. Thank the lord he didn't pull a Zoolander and light it up next to a gas station.

"Fair is where you get cotton candy. It has nothing to do with real life. Now, tell me how you found yourself in Westford as opposed to Brigham Hospital, where your ass should have been tonight."

He'd been following me here.

But how?

And more importantly … *why?*

Because you got his attention, and now he is waiting to see what you'll do with it. You burned his cash in front of his establishment, had anal sex with him in a wig and a hooker costume, and operated on his soldiers in an underground clinic. He just discovered you are a monster, too, and now wants to know how deep your darkness runs.

I quickly wiped the tears off my face, straightening my spine, and stood up.

"Shouldn't you be playing cards with my brothers at Badlands right about now? Or are you missing Cook's famous apple pie to be here?"

"Shouldn't you be answering my fucking question?" he retorted.

"The answer is none of your business," I bit out harshly.

"This old tune again." He chuckled, looking sideways as he shook his head. "You are my business. My boss' daughter. I should have kept tabs on you and tailed your ass earlier, but I didn't. So here we are. Now let's cut the bullshit, shall we? I checked everywhere worth checking and cross-examined my sources. You are not a resident at Brigham and Women's Hospital."

Merde, merde, merde.

Triple merde with a cherry on top.

He was on to me.

"Been checking on me, Brennan?" I plastered what I hoped was a teasing smile on my face. "I'm flattered, but not surprised. Still, that doesn't mean anything."

"Sure it does. For starters, it means you are a fucking liar. My least favorite trait in people. But then I thought to myself, maybe the lie isn't so big. Maybe it's about prestige. Little, perfect Aisling didn't want her parents to know she didn't get accepted to one of the most respected hospitals in the country..." he took another step toward me, his nostrils flaring, his jaw hardening so sharply it looked like it was carved in marble "...so I went and checked with *all* of the hospitals in Boston, every single fucking one. Guess what?"

I didn't have to guess. I knew.

"You're not registered anywhere as a doctor. You turned all of them down. Every single fucking offer. At this point, I got suspicious. Did you even finish med school at all?" he asked theatrically, taking yet another step, getting closer to me, crowding me, pinning me against the wall. "So I sniffed around that angle, too. You did, in fact, graduate from Harvard Medical School. So it's not that you aren't a doctor." He took the final step toward me, and now we were so close his scent and air and menace seeped into my body, hitting roots, conquering me. "Whatever you do, you're doing it under the radar. What the fuck are you playing at, Nix?"

His body was flush against mine, big and strong and threatening. My thighs clenched together, the space between them empty and needy. I drew a deep breath, trying to steady my pulse. I had to find my voice.

"You really want to know?"

He stared at me expressionlessly. Of course he did. Sam Brennan knew everything worth knowing about everyone, and I piqued his interest.

I curled my index finger, signaling him to lean down so I could whisper in his ear. He complied, his scowl deepening with annoyance. I pressed my lips against his ear, feeling his cock, hard and thick, pressing against my stomach.

"None. Of. Your. Business," I breathed.

He jerked back, his thunderstorm eyes dark and depraved, and suddenly, I had a feeling I did a very, very foolish thing taunting this man, and I was going to pay for it dearly.

"Don't play games with me, Aisling. I will win. Easily. And I'm a bad sport and notoriously unfair, just like your miserable life."

I stared at him defiantly, keeping my mouth shut. My teeth chattered. My whole body hummed with energy, but I didn't back down.

"Do you *want* to be humiliated?" He grinned, starting to enjoy this game.

"No. I want you to make up your mind about what you want to do with me," I said quietly.

"You've been running after me with your skirt up, begging to be fucked since before you got your period."

He chuckled, producing a Swiss knife from his pocket, running it up my dress and slashing a deep, long slit through its middle, right between my thighs. The dress ripped noisily. He tucked his knife back into his pocket, dipping his hand in and brushing his finger along my slit through my underwear.

"You ... you ... you ..." I panted, a mixture of rage and desire swirling in my stomach. I knew none of this was healthy or normal, and yet I craved it so much it hurt to breathe.

"Tore your pretty designer dress? Don't worry. Daddy'll buy you a hundred more. The pathetic part is you're not going to deny me because you and I both know I can fuck you whenever I want, however I want, however many times I want. Bend you over—the jewel of the Fitzpatrick crown, Princess Aisling of Avebury Court Manor—and ram my cock so deep inside your ass you'll see stars."

I turned my face away from him, squeezing my eyes shut. I hated him in that moment. Hated him beyond belief. But he was right. That didn't stop me from letting him slip his hand into my underwear, right there, in the middle of the street, behind a slimy gas station. He dipped two fingers inside of me to find me soaked and ready for him. His lips were close to mine when he spoke, but I knew he wasn't going to kiss me.

This wasn't foreplay. It was punishment.

"What do you do for a living, Nix?"

"Fuck y-you," I stuttered, feeling my hips bucking, searching for more of his touch.

"I wouldn't call that a full-time job. I usually grow bored of my fucks after a few hookups." He shoved his fingers in and out, thrusting deep, filling me while his thumb rubbed my clit in circles. My skin felt warm and tingly. My knees turned to jelly. I was suspended over the brink of disaster, about to jump headfirst into the flames he lit just to destroy me.

Keep your cards close to your chest, mon cheri. You heard his maman yourself. He is a good blackjack player.

"Illegal, experimental drugs?" he prodded, swirling his thumb faster against my clit.

I shook my head desperately, refusing to cooperate. He used his free hand to grab my butt, curling a finger into my ass through my dress.

A moan ripped from my mouth at the unexpected intrusion, and I felt so full I knew a violent orgasm was coming my way.

"The no insurance, doctors-without-borders bullshit where you treat the poor ain't flying, sweetheart." He raised an eyebrow, slanting his gaze to the apartment complex behind me, fucking me harder with his fingers, slipping a third finger in and nearly throwing me off the edge. "Whoever lives in that building doesn't get monthly food stamps. Take it from someone who looked poverty in the eye. I'd hate to blow your cover and kick in every door at the complex to find the asshole you visited and milk your secret out of them. But I'll do it if I have to. So for the last time, Aisling, tell me what the fuck it is that you do."

I shook my head, stitching my lips closed and squeezing my eyes shut, the climax washing over me, making every fine hair on my body stand on end. When Sam realized I wasn't going to answer, he let me go. Moved away from me unexpectedly.

I was so weak with desire and pleasure, I nearly fell flat on my ass, bracing myself on the wall as I struggled to gain my footing.

Sam's eyes were still on me, narrowed and full of fury. He sucked his index finger, releasing it with a pop, absorbing all the juices that coated it from when he fingered me.

"I was close," I protested.

"Tough fucking luck. For more information, go to www.lifeain'tfairandwe'vebeenthroughthis.com."

"What the hell!" I flung my arms in the air.

"The hell is you are a fucking headache and need to be taught a lesson. I am going to get the truth out of you, Aisling, one way or the other, but until I do, you lose all cumming privileges. Not by my hands, anyway, and let's admit it—your sole purpose in life is getting fucked by me."

His knowledge of just how much I wanted him destroyed me. I was too transparent, too naïve, too willing to show him how much he meant to me over the years. Now he was using it against me, and there was nothing I could do about it.

Nothing but try to show him I was my own person. That there was more to me than loving him.

"Why do you even care what I do?" I rearranged my torn dress around my legs the best I could to protect myself from the harsh weather. "You made it perfectly clear you don't give a damn about me. You spent a whole decade dodging my advances."

Not that there were many. But whenever I did muster the courage to reach out, he always shut me down in a spectacular fashion. The truth was, I was too scared to upset my parents to go after a man they didn't want for me, and Sam was too career-focused to let someone like me become a problem for his business.

He took his car keys out of his coat's pocket.

"Circumstances change," he clipped.

"Yes, they do," I agreed. "Which is why I suggest you stop assuming I am always going to be at your disposal. I'm not the same girl you met at the carnival, Sam. I'm all grown up, and I won't be treated like I'm a toy."

He leaned toward me, smirking teasingly. "Wanna bet?"

"How are we going to settle the bet? In your card room at Badlands?" I arched an eyebrow, a childish part of me desperate to let him know I was privy to the way he ran his business.

"No. You're not allowed in Badlands," he reminded me in a withering tone.

"But Sailor and Persy are." I laughed bitterly.

"Sailor and Persy are not running around looking for trouble. They stay at home with their babies. I suggest you do the same."

"I don't have babies," I pointed out the obvious. "Oh, and it's not the nineteenth century."

"You might be annoying, but I'm sure you'll find a schmuck willing to knock you up."

"What about Belle? How come she's allowed in Badlands? She looks for trouble all the time. Much more than me."

"Belle is damaged goods and also none of my fucking business. If you end up catching the clap in Badlands' restroom, your family will come crying to me."

"You're a sexist pig."

"And you are still interested. What does it say about you, Ruth Bader Ginsburg, Jr.?"

I was going to say something snarky, but apparently, Sam was through with the exchange. In a swift fashion, he turned around and sauntered over to his car, which was parked right behind me.

"Hold onto those little secrets of yours, Nix. Because I'm going to have one hell of a good time unraveling them."

He slid into his car and sped off.

Leaving me with a throbbing center, wet cheeks, and a jumbled head.

I knew something was wrong as soon as I parked the car by the fountain at my front door. Avebury Court Manor was like a body. It had bones, a heart, and a soul. I could recognize its pulse from miles away, and something felt different. Erratic.

All the lights in the house were turned on, the staff, which should be long gone, running back and forth by the window like shadow puppets. There was a commotion. My brothers' cars were also still parked by the entrance. They should be home by now.

Something happened.

Hurrying out of the car, I clutched my keys in a death grip.

Please be okay, Mother.

As soon as I flung the door open, Cillian and Hunter poured out of it, each of them holding Da from each side. My father, green and dripping with sweat, was slouched unresponsive between them, his head dangling from his neck like a pendulum.

"Where are you taking him?" I shrieked.

Cillian shouldered past me, toward his car. I followed them, my legs still shaky from my crazy night.

"Disney World," my older brother drawled, sullen. "Where do you think? The hospital."

"The hospital!" I echoed, my mouth turning dry. "Why? What happened? Where's Mother?"

"Mother is hiding in her room crying about how Da stole the show, being a real fucking adult about it per usual," Hunter filled me in, his voice playful as always, even when his words were hot and angry.

"As for *Athair*, he's been vomiting nonstop since you left, has diarrhea, a dry mouth, a rash, trouble breathing, and he fainted twice since dessert."

Cillian buckled my dad inside his Aston Martin. "How would you diagnose that, Doc?"

"Well, I need to run more tests, of course, but at first glance I would say he was poisoned."

"Ding, ding, ding," Hunter congratulated me. "When Da finished his cup of coffee, he proceeded to collapse on top of the table like a stack of cards."

All the air left my lungs at once.

"I'm coming with you."

"You just got back from the hospital," Hunter pointed out.

My face filled with heat and shame, and I curled my long coat around myself to prevent my brothers from seeing the giant rip in my dress. They thought I was at Brigham, too. Because I lied to them. To all of them. Every single member of my family and the small circle of my friends.

"It's no trouble."

"Your funeral," Cillian clipped. "Hunter, let her take the passenger seat. C'mon, Ash. We're taking the car. We don't want the headlines an ambulance would create."

"Forever the Fitzpatricks." Hunter touched his forehead with mock salute, tucking himself next to Da.

I stuffed myself into the seat next to Cillian.

"Sure you're okay leaving your baby behind?" Hunt asked from the backseat, jerking his chin toward the manor. He meant our mother.

"*Don't* start."

"No shade." Hunter raised his palms in the air defensively. "All I'm saying is she is probably writing all of us out of her will because we are driving Da to the hospital instead of telling her how pretty she is—after she poisoned him."

Hunter only knew the half of it. Jane Fitzpatrick's problems were much worse than being self-centered and prone to drastic mood swings.

Athair was unresponsive the whole way to the ER. As soon as we walked in, I found out who was the doctor assigned to deal with Da, took him aside, and explained I was a fellow doctor, relaying the evening to give him the full picture, omitting the poisoning part to prevent it from leaking to the media.

The three of us siblings spent the night sleeping by Da's bedside, huddled together like when we were kids. The blood and urine test results came back the following morning.

It looked like my father had taken an enormous amount of warfarin, a blood thinner and also an active ingredient in many rat poisons. A drug that can easily cause death if taken in a certain quantity.

My father had been poisoned by a pro who knew what they were doing.

Not enough to kill, but definitely enough to deliver a message.

The weird thing was no one at the table had any motive to kill Da.

No one other than Mother.

"It's not Mother." I shook my head, standing in Cillian's home office later that day, looking out the window as more snow fell and covered the rose garden and trimmed bushes, painting everything white. "It's not."

"Oh, come on, Ash. At the very least, it's an option worth considering. They've been at each other's throats for as long as I can remember." Hunter massaged my shoulders from behind, still in his suit from the previous night.

We'd come here straight from the hospital, as soon as my father's secretary took over and arrived there.

I whipped around, slapping his hand away. "No, Hunt. She is incapable of hurting a fly."

That was not completely true. The only person Mother was capable of hurting was herself, and she did it often, but I didn't want Hunter and Cillian to know about that side of her. They had enough on their plate, running Royal Pipelines and taking care of their families. Their wives were my best friends, and I didn't want to hog my brothers' attention by dragging them into the issues we were having at Avebury Court Manor.

"She is also the only person at the table with a hard-on to see Gerald return his equipment to the Almighty," Cillian pointed out, taking a seat in his plush leather chair and lighting up a cigar, his legs propped up on his desk with his ankles crossed.

Something about my older brother rejected vulnerability, so I learned how to become robotically efficient in front of him from a young age. I didn't allow myself to show too much emotion. Not for the first time, I found myself envying Persy and Astor. The way he looked at them so adoringly, like he was still hungry for something he already had.

I wondered if I would ever experience what my friends had. The kind of love that changes people from within.

"Let's make a list!" I proposed, snapping my fingers, remembering how Sam planned to tackle my father's sex scandal. "Of who was there. Then we can go through it and dig deeper."

"All right, Sherlock." Hunter lounged on the settee by the window overlooking Cillian's garden. "Let's see, there was Xander, Rooney, and Astor, all of them under three years old ..."

"Astor's been teething. He can be a mean little thing when he is teething," Cillian pointed out sarcastically, causing Hunter to laugh and me to roll my eyes.

"Rooney has a mean streak, too. But she usually pees on the carpet when she seeks her revenge upon us. Then there was Sailor and me," Hunter said. "Neither of us have beef with Da. And you, Ash, don't have a motive either."

"Persephone and I are out of the question. My wife couldn't hurt a fly if she tried, and I already have everything I ever needed from Gerald," Cillian continued. "And then there's Emmabelle. A distasteful excuse for a human being, sure, but I wouldn't go as far as calling her a murderer."

"Whoever did this didn't try to kill him. They tried to spook him," I pointed out. "But I agree, Emmabelle has no connection to Da whatsoever. What about Troy? Sparrow?"

"As far as I'm aware, Troy and Sparrow have no business with *Athair*. No reason to want to threaten him." Hunter shook his head.

"Devon?" I wondered aloud.

Cillian somehow managed to look down at me, even from his position sitting. "No motive."

"True, but he is not family."

"Neither is Sam." Cillian puffed on his cigar.

"I think we should keep an eye on him, too," I said honestly, something clawing at my stomach when I thought about getting him in trouble.

Hunter jumped upright. "Whoa, whoa, whoa, keep an eye how ...? We were joking, but ... he's my brother-in-law."

"He is also the most corrupt man to walk this earth." Cillian blew rings of smoke in the air. "I'll deal with him. Sniff around. See what he is up to."

"No..." I turned to face both my brothers "...I'll do it. He won't suspect me."

"*I* suspect you." Hunter's eyes flared in alarm. "No offense, sis, but even Rooney knows Auntie Ash is in *lurveeee* with Uncle Sam. And I don't mean you being patriotic toward the US of A."

"But see, that's what makes it so perfect," I said desperately. "He will never see me as a threat or think I could harm him."

"I don't want him anywhere near you," Cillian hissed.

"Well, tough luck, big bro. I'm twenty-seven. You can't shelter me forever."

"Wanna bet?" Hunter grinned. I shot him a look. Cillian sighed. We all wanted to wrap this up and go about our days.

"Fine. Ash, you can sniff around Sam. Just remember it is frowned upon to have sex with your target," Cillian clipped. "I'll check the Devon angle."

"And I'll pray for both your souls." Hunter did the sign of the cross, rolling his eyes. "Because both of y'all are dumbasses who watch too much *CSI*. It's Jane. She wanted to get back at Da for sticking his dick in the wrong hole and things got a little bit out of hand. Not the first time she did something drastic and threw a fit. Remember when he gifted her the butterfly garden after she found out he'd been screwing her own sister? Not that I ever liked this particular auntie, but she threw his Rolex collection into the food processor and set it to high."

We had a butterfly garden at our house, built by my father to show Jane Fitzpatrick his undying love for her. A love that came with the price of $670,000 worth of luxury vintage watches he parted ways with.

"Thanks for the little trip down memory lane to remind me I am the spawn of two of the most disgusting people to ever grace the planet. Now, if that is all, I'd like to go back to running my company." Cillian put out his cigar, standing up and walking briskly toward the window where I stood. "May the best man win, Aisling. You think it's Sam, Hunter thinks it's Mother, and I think Gerald has been spending too much time at the medicine cabinet and had an oopsie."

But it wasn't accidental. I knew.

Because *Athair* would never make such a mistake. He loved himself too much to overdose. As someone living under the same roof as him, I knew he was careful with his prescription drugs.

This was intentional.

All men at the table were cunning, smart, and capable, but only one of them had murdered someone before, to the extent of my knowledge, and would go to such extreme lengths with such ease.

Sam.

Six

Sam

GERALD FITZPATRICK WAS A GODDAMN MESS.

Everything about him screamed depression. He lost weight, a lot of it—at least forty pounds—had dark circles around his eyes, and looked like he hadn't slept or showered in days.

He was a dead man walking, and I savored every moment of watching him like this.

"The hostile takeover for FMK Petroleum is well underway." Cillian paced Gerald's office, hands behind his back. "We just need to finalize the small print."

FMK Petroleum had been buying off the oil fields Royal Pipelines had their eyes on for months. The Fitzpatricks were just the type of people to squash any competition before it became a threat. Monopoly was the Fitzpatrick game of choice, no doubt about that.

I knew that there were congressmen who wanted to see Gerald and his sons go down in flames for setting the pace and rules for the oil industry. Especially the Texas folks. Nobody hated the Fitzpatricks more than the Texans.

The Irish, New England outsiders who took over the industry.

"Samuel, are you ready to go?" Gerald asked.

I nodded curtly.

"Their CEO won't say no to the deal. I dug up too much dirt on him. By the time I'm done, he'll be happy to sell you his shares for a fucking Costco membership."

"That's my boy." Gerald smiled weakly.

Fuck you, old man.

The stab of rage I felt each time he called me "my boy" was enough to make me snap.

"In terms of the paperwork, we've done our due diligence," Devon, who sat next to Hunter, added. "All that's left is to hope the CEO has pull with the shareholders."

We talked shop a few more minutes before everyone said their goodbyes, shook hands, and drifted out of the room. All of them except Gerald and me.

I waited until the front door to Gerald's study was closed and the coast was clear—as clear as it could be. Nix had eavesdropped on me once in this house, and I didn't trust her not to do it again. Hell, I didn't trust her with a fucking Espresso machine. She was both an ally and an adversary, depending on the day. I suspected she wasn't even home. I hadn't seen her Prius when I parked in front of the house. It was likely she had a shift of whatever the fuck she did for a living—note to self: find out and torment her with it.

The memory of my fingers deep inside of her haunted me. It had been a few days, and I couldn't even bury myself in another warm hole because every time I went to Badlands to look for one, all the other women in the vicinity came up short in comparison.

At least none of them had stirred anything below the belt.

"Oh, Sam …" Gerald rubbed his face tiredly, flipping through his books.

"That's the point where I'm supposed to ask how you're doing, right, Gerry?" I sat across from him, lighting a cigarette.

"It is." His chin quivered. "And the answer is terrible. I am beside myself. I moved out of my marital bedroom."

"Ah, the old doghouse," I said dryly, unable to scrap an ounce of pity for the man.

"The doghouse is better than sharing a bed with a bitch. I don't want to be anywhere near her. She goddamn nearly killed me, Sam. And the worst part is she is still denying it. Trying to poison me. Damn woman."

The fact that everyone suspected Jane Fitzpatrick was the person who poisoned Gerald was a new development to me but one I welcomed nonetheless. I wanted to toy with the man, to mess with his psyche.

"Have you made the list yet?" I probed. "The faster we get to the bottom of this, the quicker we can move on from this."

I was referring to the list of mistresses he'd kept over the years. I'd insisted on him confessing to every single one. For research purposes, *of course*. "Jealousy and desperation for money are key aspects in trying to mess with someone," I explained.

"I did." Gerald puffed his cheeks. "Three nights it took me. Doing this made me realize something, you know, son? It made me see that I've been spending most of my time with women but none of it with the woman I was married to. Such a sad state of affairs. Ironically, I won't be giving Jane more attention now, after what she put me through."

"Hand me the list." I ignored his little speech. I wasn't in the mood for his fucking TED talk. If he needed to sit down and write the names of all the women he'd slept with while married to figure out his marriage was a sham, he had the IQ of the room temperature.

Reluctantly, Gerald opened the drawer in his desk, throwing me cautious looks. He clutched the papers—all fucking *three* of them—to his chest like a maiden protecting her virtue.

"There'll be some names you might recognize on the list. I trust everything in this room is confidential."

"Sure," I spat out. I was a professional, yes, but this man fucked my mother. Then killed my brother inside her. Then convinced her to leave me.

I was professional but not a dumbass.

He dragged the list across the desk, and I snatched it, my eyes roaming, looking for the name I was waiting to see.

I recognized some of the women. A news anchor, a congresswoman, the former Secretary of State's wife, and the daughter of a baseball legend.

But I did not see Catalina Greystone's name.

I skimmed again. And again. And a-motherfucking-gain.

Still. Nothing.

I looked up from the pages, scanning him silently while my blood hummed. Anger was a potent spice. Too much of it dulled your senses. But I couldn't help but feel irrationally cross. Why didn't he put her name in there? Ah, but I already knew. He must be privy to the fact she died not too long ago and figured she couldn't be behind the sex scandal leak and the poisoning since it was a little difficult to haunt a man when you were six feet under.

Truth was, Catalina posed no threat to him now, and I had no reason to call him out on it without outing myself as knowing about him. If I wanted a confession out of him, I needed to up my game.

I folded the pages and stood up, smiling.

"I'll have a look."

"Let me know if something pops up." He rubbed his forehead, looking like a less-alive version of a roadkill. "I just want this nightmare to be over. I put extra cameras around the house to make sure I am protected. I want to believe it is not Jane, but with our history …" He shook his head, heaving a sigh.

Making my way out of his office, I wondered why the fuck I was so invested in making Gerald's life a living hell. I didn't care one iota about Cat. Sure, Gerald wronged me on a fundamental level, maybe even killed my half-brother, but did he really do something to throw my life off course in a negative way? If anything, I should thank my lucky stars Cat had left me with the Brennans when she did. Hell knew where I'd be if she stuck around to "parent" me.

For the first time, as I sauntered across the shiny marble floors of Avebury Court Manor on my way out, I wondered if maybe there was another reason why I enjoyed hating Gerald so much. Perhaps the excuse to hate the Fitzpatricks and everything they stood for was just too much temptation. Or maybe I always wanted to fuck Cillian and Hunter over—these two boy-men, who had everything handed to them on a silver platter from the moment they were pushed into this world.

I stopped by the door, shook my head, turned around, and made my way back into the house. I ascended the stairs to Gerald and Jane's room. Jane was in her bed, sleeping soundly in the middle of the day. And by asleep I mean knocked the fuck out.

I strolled into his walk-in closet, took a safety pin from my pocket, unlocked his jewelry box, and went straight for the jackpot. The thing I knew Gerald valued the most.

The Fitzpatrick cufflinks he'd inherited from his dad. Seventh-generation Fitzpatricks, made of gold and engraved back in Ireland, where the family had nothing to their name other than these cufflinks.

His precious heirlooms. The cufflinks he'd refused to donate to a local museum in Boston, he loved them so much. I pocketed them, smiling.

"I put extra cameras around the house to make sure I am protected."

Now he was sure to think the traitor was within.

On my way out, I spotted Aisling parking her modest blue Prius by the fountain. Snowflakes gathered over her head like a crown.

I could easily avoid her by getting into my Porsche and driving off, but where would be the fun in that?

She got out of her car wearing scrubs, flipping me the bird in one fluid movement, somehow still managing to look graceful as she stomped her way to her house.

"Nice scrubs. Shame you only put them on so your family buys your hospital story." I chuckled. She froze for a nanosecond before resuming her walk to the front door.

I might not know every detail of her secret, but I knew enough to be able to make her life very miserable indeed.

Unsurprisingly, I made it a point to not want things that didn't want me. It was a given, considering my life experience and history.

And Aisling may have wanted me, but her family was going to keep us apart at any cost. Not that it was going to help them if I, indeed, wanted Aisling. But as it happened, I rejected things and people who thought they were too good for me.

"Have a nice evening, Miss Fitzpatrick." I tipped an imaginary hat her way.

"Burn in Hell, Brennan."

"If there's a God, that's definitely His plan for me." I ducked my head, entering my car.

"Oh, there is a God, and trust me, when He gets His hands on you, I'll be waiting with popcorn."

"Uncle Tham! Can I ride you?"

Rooney, Sailor and Hunter's daughter, not even three, flung the door to Troy and Sparrow's house open, throwing herself at me like a missile. She wrapped her pudgy arms around my leg then proceeded to crawl her way up to my torso like a mini soldier, until I scooped her, tucking her under one arm and holding her like she was a helmet. I waltzed inside the house where I'd spent my teenage years, kissing Sailor on the cheek then Sparrow.

"I wanna ride you." Rooney giggled, still tucked under my arm as I exchanged pleasantries with my adoptive mother and sister. "Puh-lease."

"After dinner, Roon Loon," I said, messing her mane of tangled red hair. She looked exactly like Sailor, who looked exactly like Sparrow. Three generations of hellion banshees. Troy clapped my shoulder, and Hunter handed me a beer, which I took with my free hand.

"Auntie Emmabelle says all the girls at your club ride you," Rooney continued from under my bicep, blinking at me in wonder.

"Auntie Emmabelle should have her mouth stitched shut." I flashed Sailor a menacing look.

"I thought I was the only girl who can ride you." Rooney wiggled free out of my hold, standing front of me. With one hand free, I reached for the table to grab an appetizer, but halfway through, Sailor tucked baby Xander into my arm so she could try to collect Rooney's hair into a ponytail. It was impossible to avoid children in the Brennan household these days.

"Samuel, could you please hold either the baby or the beer? It doesn't look good when you have both in your arms. Put one down and help me serve." Sparrow wiped her hands with a kitchen towel, padding toward the kitchen to check on the Sunday roast she was working on. A weekly tradition.

"Yes, ma'am," I said, putting Xander in his stroller by the door, following her.

I heard Sailor muttering, "A-hole," behind my back.

"I heard that."

"You were meant to!" She tugged at Rooney's ponytail out of frustration.

I leaned against the kitchen island, watching Sparrow taking out bottles of cabernet from the wine fridge to go with the roast, pouring the sky-high Yorkshire pudding, mashed sweet potatoes, and balsamic mushrooms into fancy serving bowls.

"There's something different about you," Sparrow observed, studying me through her sharp green eyes.

"Different how?" I took a pull of my beer.

"Different ... pensive." She shoved the Yorkshire pudding tray into my hands. "Put this on the table."

I did as she said. I may have been a murderer, an underground mob boss, and a savage with no morals to speak of, but I was also whipped to the bone where my adoptive mother was concerned.

"I'm the same usual shade of fucked-up as I've always been," I drawled, reappearing in the kitchen. She wasn't wrong, though. I had a lot of shit on my plate with a side of diarrhea and an appetizer of stale manure.

The Russians in Brookline were running amok, desperately trying to unshackle themselves from my claws. Operation Ruin Gerald was in full swing, and then there was his little monster of a daughter, who despite everything ran circles in my head. I couldn't stop thinking about Thanksgiving. The mystery surrounding Aisling.

Sure, I could get all the answers in the world if I just put surveillance on her, as I did on so many other people in the city, but that was admitting defeat and succumbing to the idea that I gave a fuck, and I *didn't* give a fuck.

Fuck, I gave a fuck.

Well, half a fuck.

Definitely not enough of a fuck to fuck up my entire working relationship with the Brennans, that was for sure.

Sparrow pushed Dijon-covered Brussels sprouts and a pile of sweet mashed potatoes into my hands. I went back to the dining room to unload the food. When I came back, she cornered me between the fridge and the kitchen island.

"Are you sure it's not about Cat?"

"Positive. And by the way, buying her a tombstone? Dumb move. Grow a fucking spine, Spar."

"I have a spine. I also have a son who is so deeply in denial about his feelings, he can't see straight. Have you ever heard of *Selichot*?" She tried—and failed—to tuck her crazy ginger curls behind her ear.

"No." I reached to the loose tendril, helping her.

"Every year, practicing Jews recite penitential poems and prayers leading to the High Holidays. The thirteen attributes of mercy are a central theme throughout these prayers. Instead of going to a Catholic confession, the Jews go to the people they have wronged individually and ask for their forgiveness. It's soul cleansing, they say. I have a feeling one day you'll wake up and realize you need to atone—to receive forgiveness—for your sins. I think this day is fast approaching, and having a tombstone to go visit will serve you well."

"Ask for forgiveness from Cat?" I stroked my chin, pretending to mull this over. "Forgiveness for what? Being the fastest sperm who was unfortunate enough to bump into her egg ... or expecting her to perform her motherly duties for the half second she raised me?"

"For hating her," Sparrow said, her voice steady, her chin high. "A son cannot hate his mother."

"This one can and does. Actually, it's not even hate. I'm indifferent, which is so much more humiliating."

"Neutral men are the Devil's allies." She snatched my hand from her face, squeezing, refusing to let me go.

"The Devil and I get along fine." I smirked, amused by her display of emotions, arching one eyebrow. "Anything else?"

"What are you *not* indifferent about?" she demanded.

"Nothing. Nothing matters to me."

"Bull, meet shit," she hissed. "Something is bothering you."

"It's none of your concern."

"And it's not yours either, right? Big Sam Brennan doesn't care about things. He is above emotions," Sparrow poked. I saw what she was trying to do. Make me take action, pursue what I wanted, blah blah fucking blah.

The only thing that bugged me, remotely, was the Nix thing, and I wasn't going to pursue it.

Knowing what Aisling did for a living wasn't going to make any difference. The more I knew about her, the more I wanted to *get* to know her, and there was no point in that because soon enough, I was going to kill her father.

"Mom!" Sailor called from the dining room. "Hurry up, Roon Loon is starving."

Sparrow brushed past me but not before pinning me with a look.

Dinner was uneventful. Hunter talked shop, Troy talked basketball and football, and Rooney tried to sneak scraps of food under the table for her imaginary, friendly monster. Afterward, Sailor and Troy served dessert while I crawled around on all fours. Rooney rode me, using my hair as reins, her laughter rolling down my back.

Three hours later, I was on my way to the door after completing my familial duties for the week. Sparrow grabbed my arm on my way out—because why the fuck not?—and flashed me an I'm-about-to-give-you-a-mouthful-and-there's-jack-shit-you-can-do-about-it look.

"Remember our conversation the night of?"

"Night of?" I asked sardonically.

"The night you moved in with us permanently."

The night Cat finally threw me to the curb.

"What about it?" I tensed, even after all these years.

"I told you one day a woman was going to change your mind about all women."

I cocked my head, flashing her a pitiful look.

"You were wrong."

"I'm about to be right. I have a feeling. A mother always has a feeling about her children. I was watching you today and…" she stopped, squeezing my arm tighter "…I don't know how to explain this, but it is close. I could feel it. But you are fighting this. I can tell. You can't reject fate, Sam. Whatever it is, go to her."

Petting her head, I said, "She better fucking hope I don't go to her because everything I touch, I ruin."

With that, I gave her a peck on the cheek, leaving with a playful smile on my face.

Nothing could stop me from getting what I wanted, and what I wanted was to destroy Gerald.

Not even a like-minded monster with eyes like jewels.

It was a short distance from Sparrow and Troy's place to my apartment block.

So short, in fact, after ten minutes of driving, I was starting to wonder why the fuck I wasn't home yet. I looked around and realized

I was heading straight to the clinic where Aisling had operated on my soldiers a little over a week ago.

God-fucking-dammit.

This wasn't in my plan, but I was already halfway through Boston, heading toward Dorchester, so there was no point turning around now. Besides, it had nothing to do with Aisling. I wasn't in the habit of not knowing things about my clients and their families. If Aisling was up to something stupid, I had to stop her.

I parked in front of the Victorian building, surveying it.

It was Sunday evening, so it was most likely empty. Then again, it was an underground clinic, so visiting hours may vary. When I was sure the place was deserted, I got out of the car and proceeded to break in. The front door was embarrassingly easy to tamper with, and when I descended the stairs to the actual clinic, there was a second flimsy door I only needed to shake a little to pry open.

I went for the third door—the door leading to the surgical room, where Nix treated Becker and Angus. This one was a breeze, too. Once inside her office, I started throwing drawers open and took note of the medicine they kept there, typing the long names of them on my phone so I could conduct a deeper research once I got home.

I checked every piece of furniture, examined every nook and corner until I hit the jackpot.

The patients' files.

The first telltale sign something was wrong was the fact there was only *one* folder. Yellow and razor thin. What kind of clinic only took six to seven patients?

The kind that has very specific requirements to accept people in the first place.

I began flipping through the files, reading the patients' records, their test results, their consultation recommendations.

Something didn't add up. The drugs. The number of patients. The setting. I knew a scheme when I saw one, and this was so fucking fishy it gave the Atlantic a run for its money. One thing was for sure—whatever Aisling did, there was a good reason why she wanted to keep it a secret from her family and friends.

It wasn't kosher.

It wasn't good, or innocent, or fitting for the angelic Fitzpatrick. The Mother Teresa everyone knew and loved.

I tucked the folder back into the cabinet.

I was right.

She was a monster.

A terrible monster.

A sweet, beautiful Nix.

Now I just had to find out what her sins were.

Seven

Sam

I MADE A PIT STOP AT BADLANDS AND SLIPPED INTO ONE OF THE card rooms, downing three stiff drinks to take the edge off what I saw at the clinic. Nix was a doctor, all right, but she didn't work at the hospital or any of the registered clinics around town. Whatever she did, it was secretive, illegal, and had nothing to do with people without insurance.

Stop thinking about Nix. She is just collateral.

Collateral and an inconvenience at best and a complication at worse.

I needed to get my head out of my ass and be ridden by someone who wasn't my niece. It was time for a diversion. A reminder there were other pussies out there. Just as good and warm and tight as Aisling's and not half as troublesome.

Pent-up lust.

That was all it was.

I was a busy man ruling the underworld of one of the seediest, dirtiest places in the country. It'd been a long-ass time since I drowned myself in a woman. Aisling was the last, and the woman before her happened so long ago I forgot her name, her hair color, and the setting.

A good fuck would make all of this go away.

I moseyed out of the card room and into the club, ignoring the enthusiastic claps on my back and conversation starters, and scanned the mass of sweaty, dancing figures melding together. I pressed the tumbler of whiskey to my lips.

Humans appalled me.

Despite my reputation, I didn't just fuck anything with a pulse. I had dry spells of the self-inflicted kind since fucking ultimately required talking to people, and talking to people was a punishment even a good pussy wasn't worth sometimes.

There were always whores, who didn't demand meaningful conversation, but I wasn't a fan of shoving my dick where so many others had been.

I immediately decided which woman I wanted to spend the night with. She had bleached blonde hair, a fake tan, long legs, and a pink mini-dress so tacky removing it from her would be my Christian duty.

Most of all, she looked nothing like Nix.

I snapped my fingers in the bouncers' direction, pointing at her.

"I'll have that one," I clipped then proceeded to turn around and go up the stairs to my office, past the card rooms.

In my office, I busied myself by flipping through the betting books, tugging at my hair and *not* thinking about Nix.

A knock on the door made me drop the fat book on my desk.

"Open." I sat back, sprawling out in my executive chair.

The blonde pushed the door open, giggling excitedly as she shut it behind her, and pressed her back against the bullet-chipped wood.

"Hi! I'm Dani," she squeaked, tossing her hair to one shoulder. "Your bouncer showed me up. It's my first time at Badlands. Honestly, my friends are, like, kind of freaking out about all this. You calling me here, I mean. We heard about you a lot, obvs. But we didn't even know you came to this place, like often …"

I tuned her out, focusing on how her lips moved, fast and eager. Everything about her was wrong from her juicy, probably enhanced lips to her definitely penciled-in eyebrows. Her fake eyelashes looked like a shredded semitrailer tire. Her heavy makeup and dry hair full of split ends grated on my nerves in a way that felt personal. Nothing about her felt right.

Or good.

Or delectable.

Complex, dangerous, *maddening.*

I wanted Aisling. Aisling's demureness. Her sharp little nose and aristocratic, well-proportioned lips. Her natural hair and skin and teeth. She didn't succumb to modern beauty standards, and there was something irresistible about it. Aisling had that blue-blooded look of a woman you couldn't imagine on all fours, getting fucked rough and dirty from behind. Men were simple creatures, so that meant it was precisely what I wanted to do—plow into her Royal Highness, rough and dirty, from behind while she chanted my name.

The girl in front of me continued blabbing. Hell if I knew about what. It occurred to me, now that I looked at her up-close, that she was young. Legal, yes, but much younger than me.

"… kind of down for anything, really. And, like, I know you only do casual, so that's totally okay—"

"How old are you?" I cut into her stream of words, already in need of two fucking Advils and one bullet to put me out of my misery.

"What?" She looked startled, her brown eyes widening in panic. "What do you mean?"

"Your age," I jeered, irritated with myself for apparently growing a fucking conscience somewhere between Aisling's clinic and Badlands. "What is it?"

"Twenty … five?"

"Is that a fucking question?"

"No …?"

"Then why do you keep putting question marks after your answers?"

Her generation was going to run this country one day. No

fucking wonder I had a fake Swedish passport, just in case. Say hello to Ludvig fucking Nilsson.

She blinked slowly, like this was a test. I was half sure she was illiterate.

"Show me your ID." I opened my palm, stretching my arm in her direction.

"This is ridiculous." She laughed, her neck and ears turning pink. "I'm legal! Everyone gets carded here."

Not everyone. Aisling didn't on Halloween, and now my dick wanted a subscription card to her pussy.

Never mind that I fired the bastard who let Aisling in the following day.

"You have five seconds before I blacklist you," I said dryly.

"From the club?" She sucked in a breath.

"From the *city*," I corrected. "Your ID, Dani."

She rummaged through her knockoff Chanel purse with a huff, producing her driver's license and slapping it over my palm. I lit a cigarette and sat back, rubbing my forehead as I studied it.

Twenty-two.

Danielle Rondiski was twenty-two.

A practical baby in comparison to me.

Still, legal enough to drink, to fuck, and to be here.

She was also a natural brunette with pasty white skin when that photo was taken but had since graduated from the Bimbo Academy and morphed into what was standing in front of me right now, an inflatable version of Charlotte McKinney.

I whipped the card back at her. "Get out."

"Mr. Brennan ..."

"*Out.*"

"Age is just a number."

"That's the stupidest thing I've ever heard." I tried—and failed—to find the conversation frustrating. Truth was, I was *bored*. So far from the realms of any other emotion, I couldn't muster it if I tried.

I wasn't annoyed. I was horny for something I couldn't get my hands on, and the boring words coming out of her mouth were killing my erection.

"If age is just a number, then temperature is just a number, too. And money. And cancerous cells. And war casualties. Numbers are *everything*. Numbers are what separates life from death. Numbers run this world. There's no *just* about them. Now get the fuck out."

After sending Dani on her way with my Rain Man speech, and coming to terms with the fact my dick and I were both going to bed lonely tonight, I got into my car and drove to my apartment. My instincts told me the clusterfuck of today was in full swing and to expect the worst.

My instincts were never wrong.

Because Aisling fucking Fitzpatrick was waiting at my door.

A reward—or a punishment—from Karma?

Her back was pressed against the wood, sitting cross-legged, head bent down, the cool glow of her phone illuminating the planes of her face. She looked up as soon as I stepped out of the elevator, scrambling to her feet, smoothing her black, conservative dress over her curves. Her coat was folded and rested on her forearm neatly.

"I ought to kill you." I pushed past her callously, punching the code to my door and opening it without making a move inside.

"That wouldn't be out of character for you," she murmured from behind me. "What *didn't* I do this time?"

"You cockblocked me."

"I wasn't even anywhere near you all day!" she protested, the delight in her voice giving her a cheery lilt.

"You didn't have to be. The PTSD of fucking you put me off the whole concept for life. Congratulations."

"That's why you had to finger me again, right? Just to make sure it really was that horrible the first time," she sassed back.

"I fingered you to deny you an orgasm, not because I wanted you," I replied drily.

"You really know how to woo a girl. No wonder I was obsessed with you."

"*Was?*" I turned around to shoot her a dark smile, my hand on the door handle. "Last I checked, you are still running after me like a puppy and even took it to the next level and are now showing up at my place, creeper-style."

"You show up at my place all the time, too. I don't call you a creeper."

"That's different. I work with your father. I cannot escape the sight of you, no matter how much I want to."

I was really on a roll tonight. All I needed was red-tipped horns and to sacrifice a baby or two to complete my transformation into Lucifer.

"Where have you been?" She changed the subject, refusing to be offended and or leave my fucking building.

Now I *did* feel something.

I felt ready to strangle her.

"Allow me to answer you with your favorite goddamn expression: none of your business. How did you find my address? Do *not* say none of your business," I warned.

"Google."

"Don't lie to me." I turned to face her, curling my fingers over her delicate neck and giving it a soft squeeze just to scare her. Her throat bobbed with a swallow, but she didn't back down.

I misjudged her all those years and hated myself for judging a book by its cover. Inside that lacey and elegant spine teemed chaos.

"Don't ask tough questions," she snapped back.

"My address is untraceable."

"Well, Batman, I think both of us know that isn't true." She rolled her eyes. "Can you remove your fingers from my neck? I'd hate to traumatize you further with skin-to-skin contact."

Only a handful of people knew where I lived, and not even Cillian, Devon, or my soldiers were among them. I was a notoriously private person. Came with the territory of doing what I did for a living. The only people who had my address were Troy, Sparrow, and Sailor.

Sailor.

My traistor (traitor sister) must've talked to Sparrow after I left, put two and two together, and spontaneously decided to butt into my shit.

My cat and mouse game with Aisling was starting to become a multiplayer game, spinning out of control, and it was time to put a stop to it once and for all.

I could confront her about what I'd found out today, tell her I broke into the clinic, press for more answers, but it would be useless. She looked distraught, her onyx hair plastered to her temples, her eyes shiny with tears. She would only go on the defense, and I hated fucking liars. They reminded me of my biological mother.

I removed my hand from her throat.

"Look, can I come in?" She rubbed at the column of her neck, her posture slackening all of a sudden, like a deflated balloon. It dawned on me my not wanting to fuck Dani had nothing to do with her age or ability to bore me to the point of a clinical coma and everything to do with Nix.

God-fucking-dammit.

"No," I said flatly.

"I really need to talk to someone."

"I suggest you turn to a person who cares."

"You don't care about me?" she asked, surprise and hurt marring her voice. Was she asleep the last fucking decade? Did I care about anyone, myself included? No. Troy, Sparrow, and bigmouthed Sailor were the exception. I supposed I could toss in Rooney and Xander now, too. Obviously, they had the advantage of not being able to talk fluently and therefore were in low danger of pissing me off.

"Not even a little. Go away."

She licked her lips. "I need to vent. It's about my parents. Everyone else has a horse in this race. My brothers, Mother, and Da ... even my best friends are married to my siblings, so they can't be clearheaded about it," she explained.

She had a point.

Furthermore, if she had important information about Gerald, she could help me bring him to his knees and get a confession. So while it was true that I never, under any circumstances, brought a woman over to my apartment, it was time to make an exception. For her.

For the first time since I moved in by myself at eighteen, I opened the door and let another person who wasn't Sparrow or Troy into my domain. Even my cleaning lady only had the vaguest idea where I'd lived. She was driven back and forth from my place in tinted-windowed cars.

"Fine. But I'm not gonna fuck you again," I warned.

I could always count on my pride to win over, and Aisling was a constant reminder of the fact the Fitzpatricks saw fit to do business with me but not allow me to date their daughter.

"Well, that's a relief." She smiled politely, her chin barely quivering as she tried to contain her emotions. "And I promise not to try to seduce you again. Now, shall we?"

Aisling took a seat on the plush black leather couch, spine erect, her hands demurely resting in her lap.

"May I have some coffee?" she asked shakily.

"Would you like a fucking full English breakfast along with it?" I cocked an eyebrow, still standing up. "No, you can't have coffee."

"I think we both need a few moments to gather ourselves before this conversation."

"The only part of me in need of gathering is getting my cock into someone's mouth, and since I don't want you anywhere near it, I suggest you cut to the chase."

We held each other's eyes for a few seconds. She didn't waver.

"You're not going to talk until I get you a coffee, are you?" I suppressed a groan.

She shook her head. "'Fraid not."

Reluctantly, I went into the kitchen to make it. It occurred to me midway the journey to the counter that:

One, I didn't know how to operate the coffee machine; I always grabbed Starbucks on my way out in the morning then spent the rest of the day loathing myself for consuming burnt coffee that tasted like an overflowing sewer water, and—

Two, my house, my rules, *my* drink of choice.

I grabbed a Macallan 18, poured two fingers into two tumblers, and made my way back to the living room.

My apartment was neatly and minimally designed. Bare concrete walls, black leather everything, high barstools, and chrome appliances. Notably missing from my apartment were any paintings or pieces of unneeded furniture.

Also currently missing from my apartment right now was *Nix*.

I frowned at the coffee table, confused.

I looked at the massive glass jar in the center of it.

One of the bullets I kept inside was rolling on the floor. It bumped into one of the table's legs.

Shit.

I dropped the whiskey, bolting out the door, catching Aisling punching the elevator's button hysterically, her eyes wildly scanning her surroundings. Her cheeks were wet, and she was shaking all over. I grabbed her by the wrist and tugged her toward me.

What the fuck happened? Why was she so scared?

"Let me go!" she yelled, trying to shake me off. "Coming here was a huge mistake."

"Couldn't agree with you more. Yet you're here, so you're sure as hell going to see this through. I know the Fitzpatrick clan is used to other people finishing shit for them, but this time you'll have to pull through." I hoisted her over my shoulder, stomping back into my apartment, my fingers digging into the back of her thighs with possessiveness that surprised and disgusted me.

She is not yours to keep.

She is the enemy's spawn.

She is the woman you are paid to never touch.

And she is not worth the fucking headache.

"Let me guess, there is a perfectly good explanation for the bullets, right?" She chuckled bitterly, and I was glad she at least didn't do the whole let-me-down routine women were so fond of.

"There is," I clipped, "but you are not going to like it."

"I'm all ears," she said.

I slammed the door shut with my foot behind us, planting her back on the couch and squatting between her legs, snatching her gaze and hands.

"You calm?"

"Don't treat me like a baby," she snapped.

"Don't act like one," I deadpanned.

"Why do you have bullets in a jar? Dozens of them, no less."

"Why do you think I don't want people to get into my apartment?" I answered her with a question, my newfound technique courtesy of Deidra or whoever the fuck I almost had sex with at Badlands tonight.

"Evidence." Her teeth chattered, and she hugged herself.

"I take the bullets out of the people I kill and keep them."

Sam, you fucking idiot. An admission to the woman whose father you are about to slaughter like a sacrificial lamb.

She stared at me in terror mixed with ... fascination? Of course. I kept forgetting that she, too, was a monster. I picked up the bullet she dropped on the floor, ignoring the scent of the whiskey as it soaked its way through the carpet.

I flipped the bullet, tapping it with my finger.

"See this? M.V.? Mervin Vitelli. I engrave their initials, so I don't forget."

"Why don't you want to forget?" She frowned.

Because if I start forgetting all the people I kill, nothing will separate me from an animal, and I will become a real monster.

Soon enough there would be a bullet with G.F. engraved on it, a fact that reminded me I should put some distance between Aisling and me. I stood up and walked back to the kitchen, returning with the Macallan bottle—sans tumblers this time. I took a swig straight from the bottle, passing it to Aisling. I lowered myself into a recliner opposite her, the coffee table serving as a barrier between us.

She took a small sip and winced, handing it back to me.

"I knew you killed people, but it's very different to actually see proof of how many lives you've taken."

"The first one is the most meaningful one. After that, taking lives feels the same. Like a second or third bite of an ice cream cone. Of course, it doesn't hurt to know the people I kill are pieces of shit," I replied.

"I'm not so sure," she said, and by the way her forehead creased, I could swear she was talking from experience.

"You came here to talk. Talk," I ordered, knocking the side of her sensible boot with my loafer.

She blinked as she took in the apartment, its bare walls and cold nothingness I surrounded myself with. I liked it that way. The less I had, the less I became attached to things. It was an expensive brownstone, at three million dollars, but different from Avebury Court Manor, which was laden with paintings, statues, and other luxurious symbols of wealth.

There was nowhere to hide here. It was just us and the walls and the unspoken truth sitting between us like a ticking time bomb, waiting to explode.

"My mother wants to file for divorce." Her voice cracked. She looked downward, her neck like a broken flower stem.

"I know it sounds ridiculous to you," she rushed to add. "After all, it's a well-known fact my parents have never been faithful to one another. Their marriage is considered a sham in most social circles of New England. But for me, it means something. It means a lot, actually. Growing up, I knew I had the stability of Avebury Court Manor. Even though Mother and Da weren't a functional couple, they were still a couple in their own strange way. Believe it or not, Sam, they worked. I know I'm not an impressionable teenager anymore and worse things happen to twenty-seven-year-olds. Some people lose their parents, their partners, even their *children*, but I just don't understand..." she shook her head, tears hanging on her lower lashes for dear life, refusing to fall "...how everything escalated so quickly. One moment we were leading a normal life—as normal as life could be for us—and the next everything exploded. The provocative pictures of Da and that ... that *woman* materializing out of nowhere, the poisoning. Someone is trying to ruin my father, and *Athair* thinks it's my mother."

I stared at her, offering no words of explanation or encouragement. What could I say?

Actually, now that you mention it, I'm behind the operation. Jane is merely collateral damage. Be thankful it's not you I'm throwing under the bus. And by the way, this isn't even the tip of the iceberg, so buckle up, sweetheart, because I'm about to make him remortgage your childhood house and bleed him dry of his billions.

"Do you really have no lead?" she asked, signaling me with her hand to pass the bottle.

I did, shaking my head.

She sipped the brown liquid like it was tea, returning the bottle to me. "That's weird. You are usually so resourceful. I can't recall the last time you couldn't help my family when we got ourselves into trouble."

I was marginally amused by her attempt to trick me into working harder on the case. A case that I'd created all by myself.

"Patience, Nix."

"Are *you* a patient man?"

"I don't hold myself to the same standards I hold you to."

"That's convenient."

"I lead a convenient life." I saluted her with the bottle, taking a sip. "Anyway, look at the bright side. Two houses. Two parents. Two Christmas trees. Two sets of presents and so fucking forth."

"I'm not a kid." Her eyes flared with rage.

I elevated a brow. "You sure act like one where your parents are involved."

"What would you do if you were in my position?" Her eyes zeroed in on mine, sharp all of a sudden.

Lower myself to my knees and have you take my balls in your mouth again.

"Let them sort this shit out by themselves. They are grown-ups, and you are not the parent. You're the kid."

Perhaps because I was more focused on Aisling recently, especially during Thanksgiving dinner, I couldn't help but notice how her mother had asked Aisling to pour her drinks for her and join her in the bathroom to help her with her zipper. Jane didn't treat Aisling much better than a maid. I couldn't remember when that dynamic had started, and now I wondered whether I chose to turn a blind eye to it all along or I didn't want the facts to get in my way of seeing Aisling as a spoiled brat.

"I am sort of my mother's parent," she admitted. "She relies on me … mentally."

"That, to use the technical term, is fucked-up."

"Maybe, but it's the truth. My life is … not as pretty as it seems from the outside." She scrunched her nose, reaching to pluck one of the bullets from the jar and rolled it between her fingers, examining its initials. She put it back. Took out another one. I resisted the urge to lash out at her, tell her I was now going to have to wipe her fingerprints from each of them individually, in case someone ever found them. I could tell she was close to tears and wanted to avoid becoming a wailing woman at all costs.

I grew up with Sparrow and Sailor, two women who weren't prone to dramatics. In fact, I could not recall them crying at all. I was sure a tear or two was shed at family funerals and such, but they had always carried themselves with the quiet strength of women who knew the underworld inside and out and ruled it as their unchallenged goddesses.

Usually when I heard women cry, it was in bed and for all the right reasons.

"Boo-fucking-hoo, sweetheart. You're young, beautiful, and rich enough to buy happiness. So your parents are about to get a divorce and hate each other's guts. Welcome to the twenty-first century. You are officially joining fifty percent of people in the U.S."

I really was a bottomless source of fucking sunshine, wasn't I? But there was nothing I could do to help her. I wasn't going to change my plans to spare her feelings.

Nix's eyes narrowed at me, but surprisingly, she didn't look like she was about to bawl.

"My life is not as charmed as you think," she insisted, whispering hotly. "For one thing, growing up I never saw real love. A healthy relationship between a man and a woman. At least you had Sparrow and Troy. My childhood was an endless stream of arguments, object tossing, and my parents disappearing to Europe for months at a time, together or alone, leaving me with the nannies."

I stared at her blankly, showing her she hardly mustered enough pity in me to inspire me to get up and grab her a Kleenex.

"Then I lost someone I really cared about when I was seventeen, in a pretty ... brutal way." Her throat bobbed with a swallow, and she looked around, uncomfortable all of a sudden. I didn't ask whom it was.

Rule number one was to not get attached. It clouded your judgment.

"What else have you got for me?" I yawned, leaning back, making a show of checking the time on my phone.

"My first time ..." She hesitated, biting down on her lower lip. My interest piqued, and I found myself sitting upright. "I lost my virginity to my professor."

"How old was he?"

"Forty-one."

"And you?"

"Nineteen."

"That's—"

"Disgusting?" She smiled sadly, her eyes shimmering with tears again. I was going to say hot as fuck, but of course that was out the window now. "Yeah, I know. Wanna know the disgusting part?"

"I thought I already knew. He was forty-one."

She shot me a tired smile.

"I found out three weeks after we started sleeping together that he was married with a kid. See, he didn't wear a wedding band and lived in an apartment complex on campus, alone. He looked young and stylish and hung out with the students so often..." she picked a cuticle around her fingernail, tugging on it nervously "...I wanted to lose my virginity to someone with experience, and I knew he had it. We continued seeing each other after we had sex. Until one day he just disappeared into thin air. Stopped answering my calls. Just got up and left. He didn't even complete the academic year. I needed some sort of closure, so I found him. And, well, I found out why he left. Because of me. Because his wife, who taught at another university two states away, had found out and dragged him back home by the ear. When I found his new address, I made the mistake of driving down there and knocking on his door."

Bad call. But I had plenty of life experience, and Aisling lived in a protective bubble. Of course she wanted answers, closure, and all the other mumbo jumbo you read about.

"She opened the door and threw the phone he'd used to call me. She started screaming at me in front of the entire neighborhood, calling me a whore, a homewrecker, a spoiled bitch. She said my mother is a slut, that everyone in America knows one of us doesn't belong to Fitzpatrick, then promised she would let all the hospitals in Boston know what I did. It was humiliating. Especially since I never knew this man was married."

"Is that why you never tried for a hospital here?" I asked.

She bit down on her lower lip, pulling more and more dead skin from the side of her fingernail. "Partly. Maybe. I don't know. It's not the entire reason, anyway. Since then, I limited my interaction with men even more."

"Good," I deadpanned. "We're all fuckers."

Silence hung in the air. I wanted her to leave. She wasn't going to tell me anything about her parents' relationship, about Gerald. This was pointless.

"Tell me something personal." She rested her cheek on her shoulder. "Just one thing, Sam. It will make me feel better. Please."

"Aisling, it's time for you to go."

"Why?"

"Because this is going nowhere fast. We fucked. It was a mistake. It's time you move on. Whatever you think is going to happen, I can assure you it won't happen. I don't have a soul, or a heart, or a conscience. We had fun, yes, but women are all the same to me. I will never choose you above all others. If you think life with Gerry is a nightmare for your mother, imagine your father at his worst and keep going. That would be me."

That was when it finally happened.

She finally cried in front of me.

It was just one tear. It rolled down her cheek, flying off her chin like a cliff, landing with a splash on her knee.

"Goddammit, woman," I hissed, looking away, feeling … *feeling*. It wasn't a big feeling, just a little discomfort, but I did not want to see her cry.

One time.

This would be the one and only time I was going to humor this infuriating woman. No more.

I stood up, snatching the whiskey bottle by its neck and taking a swig as I began pacing the room.

"When I was a kid, before Troy and Sparrow took me in, back when I lived with Cat and my grandmother, we had a painting in our house. Just the one. It was a very cheap painting. A faded old thing of a cabin on a lake—basic and not very good. Anyway, the painting was in front of the bed in the master bedroom. It had the tendency to fall from its nail onto the floor every time the door creaked or someone breathed in the house. Cat was the only person with a key to the master bedroom, and she hadn't figured out I'd learned how to pick a lock."

I stopped. Took another swig. Realized I was halfway drunk and put the bottle down on the coffee table, noticing Nix was fingering and touching more of the bullets in the jar, breathing the initials out with her lips. Like she was mourning those people or something.

"When I was a kid, Cat used to punish me by starving me. In order to do that, she made the spot under her bed a makeshift pantry. That's where she kept all the food. Condiments, chips, pretzels, ready-made meals. Grams wasn't strong enough to fight her on this. As you know, I was a shitty kid, so I was virtually in a constant state of punishment. That made me very hungry and very small for my age."

She pinched her lips together, and I could tell she was about to sob again. It made me feel like fucking Bambi. I didn't need anyone's pity. I rushed through the next part.

"At some point, I figured I could just break into the room and grab Ramen or a bag of chips or something. And I did. Often. But Cat had the tendency to come in at the most inconvenient time. When I didn't have time to run away from her room, I had to hide under the bed, buried beneath the junk food."

I smiled bitterly at the bare concrete wall in front of me, feeling Aisling's eyes clinging to my profile, eager to hear more.

"Cat was a whore, so more often than not, when she came home, she wasn't alone. I stopped counting after the fourth time I had to sneak under her bed and felt the springs of the mattress digging into my back as someone fucked her above me."

Aisling looked away, hissing, like my pain bled into her body.

"No," she croaked.

"Yes." I changed direction, walking toward her. "I felt the weight of my mother's sins, figuratively and literally. They fucked her over my back. Again and again and again. While I shivered, dizzy with hunger, every muscle in my body strained so I wouldn't make a sudden move and make myself known. My most distinct childhood memory is that stupid painting. Every time the headboard hit the opposite wall, it would drop, but not facedown, so I could always see the cabin and the lake staring right back at me, as if they caught me red-handed. We had a relationship, this painting and I. I felt like it was taunting me. Reminding me of my shitty life, and every time I looked at it, I could feel the blue and purple dents on my back from the rusty bedsprings digging into my skin."

"You don't have any paintings," she said slowly, looking around the room.

I tapped the bottom of my cigarette pack over my bicep, and one cigarette popped out.

I fished it between my teeth. "Nope."

"My house must be very triggering for you."

I chuckled, lighting up the cigarette. I sprawled beside her on the couch, careful not to touch her, exhaling a trail of smoke to the ceiling.

"I don't have triggers."

"Everyone has triggers," she argued.

"Not me. I let hate fester and redirect it into ambition. I welcome my weaknesses and don't shy away from them."

She leaned her head against my shoulder, pressing her palm to my heart. I froze.

This was new.

And unsolicited.

Still, I didn't move. Her hand on me felt good. Right.

"Is this why you hate women?" she whispered. "Because Cat wronged you so much?"

"I don't hate them. I just don't want much to do with them," I groaned.

"Well, I want something to do with you." She looked up, blinking at me with owlish eyes. Our gazes met. The thick humming of our pulses filled the air. I drew away from her, pressing my thumb to her lip.

"No." I smiled viciously, standing up. "Here. You got it off of your chest, and even got a little bonus with my sob story. Now get the fuck out, Nix. And don't come back."

"But I—"

She started, but I turned away, taking a drag from my cigarette and looking in the other direction.

Through the floor-to-ceiling window, I could see her standing up, dignified. She made her way to the door, her chin held high, her back straight. The minute she closed the door behind her, I let out a breath, dropping the cigarette into the half-empty whiskey bottle.

Charging to the bathroom, I all but kicked my slacks down my knees, turning on the shower spray and stumbling inside before the water turned from cold to hot.

I braced one arm over the tiles, let the water pound over my body, and started jerking off—with my dress shirt still on.

"Shit ..." I hissed as I rubbed my cock mercilessly, pumping fast. "Shit. Shit. Shit."

Her mere presence in my apartment made my balls tighten.

I came and I came and I came inside my fist. Liquid, white gel coated my fingers, and I wondered when was the last time I masturbated.

Probably when I was sixteen.

No, maybe fifteen.

Fuck you, Aisling.

I plastered my forehead against the tiles, groaning as the red-hot needles of water kept lashing my face and hair. I wasn't her savior, I was her monster. These late-night calls, me following her, her seeking me out ... they had to stop.

Before I did to her what I did to that painting.

Because I didn't tell her the whole story.

Years after I'd moved out of Cat's apartment, I came back. Paid the owner a large sum of money to get a tour around the place. I found the painting. The new tenants hadn't gotten rid of it. I stole it, burned it, and tossed the ashes in the Charles River.

I didn't know how to keep things.

I only knew how to break them.

It was time to break Aisling once and for all and ensure she would never, ever seek me out again.

Aisling

Stop choosing what isn't choosing you, mon cheri, Ms. B's voice rang between my ears as I burst out of the door of Sam's building on wobbly legs, the harsh whip of the wind slapping my cheeks.

I gasped for air, but no amount of air could satisfy my lungs.

Sam, Sam, Sam.

Broken, scarred, marred, imperfect Sam. Molded in the hands of an abusive mother, a mobster adoptive father, and a ghost of a biological dad he knew tried to kill his adoptive mother.

I wrapped my coat around my waist and jogged to the Aston Martin waiting around the corner from Sam's building, slipping into the passenger seat. The minute I slid in, I grabbed the thermos waiting for me there and took a greedy gulp of coffee.

"Well?" Cillian asked from the driver's seat, raising a skeptic eyebrow.

He didn't believe Sam had anything to do with *Athair*. Neither did Hunter. I could tell Cillian was now looking at me, trying to see if I had sex with Sam. Any telltale sign to find out if we did something sordid. Puffy lips. Flushed cheeks.

My brother didn't trust me not to throw myself at Sam.

I shook my head. "Couldn't find anything, and he didn't volunteer any information."

"Of course you couldn't. Because Sam has better things to do with his time than to mess with *Athair* for no apparent reason."

"He was the only person at the table capable of poisoning one of the guests."

"*Athair* had an oopsie visit to the hospital. Give that pretty head of yours a rest, Ash. Sam is innocent—in this case, of course. In general, he is probably responsible for every other bad thing that happened in Massachusetts since 1998. Case closed."

When I said nothing, he groaned, lowering his head on his headrest, closing his eyes.

"Tell me you'll drop it. I have enough on my plate as it is. I don't need to extinguish another fire."

"Fine," I bit out. "I won't sniff around him anymore."

"Promise?" he asked.

"Promise."

It was stupid. Childish, really, but old habits died hard, and I found myself crossing my fingers in my lap like a kid, between the creases and folds of my dress.

It was far from over.

Sam might be playing me, but now I was playing him, too.

I was going to find out the truth about what happened with my parents.

If it was the last thing I did.

Eight

Aisling

A WEEK HAD PASSED SINCE I'D VISITED SAM'S APARTMENT. A week of radio silence from his end, and my brothers trying their hardest to restore something resembling normalcy to our household.

They visited after work a few times a week to check in on Da, convinced the poisoning was either Mother's doing or Gerald's unspoken mistake.

I played along, showering Mother with attention, watching her with hawk eyes to ensure she didn't try to harm herself, but the truth was, something had shifted within me, rearranging itself into a different shape. I was beginning to change, and I didn't know how or why but the past few weeks had a lot to do with it.

Outwardly, I went through the usual motions. I caught up with Persy, Belle, and Sailor at an up-and-coming Indian restaurant downtown. I even pretended to muster an amused chuckle when Sailor frowned at her phone with a long-suffering sigh and showed us a picture of Cillian. "This is his version of sending me dick pics."

"But it's not a dick." Persy had blinked, not getting it.

"Not an anatomical one, anyway," Belle had murmured, tearing a piece of naan bread and dunking it into a mint and mango dip. Persy had protested us calling her husband a dick, but of course we all knew that he was—to everyone but her.

Mother continued moaning about how horrible my father had been to her, yet every time she ventured out of her den and he had tried to speak to her, she would make a sharp U-turn and dart back to the master bedroom, leaving a trail of tearful accusations echoing over the opulent hallway walls in her wake.

Da was still sleeping in one of the guest rooms, floating in and out of it like a ghost, his disheveled white hair sticking out in every direction, unshaven and haunted by the state of his marriage.

It didn't help that he started getting mysterious, cryptic messages threatening to drain his secret bank accounts in Switzerland—accounts that according to Da no one knew about.

The first couple days after the messages started pouring in, my father had made it a point to shower, get dressed, and go into his office. He had left his door ajar and sat there, motionless and quiet, waiting to hear my mother's door flinging open so he could talk to her.

Once he'd realized Mother was truly uninterested in talking things through, he had retreated to his current state of shambles, hardly leaving his own room.

And that, I realized, was the difference between this time and all the others. Normally, my parents entered this tango, a dance of sorts; it was difficult to follow and only they knew all the moves to it.

My father would screw up, my mother would get mad, and he would win her back. Snatch her into alcoves in the house or steal her away to the butterfly garden, whispering sweet nothings into her ear. He would court her. Make her feel desirable. Shower her with gifts and compliments. Send heated looks from across the table at dinnertime. Watch as she chipped before breaking completely and taking him back. Then he'd whisk her off on a lengthy vacation, make all these promises they both knew he couldn't keep, and superglue their relationship back together, even though it had chunks missing and was hollow from within.

Only this time, it hadn't worked. Da had been poisoned. He blamed my mother. My brothers suspected her, too. I guess Mother had decided she'd had enough and cut them out of her life. She refused to see Cillian and Hunter whenever they visited.

Which brought us to where we were now.

To the annual charity event my mother hosted.

"Aisling, could you be a darling and ask your brothers to go say hi to Mr. Arlington? He made such a substantial donation to our charity tonight, and I know he's been vying for Cillian's attention for a long time. He needs advice about his new offshore company." Mother elbowed me sharply as we stood in the ballroom of the Bellmoor, a boutique hotel in the West End.

The room glimmered in French neoclassical style—all cream, gold and ornate chandeliers, and an Instagrammable stairway with golden railings.

Guests trickled in and out, drinking champagne and laughing loudly as they looked for their designated tables. Businesspeople mingled with each other, the men in tuxedoes, the women in elaborate ball gowns. Jane Fitzpatrick had an impeccable track record of throwing lavish parties, from debutante balls to charity events, and this one was no different, even if she knew her peers never quite recovered from the last headline her husband was responsible for.

My mother was the director of *The Bipolar Aid Alliance*, a nonprofit charity group, for which she threw events often. She wore a dignified gray dress, her hair pinned up in a bun. We had never spoken about the fact she had chosen this particular charity, above all others, to give all her attention and resources to, but I knew it was telling.

I'd come to learn nothing about my mother's behavior was accidental. She was a calculated woman, and Cillian and I inherited that trait from her.

"I will, but for the record you'll have to talk to them at some point," I chided her, toying with my velvet gloves.

She stuck her nose in the air, examining her manicured fingernails.

"Have to? I doubt it. I *have* to speak to my banker at some point to settle everything ahead of the divorce. And my landscaper—the rosebushes need a proper trim. Oh, and certainly my hairstylist. But my sons? There is nothing I need from them. If I want to see my grandchildren, I can talk directly to their wives. I would actually prefer that as Sailor and Persephone at least treat me like their equal and don't believe I *poisoned* my own husband."

"Speaking of your husband, what about him?" I inquired, smoothing a hand over my cap-sleeved, dark blue gown. "Will you be talking to him anytime in the next century, or are you going to spend the rest of your life dodging him?"

"Your father and I seem to have reached a boiling point after simmering over the edge of disaster for decades. He's become paranoid and wrongfully mistrusting. Quite vulgar, seeing as I'm not the one who pops into the headlines every few months with a new affair. I hate to say this, Aisling my dear, but we might have reached the end of the road. I don't see us coming back from this particular crisis."

"Well, then I suggest you speak to him before you hand him divorce papers." I gritted my teeth.

"He won't believe me."

"Try him."

"Just tell your brothers to do as I say," Mother huffed, like I was a teenager rather than a grown woman, waving me off.

I wasn't an idiot. I knew people treated me like I was younger than my years because I let them. Because I was nice and timid and agreeable.

I shook my head, stomping over to Cillian and Hunter, who stood in a cluster with other men, smoking cigars and tutting loudly about the new tax plan.

You could tell they didn't want to be here. Normally, they took their wives anywhere worth going. If they left Sailor and Persephone at home, it meant they planned an early exit and spared their wives of boredom.

They still, however, showed up to support my mother. I wished she could see this. How we all did what we could to support her, even if she behaved like a child.

I stopped by Hunter and Cillian.

"May I borrow you two for a moment?" I smiled politely.

"*May?* I'd pay you good money to get me out of here. Extra if you agree to put a bullet in my head," Hunter whispered, taking a step away from the circle jerk he was engulfed in. Cillian, who had more finesse than that, threw an impatient smirk my way, but stayed put, a bevy of men swarming around him.

"What's going on?" Hunter asked, sipping bottled water. He barely drank alcohol, and when he did, he limited himself to one drink. "The party's in full swing and the donation box is jam-packed. Don't tell me the old bat found a reason to be unhappy again. Let me guess, the flowers are not fresh enough or someone failed to compliment her on her dress—which, by the way, makes her look like drywall."

I stomped on his foot, making him wince and clutch his toes.

"She asked if you two could introduce yourselves to Mr. Arlington, right over there." Discreetly, I gestured to a plump, older man sitting at a table across the room, enjoying the shrimp cocktail much more than anyone should enjoy a shrimp cocktail, considering its foul taste. "He made a sizable donation and would like to ask you a few questions. Offshore business-related, I believe."

"Since when did I sign up for Mother pimping me like I was a low-grade call girl in need of petty cash?" Cillian drawled in his usual, monotone voice, sidestepping away from the crowd surrounding him.

I turned to look at him, scowling. "You need to take some of the workload off of me. I'm the one she manages twenty-four-seven."

"Your choice," Cillian pointed out dryly.

"Speaking of fat checks…" a slow grin spread over Hunter's chiseled face "…the Devil himself just entered the ballroom, and he brought an expensive-looking *date*."

All heads snapped to the entrance, mine included, just in time to see Samuel Brennan waltzing in through the double doors with a tall, leggy brunette. The two doormen bowed to them. Sam wore an impeccably tailored tux, and the woman had a deep green, low-cut satin gown that made her eyes pop from across the room.

She was obviously a model.

And I was obviously—*desperately* jealous.

"And he brought a replica of our sister, no less," Hunter muttered, squeezing his water bottle until it sloshed over his hands comically, spilling all over his shoes. Cillian remained silent, his eyes narrowing on Sam.

A man I didn't know stepped in between us, gesturing to Sam with his champagne flute.

"They say he killed his first victim at thirteen. Under the guidance of his adoptive father, Troy Brennan. I worked at the DA's office at the time. Read the postmortem report. The damage he inflicted was frightening. You know, we never found the bullet he used."

That was because Sam kept all of them.

"He is my brother-in-law," Hunter said through gritted teeth. "So unless you wish to share a fate with that poor corpse, I suggest you take a hike."

"Oh ..." The man visibly recoiled, wincing. "I had no idea. My apologies."

My eyes didn't waver from Sam and his date, not even for a second. I clutched my drink to my chest, watching them move together, arms linked, her hand placed on his forearm. As if sensing my gaze, Sam spun and turned in our direction sharply, heading toward us. My heart was in my throat, and something hot stirred inside my stomach.

In all the times he taunted and provoked me over the years, and especially the last weeks, he'd never thrown other women in my face before.

This was an escalation. A new step in our screwed-up game.

He knew I'd be here.

Knew I'd helped Mother organize this charity event.

This was a blunt incitement.

Designed to get a rise out of me.

To show me how much he didn't care.

Sam and the woman stopped in front of us.

"Saw Congressman Weismann heading out just now..." Sam jerked a thumb behind his shoulder, speaking to my brothers and them alone "...your mother must've pulled some strings to get him to show his face here after the undocumented housekeeper scandal."

"I understand that you have the manners of a soiled diaper, but in cultured society, it is expected to introduce your date to your friends, which is what you will do now," Cillian bit out icily, his eyes gliding from Sam to his date. There was no approval in them. My brother only had eyes for his wife, no matter how many beautiful women had thrown themselves at his feet. But I could tell he was unnerved by how alike me and the woman in front of us were.

Hell, she could sense it, too. We both eyed each other curiously as if looking through a distorted mirror.

"Getting a little touchy, Kill." Sam looked mildly entertained. "It's just a woman. They make over fifty percent of the world's population, last I checked. Is Persephone failing in her duties to keep you entertained?"

The woman shifted on her heels awkwardly, obviously not appreciating being spoken about like mystery meat in a dodgy deli sandwich. Despite everything, I felt bad for her. She was a prop, and she deserved more than whatever Sam had in store for her.

"This is Becca..." Sam gestured toward her, without looking *at* her, like a salesman exhibiting a flashy car "...Becca, this is Cillian, the CEO of Royal Pipelines, and Hunter, my brother-in-law and the head of the PR department of the company. And this is Aisling ..." He jerked his chin in my direction offhandedly, the way you would the family dog. All eyes snapped to me. "She is their younger sibling, of undisclosed occupation. I'm sure it is something interesting, but I never mustered enough interest to find out."

"Aisling is a doctor," Cillian snapped.

"And I'm Marie Antoinette." Sam bowed theatrically. "Fancy some cake?"

"The first time you acknowledge my sister, and you talk to her like she is trash." Hunter frowned, getting heated. "Now I remember why none of us wanted you anywhere near her."

"Hello. I'm right here!" I waved my hand in the air, trying to seem unfazed. "No need to fight my battles for me. Also, I think it's time to use your right to remain silent, Brennan." I bared my teeth, rage humming beneath my skin. "Nothing that comes out of your mouth is worth listening to anyway."

He directed his gray eyes at me, and they sparkled with open delight. The first time I'd seen him happy since Halloween. Since we shared a sordid night together.

"Is it shark week for the entire Fitzpatrick clan? I hear women who live together get their period at the same time."

"I suspect you lost all rights to make blood jokes with your track record, Sam." I arched an eyebrow in his direction.

He threw his head back, full-blown laughing now.

"Touché, Nix."

Hunter dropped his water bottle. Cillian choked on his whiskey. Everything stopped, my heart included.

"*Nix?*" both my brothers asked in unison.

For the first time since Sam walked in, I forced myself to cool my jets, interested to see how he was going to get out of it. Becca octopused her arms around Sam possessively, the realization that she stepped into something bigger than her trickling into her system.

I smiled coolly.

"Oh, do tell them the story of how I got my nickname, Sam. It's a good one."

The carnival.

The kiss.

The confessions.

You're a monster and I'm a monster. We're both demons, looking for our next pound of flesh.

A platinum bullet could kill a Nix, but no, you gave me gold. You want me alive, Brennan. Well and capable of fighting back.

Becca clutched tighter onto Sam's arm, treating him as a human life preserver, not knowing his job was to make people drown. She had not spoken a word since she entered the ballroom, and I knew it wasn't accidental. He must've told her to keep her mouth shut.

Sam's silver eyes flashed with malice. "You sure you want me to tell them?"

"Now's not the time to act chivalrous," Cillian snapped. "Aisling and you have never exchanged as much as a sentence, yet you have a nickname for her? You're going to have to give me an explanation, seeing as I pay you extra not to touch my sister."

A ball formed in my throat, and I knew if I opened my mouth, I would scream.

How dare my brothers interfere with my love life?

How dare they dictate who I could and couldn't see?

And how pathetic was I that Cillian had no trouble at all saying this right in front of me?

I was Aisling. Sweet, angelic Aisling. The doctor. The nurturer. The good one.

Becca looked agonizingly embarrassed as the pieces of the puzzle started falling into place. She took a step sideways, away from Sam. He didn't even notice.

Sam turned to look at Hunter and Cillian, his expression grave.

"It was the first time I saw your sister. At dinner when Sailor and Hunter started living together." Uh-huh. Already, he was lying. That wasn't the first time we'd met. "I excused myself to go to the bathroom just as she got out of it. Her dress was stuffed inside her underwear from behind, her ass and legs on full display. I told her that she needed to untuck her dress. She cried in horror and said, 'Oh, no, my knickers!' She explained to me that underwear are called knickers in British

English. Since then, I call her Nix, because she is a goofball who can't dress properly. Isn't that right, Nix?" He winked, flicking my nose like some protective big brother.

I felt close to nuclear explosion.

Frustrated.

Humiliated.

Fuming.

Sam stared at me, waiting for me to call him out on his bullshit.

"Since when do you date?" Hunter changed the topic, obviously unamused by Sam's story.

"Since I changed my mind about marriage."

"You changed your mind about marriage?" Cillian sneered at him, skepticism all but leaking from his cold gaze. My older brother played with the golden band of his wedding ring as he spoke. "Riveting. I clearly remember you giving me a one-hour speech about the merits of staying single shortly before I married Persephone. Should I bill you for my lost time?"

"People change." Sam's eyes turned into slits. "You should know that better than anyone."

"*People*, yes. Monsters, no."

"So is Becca the one?" Hunter goaded, and I wanted to throw up all of a sudden. Because Sam was exactly the kind of psychopath to marry someone else just to spite me. I wouldn't put it past him. Buy into the idea that he could be happy with a replica of me and forget about the real thing.

Sam looked down at Becca, tugging her close.

"I hope so," he whispered, placing a chaste kiss to her mouth. "She has everything I look for in a woman. Beautiful, well-educated, and honest. Bonus points: her family is not a complete mess."

Jealousy made way to anger, and I groaned, turning my back to Sam and Becca, looking directly at Hunter and Cillian.

"Anyway, I delivered the message Mother sent me here for. Do with it what you will. Enjoy your evening."

With that, I stormed off. I could faintly hear my brothers calling Sam a jackass behind my back, which only served to make me feel worse. Like a charity case. A silly, naïve girl incapable of standing up for herself in front of the big bad wolf.

I never felt a part of them anyway. Cillian, Hunter, and Sam had their own friendship going, and Persephone and Sailor were a part of it because they were a part of my brothers. Emmabelle and I were always pushed aside, associated but not initiated into their pseudo-secret society.

I spent the rest of the night being the perfect daughter to my mother. I listened to stale jokes, laughed, clutched my pearls whenever was appropriate during longwinded, boring stories, took pictures with donors, and even introduced my mother onstage when it was time for her to deliver her speech.

No one dared to ask where Gerald Fitzpatrick was. Not even one soul. The unspoken assumption was that my parents were going through something, as they always did, and most guests thought nothing of it. This was simply the way Jane and Gerald Fitzpatrick were.

One piece of expensive jewelry and a vacation away from reconciliation.

Throughout the night, I refused to steal glances at Sam and Becca, no matter how hot the temptation burned in me.

It was unlike him to stick around for more than ten minutes at a charity event.

It was even more unlike him to show up with a date.

It was obvious this was designed to torture me, and I refused to give him the pleasure of agreeing to be tortured.

Finally, when the clock hit midnight, I told my mother I was heading home.

"I have an early shift tomorrow. I'll catch up with you in the morning. It was a lovely event." I kissed her cold cheek, heading to the cloakroom to grab my coat, clutching the wrinkled ticket to hand the clerk in exchange for my Armani jacket. When I reached the elaborate oak counter, it was empty.

The door behind was closed.

Merde.

I looked around, trying to find an available staff member to help me out. When none were found, I decided to take matters into my own hands. I wasn't going to stick around, waiting to be cornered by Sam and Becca, like a sitting duck. I rounded the counter and flung the door to the cloakroom open, taking a step inside.

I came to a halt immediately.

"Oh my gosh!" I heard a screech. It came from Becca's mouth. The first time I'd heard her voice. Shrill and nasally. I blinked away my shock, letting the scene in front of me register.

Becca was splayed across a mountain of coats and blazers, her dress pushed up her thighs—much like mine was that cursed Halloween night—with Sam standing a few feet from her, a hand on his zipper. The heat around my eyes signaled tears were on their way, and I forced myself to swallow the bile rising in my throat.

You are twenty-seven years old. Don't you dare cry.

"My, my. You give tacky a whole new meaning, don't you, Mr. Brennan." I pinched my lips, fixing my eyes on Sam, careful to keep Becca's name out of my mouth. No matter how much I despised her by association, it wasn't her fault. "You know, Samuel, that's what separates the nouveau riche from true aristocrats. Your impartialness to knockoffs. Couldn't get your hands on the real thing, so you decided to settle for a replica." I smiled sweetly.

I was angry and sad and feverish with the emotions crawling inside me.

I opened my purse and took a condom out of it—I always kept one handy for when Belle ran out and decided to end the night with someone when we went out—and flung it on the floor in Sam's general direction.

"Did you tell her you hate women? That you don't want children?

How much you loathe yourself? Did she see your apartment? Your inside? All your dirty secrets?" I was still smiling, but my heart felt like it was soaked in my own blood. I had only a few more precious seconds before they started falling. Becca's mouth hung open in fascination and horror.

I shrugged. "Yeah. I guess not. A word to the wise…" I turned in her direction "…run, don't walk. He is trouble and not the tamable kind. He will use you, play you, and discard you. That's the only thing he knows how to do. Because that's what was done to him."

I spun on my heels and ran back to the ballroom, trying to find a place where I could cry alone. Break down and let it all out. I headed straight to one of the balconies. I could see from behind the glass doors they were all empty. No one was crazy enough to sit outside on the cusp of Christmas in Boston. Not willingly, anyway. I flung open the door and ran to the stone bannister, clutching it as I gasped, the fresh, cold air rushing into my lungs like ice water.

I heaved, letting out a feral growl that echoed inside my body.

I loved him and I hated him and I loathed him and I craved him.

One thing was for sure—I was close to quitting him.

He wanted me to let go, to turn my back on him, to forget, to leave him just like every other woman in his life. Every woman other than Sparrow. And I was close to giving him exactly what he was after.

I collapsed against the wide bannister, pressing my forehead against its coolness, trying to regulate my breath as I closed my eyes.

Breathe, mon cheri. He is just a man. A bad one at that, I heard *her* voice.

I didn't know how much time I'd stayed there, but when I finally turned around to leave, I saw him.

He blocked the doorway, standing there alone, his broad shoulders shielding the party's view from me and vice versa.

"Are you done?" He sounded bored.

I didn't answer. I had to remind myself this man was about to have sex with another woman only moments ago. Maybe he went ahead and did it anyway.

"Step aside," I said quietly. "I want to leave."

"You're very prone to dramatics, know that, Nix?" He ignored my words completely, ambling toward me. He stopped when we were close, too close, and gently tucked a lock of hair behind my ear. "I am used to women who are rougher around the edges. Sparrow. Sailor. Even Cat. They have masculine strength about them. They refuse to be pushed around and never shed a tear."

"Crying doesn't make you weak," I said, sniffing and turning away from him. "It just means you're in touch with your emotions."

He cocked a brow.

"I didn't say you were weak. But you are a complex little thing, and I never know if I get the ball-busting version of you or the docile one who trails behind her mother like a toddler."

"Thank you for the psychological assessment. Did you enjoy your rendezvous with your date?"

He tilted his head sideways, studying me intently. "What's with the French words? Why not say hookup like the rest of modern civilization?"

I shrugged. "My governess was French. It stuck with me."

"You had a governess," he said, not as a question. Rather, he mulled the information over, filing it somewhere in his head. "Well, as it happens, I didn't enjoy Becca at all because you scared the living shit out of her. This is now the second fuck you've cost me, Nix."

"Nix like knickers, right?" I rolled my eyes, fresh anger coursing through my veins.

He grinned, looking like he was in a fantastic mood, which made me hate him even more.

He pushed another wisp of my hair behind my ear. "I had to think on my feet."

"I think I should go." I turned to make a beeline back into the ballroom, but he stepped in the same direction, blocking my path.

"No."

"Sam, you have a date waiting inside."

"She left. I called her an Uber."

"You still brought her here. That's the point." I took a step back, avoiding his touch at all costs. "You still paraded her. Flaunted her. Kissed her in the cloakroom."

"I didn't kiss her," he growled, his mouth twisting in annoyance.

"But when I came in you were—"

"I skipped that part," he quipped. "The kissing part. I wanted you to get the general picture."

"Well…" I smiled sadly "…I got it, all right. Mission accomplished. I now know you will go to extreme lengths to push me away. We have such a frightening ability to get under each other's skin in the worst, most terrible way. I think I'm finally done with you."

I didn't necessarily speak the truth, but my wounded pride wouldn't let me yield to my heart's desire.

He stepped forward, his heat radiating through me. I took a step back toward the bannisters.

"Why do I have a feeling you are playing me, Aisling?" he asked.

Low. Calmly. *Deadly.*

I swallowed, stepping backward for the millionth time. "Who said I wasn't?"

"Your doe-like, please-don't-eat-me eyes. But I'm starting to see there's much more to you than I initially thought."

"Your opinion of me wasn't very high in the first place, so that's not saying much."

I retreated again. He advanced toward me. This terrible tango of wills.

"I checked your IRS file. You don't have an income. Whatever you do is either voluntary or paid under the table. With your family going through audits every single year, I doubt you are stupid enough to meddle with money."

"What?" I gasped, scandalized. "How dare you—"

"Easily. That's how. Now it's your turn to answer a question. What is it that you do in this clinic, Nix?"

I felt my back hitting the edge of the bannister, the stone digging into my spine.

I lost my balance and tipped over, my arms thrashing in the air. My torso flew right over the balcony, but Sam grabbed me by the waist, the only thing to keep me suspended in the air, six floors above ground, from sure death.

A thin crust of ice covered the stone, making it even more slippery.

My heart lurched, beating wildly and hysterically.

"Pull me back!" I cried out, my hands desperately trying to clutch onto his tux. "Please!"

He dodged my attempts, pinning my waist harder against the stone but not letting me touch any part of him.

"I don't think so, sweetheart. First, you owe me a few truths. You'll start by telling me what you did outside my apartment a week ago. Because looking back, you couldn't have come there just because you needed a shoulder to cry on."

"I did!" I gasped, swallowing air. "I—"

"You took one of my bullets," he snapped, loosening his grip on my waist. My body dangled between life and death, hanging on the balance between his fingers fluttering against my middle.

He did this on purpose.

The realization hit me more violently than any slap would.

He cornered me, made me walk backward to try to get away from him, and got me right where he wanted me. At his mercy. Now he was threatening to kill me if I didn't tell him the truth.

The worst part was he could get away with it, too. It was going to look like a sure accident. I had more than a few drinks throughout the night, and Sam could easily slip out of here undetected.

"Let me go!" I wheezed.

"You sure about that?" I heard his grave chuckle. I couldn't see anything other than the black velvet sky above me, the stars shimmering like fairy dust, watching intently to see how my night played out. "Why did you take the bullet, Nix?"

"Sam, please—"

"Answer me."

"I'm scared," I whispered, my voice cold and low.

"Tell me the truth and you'll have no reason to be."

"Because I knew it was from the man you killed at the carnival!" I screamed, getting it out of my system. "My obsession with you started right after that damned carnival. I checked the news to see who was killed there, guessing correctly that they'd found the body. I found his name—Mason Kipling—and read that he was a human trafficker who had been wanted by the FBI. I put two and two together. Realized you had some beef with the guy. When I saw the bullet, M.K., I couldn't help myself. I took it. Happy?"

He was quiet for a few seconds. I was scared he'd get tired of holding my waist and would let go. A shiver ran through my body from head to toe. My tears flew downward, trickling from my forehead, as they landed somewhere under the ballroom. Probably in the empty hotel pool.

"Now tell me why you came to my apartment." His voice was silk and leather, traveling over my skin like a whip, promising both pain and pleasure.

"No."

"Tell me what you do in that clinic."

"*No.*"

"Aisling …" He began to loosen his grip on my waist even more, and I sucked in a sharp breath, telling myself that he couldn't— *wouldn't*—let me die. Not because he had a conscience but because I meant something to him.

That was why he couldn't touch other women and not for lack of trying.

That was why we kept coming back to each other over and over again, drawn together like magnets.

Whatever we had, it was screwed-up and poisonous and destructive, but it was there, and it was *ours*. It had a pulse and a breath and a soul.

We couldn't walk away from it, and it was too late to pretend as if nothing happened, but at the same time, we both had no clue where to go to from here.

"You're going to fall," he whispered, his hot breath wafting over the column of my throat, causing goose bumps to rise on my skin. On instinct, I wrapped my legs around his waist, my limbs everywhere, folding myself around him like I wanted to swallow him whole.

My mouth found his ear. "So are you. I'll be taking you with me, Monster."

"I'm not afraid of falling, Nix." His teeth dragged along my neck, nibbling at the sensitive hollow along my shoulder blade.

"Yes, you are. That's why you're torturing me. That's why you're here."

Suddenly, his mouth was on mine, hot and hungry and demanding, and he pulled us backward, stumbling unevenly as he pried my mouth with his tongue, thrusting it inside harshly. I kissed him back, deep and raw, his scent dripping into my body. Cigarettes and man and expensive clothes. Not a trace of Becca in his system. My mouth was full of his kiss, and my bones felt brittle and hot as I murmured, "Next time you pull a Becca stunt on me, I will cut your balls off."

"I'd like to see you try." His fingers dug into my ass roughly, and I moaned, desperately rubbing against his erection. "Fuck," he growled. "Why can't I stay away from you?"

I licked a path down his throat, and he yanked my head back by my hair, peppering the edge of my cleavage with intoxicating kisses.

"You really need to quit smoking. You smell horrible," I taunted.

"Never heard any complaints before."

"They were all scared of you." I sucked on his throat while he mauled the edge of my breasts. I was desperate to leave a love bite. To make him think of me tomorrow morning. And the mornings after that.

Because who knew when would be the next time we'd see each other? A week? Two weeks? A *month*? For all I knew, Sam could die in one of his street fights tomorrow. This could be the last time I saw him, touched him, felt him.

It was true for any person you were in love with, but especially for Sam, which made him even more precious to me. I was always on the verge of losing him, and sometimes at night, when I thought about what kind of dangers he was exposed to out there, I could barely breathe.

"No one wants to put a mirror to your face because they know you won't like what you see there. Everyone is afraid of your wrath," I continued.

"And *you*?" He pulled his lips from my breasts, glaring at me intensely. We were hidden by the wall next to the glass door, but I knew we needed to stop this sooner rather than later before anyone saw us. "Are you scared of me?"

"I was never truly scared of you." I rolled my thumb along his jaw, feeling blush creeping to my cheeks. "Not when I was seventeen and not a decade later. To me you'll always be beautifully misunderstood. And maybe I'm an idiot to care, Sam. In fact, I probably am, but I still want you to quit smoking because I want you to grow old and gray and be healthy. Even if I can never have you."

His eyes narrowed and something passed between us. I shuddered uncontrollably in his arms, like he'd managed to put something inside me with this one look.

"Aisling, I—" Sam started.

A blood-chilling shriek pierced through the ballroom just then, making him stop midsentence, followed by a commotion, the sound of breaking glass, and hysterical crying.

"Someone call 9-1-1!"

"We need an ambulance!"

"Oh, dear God! What's happening?"

I broke free from Sam's arms. We both rushed into the ballroom.

I stopped dead when I realized what the spectacle was all about.

In the middle of the room was my father, Gerald Fitzpatrick, dressed in his flannel pajamas and a house robe, looking like a homeless person with his hair wild and his eyes bloodshot. He held my mother by the throat, shaking her, looking drunk and out of focus, in front of an audience consisting of the cleaning crew, waitresses, and a few odd guests who still hadn't left.

"The family heirloom!" he raged. "Where is it, Jane? Tell me now. I know that it's you who stole it. You who sent those threatening letters."

My mother fainted in his arms, just as my brothers jumped in to pry him away from her.

Sam

Cillian dragged a kicking and screaming Gerald off of Jane while Hunter scooped his limp mother in his arms, shouldering past people as he rushed her out of the limelight.

British Clark Kent, AKA Devon Whitehall, appeared out of nowhere, making a beeline straight to the doors, having security close them as he demanded the staff to dispose of their phones so he

L.J. SHEN

could delete any sensitive material that might be leaked. The night had tapered off and only a handful of guests and the cleaning crew remained.

Aisling trembled next to me like a leaf, watching her family go down in flames.

Gerald had finally realized the cufflinks I took were missing, and he was blaming Jane for it.

His sanity was evaporating into thin air, along with his common sense.

The crazy hair. The pajamas and robe. The drastic weight loss. The drunkenness.

In public.

I imagined he had his driver bring him in, mumbling incoherently the whole way here. Poor asshole was probably going to get fired by Jane.

He was on the fast track to oblivion. Everything was going according to plan.

At some point, Aisling sneaked away from next to me, catching Cillian's steps, pushing Gerald out of the ballroom while people around them gossiped and gasped.

Her face was tight with emotions, her eyes glassy with concern.

Suddenly, I grappled with a feeling completely foreign to me. I never felt it before, so I couldn't exactly pinpoint what it was. It was a mixture of nausea and dread with some anger thrown into the mix.

Had I been poisoned?

Funny, because I couldn't find two fucks to give about Cillian and Hunter crapping bricks right now, even if I looked for said fucks with a search unit. I couldn't bring myself to care about Becca, for that matter, who was currently tucked in an Uber, heading back to wherever-the-hell she came from, probably cursing me all the way to next Tuesday for bailing on her ass as soon as Aisling showed up in the cloakroom.

Guilt.

That was what was seeping its way through me like poison.

After all this time, and all the sins I'd committed, it had finally wormed its way through my exterior.

It was new.

And it felt like *shit*.

At the same time, I knew backing down wasn't an option. Not like this. Not right now. Gerald had ruined my life. He had to pay.

He killed my fucking unborn brother.

Drove my mother away.

Then had me do all his dirty work—his arm bending, his illegal dabbling—all while throwing in fat bonuses to make sure I didn't touch and sully his precious princess.

"Give us a ride home." Someone clapped my shoulder from behind. When I turned around to inform them I wasn't a fucking Uber driver, I was surprised to see Troy and Sparrow, hand in hand.

"Didn't know you were here."

Troy tucked his free hand into his front pocket, glancing around the apocalyptic scene in front of us with indifference.

"Got here ten minutes ago from dinner with friends just to drop off the check. We stayed for the entertainment. Our taxi driver has left."

Sparrow smacked wet, lipstick-stained kisses on both my cheeks. She stopped, hovering an inch over my mouth, smelling Aisling. A private smirk marred her face.

"No heavy petting in the backseat," I quipped, taking out my car keys and flipping them in my hand.

"Can't promise anything," Troy deadpanned.

"Well, I can. I'll push you out on the highway without even blinking," I reminded him, meaning every word. I hated public displays of affection. "Your wife, I'll spare."

In the car, Troy asked from the passenger seat, "So, when are you going to quit your blood-thirsty vendetta?"

My eyes flicked to the rearview mirror, searching for Sparrow's reaction. She sat in the backseat, looking at me pointedly without offering her words.

Did she know? Of course she did. Fucker told her the aroma and frequency of his farts, not to mention all of his secrets. Mine too.

"I'll stop when he comes clean."

"That might never happen," Troy pointed out.

"Then I might never stop," I volleyed back.

"Are you planning to kill him?"

I opened my mouth to say yes but stopped short when I thought about Aisling.

Her unexplainable love for her shitty parents grated on my nerves. Developing sentiments for people just because they gave you their shitty DNA was a concept I would never understand. I settled for a brash, "I don't know."

"That's a first, smartass," Troy groaned.

"Huh?"

"You. Not knowing shit. You've always been like this." Troy sat back, stroking his chin, half-entertained. "Took what you wanted, even if you had to set the world on fire in the process."

"It's called being a go-getter. Not a bad thing," I pointed out, stopping in front of their place and killing the engine.

"That depends on how you look at it," Sparrow offered from behind. "It might be a very bad thing for you."

"Cut the riddles, Dr. Seuss." I turned around, scowling at her. "If you have something to say, say it, and be fast about it. I outgrew tonight about three days ago."

"What your mother is saying, and you are too stubborn to comprehend," Troy ground out slowly, the edge of his tone warning me not to give his wife lip, "is that what you want might end up not wanting you back if you slaughter everything on your way to get to it."

"Do you know what you want?" Sparrow leaned forward, her face almost touching mine, her green eyes dark and intense.

"Yes," I hissed slowly, holding her gaze. "I want you both to *fuck off.*"

"No, Sam. You *think* you want revenge. But what you want…" she trailed off, shaking her head "…what you *really* want is completely different."

"Even if I wanted the things you think I want, getting them would ruin everything. I'm a monster," I growled, feeling the invisible chain to my resolve tightening, ready to snap, unleashing all my pent-up anger.

Sparrow palmed my cheek, flashing me a sad smile. "If a monster can be made, it can be unmade, too. Good night, my darling boy." She kissed my nose and slid out of the car.

Troy followed her.

For a few seconds, it was just me and the car and the silence, punctuated by the wails of an ambulance a good few yards away.

Then I started laughing.

A good, deep laugh.

One that rumbled through my whole body.

"I don't want Aisling, you fools." I kicked my car into drive. "But I *will* have her."

It was time to take what Aisling had offered me so freely.

First, I would have what I'd deprived myself of for so long. An American Princess.

Then I would ruin her father.

It would piss him off more anyway.

Nine

Aisling

"HE IS GONE!" MOTHER BURST THROUGH MY BEDROOM door, looking like a demon right out of a horror flick—a second before it crawled its way out of a pond. "His things are gone. Suits. Clothes. Laptops. Briefcase. The only thing he left is his wedding band, the bastard!"

I sat upright in my bed, rubbing the sleep from my eyes. The world blurred into focus slowly. It was a Thursday. A few days after the charity ball. Da hadn't been back in the house since. He stayed with Cillian and Persephone until things cooled down. Or so we thought until three seconds ago.

"Mother, I—"

"I didn't do it!" she howled, pounding a fist against her chest. "You believe me, don't you? It wasn't me. I swear. Not the poisoning. Not the cufflinks. I mean, heavens, Aisling, we both know how obsessed he is with those cufflinks. I would never!"

"I believe you," I said and meant it. I got out of the bed, still dizzy, and walked over to her, putting a hand on her shoulder and rubbing slowly. "But I'm going to need some time to get to the bottom of all this. Okay?"

"You must help me, Aisling. You must." She dropped down to her knees, hugging my midsection. I stared at her in disbelief mixed with annoyance. I'd never seen her so desperate in my life. I was growing more and more suspicious, especially after the cufflinks, that whoever was doing this wanted to hurt my father specifically, not my parents as a unit. But in their quest to ruin my father's life, they also terrorized my mother, who was beyond frail and brittle and already had her own demons to battle.

Just a few weeks ago, I found fresh cuts above her wrists.

"Get up, Mother." I patted her head awkwardly, glancing around to ensure we didn't have an audience. She folded into two, doubling down by collapsing on the floor.

"I can't," she wailed. "Oh, Aisling, this is such a nightmare. I need something for my nerves." She clutched my bare toes, and I felt her tears wetting them. My stomach turned and twisted. I wanted to run away.

"I'm not prescribing you anything, Mother. I'm not a psychiatrist. You need to see a professional who will assess you. Besides, you should adopt some coping mechanisms. Bad things happen to everyone. Life is about rising to the occasion, any occasion. Think of life as a garden. You don't choose where to be planted, but you can only choose whether to bloom or wither."

"Oh but, Ash, it is hard to bloom in the storm. All I need is a little pick-me-up. I even have a list of things that might help. It's right here." She messed with the pocket of her nightgown, producing a wrinkled paper and handing it to me.

I scanned the list, my blood turning cold.

"That's a lot of pills. Some of them are strong. Zoloft. Prozac … you cannot mix them together, and you *definitely* can't consume alcohol if you take any of them."

Then something had occurred to me. Something that made me want to throw up. It was perfectly possible she had *already* taken them. Because all those things were prescribed to so many of her bored, house-wife friends, and they all loved to exchange pills like it was some sort of a hobby. If she asked for them, it might be because she wanted more of them.

"You haven't taken any, have you?"

She sniffed but didn't say anything. I stepped back, shaking her off of my feet.

"For goodness' sake, Mother!"

"Just get me the medicines and get to the bottom of this." Jane threw herself over the carpet pathetically, very intentionally wiping her snot over it.

For one brief moment I forgave myself.

Forgave myself for being so weak when it came to Sam Brennan, for going to the schools my parents chose for me, and for never quite standing up for myself. Not with my friends, not with my brothers, and not with my family.

It was obvious my role model at home wasn't exactly Marie Curie. Secretly, I wondered what I would have been like if I were raised by anyone else. By someone strong. A woman like Sparrow, who was terrifyingly direct and always made her opinion known publicly about every matter.

I redirected my thoughts quickly when I felt anger flaring in my chest. There was no time for that.

Hurrying toward the closet, I jammed my feet into the scrubs I didn't need, for a job that was a lie to please my parents.

For the first time, I wondered what it would feel like to live in my own place. An apartment where I could get precious sleeping time between shifts at work without drawing my mother baths and listening to her complain about my father. Where she wouldn't threaten to cut herself to get back at me for not giving her enough attention.

"I need to get to work. Please get yourself in the shower and brush your hair. Maybe go on a walk or see friends. You need to start taking care of yourself, Mother. I won't live here forever." I began buttoning my pea coat over my scrubs.

"No one has asked you to!" She shot me a hostile look from the floor, pouting. "And go, why don't you. Go when I need you. Just don't come crying at my grave when you lose me."

This old tune again.

Do this and this and that or else I will take my own life.

She needs help, mon cheri, and maybe you are not the place she should get it from.

"I'm calling your psychiatrist as soon as I get to work," I announced to her. She never agreed to see him. Said he never prescribed her the drugs she wanted.

"You can be mean, you know?" She stared at my ceiling numbly, zoning out. "Just like your father."

"I'm not mean." I sighed, grabbing my backpack. "But I *am* tired."

She said something else, but I didn't hear her. I walked away before she could convince me to stay. To tend to her. To give myself up for her.

On my way to the clinic, I called one of our trusted housekeepers and asked her to keep an eye on Mother, knowing I was paying lip service for my conscience.

Sam was right. A twenty-seven-year-old woman had no business living with her parents if she could afford her own place.

It was time to spread my wings.

Even and especially because Jane Fitzpatrick kept them carefully clipped.

It was a quiet day at the clinic. Full of consultations, paperwork, and research. No major decisions were made, which was always good news.

I saw Mrs. Martinez again for a checkup and accepted a new patient, a sixty-eight-year-old man so fragile he had to be carried downstairs into the clinic in Dr. Doyle's arms.

When it was time to close shop, Dr. Doyle—a tall, sixty-something man who bore an uncanny similarity to Pierce Brosnan—patted my shoulder.

L.J. SHEN

"You know, Aisling, you're a brilliant young doctor. You should find a residency and start next year. Tell your future employer you took a gap year to spend some time with your family or to do some traveling. This clinic is no place for someone as promising as you."

"I like working here." I closed Mrs. Martinez's file after making vague notes. I couldn't write anything too specific out of fear this place would be found. I tucked the document in the filing cabinet. "We've already been through this, Greg. You know why I'm doing this. This is my calling."

"And I appreciate your life experience has brought you here. I can't help but feel guilty, too…" he leaned against the wall, crossing his arms over his chest "…such medical talent shouldn't be wasted in some underground, illegal clinic. You are a Harvard graduate, Fitzpatrick. Top of the crop."

"How long have you felt this way?" I frowned at him, clearing up the table.

"Long enough," he grumbled.

I swallowed uncomfortably. I hated change, and if I didn't work here, that would be one heck of a change.

"Please don't shackle yourself in unearned guilt. You are much too pragmatic for that." I stood up, patting his cheek with a smile on my way to the bathroom before going home. From my periphery, Dr. Doyle glanced at his wristwatch. I closed the door behind me in the bathroom.

"We'll talk about it some other time," he determined.

"Fine, but if you think you're getting rid of me so easily, you have another thing coming, Greg," I spoke in a singsong. "Close the place up?"

I needed to go check on my mother. As per usual, she gave me the silent treatment after what happened this morning and refused to take my calls.

"Actually, I have to run. A patient just paged me. Mind locking up before you leave?" he called out to me.

200

"Not at all!" I answered from the restroom. "Go ahead. It's been a moon and a half since I closed shop."

Five minutes later, I found myself scrubbing medical equipment clean and locking up cabinets.

I heard a knock on the clinic's door.

Who on earth ...?

For obvious reasons, we didn't allow walk-ins.

Frowning, I walked over to the door and looked through the peephole.

Merde.

I quickly smoothed my scrubs over my body, rearranging my long ponytail.

Still, I didn't open the door. I didn't breathe. I didn't move.

Go away. Please. You are too much and not enough all at the same time.

"Too late, Nix. I know you're in there. Your car is parked directly in front of the doorway."

Double merde. I had no one but myself to blame for my lack of discretion.

Still, I didn't move. I watched through the peephole as Sam braced one arm over the doorframe, sneering down at the floor like they were sharing a secret.

"We can do this the nice way or the not-so-nice way. But you should know, my not-so-nice ways include smashing doors down, rummaging through places, and doing very dangerous fucking things."

"Go to hell."

"Can't. Satan has a restraining order against me. Now open the damn door."

"I hate you," I groaned, plastering my forehead to the door, closing my eyes.

"No, you don't."

"I should."

"No fucking shit, Sherlock. Open up."

Reluctantly, I did as I was told, stepping aside. There was no point blocking his way with all one hundred and twenty pounds of me.

We stared at each other, the threshold between us like an ocean neither of us was willing to cross. My heart beat wildly.

He did it again. He came to see me. Sought me out.

"You kill people," he said softly.

I gasped, stumbling backward. He stepped forward, walking into the clinic, not bothering to close the door behind him.

"I finally figured it out. Even though it was in front of me all this time, in plain sight. You kill people. That's what you do. Mercy killing. *Euthanasia.*"

My back bumped against the opposite wall, and I squeezed my eyes shut childishly. Maybe if I pretended he wasn't there, he'd disappear. But no. His voice hovered around me, thickening the air, making it too hot to breathe.

"That's why you limit yourself to very few patients. That's why it's an underground operation. That's why you keep all the drugs you have in here. That's why you treat them at their homes. It all makes sense. You're not here to cure people, you're here to kill them. The only question is *why*? Why are you, the sweet, caring Aisling Fitzpatrick, doing this? Your brothers always told me you wanted to be an OB-GYN or a pediatrician. Something with babies involved, they said. The exact opposite of what you turned out to be."

My eyes fluttered open on their own accord, and I met his gaze. Images of my mother earlier this morning spread over my bedroom carpet, helplessly bawling, attacked my memory. I didn't want to be her. Meek and weak and always hiding her real self from the world. I straightened my back, taking a deep breath.

But old habits die hard …

"You can't prove it."

"I don't need to. You'll tell me your truth."

"While you're keeping so many secrets from me?" I choked on my bitterness, spluttering, "Nice try. Why are you here, Sam?"

His jaw ticked, but he said nothing.

"I find it hard to believe my job means so much to you. Whether I cure or kill people, it makes no difference to you. You owe me nothing, and your job is not to watch over me. In fact, it is the very opposite—to stay away from me. So why are you pushing this?"

His nostrils flared. He took my face in his rough palm, tilting my head so our mouths were aligned.

"I don't fucking know, Aisling. I have no idea what keeps bringing me back to you, but I can't seem to stop, and you don't seem to mind, so let's just get this out of our system and fuck already."

The next thing happened like a snake bite. Sudden and fast and violent.

I kissed him roughly, this time taking what I wanted instead of waiting for it. Our kiss made me feel like we were lashing out at each other. Sam caught my lower lip between his teeth and tugged me closer to him, until there was no more space between us. He hoisted me up and carried me into the examination room, kicking the door open and spreading me flat over the table, kissing me as I toed off my work sneakers and unbuttoned his shirt.

There was nothing romantic or calculated about what we were doing. We both just needed to be physically connected as soon as possible. I tried to tell myself that it was fine. That no one had been on the examination table anyway. It was more for show. In case the place was discovered and Dr. Doyle and I needed to give the police some plausible explanation. Treating people without insurance underground wasn't half as frightening as what we were trying to hide.

Sam's tongue ran from my lips, down to my chin, heading south to my neck, licking a path between my tits. He cupped one of my breasts in his mouth through my shirt, groaning as he pushed my pants down, swirling his tongue around my erect nipple.

"*Goddammit,*" he muttered, sucking my whole breast into his mouth.

I shuddered. Something about the fact there was fabric and a sports bra between us made the act so much dirtier and erotic. I threaded my fingers through his hair—his body, hard and imposing, pressing against mine everywhere—as he moved to my other breast, giving it the same treatment.

When my pants and underwear were gone, and I was sitting on the examination table naked from the waist down, Sam pushed me roughly to lie down, using one hand to pry my thighs open and spread them as wide as he could.

"I sincerely hope you don't intend to ask me to stop."

I shook my head. "No. Don't stop."

"You know, growing up, I never played kiddie games. I graduated from formula to guns without a pit stop at toy cars and puzzles." His mouth was swollen from our filthy kisses, and he grinned at me, his fingers on my hipbones as he plastered me to the cold, metallic table.

"Want to play doctor and patient?" I quickly caught his drift.

I wouldn't bet on it, but I swore his cheeks pinked slightly.

"All right. Open up for me, Nix." His fingers skimmed their way from my inner thigh to my center. I clapped a hand over his wrist, shaking my head with a taunting smile.

"Glove up first, Doc. First drawer on your left."

He paused, then his face broke into a terrible smile. Terrible because it was the first *genuine*, giddy, hopeful smile I'd seen on Sam's face in the decade I'd known him—and how awful was that?

Sam returned in a pair of my latex gloves that were tight around his massive palms. I nodded, satisfied.

"I'm new at this," he feigned an apology, his grin turning sinister again, "so you'll have to excuse me in advance as I conduct this pap smear, Miss Fitzpatrick."

"Please, call me Nix."

"Sorry, I don't treat Knicks fans," he deadpanned.

I bit down on my lip, suppressing wild laughter. I didn't know many men who knew about pap smears, let alone how to conduct one. I let the hair in my ponytail spill over the edge of the examining table, blinking at him innocently.

"My name has nothing to do with the basketball team. It's after an enticing female monster. Does that put you at ease?"

"Definitely."

To my surprise, Sam wasn't completely off. He settled himself between my legs and pushed me open so wide I felt the delicious pain of being stretched to my limit.

"You might experience some discomfort here," he groaned, pushing two fingers deep into my core. I clenched onto them immediately, letting out a soft moan, rolling my hips to meet more of his hand.

"Miss Fitzpatrick," he *tsked*, "control yourself, please."

"S-sorry," I mumbled, half-opening my eyes to watch as he pulled his hand away, only to drive it in again, this time using three fingers, curling them upward until he hit my G-spot, his free hand still stretching me wide open.

"Oh!" I cried.

"Still can't get to that right angle. Better try again."

He thrust again, fucking me with his fingers—with his entire fist, almost—in and out, in and out. I lay there on my back and took it, wet and turned on like I had never been in my entire life, chanting his name under my breath, not caring if he knew how much of a goner I was for him.

"H-how did you learn how to do this?" I asked, bucking my hips upward. Every time I did, he pinned my waist down, his way of telling me to behave as he fingered me. "You look like you know what you're doing."

"Got accepted to premed after high school."

I let out a piercing laugh at that, but when I looked up, he seemed completely sober.

"You're serious." My smile dropped, and I felt the cloying feeling of an orgasm tingling through me. He didn't even touch my clit, and I always needed clitoral stimulation to come. *Huh.*

"Dead fucking serious." He sent me a nonchalant smirk as he fucked me with one hand and spread me with the other.

"You thought about becoming a doctor?" I wheezed.

"Hell no. I made a bet with a friend I could get into premed. Didn't study for it either. But I read a gynecology book on one of my train rides to New York City while attending an arms deal and got the gist of it."

I had a million questions to ask him, but all of them had to wait as my climax washed over me, shaking me to the core and making me cry out, grasping onto the edges of the examination table.

"Always so dramatic," Sam muttered. Instead of getting on top of me like I thought he would, he grabbed me by the ankles, tugging me until my ass perched on the edge of the table.

"Sorry, Miss Fitzpatrick, but I couldn't find what I needed. This might be a little unorthodox, but I think I know how to finish this exam."

I was all boneless desire and satisfaction. I couldn't even lift my head to see what he was doing before he squatted down between my legs, his tongue finding my clit and swirling around it slowly, teasingly, putting delicious pressure on it. I grabbed his hair and groaned so loud I thanked my lucky stars Dr. Doyle wasn't upstairs in his apartment because I could probably be heard in neighboring cities.

"*Merde*," I panted.

"I fucking love it when you say that," he murmured between my legs, and I felt the wetness of me coating my inner thighs and his face as he began to eat me out, literally.

Eat. Me. Out.

Nibbled and bit and licked me thoroughly. My eyes rolled back inside their sockets, the pleasure so poignant, so intense, the oxygen rattled in my lungs. I was close to a second, violent orgasm, I couldn't help but buck my groin, thrusting it into his face.

"Please. Ohhhhh."

I stopped breathing, every muscle in my body clenching as intense pleasure coursed over me. I reached the highest point of *la petite mort*—my own little death, as the French referred to an orgasm—just

206

when I felt him plunging into me, heavy and thick and long, in one smooth movement.

I was drenched, hot and ready for him.

My eyes opened and I saw him leaning against the examination table, between my legs, while I was full to the hilt with his erection. He closed his eyes and hissed, the pleasure too much for both of us, as he began to move inside me.

"Found what you were looking for?" I croaked, referring to his so-called pap smear.

He thrust into me with a punishing rhythm. "And then some."

Something about his movements, so sure, so nonchalantly punishing, told me that he was used to getting what he wanted not only outside of the bedroom but inside it, too.

"I can't believe I'm fucking you again." He shook his head, frowning at me.

"Believe it." My heart pounded loud and wildly. "Because I doubt you can do this with anyone else at this point."

"Shut up."

"You know it's true. That's why you couldn't have sex with that woman at the ball, who looked exactly like me. You know what you want, Sam? You just don't want to take it because the consequences would mean you'd lose my daddy's fat paycheck."

"I don't give a fuck about your daddy." He plowed into me angrily. I didn't think anyone had ever been that deep inside of me.

"Then what is it? Please don't tell me you actually convinced yourself you are bad for me. You don't have a conscience, and I can make my own decisions."

"*Shut. Up.*"

"Make me." I blew a raspberry. For a second, he stopped thrusting and just stood still between my legs, buried inside me. Then in one swift motion, he removed the latex gloves from his hands, balled them together, and shoved them into my mouth, my juices still on them. My mouth filled with the bitter taste of latex and the earthiness of myself.

"There. That's better." He resumed his thrusts. "Never have I fucked a more infuriating creature."

"*Furrryerrr,*" I offered around the ball of gloves.

"Yes, sweetheart, that's exactly what I'm doing. Fucking you."

He was close. I could feel it. The way his fingers tightened around my thighs, pushing them outward. The way his expression became less guarded and more surprised like he, too, couldn't believe it was so good.

"Are you on the pill?" he asked, mid-thrust.

I tried answering around the gloves, but my voice was muffled, and he couldn't catch that I'd said, "Yes, I was, since I was fifteen."

"Never mind." He pushed in and out with jerky movements. "Even if you aren't, you are going to take the morning after pill. Am I clear?"

The pleasure and playfulness I felt just seconds ago turned into anger again. He came inside me, holding my legs still as his face tightened. I could feel his warm cum making its way inside my body. I spat the gloves out onto the floor, roaring with fury, swinging my body upright. I pushed him off of me, kicking him for good measure. He barely moved—just enough to let me stand up fully—already tucking himself in.

"Get out." I pointed at the door. "Now. And don't come back."

He stared at me with amusement, slowly rearranging himself, buttoning his slacks, removing a cigarette from his pack.

"Lighten up, Nix. I heard you when you said you were on the pill. I just like to see you getting pissy."

"Well, congratulations, you succeeded. You think it's okay to tell a woman what to do with her body?"

"Depends on the woman." He shrugged.

"*Out!*" I yelled, louder now.

He lit his cigarette. Another thing that bothered me. He knew I hated when he smoked. I stomped to the door, flinging it open all the way.

"Out!"

"Or what?" He grinned around the cigarette. "You'll call the police to come and pick me up from your unregistered death clinic, Nix?"

"Or I will tell my brothers you've screwed their baby sister twice now, despite getting ... oh, what is it, an extra million just to stay away from me?" I blinked slowly, a sugary smile on my face.

Sam snorted, moving toward the door with deliberate leisure designed to drive me nuts.

"Don't come near me again," I bit out.

"That won't be a problem."

And just like that, he was done.

Leaving me a half-naked mess, smeared in our truths and lies and all the things we couldn't talk about.

My heart half-broken but held in his bloodied hands.

Ten

Sam

A FEW DAYS HAD PASSED SINCE I SCREWED AISLING AT HER death clinic.

I was sick as a dog and wasn't showing any signs of improvement.

My fever was up, I threw up everything I put inside my body, and could barely drag myself from my bed to the door to snatch the DoorDash delivery left there.

It was the first time I was seriously sick since I was nine. The luxury of being weak and dependable wasn't something I allowed myself. In fact, I hadn't taken one sick day from school or work since moving in with the Brennans. I'd always done my best to be worthy of their awe and admiration, a half-man, half-god. Unbreakable and stronger than steel.

This was why I never let my adoptive parents in. Not fully, anyway. Not into my apartment, my domain, my privacy.

My corner of the world was mine and mine alone—to lick my wounds, be less than perfect, quiet, uncertain.

I was content to visit Troy and Sparrow, treat them as family then retreat back to the shadows. The less they knew about me, the better. Living with them while I was a teen had been liking holding my breath underwater. Despite pretending I was going to go about my old ways and give them trouble the day I'd moved in with them, I tried hard not to fuck up.

I was the smartest, fastest, most ruthless soldier Troy had ever had, gave Sparrow jewelry for Christmas, and protected Sailor fiercely every step of the way.

And now *this* happened.

One and a half fucks with Aisling Fitzpatrick. That was all I needed to throw me off the rails. Rails? I was nowhere near the goddamn fucking train station at this point.

For a docile thing, she sure knew how to leave a lasting impression. But the raw, impossible sweetness of her called to me like a lighthouse in pitch fucking black.

Touching her was a mistake. One that had cost me more than I was willing to pay. Four days after I had her, and I still couldn't look her brothers in the face. I'd neglected all responsibilities toward the Fitzpatricks. Of course, I still showed up at Badlands, found the time to slit a Bratva member's throat for trying to sneak up on me after a business meeting downtown.

Things were heating up between the Russians and me, and I'd had to recruit more soldiers. Some of them were retired folks Troy used to work with. I needed to keep Brookline protected—and mine. Now was not the time to play house with the little doctor. Not when she could become a target, too.

On the fifth day of my feeling like a bag of steaming shit, I admitted defeat. Calling Aisling to provide me medical aid was like Johnnie Depp calling Amber Heard and asking her to be his character witness. It was time to hurl my ass into the nearest hospital and get the medical help I so obviously needed.

Reluctantly, I took a shower, jammed my feet into a pair of sneakers, and grabbed my keys, on my way to the door. I swung it open.

Aisling was standing on the other side, brown paper bags full to the brim with groceries in her arms.

I slammed the door in her face, but she was quick—or maybe

I was goddamn slow—and slid her foot between the door and the frame. She let out a yelp, causing me to open the door immediately all the way and curse under my breath.

"Her name was Ms. Blanchet," she peeped out.

I stared at her silently. She needed to elaborate for me to understand what the hell she was talking about. She dropped the groceries, cans and vegetables rolling onto the floor, and hugged her midriff.

"My governess. Her name was Ms. Blanchet. She died when I was seventeen. On the night I met you, actually, at the carnival. I drove there after I found her. She had cancer. Lung cancer. She battled it for three years. The last few months, she spent in a hospice but then decided she wanted to die at home and not in a strange place around people she didn't know and meant nothing to her. So she moved back to her apartment in the West End. She was sick, Sam. So very sick. She couldn't eat, or breathe, or laugh without feeling pain. She started peeing in her bed at night, voluntarily, after she'd woken up in the middle of the night to go to the bathroom one time and fell in the hallway, breaking her hipbone.

"But she was a proud woman and refused to wear a diaper. Something had changed after she broke her hipbone. Whenever I came to visit her—not in the capacity of a student anymore; she couldn't teach, but I would visit her to provide company, seeing as she had no one else in the States—she asked me to help her take her own life."

There was a pause. Silence hung in the air. Reluctantly, I grabbed a fistful of her dress and pulled her in, shutting the door behind us. My penthouse was the only apartment on the floor, but I still didn't want to take any chances of anyone listening to this. We left the groceries outside. Aisling twisted her fingers together, staring at her feet, determined to finish her confession.

"I said no. Of course, I said no! That was the right thing to say. My whole life I'd dreamed of becoming a doctor so I could help people survive, not kill them. But every time I left her apartment after watching her light dim, I felt guiltier for refusing her. It tore me to shreds. The idea that I was denying her something she wanted so badly. Something she truly desired. Helping her make the pain go away. And I began to wonder … wasn't it patronizing of me to make the decision of her living in pain?"

"You were just a kid," I said tersely, but she and I both knew it was bullshit. Life didn't care about your age, bank account, or circumstances. Life just happened. I was thirteen when I assumed my role as Troy's successor. I'd crushed skulls, put bullets in people's heads, tortured, killed, manipulated, and kidnapped people. Because life happened to me, and to stay alive, I had to adapt.

"She begged and begged and begged. She was slipping away from me, I could feel it." Aisling stood there, by my door, tears streaming down her face.

I made no move to console her. It wasn't what she needed in that moment, even an emotionally stunted dirtbag like me could see it. She had to get this confession off her chest. "The woman I'd looked up to since I was four, the woman whom my parents had collected from Paris to shape me into a lady—she was witty, sassy, effortlessly elegant and chic, *and* a heavy smoker," she said pointedly, eyeing me. "She'd become a shadow of her former self. I didn't know what to do. Until, finally, Ms. Blanchet made the decision for me. We had a fight. She told me to stop coming. Not to visit her anymore. Said she wouldn't answer if I visited. That was three days before I met you."

Her throat bobbed with a swallow, and she raked her shaky fingers through her hair as she took a ragged breath.

"I didn't listen. Maybe I should've, but I didn't. I couldn't not visit her. So I did. I knocked on the door, rang the bell. No one had answered. I went to a neighbor downstairs that I knew had her spare keys. An older gentleman she used to take tea with before she'd gotten too sick. He gave me the key. I opened her apartment. I found her in the bathtub…" she looked sideways then to the floor, closing her eyes "…she used whatever energy she had left to cut her wrists and bleed out. She was in a river of blood. That's why she had this fight with me. That's why she didn't want me to come anymore. She made up her mind about taking her own life. And she did it in such a painful, lonely way."

"Nix," I said, my voice gravelly. Suddenly, I forgot about being sick. I forgot about existing in general. Her pain took over the room and everything else ceased to exist.

She shook her head, laughing bitterly.

"That's why I was such a mess at the carnival. After I'd found her, I called my parents and 9-1-1. I gave a statement then drove home, put on something slutty, and started driving around until I saw the lights coming from the carnival."

The carnival where I snatched her first kiss simply because she was too sweet not to take advantage of.

Where she saw me taking a life.

Aisling saw two dead people in less than twelve hours after living a too-sheltered life. It must have been a shock to the system.

"I saw what you did to that man that night..." her chin quivered "...and something weird happened inside me. I knew you would survive, wouldn't let the guilt consume you. You looked young and healthy and intelligent. I trusted you slept well at night. Ate well. You were ... oddly okay with taking lives."

She looked up at me for confirmation, her eyes swimming with tears. I gave her a curt nod.

"I own up to who I am. I have no trouble eating or sleeping."

Except for when I touch you ... then I become a pussy-ass dipshit with a fever who can't keep a damn meal down.

She nodded.

"That's what I thought. But you have to understand, I went to an all-girls Catholic school. Euthanasia goes against every bone in my body."

"You still do it," I challenged. "Why?"

"Somehow, that night, you made it real. The possibility of taking a life. Even though our situation is vastly different. The only guilt I've felt was for not helping Ms. Blanchet when she'd needed me. Because she was too far gone, and I was far too selfish to burden myself with such guilt. I ended up feeling horrible anyway. Much worse than I would have had I helped her. That day changed my life. Our meeting was kismet. You made me realize what I needed to do. What I was put on this earth to do. And then it made me think about the rest of my relationships. The world surrounding me. You wanna know what I learned?" She sniffed.

I got it. All of it. Why she did what she did. How she had become who she was. A Nix. A gorgeous vision of a woman, hiding an enchanting monster underneath.

But I didn't agree with her. She wasn't put on this earth to kill people.

"What is that?" I asked softly.

"The thing I learned is sometimes we do very ugly things for the people we love. I do it for my mother. For my father. Even, sometimes, for myself."

I said nothing. I'd never truly loved anyone, so it didn't seem like I could contribute to that observation. She stepped toward me, the fog of death and mourning around her evaporating.

"I met Dr. Doyle in my second year of premed. By chance, if you could believe it. That clinic that you've seen? He lives in the apartment upstairs. Back then, he rented it to a few students. I was at a house-warming party there and couldn't figure out why the basement was so firmly locked. There were no less than three locks on that thing. The guy who lived there said Dr. Doyle used it, and people were coming in and out often, but he'd never asked questions because frankly the rent was too cheap to get picky or vocal about it, and he was a med student—he was hardly at home anyway. My curiosity got the better of me, and I decided to get to the bottom of the situation. I'd scheduled a meeting with Dr. Doyle. Visited his office. The real one, in the nice part of town, where he worked as a dermatologist. He had plenty of pictures of his wife, but when I asked about her, he said that she had died two years earlier. She'd had a stroke that had left her with severe disabilities and brain damage. And by damage I mean, she couldn't even eat or control her bladder. I questioned him about her death. I knew it was insensitive, but I still did it. I just had a feeling …"

"He killed her," I said, staring her dead in the eye.

Nix nodded, walking briskly in the kitchen's direction, popping cabinets open, taking out a chopping board then walking back to the door to retrieve her groceries.

"I knew I had to coax it out of him, so I told him about my story with Ms. Blanchet. It wasn't easy to convince him, but finally, he agreed to take me under his wing. The minute I graduated, I started working with him full-time. Up until then, I'd studied his work. What he did after hours. He is committed to helping those who cannot be helped anywhere else. We're not bad people, Sam."

She collected the carrots, the celery, the chicken thighs, and the broth, chopping the vegetables and meat on the board and tossing them all into a pot for what I assumed was a chicken noodle soup.

"Euthanasia means *good death* in Greek. It is about letting life go peacefully, with dignity, on your own terms. But really, it is about ending excruciating suffering. We have some ground rules we abide by, though, Dr. Doyle and I, which is why we have very few patients. What we do is provide a service for the Ms. Blanchets of the world. Medical and prescription relief to people who don't want to live in a hospice but spend their remaining time in their homes with their loved ones."

"What are your ground rules?" I asked, propping my forearms on the kitchen island between us, intrigued.

I'd met many killers in my lifetime, but all of them were like me. Decadent and soulless. Selfish and cruel. They all did it for the bloodthirst. Not for altruistic reasons. Even those who had moral codes broke them often. What Aisling did had nothing to do with what I did for a living.

"For one thing, without getting into the bioethics of it, we only do voluntarily euthanasia. Which means that if we do not have the full consent of the patient for any reason, even if they are in a coma, we will not take on the patient. For another, we only take on patients at the very end of their lives. I am talking stage four cancer, people who have very few weeks to live. And even then, we don't pull the plug, so to speak." She put the pot of soup on the stove, turning up the heat, lost in her explanation. "We don't perform the act of taking a life. No. We do something that is called palliative sedation. Basically, we keep the patient alive but under deep sedation when the time comes, until they pass away naturally. Such a thing is legal in many countries, including the Netherlands and France. It is not even considered euthanasia. Not really. But for these people—for my patients—it makes a huge difference."

"And you only do it in their homes," I said.

"Yes." She put a lid on the chicken soup, tearing open a bag of egg noodles. "We make it possible for them to be surrounded by their friends and family."

"Then what do you have the clinic for?"

"As I said, we try to prolong their lives as much as we can through medication and consultation."

"On Thanksgiving ..." I trailed off.

She bounced on her toes, looking sideways.

"Yes. And on Halloween, too."

"Jesus, Ash." I planted my forehead over the kitchen island, relishing its coolness.

"You really are my own angel of death." She sighed. "Every time I do something like this, we have a moment together. But those were the only times I did it. I swear."

"You could get into deep shit for doing this, know that?" I raised my head, pinning her with a look. Of course she knew that. Aisling wasn't stupid.

She tilted her chin up, ignoring my words. "Cillian and Hunter say they haven't been able to reach you the last few days. I put two and two together and figured you were sick and too proud to ask for help, so I came to nurse you back to health."

"Listen to me…" I slammed my open palm against the marble between us, losing patience "…you can go to prison. This is first-degree murder. It is fucking intentional. Not even manslaughter. You need to stop."

"I know you're used to obedience, doing what you do…" Nix perched her purse on the counter and took out a thermometer, sauntering over to me and sticking it under my tongue "…but you can't tell me what to do, Monster."

I glared at her like she took a shit in my bed, waiting for the thermometer to beep. When it did, I spat it out back into her hand, and hissed, "This conversation is not over."

"Please," she snorted, rounding the kitchen island and taking a few pills from her purse, reaching over to hand them to me. "Don't pretend like you care. We're too old and too jaded for that. Here, take these."

Eyeing her skeptically, I said, "I don't know, Doc, you don't have a glowing track record of bringing people back to health."

She shrugged, about to withdraw her outstretched hand. I snatched the pills, shoving them into my mouth and swallowing without water.

"The soup will be ready in about forty-five minutes. Why don't you lie down and tell me all about *your* brand of evil?"

Kicking her out wasn't going to fly. Not when I could barely crawl to the door, let alone shove her out of it. And anyway, I was tired of fighting her off. She'd finally succeeded in worming her way into my life. I saw a distinction between her and Gerald. Between her and her brothers. Nix was finally her own person in my eyes.

And what a person that was.

Gorgeous, intelligent, and compassionate. Worst of all—someone who was blindly in love with me. She didn't have to spell it out. It was radiating from every inch of her silken flesh.

I didn't deserve her.

I could have her if I wanted.

I staggered to the couch and fell onto it. Nix balanced herself on the edge, right beside me, looking at me expectedly, like Rooney anticipating story time.

I ran my fingers through my damp hair.

"Where to start?"

"The beginning would be a good place."

Rascal.

"I was born on a blistering August day—"

"Well, maybe not the very beginning. How about the middle? No. Third chapter. After the exposition, but before things get real juicy and turbulent."

Eyeing her with new fondness I wasn't even entirely sure I was capable of feeling, I chuckled.

"Things had been a shitty blur until I turned nine, after which it was all about the Brennans. I had a role to assume, and I did. I now make more than Troy did back in the day. I own more businesses, more properties, and I control more areas in Boston than he ever did."

"But you are also messier than Troy was." She ran her fingers through my hair, fixing whatever the hell I did to it, smiling. "You kill more people. You get injured. Crime rate is up. And it's a well-known fact the Bratva is a ticking time bomb waiting to explode. I read it in the news."

"Reading something in the news doesn't make it true," I pointed out.

"What about the FBI? Cillian says they are after you, too."

"They'll never catch me."

"Famous last words." She sighed.

"Quote me on them, Nix."

She smiled, dipping her hand into the bullet jar wistfully, slipping in the missing bullet she'd stolen from there.

"Thank you," I croaked, closing my eyes.

"You are most welcome, my darling monster."

I drifted off to sleep, even though I tried hard to stay awake. It reminded me of the first few Christmases I spent with the Brennans. The fight against exhaustion was like swimming against the stream, but something good was happening, and who the fuck knew when would be the next time I'd feel this elusive, intoxicating joy?

Aisling must've slept right beside me because I could still feel her heat when I woke up. Her scent of ginger and honey and my fucking undoing.

I yawned, stretching on the couch.

"Make coffee," I growled, but there was no response.

I opened my eyes, looking around.

There was a bowl of steaming chicken noodle soup by my side, a bottle of water—uncapped—and some pills.

Aisling was gone.

The next day, I met with Barbara McAllister on the outskirts of Boston.

She was a hobo-looking woman, not in the hipster, bought-that-holed-shirt-for-three-hundred-bucks way, but in the seriously-need-a-sandwich way. You could tell that underneath the bleached hair, wrinkled face, and badly applied self-tan, she'd once been an attractive woman.

Barbara was the final blow I needed to bring Gerald down to his knees. The missing piece in Operation Destroy Gerald. She held some deep secrets he never wanted anyone to know, and for a healthy sum of money, she was willing to air them out to the world.

"But I need to make sure it'll be worth my while. I'll only do it for the right price. Can I borrow a cigarette?" Barbara asked when we'd met in a small coffee shop.

She wore a black mini-dress and a cheap trench coat, and it looked like the 'right price' for her would be twenty bucks and a McMeal. I silently offered her my open pack of cigarettes, keeping my expression blank.

I still soldiered through my plan for Gerald Fitzpatrick, but I was no longer gleeful about it. Somewhere along the road, hurting Aisling, which I knew I was bound to do, felt unnecessary. It wasn't that I was going soft. It was that there was no need to be harsh to a woman as pliable as her.

So fucking pliable that she runs an underground death clinic and seeks you out.

Barbara lit up a cigarette, exhaling with a satisfied smile.

"How do you know I'll even get a book deal? There isn't exactly a shortage of women Gerald Fitzpatrick has dipped his dick into." She eyed me skeptically.

"True, but you are the only one who'd lived in one of his apartments. You weren't just a fuck, you were a mistress. He flew you places. Bought you expensive jewelry. I bet it's just the tip of the iceberg." I smirked at her, setting the bait to make her say more.

She grinned, her teeth unusually white for a smoker, and nodded enthusiastically.

"Oh, did he ever. Samuel, my boy, he adored me. Of course, I did my part, too. There were orgies. Massive orgies. He sometimes took us three at a time. I always thought it was peculiar Ger was so upset when his son, Hunter, did it. After all, he was the king of orgies back in the day."

My jaw tensed. I didn't need to hear about my brother-in-law's sexcapades before he married my baby sister.

"What else?" I asked.

"There were drugs. A whole lot of them at those parties." Barbara rubbed her chin. It struck me as interesting that although Gerald had put her on the list, too, when I asked about her, he'd lied to me. Some of the details he had given me were different from what I'd found when I conducted my own research. Addresses, where they'd met, her age. Nothing lined up, so I decided to dig deeper. I was glad I did.

"There were also a few abortions." She cleared her throat. "Gerald did not like to use protection, but he also didn't want any bastard children. He was actually adamant about that, as you could imagine. I, myself, knew better than to tempt fate. I was always on the pill. Didn't have the ambition of getting knocked up with a billionaire's kid. Too dangerous. Looking back, maybe I should've. Maybe I'd fare better than I do today." She looked around the small coffee shop with the peeling wallpaper and dusty surfaces. She lived in a small, deserted town. It was obvious she wasn't swimming in it.

"But I was privy to everything that happened behind the scenes. He was a monster, Samuel. A real monster. Ever met one?" She sucked on the cigarette I gave her greedily, ignoring the disturbed glances the barista behind the counter shot at her—though she didn't approach us or tell her to put it out.

"Yeah," I said easily. "I've met monsters before. Multiple times, actually. So, here's how we are going to do this, Barbara. I'll bring the lucrative tell-all book deal, you'll bring the juice. But whatever happens, you must remember one thing—you never met me, never saw me, and never heard of me. Am I clear?"

She nodded, finishing off her cigarette and taking a sip of the stale coffee I'd bought her.

"Absolutely. May I have another cigarette?"

I laughed, standing up and tossing the pack in her lap before disappearing back into the white blizzard.

"Sure, sweetheart, take the whole fucking pack."

Eleven

Aisling

I SMELLED IT BEFORE I SAW IT. THE PUKE.

Then when I noticed the first spot, I realized they were every-where. Vomit stains.

Yellow and faint, covering the carpets, the floor, the walls.

I dropped my backpack at the door, following their trail up the stairway, where they led. It was unlike the housekeepers to leave any sort of dirt unattended.

Unless they wanted me to see it.

It was a cry for help, I knew. And not just from my mother.

Lord, what did she do now?

I reached the second floor then rounded the hallway, my stride picking up speed. Just as I expected, the puke stains led to the mas-ter bedroom, my mother's room. *Athair* had left days ago, and even though I tried my best to keep an eye on her, I knew Mother was spiraling.

I stopped outside her door, putting my hand on the doorknob and drawing a deep breath.

"Mother?"

There was no answer. I threw the door open, flashbacks of Ms. B attacking my memories, raw and vivid.

Blood.

Bath.

Wrists.

Despair.

I scanned the room. It was completely empty.

"Mother?" I echoed, confused.

Cautiously, I made my way into the en-suite bathroom, my heart in my throat. I hoped for the best but expected the worst. Mother, rehashing that scene at Ms. B's apartment, finally making good on her idle threats to take her own life. I knew my mother was a cutter. It actually provided me a screwed-up sense of security because people who cut were less likely to perform "successful" suicide attempts.

Jane Fitzpatrick wasn't even entirely a cutter. Sometimes she bruised herself a little, well and far away from the wrists, to draw attention. But she almost exclusively did this for my father's and my viewing. Hunter and Cillian had no idea. They weren't pawns in her emotional blackmail scheme.

I found her lying on the floor by the vanity, facedown.

"Mother!" I cried out, rushing to the bathroom, swinging the door open.

I fell down on both knees, turning her over by the shoulder. She was passed out cold in a pond of her own vomit. Half-dissolved pills were swimming in the vomit like little stars, their content, powdery and thick. Like stardust.

Jesus.

I grabbed her hair, shoving my fingers into her mouth, forcing her to gag and throw up more. She came to life instantly, at first protesting weakly about my hurting her as I held her head, but then she started puking more.

More pills. More everything.

"You need to get your stomach pumped," I groaned, calling an ambulance with my free hand as I continued trying to make her throw up. "What have you done?"

But I knew exactly what she'd done and *why.*

The ambulance arrived four minutes later. I followed it with my own car. I tried to call Hunter and Cillian repeatedly. Both their phones went straight to voicemail.

I couldn't understand why. It was nighttime. They should be at home with their families. I resorted to texting both of them our code word. Our emergency code.

Clover.

And then, when there was no answer: **Clover, clover, clover! Pick up!**

Reluctantly, I didn't want my sisters-in-law to know the extent of how screwed-up my family was, especially with Da living out of the house and my parents probably getting a divorce. I called Persy.

Persephone and I always had this unspoken connection, of two, shy and romantic wallflowers forced to blossom in the jungle that was the Fitzpatrick family.

"Hello?" Pers sounded drowsy, drunk with sleep.

"Oh. Hi," I said chirpily, feeling idiotic for forcing on a cheerful tone. "It's Ash. I'm trying to reach Cillian, but he is not answering. Any idea where he might be?"

"Hey, Ash. Is everything okay?" she asked and then, processing the fact I asked her a question, she added, "Kill is at Badlands with Sam, Devon, and Hunter. It's some kind of a special gambling night. I wasn't paying attention. Can I help you in any way?"

My blood sizzled in my veins as I gripped the steering wheel to a point of having white knuckles. My brothers were *ghosting* me. They'd left me to tend to our mother while they went gambling with Sam Brennan.

Fresh anger bubbled in my stomach. How dare Cillian and Hunter so easily accept a reality in which sweet, timid Aisling took care of Mother and *Athair* while they went to live their big fulfilling lives?

I pulled up at the hospital and ushered Mother to the ER along with her designated doctor, giving him as much information as

I could based on what I knew. What drugs she may had taken, the quantity, how much of it she threw up.

They ran some tests at the speed of light and pumped her stomach, but it was already mostly empty thanks to me. Mother was put on an IV drip and was conscious now, not even two hours after she got admitted.

"Just don't tell your father. He'd think it's about him, and he doesn't need the ego boost," she moaned, reaching for the remote by her hospital bed. "Do you think they have Netflix here? Oh, this is so highly inconvenient for me. I have a facial tomorrow morning."

I stared at her through bloodshot eyes, my whole body shaking with rage.

"You're an idiot."

The words slipped from my mouth before I could stop them, but I couldn't for the life of me find a drop of remorse after they were out in the open.

"Excuse me?" Her head jerked sideways. She gave me a hard, motherly stare.

"You heard me." I stood up, walking to the window, watching snow-caked trees and dirty ice roads. "You're an idiot. A selfish one at that. You refuse to get the help you need, and you abuse prescription drugs to get back at … who, exactly? The only person you are hurting is yourself. Now let me tell you what's about to happen …" I turned back around, fixing her with my own glare, my newfound spine tingling with the need to take action. "I'm going to go back home, leave you here on your own, and empty all your cabinets of drugs. Any drugs. You won't even have an Advil for your morning migraines. Then I'm going to book you an appointment with a therapist. If you don't go, I'm moving out of the house."

"Aisling!" Mother cried. "How dare you! I would never—"

"Enough!" I roared. "I don't want to hear it. I'm tired of mothering you all day, every day. Of holding your hand through life. Of being the parent in our relationship. You know, I grew up seeing you and Da shipping off Cillian and Hunter to boarding schools in Europe and was terrified of sharing their fate. There was nothing I feared more than saying goodbye to you and *Athair*. Now, I am actually *jealous* of my brothers," I spat out, "because you gave them the best gift of all. They grew up barely knowing you and liking you very little. They are not attached to you like I am. They can live their lives, do as they please, free from the chains of loving two people who are incapable of loving anyone else but themselves. I'm done!"

I flung my hands up in the air and stormed out, bumping into a doctor who scurried into Mother's room. He called out to me, trying to find out what was wrong, but I ignored him, feeling very young and very desperate all of a sudden.

The drive back home was a blur. I was surprised I made it at all, seeing my unshed tears impaired my vision. I stormed into my mother's en-suite, opened the cabinets, and started throwing everything into a white trash bag I'd taken from the pantry.

Anything you could get high on was gone. I shoved it all in without rhyme or reason. Sunscreen, Vaseline, bandages, painkillers, and cough medicine alike. When I was satisfied with my findings, and sure there were no other drugs to be found in the house, I proceeded to stomp my way outside, hoisted the full trash bag into the trunk of my Prius, and floored it all the way to Badlands.

I tried not to think about the last time I'd seen Sam.

I told him I never wanted to see him again then went ahead and knocked on his door. Not the most consistent I'd been, but I was worried. When I'd heard from Cillian, Hunter, and Da that Sam was nowhere to be found, I figured he was holed up in his apartment and for good reason. Honestly, I'd been more afraid he'd gotten shot or had a serious wound and was too proud to ask for help.

I'd found him sick and shivering, nursed him back to health, and then gave him the space he needed.

That was three days ago.

He never even said thank you.

Not that I had any reason to expect him to. This was Sam I was talking about, a well-known monster.

While I knew he wouldn't hand me over to the authorities in a red satin ribbon, I also didn't trust him with the information of what I was doing with my medical degree. Why did I share with him my story of Ms. B, then?

Because you love him, mon cheri, and when you love someone, you want them to get to know you, so maybe they'll fall for you, too.

Well, Sam was obviously feeling much better, seeing as he was clubbing with my selfish brothers tonight.

I stopped in front of Badlands, dragged the trash bag out, and rounded the building, toward the back door leading to Sam's office.

I knew better than to knock. Which was why I took the tweezers out of the trash bag and tampered with the lock. It was a simple lock, and I had the advantage of knowing what I was doing. I'd broken into my brothers' rooms plenty of times when I was younger. I was bored and alone in the impossibly large, looming Avebury Court Manor.

Sometimes, my only company was other people's things. Toys and gadgets I had found under their beds. I'd even pretended the women gracing the covers of *Penthouse* and *Playboy*—found under Hunter's bed—were my girlfriends.

The door hissed open with a soft click, and I trampled inside. Sam's office was dark and empty. I threw the door open and headed downstairs, the music pounding from the club making the floor quake.

I wasn't interested in the club, though. I headed straight to the card rooms. As soon as I reached the junction of the four card rooms, I peeked into each of them. It wasn't hard to find my brothers. They were in the last one. It was the noisiest, most boisterous room, filled wall-to-wall with men wearing tuxedos, smoking Cuban cigars and drinking old whiskey, huddled around roulette and craps tables.

Cillian was in the corner of the room, talking animatedly with Devon, while Hunter was next to Sam by the roulette.

The Monster looked brand-new, a cigarette dangling from the corner of his mouth as he barked at his employees, no hint of his previous, sweaty, fever-ridden self in sight.

Swaggering inside, the trash bag flung over my shoulder like I was Santa delivering presents on Christmas Day, I stopped in the center of the room and emptied the content of the trash bag in the middle of the roulette table, a smile on my face.

Everyone, and I do mean *everyone,* gasped.

Everyone other than Sam.

Hunter was the first to recover from my little stint.

"Holy shitballs, sis. Way to make an entrance." He whistled low, reaching for the center of the roulette table to grab a pack of mints I'd thrown in there accidentally, popping two into his mouth. "Do you have some blow? I don't use drugs anymore, but if you have a side hustle, I'd like to financially contribute."

"Aisling," Cillian said, all ice and manners, sauntered toward me. "What are you doing here, besides the obvious, which is embarrassing yourself?"

"Great question," I chirped, all honey and smiles. "Well, brother, I started my day off at six am, worked a long shift, came back home to find *our* mother passed out in her own puke, then proceeded to shove my fingers down her throat and usher her to the hospital to ensure she didn't overdose on chewable vitamins or whatever it was she decided to cram into her stomach. At this point, I tried to call my dear brothers, but both of them were too busy playing cards to pick up the phone. You didn't even answer our emergency code word, even though I've never used it in my life before, so it should have tipped you off about the situation. Our mother is fine, by the way. But I'm not. I'm tired and in need of a shower and fed up with carrying the burden of gluing this family together all by myself."

The room turned very quiet and very still, and suddenly, I was only aware of Sam, Cillian, and Hunter. No one else registered.

Sam snapped his fingers together and barked, "Everybody out.

Family business. Phil, Jonathon, Archie..." he turned to his croupiers "...take it to room three, and get everyone a complimentary drink. Not from the vintage menu."

Sam sat back on one of the vintage armchair recliners, lighting himself another cigarette as he observed us. I turned my head toward him. I was in the mood to set fire to every single relationship I'd ever had, and he was high on my list of people I wanted to snap at.

"Wow. You mean you're not going to kick me out of your club?" I gasped mockingly.

"If you show up tomorrow, I will." He lounged comfortably in his seat, smirking. "Right now you seem to be doing a fine job ruining your own evening. No need for me to interfere."

"You're an asshole," I spat out.

"And you sound like a broken record."

"Cut this out, both of you. Start from the beginning, Ash," Cillian ordered as the last of the crowd trickled out of the room. "What happened? Since when has Mother been dabbling with prescription drugs?"

"Since forever." I threw my arms in the air. "She is a cutter, too."

Both my brothers paled in response.

"Bet you didn't know that either, huh? She mainly does this for attention, to keep Da and me on our toes whenever she thinks we don't pay her enough attention. There's a lot you don't know. I can't do this all by myself. Our family is falling apart."

"I—" Cillian started, but I was so mad I cut him off. It was the first time I ever snapped at my older brother.

"And you didn't even pick up the phone when I called you! You ghosted me."

"We didn't ghost you," Cillian maintained coolly. "We put our phones aside and didn't see your texts."

"Even if you didn't ghost me tonight, you've ghosted me our entire lives, letting me live this nightmare of tending to our mother alone!"

"Sis," Hunter said softly, reaching for my hand over the roulette table, "we had no idea. It wasn't like we ignored the situation on purpose. You were our blind spot."

"Yeah." Cillian leaned a shoulder against the wall, looking gravely serious. "Mother and *Athair* always seemed on the unhinged side, but you have to remember we've never actually lived under their roof. Not since toddlerhood, anyway. We thought it was under control. That you were the one taking advantage of the perks of staying at home and not vice versa."

"Staying at home is a nightmare!" I fell onto a nearby stool, burying my face in my hands, hating that Sam was watching this whole freak show. "Mother is a master manipulator. I draw her baths, drive her places, act as a messenger between her and Da. I'm basically her maid, and I don't want to do this anymore."

"You don't have to," Cillian said firmly. "We'll come up with a plan. I will go to the hospital and stay with Mother tonight. Hunter, you'll take over tomorrow. Aisling needs some space from her for the time being."

Hunter nodded. "Don't worry, sis, we got this. You don't have to do this alone anymore."

I tried to regulate my breaths. I could feel Sam's gaze on me. He seemed eerily quiet the entire conversation. Not that I expected him to weigh in on our family woes, but Sam wasn't a fan of gossip. Usually when he lost interest in something, he removed himself from the situation.

Why did he stay in the room?

"I just need to clear my head," I said quietly. "Her overdose was to get back at me. I'm afraid if I give her what she wants—more attention—it'll defeat the purpose of strong-arming her into getting the help she needs."

At the same time, moving out and going cold turkey was something I didn't want on my conscience. She needed me, learned how to be dependent on me, and leaving now would be cruel.

"You're right," Hunter agreed. "We don't want you near her. We'll let her know it can't carry on like this. Now that we're in the picture, too."

"I'll give Aisling a ride home." Sam stood up, his voice toneless.

I shot to my feet at the same time. "No, thanks. I'm parked outside."

"I can't believe I'm saying this, but Sam's right." Hunter gave me an apologetic look. "You're in no condition to drive. Pick the car up tomorrow morning. Your body must be flooding with adrenaline. Try to take it easy tonight. We'll tackle this clusterfuck tomorrow."

"It's a clusterfuck indeed. Which reminds me—now's a great time to ask for a raise," Devon drawled sarcastically, emerging from the shadows of the room. I forgot he was even here, which was an impossible task, seeing how gorgeous he was. "The Windsors draw less attention than you lot."

"Hands to yourself, Brennan," Cillian barked in Sam's direction. "Remember your paycheck comes with stipulations."

"Your neck does, too, *Fitzpatrick*." Sam offered me his hand, helping me to my feet, leaving my brothers behind us. He pressed his hand to the small of my back, ushering me up the stairs back to his office.

"How are you feeling?" he asked tightly. I had an inkling the mere idea of pretending to care made his skin crawl, yet I oddly appreciated his concern, even if it wasn't genuine.

"Fine." I rubbed my forehead. "Just tired. Overstimulated."

"Stay at my place. I have a spare bedroom and zero fucked-up parents living under my roof."

"And I have two brothers who'd kill me if they find out I spent the night with you." I sighed, inwardly admitting the offer was very tempting.

Sam wasn't going to go to war with Da and my brothers just to be with me. I came to terms with that a long time ago. So there was no point in accepting his offer and creating more tension between him and the men in my family.

"A dead Aisling would make life easier for me. The offer still stands," Sam remarked.

"Charming, but I'll pass. I don't go where I'm not welcome."

"Since when?" he asked, dead serious.

"Since *always*." I felt my cheeks flush. "For your information, you're the only person to bring the crazy out in me."

"Dangerous dick tends to do that to good girls." He kicked the back door to his office open. "I had no idea things were that bad at home."

We poured outside into Boston's December freeze. A thin layer of ice coated everything, from the ground to the buildings and glass panes of windows. Red, white, and gold Christmas decorations hung on the streetlamps twinkled back at us. Sam clasped the back of my neck possessively, leading me to his Porsche like I was his prisoner.

"They weren't always," I heard myself say. "There had been ups and downs. Being the backbone of the family wasn't so bad when the posture of our skeleton wasn't terrible. The last weeks were the worst, though. Ever since the media picked up the story of Da's stupid affair, things began deteriorating. Then the poisoning happened and the mysterious threatening letters. The heirloom cufflinks were the cherry on top of the crap cake."

Sam unlocked his car and helped me inside the passenger seat. The drive to my house was quiet.

The first portion of it, anyway.

When we reached the affluence of the Back Bay, a silver Bentley closed in on us from behind. Sam's eyes flicked to it in his rearview mirror. The Bentley sped up, kissing our bumper once and sending us flying forward with a jerk.

"Shit," Sam muttered. "Unbuckle yourself, duck your head, and cover it with both hands, Nix."

"What?" My blood froze in my veins. "Wh-why?"

"Just do it."

"But—"

Sam didn't wait for me to finish my sentence. He took a sharp left turn, driving over the manicured lawn of someone's front yard as he sliced through a junction, not stopping at a traffic sign, and sped through a side street. The first bullet pierced the rear window and popped into the AC unit, where it got stuck.

"Motherfucker," Sam hissed, still completely calm. He grabbed the back of my head roughly, dipping it further down, leaning toward me to ensure I was tucked away as carefully as possible. The car skidded, and I knew that the fact it had been snowing and the road was extra slippery didn't work in our favor.

"On the floor, Nix."

"Sam," I screeched, terrified, "don't lean toward me! They'll shoot you if you do."

"Better me than you."

Another shot pierced through the rear window. It made it shatter completely. The glass came down in a sheet. Sam jumped on top of me, his torso covering my body, blocking me from harm, but still somehow driving.

"What are you doing!" I moaned. "You're going to get yourself killed. Drive!"

He floored the accelerator. The car started to sound like a plane taking off. Then, without warning, he swiveled, making a sharp U-turn and speeding up again. Since my head was tucked firmly below my seat, I couldn't tell if we lost whoever was after us or not.

"You okay?" he asked.

"I'm fine." I chanced a look at him through my periphery, noticing that his arm was bleeding. He caught a bullet while pushing me down to the floor. He took a bullet for *me*.

"You're bleeding," I said.

He groaned but didn't say anything.

"Are we safe?" I asked.

Sam didn't answer. I could tell he was concentrating on deciding which turn he was going to take next. I guessed driving home was out of the question. He was hardly going to lead his enemies to his doorstep.

"Who are they?" Tucked under the passenger seat, I pressed, my knees knocking against my chin as my teeth chattered. I'd never been this scared in my life. The kind of fear that seeps into your bones and burrows into your soul.

"Bratva. The Russians."

"They own Brookline," I murmured. I knew that. Everyone knew that. My parents hadn't allowed me into their neighborhoods fearing I'd get kidnapped for ransom.

"Not anymore."

"They're trying to kill you because you took over their territory?"

"Conquered, fair and square. If they find you in my car, they'll have a merry good time milking your daddy for money. But they'll gang-rape and torture you first. Which is why you need to stay the fuck down and let me handle this."

I heard another shot fired toward us. I squeezed my eyes shut, keeping my head bent, just like he told me. Sam took another sharp turn. He opened the glove compartment above my head, knocking my forehead in the process. He took out a gun, stopped the car, then reversed fast. He turned around and started heading in the Bentley's direction, releasing the gun's safety, a devious smirk on his face, his eyes zinging with determination.

He is playing chicken.

I wanted to claw his face to ribbons.

The buzzing coming from the Bentley became louder, and I knew they were close. Sam stretched his arm outside his open window and fired two shots.

Time and space hung above our heads, suspended.

I heard a scream. A moan. Then footsteps over damp concrete, the crunching of the snow underneath someone's feet. Someone running. Fleeing. Sobbing.

"You can come up now," Sam murmured, stone-cold. Numb, I slid back to my seat, buckled up, and moved a shaky hand over my raven hair.

Sam slowed his vehicle, and I noticed he was following a man. I only saw the back of him. A scrawny figure with blond messy hair and a prominent limp. He wore baggy sweatpants and matching hoodie. The glow-in-the-dark type. Sam directed his gun at his head, holding it steadily.

"Are you going to shoot him?" I whispered.

"Only cowards shoot people in the back, Nix. I'll shoot him in the face. Respectfully, of course."

I didn't know if he was being sarcastic or purposely crass. Either option seemed completely unsuitable for the ears of a lady. But that was the essence of Sam Brennan. He would take a bullet for me without even thinking twice about it but trash-talk to the moon and back in my presence.

The man stumbled on the uneven cobblestone of the sidewalk, trying to pick up his pace when he heard us driving by his side. It was futile. Sam had already caught him. The Monster was now playing with its food.

The man's shoulders quaked, and he sniffled loudly.

"Please." I put a hand on Sam's arm, the one that wasn't holding the gun. "Don't make things worse."

He ignored me, passing the man and parking in front of him, blocking his way.

Our victim stopped. I leaned forward, taking a good look at him. Sam must've killed his armed companion.

The man was not a man at all.

It was a *boy*.

Of fourteen. Maybe fifteen at most.

Gangly, long-limbed and wide-eyed, his pasty face sprinkled with acne.

My heart lurched and twisted behind my ribcage. He was obviously a minor. Maybe even an innocent one. I imagined he was born and initiated into the Bratva. It was hard to believe he would choose such a life for himself.

Sam got out of the car, blocking my view with his body, still protecting me, his gun aimed at the boy's head. The boy dropped to his knees, raising his arms in the air in defeat. He didn't seem to even realize there was a second person in the car.

"P-p-please," he sputtered, weeping so openly, so loudly, it felt like he tore my chest in two and watched while I bled out. "I didn't want to do this. I begged them not to. He was ... I was ... my father, I mean, put a gun to my head. I couldn't say no. I couldn't. You know what it's like with dads like him. You know. You have one, too. You're a Brennan." He swallowed air, hiccupping, his face twisted in so much agony, it was hard to make out his features.

"You fucked up. Now it's time to pay," Sam ground out.

"No!" I gasped.

I shot out of the car, desperate to do something, anything to save this boy.

I tackled Sam without thinking, trying to bring him down to the ground with me. But he was much bigger and heavier than I was. It felt like slamming headfirst into a concrete wall. I flew backward from the impact, but Sam snaked his free arm around my waist, jerking me behind him, like the boy still posed a threat to me.

"Please, Sam, please." I wrapped my arms around his chest and stomach and felt his muscles tensing against my fingertips through his shirt. A soft, barely audible groan escaped his lips. I took that as a sign.

"Please, he is just a boy. Young and misled. Like you were. If you don't do this for yourself, do it for me. For what I did for your soldiers. For ... for ... for the chicken noodle soup!"

I held my breath, waiting for another stinging rejection and the pain that came with it. To my surprise, all I felt was a brief shudder passing through his torso. Goose bumps rose on my skin. I didn't know why, but I felt this moment was monumental for both of us, though in very different ways.

"You have one thing going for you, and that is that I don't want the fucking headache that comes with the territory of blowing your brains out in front of her." Sam bared his teeth, lowering his gun just an inch.

I let out a relieved breath, feeling nauseous with relief.

My throat burned as I exhaled. I must've screamed bloody murder while we were being chased in the car.

"But I'm sending you with a message and a souvenir. The message is as follows: tell Vasily that I am going to have his head on a plate if he as much as tries to breathe in my direction again. Last time, I cut his face. Next time, I am going to decapitate him completely."

The teenager nodded almost violently.

"W-w-what's the souvenir?" He peeked at Sam through one eye, the other one squeezed shut in fear.

Sam smirked crookedly.

"This one is something to remember me by. A farewell. A reminder. A warning. Are you left or right-handed?"

The kid didn't try to beg for remorse. He bent his head obediently. "Right-handed."

Sam fired a shot, the bullet grazing the teenager's right arm, going straight through his nerve system.

"Here. This'll ensure you'll be a crappy aim for the rest of your life and choose a different occupation. In case you're thinking of finishing your daddy's job ..." Sam chuckled.

Blood pooled beneath the young man, but he didn't make a move to press a hand to his wound.

"Thank you for sparing my life, sir."

Sam hoisted me over his shoulder, blood still trickling down his arm, and led me to his car. His blood ran the length of my thigh, and I shivered with unexpected desire.

I felt protected and wanted to protect him, and if that wasn't majorly screwed-up, I didn't know what was.

"Never interfere with my business again, Aisling, and never, *ever* show your face when we bump into my enemies." He tugged my pants and panties down my upper thigh, the cold night air stinging my skin. Sam sank his teeth into one of my ass cheeks, biting hard.

"They're your enemies, not mine." I involuntarily thrust my thighs against his shoulder, begging for more. He opened the passenger door, tossing me inside and buckling me up like I was a toddler.

"They'll think you're my weakness."

"They'd be wrong." I crossed my arms over my chest.

"Very astute of you, Einstein," he snapped. "But I've never been seen with women before. They'll jump to conclusions."

"Is that why you won't marry Becca?" I challenged. "Because you wanted to spare her precious life?"

"First of all, who the fuck is Becca?" He rounded the car then started it.

"Are you serious?" A hysterical laugh bubbled from my throat. "Becca is the woman you took to the charity event."

He drove away from the Back Bay and outside city limits. Boston's skyline slid away through the windows, giving way to wildland. It made sense that Sam wanted to lie low for tonight, but what did that mean? Were we going to stay together, wherever it was? Where was he taking me?

"I thought her name was Bella," he said.

"Nope," I snapped.

"At any rate, yes, part of the reason why I'd never take a wife is because watching an innocent woman die because of me is not on my to-do list."

"Sparrow didn't die," I pointed out.

"Troy was a fixer. A mostly good guy doing bad stuff. I'm an underboss. An all-around monster. I dabble in many things and have enough blood on my hands to fill up your Olympic-sized pool."

"Where are you taking me?" I asked, tired of being repeatedly reminded how far from the realms of commitment Sam was. He didn't want a wife, a family, children; even though he protected me, prevented me from dying tonight, it was more about his newly found moral code than his affection toward me.

"The Brennan cabin." Sam tapped a cigarette pack flat against his muscular thigh, fishing one and tucking it into the side of his mouth. "A nice reprieve for you from your family."

"Yeah..." I turned my head to the window "...I already feel so much more relaxed."

Sam chuckled, lighting up his cigarette, yet again ignoring my acute disapproval of what he was doing to his body.

"You saved me tonight," I said throatily, bracing myself for disappointment when he shut me down. I knew he would, too. Sam Brennan didn't allow himself to feel anything. Especially toward women.

His eyes remained fixated on the road.

"Why?" I demanded.

"Because you're my boss' daughter."

"You don't care about my father," I said.

"True. But I do care about his money. I'm on the fast track to becoming one of the richest men in Boston. Keeping you protected is in my best interest."

"So it had nothing to do with me," I muttered.

Why was I doing this to myself? *Why?*

"None whatsoever, Nix. I would do the same for Hunter. For Cillian. Even for your deranged mother. You are business to me, sweetheart. With a side of pleasure every now and again."

I didn't say another word the entire journey.

I'd already heard everything I needed to know.

Sam may have been a good underboss, but he was a terrible potential realtor.

He was being modest calling the place a cabin. It was more of a ranch, one like my brother, Cillian, owned. It was smack-dab in the middle of the woods.

The place was so remote, there wasn't even a paved pathway for the car to get there. The Porsche trudged through gravel and sleet the last few miles to get to the front door.

Sam got out of the car and threw the door open for me. I followed him inside as he began flicking the lights on. He turned on the central heating, scanning the living room and open-plan kitchen for any signs of a break-in.

The place was freezing. First, I tended to the wound in his arm. Removed the bullet and did some light stitches. Then, I hugged myself, realizing all of a sudden that it was the middle of the night—two maybe three in the morning—and I still hadn't had lunch, dinner, or a shower. The last thing I ate was a Nature's Valley granola bar in the morning, and as we were all aware, those bars tended to crumble so badly you only consumed about thirty percent of them. My stomach growled, demanding to be fed, giving zero F's about the life or death situation I'd just escaped.

"I'll see what we have in the fridge," Sam said without turning around, and my skin prickled with heat when I realized he must've heard my stomach.

As it turned out, there was absolutely nothing in the fridge.

The heating was taking too long—maybe it was broken; Sam said the place hadn't been occupied in years—so as far as a relaxing retreat went, this resort got one star and a scathing review on Yelp.

"You'll have to settle for something canned," Sam clipped. "Refried beans."

"I don't know how to make them." I stood on the opposite side of the room, looking down, humbled by my own privilege.

Sam spun in my direction. "You don't know how to heat a can of refried beans?"

"I'm guessing you do it without the can." I looked sideways, wanting to die of embarrassment.

"You made me chicken soup," he reminded me. I nodded seriously.

"Ms. B had taught me how to make it. It's the only thing I know how to make because it was the only thing she could keep down when she was sick. I can't even make an omelet."

With a growl, Sam opened a tin of refried beans using his metal key, tossing the can-shaped congealed beans into a pan. It looked about as appetizing as fresh manure and smelled similar. Still, I stood close to him as he prepared the food, mainly to catch the warmth of the fire coming from the stove. I ate straight from the pan. It was horrible, but I knew better than to complain. I imagined canned food was a luxury for him before the Brennans officially adopted him. I had no right to complain.

As for me, I suspected this was the first time I'd eaten anything from a can. I always had food made from scratch, prepared by our cook who used fresh produce, seasonal vegetables and fruit, and herbs.

Of course I didn't share this with Sam. Already, he mockingly referred to me as a princess. There was no need to give him any more ammo.

"The heating is not working properly. I think at this point, it's a given." I took the pan to the sink and began to rinse it clean. The water was freezing cold. Sam sat at the dining table across from me, looking mildly entertained. I think he took joy from watching me do everyday chores. Little did he know I was my mother's maid.

"My apologies. There's a Waldorf Astoria across the road," he drawled.

"Very funny. Thanks for the ride *home*, by the way. Highly appreciated," I said sarcastically, drying the pan and putting it back in the cupboard where it belonged. There were some refried beans still stuck to it. Call it my little revenge. I liked to take my wins where I could get them.

"Stop being a brat." His tone had an edge now.

"Why? It's exactly what you expect from me," I sniffed. "Admit it.

You think the worst of me and my parents. And while I suspect you don't hate my brothers, you are far from the realm of respecting them."

Rather than answering me with words, Sam got up, snatched a few throws from the couch, and stomped into one of the rooms.

"Master bedroom is the first door to your right. Don't bother trying to seduce me in the middle of the night. I fucked you out of my system and don't need a repeat."

I watched his back retreat, stunned with his brashness. He slammed the door behind him. I wondered why he'd given me the master bedroom and not the extra one.

Because, mon cheri, even though he says he doesn't like you, I suspect he really quite does.

It was the first time Ms. B and I weren't in complete agreement.

Shaking my head, I carried my purse to the master bedroom, slipping under the blankets, which were cold as ice and did nothing to warm me up.

For the next hour, I tossed and turned, staring at the patterned ceiling, wondering how they'd decorated it.

Sleep didn't come, even when I willed it, *begged* for it. Adrenaline ran through my bloodstream like poison.

The brush up with the Bratva.

Sam saving me.

The way he'd rejected me before I'd even offered myself up, all while cooking me dinner and giving me the master bedroom.

Was he my protector or adversary?

I was tired of sorting through his mixed signals like it was Halloween candy, separating his actions by brand, intent, and flavor.

Whatever his reasons might be for treating me this way, I intended to keep away from him.

I was tired of chasing him around. Even though he'd done his fair share of showering me with averse, cold attention every time he wanted to get in my pants, there was always a static undercurrent between us. I was the pursuer, and he was the somewhat amused, precious prize. He tossed me around and played with me whenever he had a few minutes to burn but always went back to ignoring my existence.

This had gone on for a decade, reaching its peak these past weeks.

And I knew, with a clarity that stole my breath away, that I could spend the next decade being his casual plaything just as easily if I let it happen.

But I wasn't a teenager anymore. I had aspirations. Dreams. Goals.

It was time to cut the cord. Not just with Sam but with everyone else in my life who assumed I'd cater to their every need and whim.

An hour and some change after I tucked myself into bed, I heard the door to the master bedroom creak open. I rolled in bed, turning toward the door.

Sam stood on the threshold, fully clothed in his suit, his hair a tousled mess, like he ran his hand through it a thousand times.

"Fine. I'll fuck you one last time."

I rolled onto my back, sighing as I whispered to the ceiling.

"Romeo, oh Romeo, wherefore art thou?"

He chuckled, stepping inside, interpreting my sarcasm as invitation.

Why wouldn't he? I'd never denied him anything. Not when he intended to sleep with someone else the night I showed up at his apartment. And not at the charity event, when he brought a date who looked freakishly similar to me.

And tried to sleep with her, too.

"This'll be the last time, Fitzpatrick. A farewell. There's a reason why your brothers pay me extra not to touch you, and you just got a taste of it tonight. I'll make your life a living hell and a short living hell at that."

"Newsflash, Sam, you're already doing that."

He shifted closer but still far enough that I realized that despite everything—who he was, what he did, the general callousness of him—he was waiting for an explicit offer. He didn't want to pounce and take me on his own terms. He wanted me to come to him willingly, desperately, lovingly.

Neither of us made a move.

I didn't invite him into my bed.

He didn't leave the room.

My thoughts swirled around in my head like the snowstorm outside, and I dug my heels into the mattress, refusing to give in to the urge to feel his body over mine, his skin against my own, his hot, sweet breath everywhere. His heat was irresistible in more ways than I could count.

"Well?" he spat out, all but sneering. "Am I going to stand here for long?"

Kicking off the blankets, I darted past him, out the door. He whirled, his brows pinching in a frown, following me to the living room.

I plopped down on the carpet, jamming my feet into my sneakers, lacing up.

"What are you doing?" he growled.

"I'm tired, Sam. Tired of you. Tired of us. Tired of this cat and mouse game. There's only so much push and pull I can tolerate before it gets repetitive and abusive. You want me? You'll have to get me. The hard way. I'm going to run, and you are going to catch me. If you don't, you've missed your chance. How about them apples?"

He stared at me like I was crazy.

It was nighttime, and we were in the middle of the woods, in the midst of a never-ending snowstorm, with no cellular reception, no heat, and no food.

He had a point.

Scooping my phone, I slid my arms into the long plush sleeves of my coat. Sam stood there, motionless, watching me.

"You're not roaming the woods," he said dryly.

"You can't tell me what to do, Brennan. You're the hired *help*," I spat out, bitterness exploding on my tongue. I was hurting because of him, so I wanted to hurt him back.

That was the excuse I gave myself, anyway, yet it didn't make me feel any less horrible.

It was probably exhausting to be him. To constantly look for people's weaknesses, press them where it hurt, and never allow yourself to be exposed.

The word 'help' seemed to set him off. He pounced on me so quickly his movements were a blur as he slammed me against the floor, my back plastered against the parquet wood. His arms bracketed me on either side of my head. His body was flush against mine. I tried to kick him in the groin, but he dodged me easily.

"I don't fucking think so, Nix. You don't get to call me the help and live to tell the tale unharmed."

Feeling my eyes flaring, I was surprised to discover I didn't fear him. I knew he wasn't going to hurt me. Not physically, anyway. After all, he said it himself—his kingdom was on the line. His fate was entwined with my family's. This was the way it had always been.

It boggled my mind that I'd ever thought he would stand against my father and my brothers. Insist on being with me. Even if he hated my family, he still needed it. For more money and power. We were his door to Boston's upper crust, and he wasn't going to let it slam in his face. Not because of me.

If the men in my family paid him to keep his hands off of me and found out what we did in secret, in the dark, it would be the end of their business relationship.

I also wouldn't put it past Sam and Cillian to try to kill each other.

"You can't harm me more than you already have, you fool." I writhed underneath him, attempting to push him away. "Unfortunately, I'd never be able to hurt you the way you hurt me, but at least I can stop loving you."

"Don't be so sure about that," he said grimly, reaching for his boot and yanking out a small dagger. He took my fingers and curled them around the handle. He directed my hand to the center of his throat.

"You want to hurt me? Go ahead. You should know where my carotid is, Doc."

I slid the blade across his neck, to the pulsing artery calling for me, faint blue against his endless, smooth brown skin. My hands shook and my teeth chattered.

His eyes bore into mine. "Now be a good monster and kill me, Nix."

I tried to poke the blade against his skin, to push it through, to cut him, even a shallow nick, but I couldn't. I couldn't inflict pain on him. I caught my lower lip between my teeth, struggling, panting, trying desperately to push through, to make him bleed.

I shook all over.

The knife fell to the floor with a dull thud beside us.

"I can't!" I roared. "I can't hurt you, no matter how much I hate you. And I do hate you. Because I love you. I love you and you treat me like garbage. What do you want me to say? That I'm jealous of your dreams because you belong to them at night? Because I am. I cannot breathe, eat, or blink without thinking about you, Sam Brennan. You've conquered every inch of me before you'd even touched me. After you did, things got worse. Way worse. I've always loved you, Monster, but the more I get to know you, the more I wish I didn't."

Getting it out there, in the open, felt like shedding old, dead skin. Even if I knew I was putting myself in a position of weakness, I was still happy that I did.

If my confession stirred anything inside him, Sam didn't let it show.

In fact, he made it a point to keep my arms pinned with one hand as he jerked down his slacks, kicking my legs open and pushing my pants down.

"Rape? That's the only thing you haven't done to me yet," I spat in his face, seething. Having him was a torture because it reminded me he would never be mine.

He stopped undressing us.

"You think I'll rape you?" His eyes were hooded, the hint of a sneer on his face.

"I know you will, if you enter me," I kept my voice steady, "because I don't want you to touch me."

"Then what the fuck was that love declaration a second ago?"

"A confession, not an invitation, you moron. I don't trust you. I don't know what you want from me. I'm not even sure what part you play in my life. My father is MIA. My mother is an addict and a cutter. My brothers left me with this mess. And the only thing I know for sure is that the person I've been pining for over a decade doesn't want me back but is willing to play with me whenever it tickles his fancy. I'm done." I shook my head. "Let me go. I don't want this anymore."

We stared at each other. He knew this time was different from all the others. Because all the other times I tried to make light of things, to playfully banter with him while drawing closer and closer to him.

Now, I wanted to leave.

"You're serious," he rasped.

I jerked my head in a nod.

He sat up and let me go, allowing me to scurry backward toward the wall. I tugged my pants up.

The truth of my statement hit me all at once.

I was done with his games. Done with giving him what he wanted, whenever he wanted it. Done hoping he would someday wake up and realize he cared for me, too.

He stood up and stared at me, blinking somberly, like I'd just slapped him in the face. Maybe it felt that way. I doubted a man like Sam was used to hearing the word 'no.'

"We're done?" he asked, businesslike. The icy edge to his voice made me shiver.

"Yes," I said, quickly retying my shoelaces. "Leave me alone. Don't show up at my clinic anymore and don't steal kisses from me when we see each other at family functions."

"Why? Because I don't *love* you back?"

He let the word 'love' roll out of his mouth like it was profanity. I licked my lips. Dawn was breaking outside beyond the pine trees, and the room began to wash with cool pinks and royal blues, the shadows framing his face making him look even more breathtakingly beautiful than usual.

"No. I can handle it if you don't love me back. But I won't accept indifference, humiliation, and unstableness. I am not your plaything. The little teenybopper who stared at you with starry eyes at a carnival. Those days are over. I deserve respect and consideration, and you know what? I changed my mind." I frowned then began to laugh. A throaty, screechy laugh, not even caring how unhinged I looked anymore. "Yes. I don't want to have sex with you anymore because you don't love me back. Is that bad? Immature? Anti-feminist? I expect love. I want it all, so if you don't intend to give it to me, I suggest you leave me be or I am going to tell my family how you dipped your hand into the honey jar, tasted the forbidden sweetness, then came back for third and fourth helpings."

"I told you I will never settle down."

"Then that means you are letting me go."

He nodded once, sauntering over to the door and throwing it open. A chill rushed into the cabin, biting and claiming every inch of my exposed skin.

"Love is not a price I am willing to pay for pussy, no matter how tight and aristocratic. Goodbye, Aisling."

He was letting me go.

Maybe I was on a roll because of my own speech, or perhaps the adrenaline still pumped in my blood, but all at once, I gathered my courage, stood up, grabbed my purse, and fled out the door.

He didn't chase me. I knew he wouldn't.

Men like Sam never did.

I followed the faint tire signs of the Porsche to find my way out of the woods, clutching my cell phone in a death grip. I slipped several times, and my knees and hands were soaked with melted snow. When I reached the main road, I called an Uber then continued walking. The foolish, desperate hope flaring in my chest that Sam would find me shrank more and more with each step I took.

My toes were numb, my fingers had frostbite, and I could feel myself coming down with something.

I played with the monster under my bed and felt the wrath of its claws on my skin.

This was all on me.

But that didn't mean I had to put up with it anymore.

It was like my love for him had snuffed out after teetering on the brink of death for a while. A love that started as a sun-shaped blaze when I was seventeen, big and hot and impossible to extinguish, but as time passed, Sam's actions doused water on it until there was barely anything left.

I slipped into the back of an Uber, thinking about that night at the carnival.

About the text I'd seen scribbled on that bathroom.

Maybe it wasn't meant for me.

Maybe it was meant for someone with a happy ending.

Twelve

Sam

A FEW DAYS AFTER AISLING FLED THE CABIN, TROY BREEZED into my office, tossing a newspaper onto my desk.

"Checkmate."

I was sitting in front of a pile of Excel spreadsheets, trying to concentrate on the simple task of finding a way to help a client launder a couple of millions. Normally, I could do it with my eyes closed, hands tied, and dick buried deep inside a random. Shuffle the sum from place to place. Blow up expenses. Tamper with bank statements. Making money untraceable was an art form I'd perfected from a young age. It made me a darling in certain corporate circles. Nothing bought your way into a rich man's heart better than helping him screw the IRS over.

These last few days, however, my head was so deep inside my ass, I was surprised I didn't drop dead from lack of oxygen. My thoughts were on a loop, getting stuck on the same thing over and over again.

I saved Aisling.

Put my life in danger to keep her from harm's way.

And what did the bitch do? She turned me down and cut me off.

I glanced at the newspaper Troy threw at my desk. The headline smeared in cheap, black ink.

Busted! Billionaire Gerald Fitzpatrick's Mistress Writes an Explosive Tell-All!

Barbara McAllister's testimonies could be a game changer for the royal American family. The company's stock has dropped significantly since yesterday.

It did nothing to improve my sour mood, even though I knew, in all probability, that Gerald was on the verge of hurling himself out the window from the skyscraper he was currently holed up in.

Troy fell into the seat in front of me, lounging back, rolling a toothpick in his mouth.

"Time for a quick and efficient K.O., Sam. I will not sit here and watch you destroy a perfectly good family just because you have a boner for Gerald's blood. Don't forget your sister's marriage and happiness is on the line, too. You are taking this God complex too far."

"There's nothing complicated about my godly gift to distribute pain. I'm merely giving Gerald what he deserves." I dropped my pen, sitting back. "He—"

"Yes, I know. Killed your unborn brother. Made your mother leave you behind. No one is propositioning Gerald Fitzpatrick for knighthood." Troy raised his palm up, cutting through my words. "Yet here you are, alive and fucking well, much to the Bratva's chagrin. This means whatever damage he inflicted on you didn't finish the job. So why don't you get it over with, give him the final blow, call it even and move on?"

Because then I'll have to face my other Fitzpatrick problem.

The pressing one I've been trying to ignore for weeks.

Their daughter.

Aisling stayed far away from me since she fled the cabin in the middle of the night like a dumb horror flick side character, the first to get murdered ten minutes into the film.

I knew she survived our little showdown because I drove by her clinic the following afternoon, just to make sure she hadn't been chopped up by an axe murderer on her way out of the woods.

Her Prius was parked in front of the main door. She was alive, even if not well.

Consequently, she was also done with my ass.

"I want a confession," I insisted.

"And I want to fuck my wife ten hours a day. Guess what? Looks like we're both not getting what we want," Troy snapped. "What makes you think Gerald is willingly going to come to you and tell you all about how he fucked your mother then fucked *you* over?" Troy stood up, spitting his toothpick on the floor. "Grow the fuck up, Sam. Your story doesn't add up, and frankly, with each passing day, I'm starting to think there's more to this than you're letting on. You've never given a damn about Cat, and yes, she left you, but she'd tried to contact you and you shut her down without a blink of an eye. It's not the first time you've been wronged by one of your clients. You are a pragmatic person. You take things in stride. This is a part of you I don't know and don't care to discover. Emotional, messy, and above all—strategically faulty. You are about to make some pretty grave mistakes if you are not careful. I can see it. Be upfront with Gerald or drop it altogether. But this is the last prank you pull on him. Your sister is married to his son, and now that Hunter and Cillian are watching their mother and paying attention, they'll be on your tail in no time. You understand?"

"Are you done?" I asked, sitting perfectly still in my seat, rejecting any sentiment that stemmed from Troy looking royally and thoroughly pissed at me. This was a first. We'd had our arguments before, of course we had, but we always ended up seeing eye to eye. Not this time. "Because if so, you know where the fucking door is. I'm sorry the student outdid the master, but sometimes, old man, that's just the way it is."

He stared at me with a look of complete disbelief. Despite myself, I felt my stomach roiling, turning over and over, like it was folding into a small origami square.

He offered me a noncommittal grunt and dashed away, leaving the faint scent of his cologne and a hell of a headline on the newspaper.

I turned my attention back to the Excel sheet, noticing, for the first time, a company trip to the Maldives I could use to max out the expenses proportion. An easy eight-hundred-thousand-dollar hole in the budget to throw the IRS off.

I started making the necessary moves.

Gerald would pay for what he did with his blood.

Even if it cost me my relationship with my adoptive father.

After working into the wee hours, I stopped by the card rooms again, checking on the tables, making sure we were making killer profits before locking up my office door.

The night turned from black to blue by the time I made my way to my (newly fixed) Porsche. I unlocked the doors and put my hand on the handle when the cold barrel of a gun dug between my shoulder blades, biting into my skin.

The voice that came after it was unmistakable.

I would recognize it anywhere because I'd spent nearly a decade listening to it wail.

"Busted, kiddo."

Gerald.

"Now get into the car, nice and easy. I'll take the passenger's seat," he instructed, his voice and the gun quaking with both adrenaline and fear.

I lifted my hands haphazardly, smirking.

"Do you even know how to use a gun, Gerry?"

"Don't call me Gerry." He dug the metal into my skin. "My name is Gerald. You're the only person to call me Gerry, and I despise it. I only let you get away with it because I thought it was a term of endearment."

"You were wrong," I deadpanned.

"Tell me about. In the car. Now. No funny business. I will shoot to kill, Brennan. You've left me with nothing. Not my family, not my business, and not my pride."

I slid into the Porsche calmly, not breaking a sweat. My fear of being shot by him was somewhere below zero. Firstly, because I didn't think he had the guts to pull the trigger, and, secondly, because even if he did shoot, which was unlikely, he would miss. He didn't have a steady hand, and all I needed was one small error to snatch the gun from between his sweaty fingers.

Thirdly, and most importantly, I didn't care if I died. I never was much of a fan of living in the first place. I enjoyed very few things, and one of them was Gerald's daughter, who did not want anything to do with me anymore. My fault, of course, for pushing her away, knowing beyond reasonable doubt that her family would never let her flaunt the help in high society.

"Put the gun down, Gerry. I'll take us to your apartment, but not because you're threatening me with a gun. I can grab it from you blindfolded with my arms tied behind my back. I'll come willingly because I'm interested in what you have to say and how much you know," I said, my voice soaked with amusement. It was high time we had a conversation about what mattered.

"B-b-bullshit!" he stuttered. "You will do as I say because I—"

I had no interest in letting him finish that sentence. I turned around quickly, elbowing the gun and sending it careening across the road. Gerald let out a high-pitched moan of surprise, making a bee-line to seize it, squatting down to the ground. I was taller, leaner, and faster. I sauntered my way to him as he bent down to take the weapon, pressed my loafer onto his hand—breaking a few small bones in the process, no doubt—just as his fingers curled around the base of the gun.

I smacked my lips together.

"You rich pricks aren't very good at listening."

"You will do as I say, goddammit!" He wiggled under my foot desperately. I grabbed him by the shirt, dragging him toward my car as he kicked and grunted in annoyance, pocketing his gun after checking if it was cocked (shocker: it was not).

I hurled Gerald inside and slammed the door, getting into the driver's seat next to him and starting the car.

"Where to?" I grumbled.

"The penthouse. The one Hunter and Sailor lived in before moving into their own house."

I nodded, noticing that he shook beside me. Unbelievable. I put his daughter through so much shit, and she always gave me one hell of a fight. But this guy, he couldn't even sit still without wanting to piss his pants. I didn't know where Aisling got her strength, but it sure wasn't from her fucking parents.

When we got to the penthouse and Gerald pushed the door open and started his verbal diarrhea, I pressed my finger to my mouth then started looking around the living room to see if it was bugged. As far as I could tell, it wasn't. I sat at the dining table, smiling sardonically at him.

"You may continue with your meltdown now, Gerry."

Gerald erected himself to his full height, jutting his chin out, trying to appear braver than he was. The weight loss made him slightly less deplorable physically, but I still knew that behind the exterior was a man who deserved a slow and painful death.

"You've been caught, Sam Brennan. I set a trap for you, and you fell for it," Gerald boasted, still standing up, for some reason beyond my grasp.

"You already said," I yawned. "Care to elaborate?"

Gerald leaned forward, pressing his fingers to the oak dining table as he spoke.

"When you asked me to give you a list of all the women I'd had an affair with, I got suspicious. It seemed farfetched, and as time went by and you dragged your feet about my little problem, I got even more suspicious. You'd never failed a mission I'd given you before, and suddenly, you didn't have as much as a lead. I couldn't understand why you left me to drown. Then the poisoning happened. And the cufflinks ..."

"Christ, Gerry, I was there when all of this happened. Get to the juicy part. My time is precious." I looked around, wondering if he had any good coffee.

He straightened his spine.

"Aisling made me do it. She told her mother and me what to do, that way we could know for sure."

"Made you do *what*?" I spat out, losing patience.

The mention of her name made me nauseous. This was outrageous. I couldn't be nauseous. I wasn't a fucking damsel in distress.

"Plant a bug. A mole. A trap. See, Aisling said that the only way to outsmart you is to beat you at your own game. Together, we found a woman from my past—Barbara McAllister, in this case—and had her assist us. We knew if you contacted her, that would mean that you were after my throat and not those who harmed me."

I stared at him, speechless.

Aisling played me.

And she fucking won, too.

She loved me, yes, but not so much that she was blinded by my actions.

Even more than her affections for me, she was loyal to her family, and hell if it didn't make me miss her even more.

"The newspaper—" I started.

Gerald shook his head, walking over to the coffee table, picking up what looked to be today's newspaper, tossing it into my hands. I picked it up and glanced at the headline.

Keaton Hints at Firing Clayborn After Elections: What's Next for the White House?

Motherfucker.

"The headline was fake." I let the words churn in my mouth, deciding I fucking hated how they tasted.

Gerald plopped down next to me, rubbing at his face tiredly as he reached for a whiskey with two tumblers at the center of the table, pouring us drinks. I took out a pack of cigarettes and lit one up, making myself comfortable. This bullshit wasn't going to be over anytime soon.

"Quite." He nudged my drink in my direction, his fingers still trembling. "I didn't believe Aisling when she said you were probably a double agent, so I came to see you a few times at Badlands. Each time, I turned around, losing my nerve. But I noticed the same newspaper was rolled and left at the entrance each time, so I figured that was your media outlet of choice. From there, faking a headline wasn't too hard."

Then Troy picked it up at the entrance to my club, on his way in, and showed it to me.

Goddammit, Nix, you're a clever one.

"Now, Barbara McAllister is a college friend. She is not at all what you believed her to be. But for the purposes of helping me, she put on a show. Her sister has an address in a shithole part of the city. I added her name in the lease, knowing you would find her, see the poverty she so-called lives in, and decide to press her because she is easy prey," Gerald continued.

"Aisling said that if I gave you information that didn't match what you'd find on your own, it'd raise a red flag and you'd take the bait. She was right."

"Did you decide to do all this or did Ash?" It seemed like a sophisticated operation, and Gerald was only good for managing a company that'd been handed to him by his own father. Even that, he half-assed. Cillian was a much better CEO than Gerald ever was, something Gerald secretly resented his son for.

"Well, Aisling did, bless her heart. She is my child through and through, that one. So delicately cunning. So smart."

So hot.

Though I doubted he'd appreciate that specific input.

Gerald took a sip of his drink, his shoulders rolling as he visibly relaxed.

"Aisling knew Barbara would stand out with her zip code. We wanted to ensure you'd approach her, so we made certain her address led to a trailer park. You took the bait. When you called Barbara, Aisling and I instructed her beforehand. What to say. How to act. We couldn't chance her blowing her cover. She did a remarkable job, didn't she? And by the end of the day, you were already on the phone with publishing houses and literary agents, hooking her up with people who wanted to hear her story about the sordid Gerald Fitzpatrick. The new Jeffrey Epstein, right? The fall from grace of the tycoon who wanted too much from too many."

This was pretty much spot-on, so I couldn't dispute it. I played into Ash's hands, and even when we'd met, even when I'd been balls deep inside her, when she cried my name, when she told me she loved me, when she offered me herself on a silver platter, she still plotted against me.

Tried to uncover the truth.

Was an active participant in our mental chess game.

"We got three offers from three different publishing houses," I said tersely, trying to understand how they managed to cover the last part of their plan.

This was why the headline made sense. Because Barbara told me she had taken one of the deals. That she was going to write the tell-all. The plan was to have Gerald beg me to step in. I, in turn, would have a confession from him, throw my weight a little around Barbara, pay her to keep her mouth shut, and the whole thing would be canceled.

Then, depending on Gerald's version of what went down between him and Cat, I planned to shed some Fitzpatrick blood. Not a lot. Just enough to satisfy my bloodthirsty nature.

"You didn't get an offer from anyone." Gerald shook his head. "Your calls to the publishers went straight to Emmabelle Penrose's phone."

I could feel my face morph from anger to disgust. I was played not only by Ash, but by that airheaded Barbie.

As if hearing my internal thoughts, Gerald offered a quick nod.

"Aisling didn't want you to recognize her voice. She had your calls redirected to Emmabelle's phone each time you made an inquiry. And once the so-called contract between Barbara and the publishing house of her choice was signed, you were out of the loop. You only ever saw the contract. You didn't actually speak to any of the people Barbara had spoken to."

That was true. The minute I hooked Barbara McAllister up with a so-called literary agent—who was probably Emmabelle, too—I stepped aside and tended to my own business, secure in the notion everything would run smoothly.

"How did Ash redirect the calls to Belle?" I narrowed my eyes at Gerald. Everything seemed too flawless to be done without any help.

Gerald smiled a smile that sank into the pit of my fucking stomach.

No.

"Yes," Gerald replied, and I realized I said the word out loud. "She used the man who knows how to be Sam Brennan better than Sam Brennan—Troy Brennan."

For the first time in a long time, I had nothing to say. Nothing other than *where the fuck was Aisling?* Why wasn't she the one confronting me? Only the answer was obvious. She didn't want anything to do with me. Every time we were alone, I'd somehow find a way into her pants before pushing her away and telling both of us it would never happen again.

Fucking pathetic.

And this time I didn't mean her.

"If it makes you feel any better, your adoptive father had no idea this had anything to do with you. He would never betray you like this. Aisling told him she needed a few certain numbers to be redirected to Belle because, as you know, Belle is the owner at Madame

Mayhem, a local nightclub, and she said someone was trying to target the club and write a damning tell-all about the managers and goings-on inside," Gerald continued, taking another generous sip of whiskey.

I took a drag off my cigarette. My drink remained untouched.

Through the curtains, the oranges and pinks of a winter sunrise colored the sky. I tapped my cigarette to the side of my lip, mulling it over.

"It was airtight," I said eventually.

"Yes," Gerald agreed. "Aisling did all the leg work. When Troy asked why she didn't come to you directly to deal with the publishing companies, she explained that because she was infatuated with you, she wanted to limit your communication to the bare minimum."

She even used her weaknesses to her advantage.

"We communicate often," I bit out harshly, childishly, the need to fuck her over right back overwhelming me. "If that's what you want to call it. So where is this Barbara woman now?"

I knew where she was going to be soon.

Six feet under.

Actually, that wasn't true. I wasn't going to kill Barbara, but not because she didn't deserve it for double-crossing me. I wasn't going to kill her because it was obvious Aisling fucking Fitzpatrick was going to go after my ass, knowing I had one hell of a motive. It wasn't a cold day in Hell, but finally, I found someone who held me accountable for my actions.

It wasn't the police, the sheriff, the FBI, or the mayor, although all of them had tried.

It was a petite Irish girl with a smart mouth and eyes like bluebells who wanted to give me everything she had until I made it very clear to her I wasn't worth any of it.

"That's a great question." Gerald grinned smugly, his face so punchable I was surprised it didn't curve inside out.

He snapped his fingers, and just like that, Barbara materialized from the hallway, no longer looking like a day-shift stripper. Her hair was coiffed back, her attire a black velvet Prada suit and Chanel purse.

Yeah, she definitely didn't need any food stamps or half-finished cigarette packs.

Barbara smiled at me apologetically, giving me a quick nod.

"I wanted to be here just to say I was sorry in person. I never meant to complicate things for you, Mr. Brennan, but Gerald is an old friend, and when he told me he was in trouble, I simply couldn't turn my back on him. Surely, you can understand."

Only I couldn't.

Because I didn't have any real friends. Only people I had business with and met with socially—only to make sure they didn't screw up any of our mutual business shit.

"Well played, madam."

She smiled and dashed out the door after saying her goodbyes, leaving Gerald and me to face each other. I took out another cigarette, waiting for the question on the tip of his tongue.

"So now it's your turn to tell me … why?" he asked quietly, dropping his elbows to his knees. He looked broken. Wilted and weak and somehow still angry.

"Why did you put me through this? Why did you take everything I've ever cared for? What did I ever do to you, Brennan? Up until two months ago, I would name you as one of my closest business partners. *Openly.*"

Openly my ass. If he was so open about his business with me, he wouldn't have forbade me from taking his daughter out for a coffee.

Not that that was what I wanted.

Or had anything to do with this bullshit.

"I found the letters," I said, flicking ash into an ashtray on the table. "Catalina's letters. Back in November. The old bat finally conked out, and her neighbor invited me to sort through her shit and see if there was anything of value there. Spoiler alert: there wasn't. But she kept the letters to you. The ones you redirected back to her. And your photos together…" I took a deep breath "…*and* the pregnancy test. I know all about what you did to her, to me. How you drove her away from me. How you killed the child in her womb. My brother. I know everything. *Everything. Everything.*"

I said it three times, so he'd understand I meant business.

Gerald stared at me for a long beat. When he finally opened his mouth, no words came out.

He started to laugh.

Cackle was more like it.

And I mean, really go at it, slapping his thigh as he tried to regulate his breath, wiping a tear from the corner of his eye, shaking his head.

"You bought that bullshit?" He heaved. "Are you serious, son?"

"There were pictures, Gerald. Lots of them. Of you and Cat together. By the way, you should probably stop the habit of documenting every single fuck you have with women who are not your wife."

The pictures were genuine. They were real. And they were damning. I knew a photoshopped work when I saw it, and this wasn't it.

So why was I feeling like an idiot right now?

"No, I *did* have an affair with Cat, I'm not going to deny that part. Hell, Sam, you were a child, barely even old enough to wipe your own ass. I didn't know you. And Cat was a gorgeous woman in her prime. Besides, she needed the money, and I paid her well for her … uh … company." He looked away now, rubbing the back of his head.

There was no well-mannered way to point out someone's mother was a whore, so I didn't necessarily fault him for that. He carried on, exhaling quickly.

"I had an affair with her, yes, but everything else was a complete and utter fabrication. Catalina was never pregnant with my child, and I never raised a finger to hurt her. I did not cause her to miscarry. When we started seeing each other, she told me she had her tubes tied after she had you. I asked her to show me the doctor's note—I knew

Jane would rip my head off if I ever got any of my mistresses pregnant—and Cat provided it to me within the day. Not only that, but I went ahead and double-checked it with her OB-GYN."

"Then what the fuck was that pregnancy test?"

"My guess is she took it from one of her friends. Catalina had a lot of friends in the … uh … industry she worked in. Kept women who messed around with rich men. We provided for them, but the main incentive was, of course, to fall pregnant with our children. That would tie us to them for life."

I did not take that into consideration.

"So you are saying she was never pregnant with your child?" I drawled, trying to keep my cool.

He finished his whiskey in one go. "Correct."

"That's all nice and well, but I distinctly remember Cat coming back home around the time of the alleged miscarriage, disoriented and bruised. I remember her crawling into her bed, curling up into a ball, crying. I remember her being ushered to the hospital in an ambulance. How would you explain that?"

Gerald stared at me through beady, liquid black eyes, his lips sneering in distaste. "Does the name Donnie ring a bell?"

I shook my head slowly.

"Tall, muscular, an underwear model type. He was Cat's real boyfriend at the time. The man she fucked without leaving an invoice on the nightstand afterward. Real good-looking guy, I'll give him that, but he never came to terms with what she did for a living. Every now and again, he would rough her up if she showed up to meet him smelling like the man before him. As it happened, that man before him that night was me. I know, because I met your mother at the hospital and even paid for her hospital stay. I told her to press charges. She didn't want to. I still have the receipt for that hospital bill, and I can show you none of the things listed there have anything to do with Cat's womb or any of her reproductive organs."

Suddenly, I had a really bad headache. Because through foggy memory, I did remember Donnie. A tall, blond fuckboy. I remembered internally referring to him as Captain Potato Head for having the combined IQ and wit of a used condom. He was the first person to give me a cigarette.

"Hey, Cat's kid, bring me the pack of Marlboros over there, will ya?"

I did as I was told, mostly because I was too distracted to tell him to fuck off. The man left the pack open, jerking it in my direction.

"Here, boy, take one. I'll show you how it's done."

"I don't smoke."

"Oh, you will, buddy. With your fucked-up life, cigarettes are a question of when, not if."

"Explain the letters." I turned to Gerald, the biting pain of being played closing in on my throat again. This time not by Aisling, who was at least smart and intelligent, but by Cat, whom I wouldn't trust with a goddamn Snickers bar.

All the pieces of the puzzle were falling together.

"Easily, Sam." Gerald poured himself more whiskey, seeming more relaxed than he had in weeks. I knew he was telling the truth, and it fucking killed me. "Sometime after Donnie roughed her up, Cat realized her line of work was just too dangerous. She asked me for money. A lot of it. To keep silent. I said no, and that's when the blackmailing began. Each and every one of her letters was part of an extortion scheme. She threatened to out us, to spread terrible lies, to ensure Jane knew about what we were. What we did. She wanted to skip town, but she never wanted to take you, Sam. You weren't in her plans. Not even for a second. At some point, I realized she wasn't worth the heat I was about to get from Jane. I became open to giving her money. I kept asking her how she could leave you behind. Tried to convince her to take you with her—kids need their mothers. By God, Sam, she just wouldn't. Finally, I handed her 150k just so she would shut up and leave me alone. I remember the day she left. She was so happy, and you know what, son? So was I. She almost cost me everything. I'm not going to lie, Sam, seeing the back of your mother as she skipped town was one of my favorite sights. It should have been a happy day for you, too."

I began peeling the soft paper around the cigarette pack, feeling like a thirteen-year-old again.

"You never told me about your history with my mother," I said coldly.

"No. Not because I did something horrible to her but because I didn't want you to think I see you as the spawn of this money-grabbing idiot. I didn't want our professional relationship to be tainted by that. Besides, I truly didn't and don't see you as Cat's. You are a Brennan through and through. A Brennan is the best thing a person in Boston can be, other than a Fitzpatrick. You had a good childhood once she gave you up. You shouldn't be thinking about her. Not for one second."

"I don't," I hissed. "I'm thinking about how *you* wronged me."

"I didn't *know* you," Gerald emphasized. "You were a kid. Still, I felt some sort of responsibility toward you. After I'd heard Cat had left, I looked you up. Found out that Sparrow sent you to this fancy Montessori school. I had my driver drive around it sometimes to see if I could spot you during recess. Sometimes I did. You sat in the middle of a circle, and all the boys looked up to you, captivated by you. You became strong, and prominent, and unbeatable. After a while, I was satisfied with how it all turned out. Pleased with my decision to give the wretched woman what she wanted to leave you behind. It worked out well for you."

"So well you later on hired me as the help."

"No, as my fixer," Gerald corrected. "A savvy businessman whose expertise I needed and was willing to pay for handsomely. Admittedly, I wasn't surprised to see you on my doorstep. I stitched together the Sailor and Hunter plan with Troy, tightening our ties with the Brennans had always been the plan for me. You were too prominent a family in Boston for me not to acknowledge you somehow. But I hired you because you were the best in the business and not for any other reason."

There was silence. I knew more needed to be said, but I wasn't sure what. I believed Gerald, and that should have been enough. I should have felt some sort of relief or contentment with this information.

Cautiously, Gerald continued, drawing a circle with his index finger around his tumbler of whiskey.

"But I have a feeling this doesn't have much to do with Catalina and me. You wanted a reason for me to become your enemy. Otherwise, you would have come straight to me with those letters. What's going on, Sam?"

And just like that, he hit the nail on the head.

I created this mess.

Troy was right.

Gerald was right, too.

I wanted it, needed it, manufactured it the day after I slept with Aisling to distract myself from the hard truths.

Aisling Fitzpatrick could never be mine.

She was too innocent, too precious, too blue-blooded for a man like me.

I couldn't have her—and not just because her family paid me not to.

The extra money didn't matter much to me. But also because I couldn't give her all the things she needed—monogamy, a wedding, a family, children. And most importantly because I knew being with her would put her life at risk.

She is already putting her life at risk, doing what she is doing. She could end up in jail tomorrow, which means you played savior Jesus for nothing.

The truth hit me hard.

I wanted Aisling Fitzpatrick.

There were no more distractions.

No more excuses.

No more reasons to stay away.

Especially now, when both Gerald and I had each other by the throat.

It was time to make a bargain.

"You deprived me of my mother, Gerald, and I deprived you of your sanity for weeks. I think it is high time we cut a deal." I sat back, nailing him to his seat with a stare.

"Don't turn this around on me, Brennan. You were caught red-handed, meddling with my business and ruining my relationships with my loved ones. I know it seems like Jane and I have a lot of issues to work through, and truth be told, ours is less than a perfect marriage, but I still care about my wife. I love her in my own way, and I am definitely not impressed with the way you interfered in our marriage."

"Regardless of that speech, the truth of the matter is, I have a lot of dirt on you, Gerry boy, and I fully plan to unleash it if I don't get what I want. The letters are still real. The pregnancy test is still in existence. All those things you ran away from with Cat are now in my possession, and trust me, I make my birth mother look like a kitten in comparison."

He groaned, rubbing his face tiredly.

"What is it that you want?"

"Your daughter," I replied simply.

He laughed. This time it came out metallic and scratchy. His whole body rejected the idea. Like a failed organ transplant.

"You'll never stand a chance with my daughter after what you did to us. This is the ultimate betrayal. She cares for her mother dearly, and in her eyes, you are to blame for the destruction of her family. In fact, I will be meeting her for breakfast in…" he flicked his wrist, checking his Rolex "…about two hours to tell her all about this little conversation. I cannot give you what is not up for offer."

"Leave the persuasion to me," I clipped. "Give her your blessing to be with me."

"My *blessing*?" he spat out, his eyes widening. "You tried ruining my life!"

"You ruined mine first." I waved an impatient hand his way, standing up and collecting my things.

"I'm paying you extra to stay away from Aisling!" He shot up to his feet, jabbing a finger in the air in my direction.

I shrugged. "Don't worry about my bank account. I'll survive without it."

"It's not your bank account I'm worried about. It's my daughter." He paused, a flicker of interest crossing his face. "How well off are you, anyway?"

"Triple digit millions well off. Your daughter will be provided for."

"You will not have her!" he cried desperately. "Aisling is beautiful, smart, delicate, and well-bred. She—"

"Is also fucking single because the only man she wants is forbidden," I cut him off, shouldering past him toward the bathroom, where I yanked his gun out of my pocket and wiped it clean of my fingerprints with a towel. "You are doing her a disservice by interfering with her love life. She knows what she wants."

"And you?" He eyed me skeptically through the bathroom mirror. "Do you know what you want?"

Yes.

I wanted Aisling.

I met his gaze head-on in the mirror.

"You will tell her she has your blessing to date me. To be with me. To *marry* me," I enunciated. "Understood?"

He looked close to hitting me. It surprised and delighted me to know Gerald cared so much about his daughter.

"She is my flesh and blood," he hissed.

"Don't remind me." I pretended to gag. "Look, I don't need your dirty money. I plan on courting her and touching her—a lot, in ways you don't want to think about—and I would like to do that very openly. She deserves dinners, and restaurants, and vacations. Things

269

I cannot give her in secret. You either roll with the plan or I run you over. Your pick."

"I have conditions, too."

I put his gun down on the sink's edge, turning around and folding my arms over my chest. "Let's hear them."

"I'll be going back to Avebury Court Manor in a few to give Jane and Aisling a rundown of everything we discussed. All facts. You will not deny what happened. You will own up to tampering with our lives. To poisoning me. To dragging out those awful pictures."

It seemed straightforward enough.

"You will also hand me back my cufflinks. My family heirloom."

I gave him a curt nod. "That it?"

"No. One more thing. If you hurt her …" He didn't finish the sentence, shaking his head to rid himself of whatever horrid image played in his mind.

"I will not hurt your daughter."

"I'm already regretting this bargain."

I turned around and left him there.

Now there was only one slight matter.

The matter of making Aisling not hate me with a burning passion of a fucking million suns.

Thirteen

Aisling

"**D**O YOU THINK HE IS OKAY? SHOULD WE CALL THE police?" My mother tore her croissant into miniscule pieces on her flowery plate, demolishing the poor pastry. "Does my hair look okay?"

I sat across the table from her, staring into my oatmeal like it had wronged me in some profound way. I didn't want *Athair* to deal with Sam by himself, but he had insisted, and considering the fact he was the main victim of Sam's vicious plan—a plan that I followed closely without telling anyone from my family—I tended to agree with him.

Besides, there was nothing I could possibly say to Sam that I hadn't already.

I confessed my love to him, gave him my body, offered him my soul, sought him out over and over again.

I needed to gather whatever was left of my pride and move on with my life.

"Da will be fine," I said unconvincingly, taking a sip of my pulpy, freshly-squeezed orange juice. "And your hair looks great."

"What if he kills him?" Mother slapped a hand to her chest. "Don't get me wrong, I appreciate all you did for us, uncovering all this, Aisling, but maybe this should've been handled by the police."

"Samuel Brennan would have slaughtered Da if he brought police officers into his club, and you and I both know it."

Mother's fingers strummed over her Swarovski necklace, letting out something between a wail and a moan. The door behind my back swung open. I didn't have to turn around to see who it was. My father stalked inside, his steps heavy and wobbly. It was the first time he'd seen my mother in weeks.

After my idea to set Barbara as a trap for Sam and put our plan into motion, I had gotten my parents to talk a little on the phone but couldn't get them to meet in person. They were both still wary of one another, even when I clearly established the only dirty player in this whole situation was Sam.

"Hello, Jane." Da stopped cold to take in my mother.

They'd both lost so much weight and vitality over the last weeks, it was almost like looking at their ghosts.

It hit me like a brick just then. How love was like Lady Masquerade. It could take on many faces. My parents cheated on each other. They lied, backstabbed one another, and failed to communicate with each other. Still, they couldn't bear to be apart.

They loved each other in their own backward way, and maybe love wasn't a beautiful thing, after all. Most things in life weren't.

Mother stood up. They both stared at each other, neither of them wanting to say anything to ruin this precious, fragile moment.

"You look well," Da said finally.

Mother pressed her palm against her cheek, actually blushing.

"Liar. I look awful. So do you."

"I feel awful, too. You were at the hospital."

"I was."

"I missed you," he said.

She motioned to the dining table laden with pastries, oatmeal, and fresh fruit.

"Join us for breakfast?"

"Don't mind if I do." He slipped into his usual seat, piling pastries onto a plate.

I didn't ask him how it went with Sam. His appetite alone told me everything I needed to know. My worst fears and suspicions about my personal monster had turned out to be true.

He almost ruined my family. *Almost*, because I wouldn't let him.

But he'd intended to do that nonetheless.

I took another sip of my orange juice, studying Da.

Finally, he whipped his head to look at me.

"You were right, Aisling." He put a butter knife streaked with marmalade on the side of his plate. "It was him. The cufflinks. The poisoning. The pictures. Barbara, *obviously*."

My heart hurt so much it felt like he ripped it straight out of my chest, breaking a few ribs in the process.

Why, Sam, why?

"Why?" Mother asked tentatively, echoing my thoughts. Da turned to look at her.

"I'll tell you in a little bit, my sweet, when Aisling leaves for work. I'll give you the truth. Nothing but the truth. I swear. But first, I want to tell you something." Da turned back to me.

Smiling and trying my best to appear calm, I waited for more.

"I was wrong in forcing you and Samuel apart. I thought I was doing you a favor. To be honest, I still think I did. Your brothers and I knew you liked him from the moment you saw him, and we wanted someone better for you. You deserved nothing but the best. But if what you want is less than the best, if your heart desires Sam…" he took a deep breath, as if he was about to rip a Band-Aid "…you have my permission to be with him, honey. I will not stand in your way, and I will not pay Sam an extra fee not to touch you. You are free to do as you please. Frankly, it's been a long time coming, considering you are showing signs of being the smartest person in the family."

I waited to feel all the feelings I thought I'd associate with this speech.

Relief, happiness, and elation.

But all I could feel was the bitter taste of irony exploding in my mouth.

Because Da's acceptance of my relationship with Sam was too little too late.

Sam would never be mine. He'd made that perfectly clear. Even if he was open to some sort of a relationship, he wouldn't offer me love, and I wasn't going to back down from my demand—it was all or nothing.

Besides, what kind of woman was idiotic enough to be with a man who wished to see her family burn?

Standing up, I excused myself, curtsying like Ms. B had taught me, and gave them the one-on-one time they needed.

"That is very nice of you, *Athair,* and I appreciate you finally seeing the error in your ways, but I'm afraid it doesn't matter anymore. I will not be touching Sam, dead or alive. Have a great morning." I grabbed my coat and dashed out to the freezing cold of winter.

To the lonely arms of heartbreak.

Later that evening, when I came back home, Sailor, Belle, and Persy were waiting for me in my room. They were wearing Christmas-themed pajamas. An unholy amount of takeout food and wine was sprawled on my bed, stinking up the place.

Merde. Christmas was only a few days away. How did it slip my mind?

We hadn't made any plans together, so I was caught off-guard by the spontaneous meet-up, but after a long day at work, I couldn't exactly be mad at them for providing a much-needed distraction.

"Hi?" I dropped my backpack, scanning the three of them huddled in my bed like kids, watching *It's a Wonderful Life,* stuffing their faces with maple-covered popcorn.

"Hey, girl! We brought Vietnamese." Persy drummed chopsticks over takeout boxes, wiggling her brows.

"And good spirits," Sailor added, showing me exactly what she meant by waving around a bottle of gin. I laughed.

"And sexual innuendos," Belle murmured around a mouthful of popcorn. "But first take a shower and join us in a pre-Christmas celebration. These bitches didn't chain their husbands to their babies' cribs for nothing." She tossed a matching pajama set my way, and I noticed there was a red lettering on the green PJ's: *69% Nice.*

I scurried to the bathroom and enjoyed a quick but steaming hot shower. When I got out, they were already settling all the food on the floor, including plates and utensils. Belle cracked open a bottle of champagne, leaving the gin unopened behind her back. I frowned.

"Are we celebrating something? Did you finally sell Madame Mayhem?"

Belle was the owner of a nightclub, much different than the one Sam was running. Recently, though, she wanted to sell it and soul-search across the globe. Travel. See things. Taste things. She always went against the grain, always did things her way—independently. Belle shook her head.

"This has nothing to do with me."

"What's going on?" I looked between them. I had an inkling I was being ambushed, and after the morning I had today—after giving up on my dream of being with Sam once and for all—I was in no mood to receive a lecture.

Belle sighed, tossing her blonde hair over one shoulder.

"I should've been more observant, that's what happened. I'm so sorry. This week, the penny finally dropped. Halloween night at Badlands when I left you alone there. Then Sam asking Sailor for your number. The way the two of you disappeared at Thanksgiving around the same time ..." she trailed off.

"Look, Aisling, we know," Sailor said gravely.

We hadn't exactly disappeared at the same time. Sam had tailed me without my knowledge. I blinked, waiting for the other shoe to drop.

How much did they really know? I was always careful not to tell my friends anything about what went on with Sam. I knew how unlikely it was that something real would grow out of it, and didn't want to be judged. More than I already was anyway.

"You're having an affair with him," Sailor said flatly. "With my brother. Sam Brennan. Underboss extraordinaire. The most ruthless man in Boston. I should have known. He'd always refused to talk about you, but recently, he's become almost touchy every time your name comes up."

Touchy? I wanted to laugh. Surely not. He didn't care. He'd made that abundantly clear.

"No," I said flatly, relieved that they didn't know more. "I'm not having an affair with Sam Brennan."

"Do sit down," Persy requested, patting a spot on the carpet next to her. "And you don't need to lie to us. It's okay. God knows I did my fair share of chasing after Cillian when we first started out." She sighed wistfully.

"It's not the same. Cillian hounded you then forced you into marriage. The grain of want was always there. You helped it bloom into a magnificent garden, but he was a willing participant all throughout," Belle pointed out, dumping a mass of noodles, beef, and vegetables onto a plate then handing it over to me. "We're not going to sugarcoat it, Ash. We're worried about you. Sam Brennan is a more-than-you-can-chew type of guy."

"We also have something to tell you." Sailor bit her lower lip, looking downward at her food. I sank to the carpet next to Persy, my eyes drifting among all of them as the pit in my stomach grew deeper and darker, as if bracing myself for the pain that was about to come.

"Something we probably should have said to you a long time ago," Persy added, slurping a noodle between her pink Cupid lips.

Oh, *merde*. I couldn't possibly handle any more bad news or sensational revelations today. Already, I felt like my heart was in my throat, ready to be puked out any minute now.

"What is it?" I asked.

"The evening we'd met you…" Sailor cleared her throat, amending as she chewed on her broccoli "…remember when we all made a pact that we would only marry for love? Not for money, not for power, not for fame, and not because it seemed like the safe thing to do. We only have eighty or so years on this planet, and it would be foolish to spend them with someone less than phenomenal. Well, it was your idea, which was why we thought it would be unfair to try to persuade you to stop pining after Sam. After all, you were going after your own heart. Doing as you preach. But … we had talks, Ash. And we all think that bet was not thought-through. Sometimes … well, sometimes it's not so bad to let go." Sailor nibbled on the broccoli nervously.

I did my best not to laugh at that. They had lengthy conversations about my obsession with Sam. Behind my back. I always knew that Sailor, Emmabelle, and Persephone were one unit, and I was an addition. A bonus epilogue to an already perfectly finished book. They'd all met at elementary school, while I'd been added to their girl-gang when I was seventeen. By then, they were best friends for a very long time and ticked off all the milestones together: first period, first kiss, first guy, first love, first heartbreak. Emmabelle and Persephone were sisters, with Belle being the oldest. And Sailor? Sailor was like Persy's twin.

They didn't tell me about the pact because they didn't think to include me in it.

"And I love Sam with all my heart," Sailor continued, "I mean, how could I not? He is my big brother, the boy who shooed the monsters away when I was a kid before becoming one himself. But I would never live with myself if I don't get this out of my system. Sam is incapable of love, Ash. And I think it is time for you to move on. You cannot marry for love if you marry him because he is not the loving kind."

"Not to mention, Sam doesn't want to get married. He says that all the time. Boasts about it, too," Persy pointed out heatedly, and I knew their hearts were in the right place, but I so didn't need to hear this right now.

"I'm not having an affair," I repeated again, dully though my body temperature climbed up steadily. They were patronizing me. Again.

"Honey, I'm not saying you can't screw him out of your system a few more times." Belle threw her arms around my shoulders, pressing me close in a hug. My plate nearly tipped over, some of its contents spilling on the carpet. "Just make sure you know he is not your forever. You're a romantic one, like Persy."

"Yeah. Just guard your heart." Sailor smiled awkwardly. "You know? Because love—"

"Yes, I know," I bit out, pulling back from Belle. "Love is not something your brother has to offer. So you've mentioned. I suppose it doesn't matter if I repeat for the third time that I'm not sleeping with him?"

Technically speaking, I wasn't. I had in the past, but I ended things, coming to the same conclusion they did—a decade after giving him my heart on a monster ride.

Belle gave me a pitying look. "Oh, honey."

That was it.

I snapped.

Jumped to my feet, sending my plate in the air.

"Let me get this straight, you staged a whole intervention because you thought I was having an affair with Sam and couldn't handle him?" I laughed incredulously, my teeth clenching with anger.

Sailor winced. "I wouldn't say can't handle ..."

I squeezed the bridge of my nose, willing myself to take a big, cleansing breath.

In. Out. That's it.

Nope. It didn't work.

"All right, let's see about your green, green grass, shall we?" I opened my arms theatrically, making a show of it. "Starting with you, the almighty Sailor, the first of us to get married. May I remind you your relationship started when you were Hunter's *babysitter*? Because that totally happened. You were in charge of keeping him in line because his dick was not to be left unsupervised for longer than five minutes. I've met *toddlers* with more self-control than Hunter's junk before he met you; he was hardly marriage material. That didn't stop you from jumping into commitment with him. And you ..." I turned to Persy, who shrank into herself visibly.

She was the least judgmental out of my friends, but she wasn't lily white or guiltless. "You were literally *bought* by my brother, like cattle. Actually, scratch that, he conducts more research before he buys a steer. He'd treated you horribly for months. You broke him the way you break an unruly horse. Through trials and tribulations. You should know better than anyone that the most stubborn mares make the best riding mates once you tame them. And, of course, there is you, Belle ..." I turned to Belle, smiling at her sweetly.

Out of all of our friends, Belle and I were the most unlikely pair and also the closest. Probably because we were the only two still single.

"You cannot even spell the word 'relationship,' let alone make one work. You are scared to death of love, for whatever reason, and have never once let anyone into your heart since I've known you. Who are you guys to tell me where my relationship—or lack of it—is going? You know better than anyone bumpy starts don't guarantee a terrible journey. In fact, the paths with the best scenery are the ones where you have to go through the mud."

By the time I was done, I was panting and sweating under the flannel pajamas.

I lost all appetite for the takeout, and even the Christmas movie binge session seemed unappealing. "I would like you to leave now..." I folded my arms over my chest, shifting my weight from foot to foot "...please."

Persy was the first to oblige. She smoothed her jammies, her eyes filled to the brim with tears. "You're right," she whispered. "We have no idea what goes on between you and Sam. In our quest to try to protect you, we've been pushing you around, belittling you." She looked around for support and found it from Sailor and Belle, who nodded, shuffling up to their feet also.

"Reforming bad men seems to be the theme of our girl-gang." Sailor smiled crookedly, and in that moment, I could swear that even though they didn't share DNA, she was all Sam. Same mannerisms and lopsided smile. "So I'm really not sure why we're even worried about you."

"You also happen to be annoyingly right." Belle rolled her eyes with a huff. "We all have our ten-ton baggage. Our dark fears. The things that made us who we are today. So what if you're a one-man woman? At least that man can wear the heck out of a pea coat, is tall as fuck, and richer than sin."

"Let's start this again," Sailor said tentatively. "This time without the judge fest. Ash, would you like to spend an evening together? Just eating junk, getting drunk, watching TV, and sharing tea that has nothing to do with the hot liquid?"

I smiled softly, feeling like a stone had been lifted from my heart, and it was my friends that had pushed it off through teamwork.

"I'd like that, thank you."

And just like that, I knew I would no longer get shit for whatever happened or didn't happen with Sam.

Fourteen

Sam

THE BRENNANS AND THE FITZPATRICKS DID NOT CELEBRATE Christmas together that year for the first time in a decade.

Sailor elegantly addressed the subject after Jane and Gerald's invitation arrived at her house, excluding Troy's, Sparrow's, and my name.

It was during Christmas dinner, with Hunter looking so emo he gave that asshole from Panic! At The Disco a run for his money.

"What did you do, you class-A fuckboy?" Sailor shot poisonous arrows across the table with her moss-green eyes.

Entirely unwilling to discuss the subject publicly, I shoved lukewarm yams into my mouth.

"What do you care? I saved you from a night of boredom at the Fitzpatricks'."

"First of all, it is my family you are talking about," Hunter stated the fucking obvious, as per usual. "Second, I was looking forward to seeing Cillian and Ash."

"You're welcome to join them, Hunter. No one is forcing you to be here," Troy said matter-of-factly, though I knew he was still pissed with me for screwing up the entire Gerald operation.

I'd given Nix a few days to come to terms with what had happened between her father and me, letting her cool down. She was upset. That was a given. But she would get over it.

I imagined her overcome with joy as I told her I'd come to terms with the idea of being with her.

Tonight, I had every intention of putting an end to this nonsense and claim her.

As the evening unfolded, and Hunter hit the eggnog like it was vintage whiskey while Sailor watched over her kids to ensure none of them caught on fire, and Troy and Sparrow looked ready to undress each other, I took my cue and said my goodbyes. Rather than drive back to my apartment, I headed straight to Avebury Court Manor.

I wasn't so dumb as to think Gerald and Jane Fitzpatrick would share their daughter's enthusiasm at seeing me on their doorstep. That suited me just fine. I was more than capable of climbing into windows, which according to all the movies and shows I had definitely *not* watched with Sailor and Sparrow, it was deemed hopelessly romantic.

Nix was a romantic.

I was in the best shape of my life.

It was a no-fucking-brainer.

Parking in front of the mansion, I noticed the lights were already out. The Fitzpatricks wrapped up Christmas early. I rounded their house, detecting Nix's window. The light was turned off there, too.

Breaking into her room was like taking candy from a baby. Avebury Court Manor was built low and spread out rather than tall and narrow. And there were columns fucking everywhere. The snow was not ideal. Then again, I'd managed climbing my way into places in worse conditions.

I threw a rope over the bannister between her window and one of the columns, and when it fell back through the other side, I tied a tight knot, tugging at it to ensure it was firm before ascending up the column while holding onto the rope, rock-climbing style.

When I reached her window, I knocked on it a few times, peering in through the double-glazed glass. She was sound asleep, unmoving in her bed, her midnight hair fanned across her shoulders and face. A dark angel.

I rapped the window again, watching as she stirred awake, her eyelashes fluttering before swinging her long, lean legs over the bed and walking over toward her door.

For the third time, I banged on the window, exasperated. Pretty sure Romeo didn't have to deal with a woman who had the hearing of a fucking air fryer.

She jumped in surprise, turning around, her eyes meeting mine from across the room. When the sight of me registered, she ran toward the window.

Atta girl.

Nix was coming back to the arms of her favorite monster.

She unlatched the window open, and in one swift movement put her hands on my shoulders and pushed me with all her power, sending me flying back down. Quick on my feet, I grabbed onto the gutter, hanging onto it for dear fucking life, my legs swinging in the air.

"Merry Christmas to you, too. I see you decided to gift me a crazy bitch this year. I'll take it."

"You expected a gift?" she spat out from somewhere above my head, sounding … well, not half as glad as I thought she'd be to see me. "What on earth are you doing here, Brennan?"

Luckily, I put a lot of effort into ensuring my upper body was strong and did suspension exercises and pull-ups with Mitchell four times a week, so I knew that as long as the gutter wasn't going to split in two, I could hang on it for a while.

Of course, I might lose my fingers in the process because of fucking frostbite.

"Well, I thought it would be a good time to talk now, after you've processed everything that's happened."

I was fucking obsessed with her. It made no sense at all. You were not supposed to crave what was offered to you in abundance.

"You mean you backstabbing my family and me, making my life a living hell, causing the very near wreckage of my parents' marriage, and bringing destruction upon us that would take decades to emotionally reconstruct?"

When she put it *that* way …

"Grow the fuck up, Nix. I played with your daddy a little. It had nothing to do with you."

"It had *everything* to do with me! You hurt the people I love and care about the most, knowing how many issues I had with my mother and about her mental state, and you kept it from me."

"I had a good reason," I grunted, pulling myself up and settling on the roof outside her window like a goddamn dog since she wouldn't let me in. Aisling crossed her arms, arching an eyebrow. She wore horrible flannel pajamas with ferrets on them. I knew she used to have a ferret—Shelly—and wondered how the fuck I ended up being consumed by a woman who, despite her declarations of love for me, never tried to change her quirky weirdness to fit the mold and please me.

"Aw, you had a reason." She clapped sarcastically. "This should be good. Let's hear it."

"Your father had an affair with my biological mother."

"So did the rest of Boston. *Allegedly*," she drawled. "Didn't she work in the most ancient profession in the world?"

Ignoring her snark, I trudged through with the story that was frankly beginning to bore even me to death.

"Earlier this year, in November, the day I bailed on you—"

"Another prime example for why I shouldn't give you the time of the day," she added, "*or* night."

I ground my teeth together, trying to keep my cool.

"I didn't show up because Catalina had died, and I needed to fly to Atlanta to sort through her shit. I found some letters she wrote to your father. Letters in which she accused him of impregnating her then causing her to miscarry through beating her up. She claimed he was the one who forced her into leaving me behind when she left."

That stopped her from unleashing another unhelpful remark my way. Aisling's already milky skin paled further. She stepped back, biting her lip to prevent her mouth from falling in shock. I raised a hand, shaking my head.

"Are we…" she cleared her throat "…related?"

I was very close to falling from her roof and breaking my spine.

"What? Aw, fuck no, sweetheart. I'd be puking buckets into next year if that were the case. No offense. Their affair happened way after I was born. Point is, I discussed it with your father. Most of it wasn't true, but some of it was. At any rate, that was why I wanted to torture him."

"You could have told me," she said finally.

"No, I couldn't," I groaned. "What would I have said? 'Oh, by the way, I'm responsible for all the shit your family is going through. Now must be a good time to put my dick in your mouth.'"

"No need to be crass."

"Look, I'm sorry it happened this way. I don't apologize often—correction, I don't apologize at *all*—so I suggest you take it, run with it, and accept it. I came here today with a proposition I think you would very much like."

She pursed her full lips in dissatisfaction, and again I hated myself for taking her for granted all these years. Even when I didn't touch her, I knew she was there, waiting for me, fantasizing about me. It was almost as good as having her. Knowing that I *could*.

Now, she looked like she wanted to finish the job the Bratva started that night she ran away from the cabin.

"A proposition?" she asked.

"I'm ready to take our relationship to the next level."

"I'm afraid you'll have to spell it out for me, seeing as with you it could also mean anal sex."

I chuckled. "I'm willing to have you."

"You're willing to have me," she repeated flatly.

"Yes. As whatever-the-fuck. Girlfriend? Partner? What's the correct term for people who are over twenty-five?"

"I don't know, and I don't care. I'm not your anything, Brennan. You had your chance. You blew it. Ten whole years I waited for you to make me yours. All you needed to do was give me the time of the day.

I've wanted you for so long, I don't even remember what it feels like *not* to want you. Well, I'm about to find out."

She didn't want me.

I had never taken a scenario like this into consideration.

Nix's love was always in the background for me. Available and ready whenever I was.

Now, I'd fucked up and needed to deal with the consequences.

"I'm not the type of guy to take no for an answer," I warned, meaning it.

"I'm not the type of girl to give a dang about what kind of guy you are. You want me, you'll have to win me."

Feeling my jaw ticking with annoyance, I took a deep breath.

"That should be easy. I only win."

"You'll have to *chase* me," she corrected.

"I don't chase," I reminded her quietly.

"Well, then I guess you won't have me. Work for it. Treat me as your equal. No. Know what? Treat me as your better. Because I am. I know you hate women. I know you are leery of them, but unfortunately for you, I am one. I will not accept anything short of a fairy tale, Brennan, even if it's with the monster in the story."

Dumbfounded, I stared at her, waiting for … what exactly? Her to change her mind? She wasn't going to. She wanted a fucking fairy tale, and so far I gave her a nightmare with a side of betrayal.

"Now leave," she said primly.

"Nix—"

She slammed her window in my face, drawing the curtains shut for good measure.

She kicked me out.

Made new rules for our game.

Now I needed to play by them or admit defeat.

The first thing I did when I got back to my apartment was fling the pantry door open, nearly sending it off its hinges. There wasn't much food there. And by 'much' I meant at all. There wasn't any food there period. Only packs upon packs of Marlboros imported from Europe, because American cigarettes tasted like farts on fire.

I stared at the piles upon piles of what Aisling had referred to as cancer sticks, wondering if I was really about to do what I was about to do.

I was.

Fuck it. I took six bullets in my lifetime. I could do this.

I grabbed all the packs and shoved them into four recycling bags, including the pack that was in my pocket, and tossed everything into the building's dumpster.

Then I went back upstairs and stared at the empty ashtray on my coffee table.

Proving to Aisling that I took her seriously just might turn into my idea of a nightmare.

And so help me God, she better come around fucking quickly or heads were going to roll on the streets of Boston.

Fifteen

Aisling

MY PHONE STARTED RINGING IN MY SKIRT'S POCKET WHILE I hugged Mrs. Martinez goodbye at the clinic door. Tugging it out, I was surprised to see Sam's name flashing on the screen. I had saved his number that time he came in with his injured soldiers just in case but never expected him to call me. I drew a firm line between optimism and stupidity, and that seemed like the threshold for it.

What did he want?

"Everything okay?" Mrs. Martinez's face clouded as she drank in my expression. Her hair had begun to grow again, fluffy and strewn about her head like little clouds now that she'd stopped her chemotherapy treatments. She was feeling better. Sometimes it worked that way after chemo. She opted to stop because her doctor had told her there was no hope for remission. But we now had new hope. She was taking an experimental drug that was supposed to shrink the tumor on her pancreas.

I was feeling hopeful she could live a comfortable life for months, maybe even a couple years.

"Yeah." I smiled brightly, nodding as I all but pushed her out the door. "Sorry. I just had a moment there. Everything is fine."

"You know ..." She stopped, digging her heels into the floor, grinning. "I never asked you if you are married. Are you, Dr. F?"

I hadn't given any of my patients my real full name. I needed to take safety measures to ensure my tracks were covered in case things went south.

"Not even remotely." My fingers tightened around my phone, which kept buzzing. "I'm morbidly single, I'm afraid."

"Hmm." She looked thoughtful. "There is nothing morbid about your situation, dear. You will be married soon." Mrs. Martinez winked. "I know about things like that."

"You do?" I asked, my smile thin and distracted.

Please, lady, let me answer this.

She nodded enthusiastically.

"Absolutely. I was a fortuneteller my whole life before I retired. Traveled around with Aquila Carnival. Do you know it? They stop every summer just outside the city."

Aquila Festival was where the most monumental part of my life had happened. Where I met Sam.

"I predicted I'd get cancer, all the royal weddings and divorces, and the exact order of Kate and William's babies by gender..." her chest puffed proudly "...and let me tell you, my sweet, you will get married and soon. Maybe even to the person who tried to call you right now." She jerked her chin to the phone I was clutching.

I dropped my eyes to it and realized I missed the call.

"Don't worry." Mrs. Martinez rose on her tiptoes, kissing my cheek. "He'll call again. He has something important to tell you. Goodbye."

I closed the door after her, frowning at my phone, willing it to ring again.

Sure enough, it did.

He has something important to tell you.

Swiping a finger across the screen, I received the call.

"What do you want?" I put on the most bored tone I could find in my arsenal of voices.

"You, spread eagle on my bed, wearing nothing but whipped

cream and my favorite please-fuck-me-Sam expression," he said darkly.

I did not reply. Responding to his banter would suggest I'd forgiven him.

"I need your help," he said after a beat.

"You need help … I can agree with that. But it won't be mine, Sam. I'm done handing you favors just to watch how you screw me over." I ambled back into my office, pinning the phone between my ear and shoulder as I scrubbed my hands clean in the sink.

"Actually, you seem to have a dog in this fight. Remember that Russian kid from the night we stayed at the cabin?"

"Yes," I said immediately. Of course I remembered him. He haunted me in my dreams. The liquid fear in his eyes. The way he shook and begged for his life. The pain Sam had inflicted on him when he shot his arm.

"Well, he is right here with me, suffering from a chest wound. Shallow, I think. Things went a little sideways with the Russians, and he got caught in the middle of it." Sam delivered the information blandly, like he was reading me food options from a menu.

"Bring him over," I ordered.

"We're just pulling up in front of your clinic," he said and hung up.

I prepared the examination table for the new patient as I mulled over how odd Sam was. He'd promised he would court me on Christmas, and I suppose he did, in his own way. He sent me flowers yesterday with a simple unsigned note bearing his name, and a piece of jewelry, I suppose as a late Christmas gift.

But he didn't cower or beg. Didn't come knocking on my door.

He wasn't exactly chasing me. More like speed-walking while taking frequent water breaks. He still had a long way to go. But he was still in training.

A few moments later, there was a knock on the door. I opened it, finding Sam and the Russian kid leaning against the gigantic man I hated to love.

I slanted my head toward my office. Sam followed me, dragging the tall, scrawny boy along. I tried to ignore the acute beauty of my favorite monster. How tall and strong and corded with muscles he was. The deep tan of his skin and those full-moon eyes that always looked tranquil and cold, like a crisp December night. There was something else about him I found attractive today, but I couldn't put my finger on it.

Something had changed, even if it was subtle.

Sam unloaded the gangly kid onto the examination table, and I took scissors to the boy's shirt and started cutting it off of his chest.

"What's your name?" I smiled at the boy.

"Ruslan," he breathed, wincing as he spoke, wetting his lips with his tongue. "Ruslan Kozlov."

"How old are you, Ruslan Kozlov?"

"Fourteen." His teeth chattered, and a few acne zits were gushing blood, probably from the stress. He was as pale as snow, and I knew he needed a blood transfusion fast.

"Tell me about the wound," I murmured, keeping calm as I put on latex gloves.

He did. It was one of Sam's soldiers who had shot him in Bratva territory—or what used to be their territory before Sam butted in. Ruslan was running errands for Vasily Mikhailov, whom I gathered was the local underboss. Sam came in with his entourage to threaten Vasily, and things got out of control.

"So why didn't Vasily get you medical care?" I frowned. "You are his soldier, not Sam's."

The boy smiled. "Yeah. Mikhailov is not like Brennan. He doesn't care about his soldiers. He is a real monster."

Something warm flooded my chest. I tried telling myself it meant nothing.

Luckily, Ruslan knew his blood type, so I was able to call a friend of mine from med school who worked at the hospital and some-times—on the rare occasion I asked him—provided me with blood units for transfusion. I sent Sam to pick it up with a cooler I had stashed in the clinic while I stayed and tended to Ruslan.

When Sam came back with the blood donation, he wanted to hang around in the room, but I barked at him to leave.

After I took care of Ruslan's wound, I put him on sedatives and took off my gloves, joining Sam in the waiting room. He was sitting on the couch, messing with his phone and hair at the same time. He stood up alertly the minute I appeared.

"He'll be fine." I tried smoothing my hair into something that resembled a ponytail. "I'm glad you brought him in, though."

He stared at me quietly, like he was looking at me for the first time. The heat flooding my cheeks was unbearable.

"Move in with me," he said suddenly.

"What?" My breath caught in my throat. "What are you talking about? We haven't even gone on a date yet."

"A date?" He spat out the word like it was dirty. "We don't need to go on dates. We've known each other since before you were allowed to vote. I'm picking up from where we left off after your little cabin stint, Aisling. I'm not starting from scratch."

"You're starting from wherever I want you to start or you are not starting at all," I announced, giving him the stink eye. "And I can't move in with you."

"Why?" he demanded. "You want to move out. And you should. You are kissing thirty, Nix. Twenty-seven is no spring chicken. And your parents don't need a babysitter anymore. They're sorting their shit out, like they should have done three decades ago. Your mother is going to therapy. Your brothers told me. You're welcome for that little push, by the way."

Welcome?

He was now taking credit for the fact my father moved back into Avebury Court Manor and both my parents attended therapy together? *Unreal.*

I took a step back, staring at him like he was a complete loon.

"First of all, they are attending therapy because you scarred them for life, not pushed them together."

"To-may-to, to-ma-to."

"*Secondly*," I hissed, "I don't make any money of my own and can't afford to pay rent."

"You paying rent was never on the fucking table," he quipped. "I own my place."

"I will not be freeloading."

"Nothing about this arrangement is free, Aisling. There's a heavy price to pay when you are shacking up with a man like me."

"You're still being a chauvinist pig." I folded my arms over my chest.

He took a step forward, crowding me as he brushed a fly-away from my cheek. "No, Nix, I'm taking what I want. What's mine. And what I deserve."

"You don't deserve me."

He smiled. "I used to think that was true, too. Then I found out what you do here in this clinic. We are not so different, you and I. The only thing separating us is semantics."

I gasped. "Don't you dare. What I do is—"

"Beautiful. And also *illegal*. In a saturated population, life is always cheap," he replied, his breath fanning across my face, making every cell in my body tingle with need and anticipation.

"You're still being an asshole," I informed him.

He leaned forward, saying the words as his lips traced mine, speaking into my mouth. "I never promised not to be an asshole. I only promised to be *your* asshole."

"What about other women?" I was starting to feel it. The way I liquefied in his arms. "What happens when you grow tired of me?"

"I will never grow tired of you." His tongue glided between my lips, prying them open as he kissed me deeply. I let him, despite my inhibitions, and my better judgment, and the fact that I knew this was the opposite of what I was trying to do.

I became lax in his arms, enjoying the steadiness of him as his tongue rolled around mine. His fingers dug into my skull, gripping my hair.

"All these years, Nix, I thought about you. Every time I fucked someone else. Every time I brought someone into my office. I'd close my eyes and it was you I'd see. Then I'd remember your family would destroy us if I had you. They would never let that fly. I would remember how I'd fuck your life up if I touched you. If you became mine. If you were privy to all the blood I shed. I didn't want to bring you into my mess, but now that I know that we're both screwed-up and imperfect, it changes things."

"And you have my father's approval." I put a hand on his chest, pushing him away. "How?"

He grinned. "I think your father figured out I am willing to go further to get you than he is willing to go to protect you. He is not a stupid man, Ash. He knows I always get what I want. And what I want is his daughter."

"Your kiss." I frowned. "It tasted different."

"I quit smoking." He arched an eyebrow, looking more annoyed than gloating.

"You did?" My heart did a weird flip in my chest. "Why?"

"You said you hated it. You said you don't want to feel like you're kissing an ashtray."

"You should have done it because you want to live to a ripe old age."

"Well, that might not be in store for me with my line of work anyway, but while I do live, I'd rather do it with you by my side."

He said all the right things, and did all the right things, and still, I couldn't forgive him. Not now. Not yet. Not when I knew that he was so close to destroying my family.

I took a step back, sobering up.

"What about my ban from Badlands?" I asked. The change of topic seemed to have thrown him off, too, because he cocked his head, examining me coldly.

"What about it?"

"Lift it." I tilted my chin up.

"Nix," he said darkly, narrowing his eyes. "I will not have you parading around in skimpy clothes in close proximity just to make me suffer."

"Yes, you will," I said airily. "Because you want me, and when you want someone, you make sacrifices for them—and don't try to control them. Better get used to it."

He considered my words, his face twisting.

"One condition."

I rolled my eyes. "Yes?"

"Have dinner with me."

"I thought we were past dating." I couldn't help but grin.

"We are," he said dryly. "No one said food is going to be the only thing on the menu. I'll come pick the kid up in a few hours." He leaned down, kissed me hard, turned around, and walked away.

It was only when he was gone that I realized the bastard had managed to snatch a piece of my heart in his fist yet again.

Thief.

Sixteen

Aisling

SAM PICKED ME UP ON NEW YEAR'S EVE, WEARING A FULL-blown tux and a solemn scowl that suggested Satan himself had blackmailed him into doing this at gunpoint.

"For you …" He shoved a bouquet of flowers into my hands when I opened the door, all dolled up in a sheer white mini-dress paired with Louboutin boots.

They were a mix of lilies, sunflowers, and roses, in all shades and colors.

I pressed them to my nose and grinned.

"Thank you. Let me put them in water."

"What's the point?" He groaned, still obviously struggling with nicotine withdrawal. "They'll die at some point anyway."

"Just like us," I answered with a small smile. "Death is not a reason to stop living."

I let him into the foyer and went to the kitchen to find a vase.

When I rounded the corner to come back to the hallway, I stopped dead in my tracks at the sound of my father and Sam speaking.

"… treat her well. She is still my daughter. Nothing will change that, Brennan, even if I have to go down in flames. She comes first," I heard *Athair* say.

Merde.

Sam was bound to say something provocative and crass just to piss Da off. That was the way he operated.

To my surprise, Sam replied, "I'll treat her well, Gerry. Better than you and your wife have for the past twenty-seven years. But I'm letting you know right now, I'm moving her in with me in the next few weeks. I can't stand how she is here to cater to your wife's every whim like she's a newborn baby."

"That's up to her," Da said. "And I don't think it's as bad now. Not since the hospitalization. Cillian and Hunter have been taking a more proactive approach with their mother."

Da wasn't wrong. I did have a bit more free time, but Mother still had a long way to go.

"Give me a couple weeks and she'll be more attached to me." Sam put a lid on the conversation, firm but not crass.

I cleared my throat, stepping from the kitchen and making myself known. Both men froze. Sam's eyes landed on me.

"Ready to go?" he asked.

I nodded, my heart missing a beat again to the sight of him in a tux.

"Make it fast, though, Brennan. I want an early evening. I have work tomorrow."

"You're kidding me." I sat in his car, speechless and dumbfounded.

Sam threw the Porsche into park and got out. Fifty minutes after he picked me up, we were at Canobie Lake Park, the closest serious amusement park to Boston. Sam rounded the car and opened the door for me. I stepped out, wrapping my coat around me.

"It's freezing outside," I complained.

"I'll keep you nice and cozy." He tugged at my hand, leading me to the entrance.

"Bulletproof plan to cop a feel," I grumbled.

"You wound me," he said flatly.

"No, I don't."

He walked right into the open gate, not bothering with purchasing tickets at the cashier.

"The place is empty." I blinked.

Sam scanned the park around us absentmindedly, not bothering to look remotely surprised.

"It appears that way. Did I fail to mention I rented the entire thing? I thought it would be nice to have some privacy for a fucking change. There always seems to be too many people around us."

"And the rides?" I turned to look at him, my heart twisting in my chest.

He chucked my chin with a smile. "All manned up and ready to roll."

"That must've cost a pretty penny." I cleared my throat.

"Well, the woman I am dating is kind of used to the best."

That wasn't true. Even though I came from money, I never enjoyed it quite as much as people thought I did, and that made me even more emotional.

"Oh, Sam." I looked away, so he couldn't see how deeply I blushed.

Ten years ago, I came to a fair all by myself, lonely, lost, and sad.

Now, I was at a theme park with the man I fell in love with by my side.

He wanted me to have a do-over.

A different spin on the monster ride.

"You got me good with the tux. I thought we were going somewhere expensive." I grinned, taking a step back from him, because yet again it was hard not to jump his bones when he was being sweet—or at least not a full-blown asshole.

"It *is* fucking expensive, Nix. Ever rented a theme park on New Year's Eve? Now where do you want to start?"

We stared at each other, smirking.

My reply was immediate. "Whatever's scariest. Something with monsters in it."

"The Mine of Lost Souls," he said.

"Mine's not so lost anymore," I murmured, taking his outstretched hand.

He led the way.

We boarded a train resembling a mine cart. I knew the ride was themed around a fictional mine that was about to collapse.

The teenager who manned the ride approached us to check we were secure in our seats, grinning at Sam and offering him a fist bump that remained unanswered in the air. I rolled my eyes.

"He was being nice."

"He was ogling you and imagining what I'll do to you when the ride is done."

The ride started and Sam's hand, which I didn't even notice was resting on my knee, slid up my thigh, making my dress hike up to my waist. His face was still turned to the other side. To the miners and monsters around us. The story of the collapsing mine unfolded.

"When?" Sam asked, his fingers biting into my thighs, skimming my underwear.

"When what?" I swallowed.

"When did you figure out who you were? In the timeline between seventeen and now. It couldn't have been the night we met. That was the beginning of things. You're a fully-formed person now."

I gave it some thought, even though his fingers pushing my underwear sideways, dipping into my wet core, made me shudder and lose my train of thought. I started breathing hard, feeling my nipples puckering under my bra.

"Honestly?" I heard myself say. "Every single time I met you, you chipped at something in me. I don't know how to explain it, but there is something about you, something formidable and scary and impossible, that makes a person realize who they are when they deal with you. It's like looking death in the eye."

I turned quiet for a second then said, "I know she is dead and it might not mean much, but do you think you'll ever forgive Cat?"

My underlying question had nothing to do with Catalina. What I wanted to know was—would he ever be able to love a woman?

Sam's finger curled inside me, pushing in deeper and harder and faster. I began to pant. He turned his head toward me, his mouth finding mine in the dark, slanting over my lips possessively.

"I don't need to forgive Cat. Somewhere along the road of screwing everything up with you, I found out that I don't hate women all that much. I love Sparrow, and Sailor, and I'm pretty sure I will fucking kill anyone who gets anywhere close to Rooney until she hits thirty."

I moaned into his kiss, half-laughing, half-groaning, clutching him close as the ride drew to an end, spinning and sliding from here to there.

The only people in the world were me and him.

My orgasm was within reach. I could feel my body humming to the rhythm of his fingers inside me.

"I still want revenge," I croaked into his mouth. "Don't think you've won me over just yet. You haven't."

"I know," he grunted, letting me ride his whole hand now beneath my dress. My hips bucked toward his arm, and I thrust and moaned shamelessly, the climax taking over my body like a tsunami.

"*Monster, Monster, Monster,*" I chanted, breathing his nickname in, thinking how he was right all those years ago, when I asked him what his name was.

It was always Monster.

And I was his Nix.

Maybe it was the best night of my life.

The thing about magical moments is that they wrap around you like a cloak, shielding you from reality, numbing your senses.

But it felt like everything was illuminated. The air was fresher, my lungs fuller, and my skin tingled with adrenaline and warmth.

From the junk food we consumed—sweet and salty popcorn, candy apples, and hot spiked ciders—and the rides. Ten seconds before midnight, we made our own countdown and kissed on the merry-go-round, each of us sitting on top of a unicorn. By the time we left the amusement park, it was half past two in the morning, and I knew I was going to hate both myself and Sam when I woke up in a few hours for another grueling shift at Dr. Doyle's clinic.

I buckled up next to Sam in the car, still riding the high of the evening.

"You need to quit your job," he said out of nowhere, starting the car.

I whipped my head in his direction, my mouth going dry. It was like he threw a bucket full of ice water on my face.

"Excuse me?"

"You're excused, but this week is your last at the horror clinic." He kicked the vehicle into drive, his eyes cool and disciplined on the road. "It's too dangerous. There's too much at stake here. I won't let you put yourself in a vulnerable position."

"What I do with my life is none of your business," I reminded him.

"Everything you do is my business, and you will not continue doing illegal shit that could lead to you spending the rest of your life in prison, no matter how good your intentions are. Either you concede willingly or I will have to go to Dr. Doyle myself and tug at a few strings. Spoiler alert: I've been known to tear apart things I don't like."

"If you go to Dr. Doyle, I will never speak to or see you again." I trained my voice to sound blasé, keeping my raging emotions out of it. I had to remind myself he was trying to protect me, even if he had a weird way of going about it. "And I'll ask my father to fire you just to spite you, making sure we are even. You know he will, after everything that went down. Two can play this game, Brennan. I will not be pushed around by you. Not anymore."

"It's a disaster waiting to happen," he hissed, trying to keep himself in check. I knew Sam wasn't well-versed in negotiations. He normally just took what he wanted, when he wanted it. He was trying to make an effort.

"It's not even that bad," I argued. We slid onto the highway. December gave way to January. It seemed like everything in the world—the trees, the roads, the buildings—was coated with a thin layer of crystal-blue frost, including Sam's heart. "What I do is perfectly legal in a variety of countries. Switzerland, for instance. But also Belgium, Western Australia, Columbia—"

"Notice what country you omitted from the list?"

I turned to look at him.

"The United States of fucking 'Murica. Here it is illegal, ergo you will not be doing it."

"You're right." I chewed on my lower lip. "Maybe I should move to Switzerland."

"Your backward logic never ceases to amaze me," he grunted. "We aren't moving to Switzerland, sweetheart, no matter how much you like killing people."

There was a we? Since when was there a we? And why did it make my heart squeeze inside my chest?

Because you still love him, mon cheri. You've always loved him. He is your forever, even if you are only his right now.

"Why?" I feigned innocence. "You can do what you do anywhere. I don't remember being a mobster requiring high SAT and IQ scores. And it's not like you'll have a job interview to fail."

"You done being sassy?"

"Not quite." I grinned, pleased with myself for holding my own.

"I own too much of Boston to let it go," Sam explained, letting another verbal attack from my end roll off his back.

"Does ruling Boston make you happy?" I gave him a sidelong glance. "Does anything make you happy?" I added quietly.

"You make me happy," he snapped, disgusted with himself. "You, and your blue, blue eyes and throaty voice and good, fair heart and dark, depraved soul."

It was fascinating to see him like this. An injured animal cornered into talking about his feelings. I didn't want to push him, so I turned to look at the view from the window, smiling to myself.

When we got to Boston, I noticed he was driving to his place, not mine.

"What are you doing?" I demanded. "I told you, I have work in the morning."

"I already packed half your fucking room and moved it into my place, Sherlock. Chances are whatever you were planning to wear in the morning is already at my apartment. Bonus points … you don't have to pretend to wear scrubs and change when you get to the clinic because I already know your secret." He killed the engine and got out of the car.

I followed him, my mouth hanging open in astonishment, delight, and irritation. Only Sam could set all three on fire at the same time.

"How?" I demanded. "When?"

Sam took out a pair of keys from his pocket, dangling them between his fingers in front of my face. I recognized them to be my house keys.

"How? Duplicated these puppies a few days ago. When? Mostly when you were at work. Sometimes when you were asleep. It's amazing how much can escape you. Remind me to never trust you with a safe. The burglar would steal it *and* you and you wouldn't even notice."

Sam

That night I fucked Nix the way I'd always planned to.

In leisure, without feeling her family breathing down my fucking neck.

Bent her over my desk and plowed into her while she screamed my name.

Then again in my bed and another time on the kitchen counter.

After the fifth time, we both fell into bed, exhausted and sweaty.

For the first time in my life, I fell asleep with someone by my side. Felt a woman's warmth next to mine.

There was still some way to go. She had to quit her god-awful job and take a more traditional position as a doctor. But we were going places.

When I woke up in the morning, I turned over on my back and flung an arm out to her. Her side of the bed was cold.

I opened one eye, frowning.

She was gone.

She left a note on the nightstand.

Thanks for the sex, but you are still not off the hook.
—Nix.

Sam

Aisling refused to see me the next day.

And the day after that.

And the day after.

She didn't take my calls, didn't show up when I drove over to her house, and wouldn't read my text messages.

And there were so fucking many of them.

Much more than I'd ever sent anyone else.

Sam: Stop acting like a child.

Sam: All I need is to show up at the clinic if I want to see you.

Sam: You proved your point. We can renegotiate your job.

Sam: You're getting on my last nerve, Nix, and you don't want to see what happens when I finally snap.

Sam: This is why I never wanted a relationship.

For better or worse, the last sentence triggered her, because she chose to reply.

Nix: No one is forcing you to be with me.

Sam: That's not entirely true.

Something was, in fact, forcing me to be with her. My lack of ability to keep away from her. Ignoring her was manageable before we fell into bed, before we spent time together, before I found out things about her. Pussy was pussy, and with my eyes closed, it was easy to imagine fucking Aisling when I was deep inside someone else.

But no one else was going to cut it now, no matter how much I wanted to turn around and walk away from her.

It was going to be difficult and maddening and definitely take me out of my comfort zone, but I couldn't not have her, however how much I tried.

Nix: Are you going to elaborate?

Sam: No.

Sam: Have dinner with me tonight.

Nix: Not until you apologize. You moved my things into your apartment, Sam. Without asking. Who does that?

Sam: I'm assuming this is a hypothetical question.

Nix: We'll do things my way now. And my way might be frustrating to you. It's about what I'm comfortable with, not about making you pay.

Sam: You're already making me pay. I'm not accustomed to not getting what I want.

Nix: Life is hard.

Sam: So am I.

Nix: You sound like Hunter.

I was.

I finally realized why Hunter was so obsessed with my sister. Why Cillian couldn't tear himself away from Persephone. There was something addicting about a woman who gave you her everything. Something that was hard to walk away from once you'd tasted it.

Sam: I will have you, one way or the other.

Nix: We'll see about that.

That was what she didn't take into account.

It took a monster to destroy a monster.

And I was going to devour her whole.

Seventeen

Aisling

SAM AND I SPENT THE NEXT TWO MONTHS PLAYING THIS CHESS game.

Whenever he'd make a move too bold, I'd retreat.

I made him work for it. Work for it like he hadn't in an entire decade. There was something to be said about unrequited love. It taught you resilience and bravery and strength. Now, the tables had turned, and I wanted him to show me I wasn't the flavor of the month. That I was worthy of his attention, his affection, his *everything*. I couldn't allow him to take what I had offered for free for ten years.

I had to put a price tag on my absolute devotion.

And that price tag was love.

I wanted to feel loved.

As with everything he did, Sam brought his A-game to the table.

He would corner me in places, follow me, steal dirty kisses when no one was watching. Maybe another girl would have been alarmed by it, but I relished his attention. His new desperation for my touch.

He waited for me outside a Thai restaurant when I went out with Persy, Sailor, and Belle, snatching me into a dark alley and kissing me roughly, his hands between my legs pushing my skirt up.

Three days later, he ambushed me outside the clinic, dragged me into his car, and fucked me raw in the backseat, giving me a small heart attack and a raging orgasm.

Four days after, I visited his apartment to grab a dress I wanted to wear for a charity event. Most of my clothes were still at his place, and even though he'd left me the code for his apartment lock, he refused to let me take my things back to Avebury Court Manor.

One day, I caught him sitting on a stool by his kitchen island, catching up on some work on his laptop. When I trudged in and yanked my desired Armani dress from the closet, he raised his eyes from the laptop coldly. I expected him to stop me and have his way with me before I made my way out of the apartment, but all he did was salute me with a touch of his fingers to his forehead, bidding me goodbye.

I stopped by the door, confused.

"Aren't you going to try to sleep with me?"

The subtext was obvious: *I am going to sleep with you, but I'm not going to move in with you. I will not commit to you. I will not give you more than I am ready to give.*

Sam kept his eyes on the screen.

"Do you want me to try to sleep with you?"

"No." *Yes.*

He smirked, his eyes still on the screen. "Seems like we don't have a problem, then."

"That's a change I didn't see coming."

For some reason, my feet were glued to his floor. I couldn't leave without figuring out what had changed.

Had he finally given up on us? Maybe he decided I was simply not worth the effort. I wanted to punch my own face for putting him through so much. But then again, I didn't regret any of it. He deserved to repent for what he'd done to my family, and I wasn't sure he was done paying.

"Maybe I decided to save myself for marriage," he murmured, taking a sip from the glass of brandy sitting next to him.

Staring at him dumbly, I shifted the dress on the hanger from one shoulder to the other.

"Usually you do that *before* sleeping with enough people to break a Guinness World Record," I pointed out.

He finally lifted his eyes from the screen.

"Well, I'm an unorthodox guy. Better late than never."

"I guess this is where our journey ends, then." I put on a brave face, forcing myself to smile. Internally, I was shouting, "*Merde, merde, merde*" to the moon.

He was dumping me. I knew I was making things hard for him, but Sam never showed any signs of looking tired or distressed. If anything, he took our new game in a stride and always had that dangerous, mischievous glint in his eyes of a man entertained by having to work for it for a change.

"Guess so." He took another sip of his drink, his eyes never wavering from mine. "Unless we get married."

I threw my head back and laughed hysterically.

Get married. Us. Good one.

"Never gonna happen," I provided.

"Unlikely," he agreed. "You can still suck my cock every now and again, but sex is off the table."

"That's something I can live with," I said with more conviction than I felt. "And thanks for the offer, but I'll pass."

He'd nodded.

"Have a great night at the Fishers' charity ball."

"How do you know that's where I'm going?"

"I know everything about you, Nix, including where you take your lunches at work—the little backyard on a white bench—and what you eat—hope you enjoyed your oatmeal bar today."

I didn't dance with anyone at the charity ball.

I was nailed to my seat, punished, thinking about one thing—*marriage*.

After that night, Sam did seek me out again and we never went all the way anymore. Never clawed at each other's clothes or had wild sex.

He showed up in places I went to but only enjoyed heavy petting and kissing. Every time I tried to stir him into full-blown sex territory, he would clap his hand over my wrist and say, "You can't sample the goods anymore, Nix. You break it, you pay for it. Move in with me."

"No."

It went on and on and on, week in and week out, to a point where I wasn't sure if I was not done hating him for what he'd done or if I was just enjoying the chase too much. It was entirely possible I lost myself somewhere in our game, and I didn't know how to find my way back to what we were.

The truth was, I *did* want to move in with him.

I wanted to move in with him very badly.

Not because taking care of Mother was daunting—on the contrary, she had actually been quite okay, everything considered—but because I missed him terribly every time we were apart.

I was just afraid he was going to break my heart again, and this time, I knew I wouldn't be able to mend it back to health.

Right now, we were in the twilight zone. On the edge of something deep but still with the possibility of swimming back ashore. I was afraid if I lost that edge, my resistance as a result of being pushed around by him, he would conquer what little I'd kept for myself, and it would be game over for me.

I think Sam knew it, too. That we were stuck in limbo, and we didn't know how to stop. Even our families, who little by little began to see each other again for dinners, looked at us with puzzled bewilderment every time Sam treated me gently in public and I gave him the cold shoulder.

One day, when he came to my house to drop off some paperwork for *Athair* and stayed for coffee, he grabbed my hand from across the table and frowned.

"I don't mind waiting, Nix. I just want you to know I appreciate you not coming to Badlands and defying me."

"Defy you?" I yanked my hand away from him like he was made of fire, taking a slow sip of my too hot coffee. "How do you mean?"

"I asked you not to come to Badlands, and you agreed, even though I lifted the ban. I'm glad you still take directions well. You are an obedient girl deep down, aren't you, sweetheart? You'll be easy to manage."

My blood bubbled with rage. So much so I didn't take a second to decode his words or figure out if he was goading me, deliberately moving another piece in our chess game.

"I'm not easy to manage." I stood up abruptly, yanking my coffee from the table. "And the only reason I haven't showed up at Badlands yet was because of my workload. In fact, I think I'll hit your club this weekend, just to get on your nerves." I smiled, feeling much better about provoking him back.

Oui, mon cheri. Always showing the maturity level of a wet tissue.

"Can't fucking wait," Sam drawled, getting up from his seat.

Just then, my father came into the kitchen, holding his ledgers under his armpit, looking between us.

"Everything okay?"

"Perfect." Sam grinned at me. "Absolutely fucking perfect."

Staying true to my word, I showed up at Badlands the following weekend.

As always, I invited Belle to join me. I didn't tell my friends about Sam yet, but this time it had nothing to do with my fear of being judged by them. Things were still complicated between him and me, to say the least, and my brothers weren't privy to what was going on.

I knew Sailor and Persy were going to confide in my brothers no

matter what, and I didn't want to complicate things for all of us for
something that might not materialize.

Belle looked to be in good spirits and ready to tackle the night in
a skintight red leather mini-dress and matching lipstick. As soon as we
got into the club—this time I *did* show my ID to the bouncers—she
headed to the dance floor.

I was still shocked by the fact they let me in.

The balance of power had shifted, and true, I didn't have most of it,
but I didn't have any less power than Sam did in our relationship either.

He said I didn't come here out of obedience, and I wanted to show
him it wasn't true. At the same time, texting him I was here was too
blatant, too transparent, and I knew that if Sam was here on the premises
chances were he wasn't going to come to the dance floor.

I wanted to press where it hurt. To show Sam I wasn't his little
plaything. And so after seeing Belle was content on the dance floor, I
marched toward the narrow hallway through which Sam had led me all
those months ago, on Halloween, when I desperately got on my knees
for him, taking the scraps he threw my way while masquerading as a
stranger.

Two burly bouncers stood at the edge of the hallway, arms crossed,
blocking my way.

"Let me in." I tilted my chin up.

They looked at me in amusement but didn't move. As if the mere
idea was ridiculous.

Women weren't allowed in the card rooms. Cillian once told me the
official reason for that was because gambling and whores went together,
and Sam didn't want respectable ladies getting harassed if his gamblers
got the wrong idea.

"Hey. I'm talking to you." I waved my hand in front of their faces.

"No women allowed," one of them spat on the floor.

"I'm not just *any* woman."

His eyes raked over my body, head to toe, halting when he reached
my breasts. "Seems to me like you are."

I took out my phone, gliding my finger on the screen until I got to Sam's contact information, showing them his phone number. "How about I call Brennan and clear it with him? I'm sure he'll have something to say about you not letting his girlfriend in."

"Brennan doesn't have a girlfriend," one said.

"He doesn't?" I snorted, my confidence wavering a little. "Didn't know he spent a lot of time talking to his bouncers about his love life. My name is Aisling Fitzpatrick. Check with him if you want."

The one who seemed hell-bent on not letting me in fished his phone out of his front pocket reluctantly, punching in Sam's number while glaring at me. My heart was in my throat. This was the make or break moment. Sam would know I was here. The bouncer said my name. Asked if I could come in. There was a pause on the other line. The air was still despite the hustle and bustle of people, drinks, music, and the lights around us. After a second, he hung up and bowed his head, stepping sideways. His colleague widened his eyes.

"I'll be damned. I thought pigs would fly sooner."

"Keep the dream alive." I patted his shoulder, shouldering past them.

I entered the hallway and picked the busiest, loudest, rowdiest card room. This time, I observed my surroundings more carefully than I did the night I came to fetch Cillian and Hunter. I had to look behind my shoulder for the bouncers and was too filled with white-hot rage to pay attention to anything back then.

Round, deep oak tables with green centers sat across the room with men in expensive suits huddled around them, smoking fine cigars and drinking brandy. They all looked like variations of the men in my family—privileged, corrupt, and desperate for cheap entertainment. There were also waitresses wearing tiny, black baby dolls, leaning down and tending to the clientele.

Scanning the room, I looked for the blackjack table. I knew how to play Texas hold 'em and seven-card stud, but my real specialty had always been blackjack. It was the first card game Cillian had taught me, and he made it a point to practice with me during Christmas Eves, after everyone had retired back to their rooms.

We kept that tradition alive for decades, this year included.

I found the table I was looking for and waited. I knew gambling in Sam's establishment was going to make him explode with anger. My heart pinched a little when I realized he most likely was not around, but I forced myself to find the silver lining. The mere idea of me being here without him was going to bring him closer to asking me to move in with him again.

When the game drew to a close, I wedged myself in the middle of the semicircle of Prada-clad men, beaming at the dealer.

"I'd love to play."

"I would love to play *you*," a middle-aged man beside me jested, making the entire circle of men laugh crudely. I refused to let my smile drop.

"Wait, isn't this …?" One of them frowned at me. I kept my gaze carefully on the dealer. "Whoa, it is. Aisling Fitzpatrick. Isn't it your bedtime? Does your daddy know you're here?"

I was three years shy of turning thirty, so this definitely stung, but maybe I deserved it for putting my parents' needs before mine for almost three decades and still living at their place.

I stared at the dealer, ignoring the idiot talking to me. The older employee cleared his throat, widening his bowtie with his finger.

"Ma'am, I'm afraid—"

"Don't be afraid. Fear is never a good look. Let me play," I demanded, clinging onto my false confidence.

I was becoming aware of a warm, tingly sensation that spread from the top of my head down my spine. I knew exactly what it meant, and who just entered the room, but he didn't make himself known.

"I'm not sure it is up to me, ma'am. See, there are rules regarding—"

"Me. Yes. I know. Brennan rescinded all of them." I rolled up the sleeves of my Balmain mini-dress. "Same goes to women gambling in the card rooms. I'm not just any woman. I'm the woman Sam Brennan is engaged with in a battle of the wills. The rules do not apply to me. You can call and ask him yourself. That's how I made it here in the first place."

"There's no battle, sweetheart. I won before I laid a finger on you, but nice try," a low voice mocked behind me. My head snapped toward the door. Sam stood there, wearing a pale gray suit with a burgundy Hermes pocket square poking out of his blazer. A gorgeous sin in Italian loafers. He looked ready for a date. Ready for me, his skin gold and warm, his eyes gray and cold.

He knew I was going to come here the minute he challenged me to do so, and I fell right into his trap.

I looked away, ignoring him and turning my attention back to the dealer. I remembered what he told me all those years ago.

"I wouldn't bet with me."

"Why?"

"I always win."

For the first time in a long time, I didn't feel the warm excitement that came with seeing him, and my insides didn't turn into baby food as they usually had. Something about him felt daring, quiet, and on edge tonight. Like the old Sam, the one who didn't want me. I felt like he was on the brink of showing me very publicly how much I abused his patience. I shifted from one foot to the other on my high heels.

"She can play, under one condition." Sam sauntered deeper into the room behind me, his voice drawing closer, and I was aware of the curious glances thrown my way.

I refused to turn around and give him the audience he demanded.

"Usually when a man gives you his word, it doesn't come with stipulations," I muttered, feeling the color rising in my cheeks.

"I'm not a man. I'm a monster." He stopped beside me, not removing his gaze from my face for a second. "Look at me, Nix."

I didn't.

I looked anywhere *but* at him.

"I will let you play, if we play each other," he finished.

"It's blackjack. I won't be playing against you. I'll be playing against the dealer." I turned around, facing him.

Men whistled and chuckled, enjoying their front-row seat to our exchange. They obviously weren't used to seeing anyone stand up to Sam Brennan, let alone a dainty woman in a dress.

Sam smiled calmly. "We play high stakes here, Miss Fitzpatrick."

"My Spidey senses tell me I'm good for it," I deadpanned, making everyone in the room erupt into rowdy laughter. Did he really just try to financially intimidate me? I had more money than all the men in this room combined.

"A million dollars a hand. Five hands. Sound acceptable?" I asked, my voice prim and proper, offering him my hand for a shake.

The place exploded with hoots, laughter, and shrieks. The men were on fire. Everyone looked at Sam expectantly, knowing he was not a man to bow out of a challenge.

Sam glanced at my outstretched hand, hands still in his pockets, his posture lazy. He was in no hurry to answer.

He obviously savored this moment. Our first public exchange in the ten years since we'd known each other.

"You mean five million dollars a hand." He smirked.

"Dang!"

"Oh my!"

"Bryan, you gotta come here."

Our audience grew as more men yelled and gasped to each other, people trickling from nearby rooms, craning their necks as the thick circle of bodies around us grew bigger and tighter. I felt the ring of men around me, like it was squeezing my neck. Cigarettes were put down, drinks were left unattended, everyone waited to hear my reply.

"Famous last words." I hitched one shoulder up, raising my un-touched hand an inch, hysteria clogging up my throat. Just because I had this kind of money didn't mean I wanted to see twenty-five mil-lion dollars flushed down the drain in half an hour.

I felt my armpits dampen and started second-guessing my coming here.

Why did I want to push him so much?

"And if I win…" he raised his palm up to stop me "…you marry me."

The dealer looked between us, dropping the stack of cards in his hand in shock. The middle-aged man who propositioned me rubbed his hands together.

"This is gonna be a story to tell my grandchildren."

I stared at Sam silently, stone-cold sober, searching for mockery in his eyes. I found none, but I still couldn't believe my ears.

"It's not funny." My voice came out gravelly, crawling its way out my throat.

"I'm not laughing," he countered softly, his eyes never leaving mine, delivering the final blow. "Oh. And no prenup."

"Ohhhh!"

Men bent backward, slapping their foreheads dramatically. I was lucky I was propped against the table because every muscle in my body ceased to work.

I wondered if it was another stop in his destination to full domination over Boston, marrying into the richest family with no prenup. Was I just a pawn in his game? Another juicy deal waiting to be sealed?

"Sweetheart, Brennan's a top-notch mathematician. Crazy good with numbers. Run, don't walk," one man hollered from the depths of the room.

Sam smirked, neither confirming nor denying it.

"I know your older brother, little Fitzy. Say yes and I'll have no choice but to call him," another young man shouted.

Smiling and refusing to withdraw my hand and cower like everyone expected me to, I said, "Wouldn't you like that, Samuel Brennan? The son of a whore, born without a dime to his name, married to one of the richest women in the western world. You'll be eligible to half my fortune."

"I know," he said calmly. "Which means you'll think twice before leaving me."

Our audience laughed and hooted loudly.

"I'm not giving you half my kingdom," I enunciated, my voice clear and unwavering.

"I don't give a fuck about your kingdom, sweetheart. Mine is bigger in all the ways that matter. Believe it or not, the number in your bank account is not as powerful as my hold on the East Coast."

"I don't believe you," I lied.

"Take the stakes or leave this room, Miss Fitzpatrick, but do it now. I'm running a well-oiled operation here, and every moment people don't spend their money on these tables costs me."

"Marry you," I mouthed the words rather than said them aloud, shock still gripping me. My father was going to kill me. Cillian and Hunter were going to burn whatever was left of me. Yet somehow I believed Sam's motive wasn't money. He had enough of it.

He wanted to trap me. And me? I wanted to be trapped.

"Fine," I said shakily, my stomach turning a hundred times over.

Sam finally clasped my hand in his, but instead of shaking it, he used our entwined fingers to jerk me toward him, pressing a very public, very possessive kiss on my mouth.

"We have a game. They're going for it!" A young man in a sage green velvet suit jumped up from his seat. There was chaos in the room for the next few minutes, and I tried to gulp deep breaths and tell myself it didn't matter. None of it did. I could dig my way out of this. Maybe.

The stakes for a game were never this high in the history of Badlands. Bookies rolled in from other rooms to take bets on the game, holding clipboards with spreadsheets, taking names and numbers and odds. I recognized Becker and Angus, the soldiers I had treated last year, shuffling about, whispering between them as they placed their bet against me.

There was a human traffic jam outside the door to the card room, and I could barely breathe when I heard the bouncers physically pushing people away.

We both took our places in front of the dealer, whose golden nametag said Daniel. I drummed my fingers against the green felt of the table. Sam stared at me. I refused to look back at him.

"Smart move. Your club's about to become legendary after this." I flicked my hair behind my shoulder.

"I never let a good scandal go to waste," he replied wryly.

"Are you really that good at math?" my voice quivered.

"*Better.*"

Everyone settled, and Daniel started shuffling the cards, reciting the rules of the game loud and clear. He made a show of it. First with an overhand shuffle, a riffle shuffle, then a pile shuffle. By the time he was done, the cards were thoroughly mixed, even I couldn't deny that.

Daniel put the neat stack of cards down, glancing between Sam and me.

Sam jerked his chin toward me, deciding now was a good time to become a gentleman.

I refused to remove my gaze from the cards, splitting them into two stacks.

Why was I so hysterical? Wasn't it my longtime wish? To marry Sam Brennan?

Oui, mon cheri, but not like this. Not as a part of another elaborate game between you two.

I withdrew my hand and indicated for Daniel to choose from the right-hand stack. We were each dealt two cards. Daniel also dealt himself a hand. One exposed, one hidden.

The first round was a quick win for me, allowing me to breathe again. I spluttered around an exhale, wondering if it was Sam's way of making me lower my guard. The second round went to Sam, after I doubled down and lost, making my rival flash a devious smirk. The third—to me. The fourth—to Sam.

The eerie feeling everything was premeditated took root in my stomach. Perhaps Sam had intentionally made this game a close call to make people more interested. Statistically, the neatness of our wins, and losses, seemed highly unlikely. He was engineering a narrative where anything could happen, and it made me even more nervous because that meant he knew he would win.

I never lose.

Sam played against casinos and won repeatedly. The chances of him losing twice, out of four times, were slim to nonexistent.

By the time we were dealt our fifth hands, I was a sweaty pile of mess. My hair was plastered to my temples, and everything in me shook. No matter the result, I was going to be devastated.

I didn't want his money, but marrying him right now seemed as impossible as kissing the moon good night.

"Don't worry. I'll make it fast and easy for you, Miss Fitzpatrick." Sam shot me an impersonal smile as Daniel cut the cards. The whole room held its breath.

I got confused and didn't stand with a pair of nines when Daniel's up-card was a seven, even though Cillian had taught me to do so.

Sam split a pair of eights and aces.

Sam *won.*

Three to two.

Fair and square.

The whole room erupted in screams, arguments, and laughter as hands exchanged thick stacks of money. People huddled over the betting books. Others clapped Sam's back and whistled, shaking his hand with a smug smile.

"The deal of your life, Brennan. Next stop, world domination."

"Make sure you get your hands on those Royal Pipelines shares, man."

"You delicate fucking genius."

"Better take her for a test drive, eh?"

Nausea washed over me, and I gripped the edges of the table with force.

I lost.

Not only tonight but the last decade.

We were always playing a game, at least that was how it felt, and this was the pinnacle of a ten-year battle.

It didn't matter that I wanted it. That I wished for it. That I longed for it.

Sam Brennan won me, but he didn't *earn* me.

What kind of marriage would I have to a man who didn't want to have children and hated women?

Sam ignored the congratulations, strolling the short distance to meet me, his face unreadable. Everyone stopped to see what happened next. I couldn't blame them. I wanted to know, too. I didn't move. Didn't run away. The least I could do was handle the situation with dignity. A Fitzpatrick never bowed down.

Sam stopped a foot away from me.

"Well done. I knew you were a talented mathematician and blackjack player, but I still underestimated you." I offered him my hand again, my voice quiet and resolute.

He narrowed his eyes at me, like we were enemies. Maybe we were. I never knew where we stood. He cupped my throat, angling my face up to look him in the eye. When he spoke, it was to the room, not to me, but his words were loud and clear, filling the air with poison.

"I want every single asshole who witnessed this game to go and tell their friends. And tell your friends to tell *their* friends. I want this to hit Cillian, Hunter, and Gerald's ears tonight. I want this in the papers. Aisling Fitzpatrick is now mine. I won her, and she is going to be my wife. If anyone has a problem with that, he will have to go through me, and I sincerely don't recommend it. It's a terrible way to die."

With that, he crashed his lips down on mine, sealing our deal with an animalistic kiss. People cheered in the background, but we paid no attention to them. I paid no attention to them, completely immersed in this thing between us, my heart soaring to the sky. Sam hoisted me up and carried me out of the card room, shouldering past dozens of men, heading straight to his office. My legs wrapped around his waist, my tongue dancing inside his mouth.

We reached the point of no return.

There were no more games to be played.

We were together.

"You will keep your word to me," he growled into my mouth, kicking the door to his office open and slamming it shut behind us without touching the handle, his fingers digging into my behind.

"No," I insisted breathlessly, peppering his neck with kisses. "Not until you tell me that it's real. That I'm just not a conquest. That I mean something to you."

"You don't mean something to me," he countered. "You mean *everything* to me. Jesus Christ, I need to get inside you before I fucking die." He let me down, turned to his desk, and in one go wiped it clean of his laptop, ledgers, and paperwork.

He grabbed my waist roughly and turned me around to face the desk, bending me over as he hoisted my dress up, tugging my panties to the side.

"Belle is waiting for me outside," I warned, panting hard, so wet my thighs were sticking together.

"Belle can go fuck herself. You're mine now, and I'm celebrating our engagement in my favorite place—inside you."

He thrust into me from behind, and the unexpectedness of it, the sheer surprise made a loud moan slip between my lips. He snaked one arm between my legs and started playing with my clit as he entered me mercilessly, picking up pace, driving me mad as he hit my G-spot again and again.

"Oh, Monster."

"Mine." He leaned down, brushing my hair from my ear, biting the lobe softly.

"Mine, mine, mine. Forever mine," he chanted, moving his

fingers from between my thighs, up to my breasts, kneading them. His fingers traveled north again, and he pushed them into my mouth, coated with my arousal, to stop me from moaning loudly.

"There, there, little Nix." His breath tickled the back of my neck and my ear, sending goose bumps down my body, making me clench around him even more. "You will now have this dick on a daily basis. Starting tonight, you'll be moving in with me. I'll have no lip from you, Aisling. I won. You lost. Understood? Nod if you do."

I nodded jerkily, my body quaking with an impending climax that threatened to tear through my bones. From this angle, he was so deep inside me, I felt impossibly full. I swear the man was rearranging my guts.

My fingers dug into the wood of the table, my teeth sinking into Sam's fingers in my bid to stifle a groan. The orgasm racked through me like a tornado, ripping everything inside me in its wake. He must've sensed my orgasm because he, too, let go of the sliver of self-control he still possessed and began thrusting erratically, coming inside me in warm spurts, grabbing the base of my neck and pulling me to his mouth for a kiss full of tongue.

We stayed in this position for a few moments, him deep inside me, the last of his cum dripping into me. He placed a chaste kiss on the top of my head.

"Better than cigarettes," he said dryly, his face turning cold and expressionless again, putting his mask back on now that we were done.

This time, I smiled, knowing it wasn't personal.

"Aren't you glad you quit?"

"No." He pulled out slowly, massaging my butt in the process. "But I'm glad you took the bait and got lured back into Badlands. A few more weeks of being celibate and the cemeteries in Boston would be overcrowded. Now go say goodbye to your friend. You have exactly five minutes before we go back home and I fuck you all over again." He squeezed my ass, pushing me toward the door playfully. "Make it quick and make it count, Nix."

I was marrying a bastard.

But he was *my* bastard.

"I heard the news." Belle waited for me by the bouncers, leaning on the balls of her feet, just outside the card rooms. They wouldn't let her in. By the looks she sent them, I could tell no love was lost between her and the two burly men. "On a scale of one to Lindsay Lohan circa 2010, how drunk were you when you said yes to the bet?" she raged.

I threw myself between her arms, even though they weren't technically open, squeezing her in a hug.

"Not drunk at all, Belle. It's the real deal. I didn't want to tell you because I wasn't sure where it was going, but ... we're kind of together now."

"Kind of? Ya think?" Belle gave me a sarcastic look, still in shock, pulling away from me while patting my shoulder to show me she wasn't mad. "We all know where it's going now, and let me tell you, people called your brothers, who then told their wives, who told your *parents*. Needless to say, no one's happy you kept it such a secret. They're suspecting you've been lovers all along. The entire ten years you've known each other."

Let them think that, I thought.

In a way, it was true.

Sam and I were always lovers.

Even when we didn't speak or touch each other at all.

That night, I went home with Sam. It was only when we entered his apartment that I realized that the place felt completely and irrevocably mine. Somewhere down the line, his place had become my home. It housed my clothes, my shoes, my toiletries, and the man I love.

Still in a daze, I walked around the living room, brushing my fingers over the minimal furniture, the bare walls; I knew there was a good chance our house was never going to have any art in it, no paintings, no beloved vintage knickknacks to fill the place with personality and warmth. I was oddly okay with that. With the loss of art in the name of love.

I was facing the window overlooking Boston's cityscape, sparkling in the nighttime like masses of tiny stars, when I heard Sam's voice behind me.

"Don't turn around. Stay like that."

I did.

Our phones were both blowing up with calls all the way from Badlands.

At first, we shoved them into my purse, but when that didn't help, and the buzzing and lit screens kept taunting us, we turned them off completely. I was pretty sure my brothers and parents were fully intending to knock this door down any minute now, only they couldn't because they didn't know where Sam lived.

I found that little fact strangely liberating.

The irony of living somewhere my parents couldn't find me, after being under their thumb for so long.

His footsteps pressed down on the floor underneath us. I felt him stop right behind my back. He took my left hand while I was still facing the window, sliding a ring onto my ring finger. My breath caught, and my heart stuttered, the unreliable monster that it was.

"Don't look yet," he whispered into my ear. I nodded, waiting.

He dropped a kiss to the crown of my head, and I felt dizzy with pleasure.

"Sam," I breathed.

"Yes?" he asked, catching the zipper of my dress, sliding it down seductively.

I cleared my throat. "I want children."

He stopped unzipping me. I found my voice again. I couldn't not talk to him about it.

"I know you are not a fan, but I want them very much. Is this going to be a problem for us?"

Holding my breath, I waited. After a few seconds, he resumed the work of undressing me, sliding the zipper down all the way. The dress pooled at my feet like a shimmering lake of burgundy blood and glitter.

"No." His lips skimmed the hollow of my neck. "I will give you children, if you quit your job. Do something legal, Aisling. I cannot bear the idea of something happening to you."

I swallowed hard, closing my eyes.

My patients were so dear to me.

Their well-being, supporting them meant everything.

But he was right. If someone caught me, I'd be locked up for life.

Becoming a mother and doing something so dangerous simply didn't go together. Especially since my future children's father had a less than respectable job, too. Someone would have to be their anchor. The reliable parent who goes out to work and comes back every day, no matter what.

I felt my eyelids drooping.

"I'll tell Dr. Doyle tomorrow."

"Good girl." He kissed my cheek, unfastening my bra. "Now take a look at your ring."

I turned around to face him, wearing nothing but my underwear and the ring. I blinked at it. A gasp of shock and pleasure escaped me. I looked up to Sam with eyes full of tears.

"Troy gave Sparrow a ring with a blood red diamond. It reminded him of her hair. I wanted to do the same, but when I think of you, I don't think about your hair. I think about those eyes. They taunt me. The absolute blueness of them."

He took my hand and kissed the ring, a huge halo ring of diamonds surrounding the center stone—an emerald-cut octagon-shaped sapphire. I kissed it, too, laughing and crying at the same time.

"You were going to win all along, weren't you?" I whispered, referring to our blackjack game. "You knew you were."

He cupped my cheeks, pulling me to him.

"I was never going to lose you, Ash. That wasn't in the cards, or on the table, or part of the agenda. You were always going to be mine. You had to have known that."

Eighteen

Sam

"I AM GOING TO KILL YOU, BRENNAN." CILLIAN FITZPATRICK stormed into my office at Badlands the following day, with Hunter trailing behind him. "You have some nerve cornering my sister like that. Your bet with her is off. We'll pay the money."

I sat back in my seat, smirking as I tapped my fingers over my mouth. It had been three hours since I dropped Aisling off at the clinic to hand in her resignation, and already I missed her like crazy. The idea of giving up on the engagement after she'd agreed to it seemed as far from reality as letting Cillian and Hunter shove a ten-foot spiky dildo into my ass while I watch reruns of *Hannah Montana*.

"I don't want the money," I drawled.

"Well too bad..." Cillian stopped in front of my desk, his fists clenched "...because buying my sister is not an option."

"I didn't buy her, I won her. You were the one who bought your wife, while we're on the subject, and you..." I turned to Hunter before he opened his mouth "...you don't even have a say in this. You're having sex with my sister. Count your blessing that you are still alive. I still have no idea what she sees in you."

Hunter lifted his hands up in surrender. "Same here, bro. I have no idea why she is with me. I just know I'm not letting her go."

"How did you get in here anyway?" I frowned. The entrance was manned by two bodyguards.

Cillian took a seat in front of me, and Hunter occupied the chair beside him as they both invited themselves to stay.

Cillian and Hunter had no idea what went on between me, their father, Aisling and Jane, and I intended to keep it that way. Not because I gave a fuck about what they thought but because I knew it would hurt Aisling if her brothers doubted my devotion to her. And she would be upset when Hunter and Cillian passed the information along to Persephone, Sailor, and Devon, making the fact I stabbed her in the back a well-known matter.

"Oh, I know Johnny and Grayson from way back." Hunter waved his hand around dismissively, referring to the bouncers standing at the front door. "I told them we came in to congratulate you on your engagement."

"When really we came here to tell you that you will not blackmail our sister." Cillian lit up a cigar. The stench of the burning rolled tobacco drifted around the room, and I tried to remember what I liked about smoking. Cigars smelled like feet on fire, and cigarettes were their cheaper equivalent.

It was peculiar. How both bad and good habits were born from boredom. How they turned into an obsession, an addiction, before you knew it. And how taking back control from them became a habit in itself.

"Your sister is a big girl." I laced my fingers together on my desk, trying to keep the disdain from my voice. "She came to me of her own free will. As you recall, you paid me not to get anywhere near her, which should tell you something about her reaction to *me*."

"And as you recall, you crapped all over your promise not to touch her, if you are getting married now," Cillian retorted.

Cillian wasn't wrong, but he couldn't prove his suspicion either, so I just flashed him a barely tolerant smile.

"Do you have proof?"

"No, but—"

"Then I suggest you keep your opinion where it belongs, in Reddit conspiracy theory threads. Aisling and I are engaged to be married. The marriage will take place sooner rather than later. I've already spoken to your father about deducting the annual bonus for not touching her as I intend to touch her very often—and very inappropriately. I understand that the Fitzpatrick family enjoys seeing Ash as the prized, devoted daughter who dotes on Jane and fulfills her father's every whim, but this stops now."

"Which brings us to our next topic." Cillian narrowed his eyes at me. "Seems to me like the entire divorce ordeal between my parents, along with the stolen cufflinks and poison case disappeared into thin air. As the person in charge of the situation, would you care to explain it?" He held his cigar between his teeth, half-smiling.

The problem with Cillian was that, unlike most of my rich clients, he was smart and observant. Those things were definitely a thorn in my side.

"Gladly." I smacked my lips together. "We found the person responsible for all those things. For obvious reasons, your father swiped it under the rug. Didn't want your mother to become even more upset with him when another lover came to light. How is Jane doing, by the way?"

"Don't pretend like you care," Cillian yawned. I doubted he cared, too.

"Fair enough." I chuckled. Hunter, the only one out of us three who actually gave a fuck, confirmed that she was still attending therapy. Good for her. She needed all the help she could get because I was never letting her emotionally manipulate Aisling again.

"You quit smoking, huh?" Hunter's gaze flicked to my desk, which now lacked the usual mountain of ashtrays, cigarette packs, and Zippos. "From one addict to another, let me tell you, I'm really proud of you."

"That warms my heart," I said.

"Really?" Hunter's eyes lit up.

"No," I deadpanned, looking between them. "Did you get everything you came here for? I have a busy day. It's called work…" I snapped my fingers, making a show of reminding them "…you know that thing people do to make money when they are not born into royalty."

"You are about to marry into royalty," Hunter jested, wiggling his brows.

"Which reminds me," Cillian put his cigar out, standing up and buttoning his blazer, "there is no way I am letting you marry my sister without a prenup."

"I'll sign the goddamn prenup," I bit out, "but she can't know that."

"She can't know that?" Hunter frowned. "Why not?"

"It's not the money I care about, it's keeping your sister," I grunted, annoyed that I had to spell it out for him, like he didn't know what it meant to be pussy-whipped.

"You really do love her, don't you?" Hunter grinned smugly.

"Give us a smart-ass answer and I will kill you," Cillian warned.

I was about to answer when someone kicked the door down, sending it flying off its hinges and skating along the floor. I reached for my gun in my desk's drawer, but the two men in the balaclavas were faster.

"No need to kill him," one said in a thick Russian accent, pointing his gun at me. "We'll do it for you."

He shot two bullets into my chest.

Everything went black.

I slipped in and out of consciousness as they rushed me to the hospital. I couldn't feel any pain in my chest or my shoulder, which couldn't have been a good sign. Everything was blurry. The white punishing florescent light forced me to close my eyes as soon as I opened them.

In the background, I heard Cillian and Hunter's voices, and Devon's.

"Johnny and Grayson are dead," Hunter said, unaware that I was half-conscious. "We need to take care of that."

"Troy's on it," Cillian quipped. "He'll clean up the scene. He has people working on it right now. They're boarding up the card rooms in case the police get tipped off."

In that moment, I was glad my friends weren't total dumbasses. I must've groaned because Cillian's head snapped in my direction. The doctor and nurse behind me shooed my entourage away. We must have been heading into the operating room.

"Call Ash," I tried to say, but even though I could move my mouth, it didn't produce any sound.

"What?" Hunter reached over to squeeze my hand. For fuck's sake, what was he going to do next? Cut the cord when I delivered his fucking baby?

"Call Ash!" I roared, hoping my hearing was impaired due to the gunshots and that I didn't lose my fucking vocal chords.

Cillian and Hunter stopped dead in their tracks behind the medical staff as my gurney burst through the double doors.

I had to stay alive.

I had to.

Not for me.

For *her*.

I closed my eyes again.

For the first time in my life, I was losing a fight.

Aisling

"I quit."

Dr. Doyle and I were sitting in front of each other, filling out charts.

I blurted the words before I chickened out, making the older man straighten in his seat. He watched me through the thick rim of his reading glasses.

"I'm very happy to hear that," he said finally, and all the air rushed out from my lungs in a desperate sigh. Even though I knew Dr. Doyle had been wanting me to explore more legal and accomplishing means of medicine, I also knew he had his hands full here at the clinic, and he needed help.

"I feel terrible." I covered my face with both hands, shaking my head.

"Don't." I heard the smile in his voice. "I want more for you than this. That time you came to my office, when you found out what it was I did, I knew how passionate you were about this job when you told me about Ms. Blanchet, but I never hoped for you to come work here full-time."

"But what about Mrs. Martinez—"

"She'll survive," he hurried to say. Then, realizing his poor choice of words, he gave a small chuckle and added, "I'll take over. I have my own ideas about her treatment."

I swallowed. He was a great doctor. I wasn't worried about his abilities, I was worried about his workload.

"What are you going to do?" I asked Dr. Doyle, peeking at him through my fingers fanned across my face. The engagement ring still felt heavy on my finger. Strange and foreign and yet like a cloak of security I'd never worn before.

Dr. Doyle's eyes halted on the huge sapphire ring, but other than his smile tugging wider, he didn't mention it.

It was obvious he put two and two together.

Engagement meant marriage, and marriage oftentimes meant babies, and if there was one thing my children deserved, it was at least one parent who wouldn't be at risk of being thrown into prison.

"I'm going to cut back on the work eventually, too, starting by turning down new patients." He dropped his pen on the chart he was filling out. "You know, I thought about this long and hard recently. Why we do this..." he motioned around the room "...and I've come to the conclusion that we are trying to repent. We've both lost people we loved very dearly in the most horribly painful ways, but it is not our fault. It is time to let go of the guilt, my dear. You cannot change history. But you can write your next chapters. You are doing the right thing by quitting, Aisling. You have a beautiful life ahead of you. Ah, to be your age again," he said wistfully, staring at an invisible point behind my shoulder, looking far away all of a sudden. "The world is spread before you in all its glory. Make the most of it. You've worked hard here, and you weren't paid a penny. You've helped others. Now it's time to focus on yourself, child."

I looked down and noticed my phone was beeping with an incoming text. I slid the screen with my thumb.

Cillian: Clover.

Hunter: Cloverrrrrrrrrrrrrrrrrrrrrrrrrrrrrrr.

They could wait. They sure made me wait when I needed them.

"Do you think I can handle a residency?" I gnawed on my inner cheek.

I'd been so far removed from mainstream medical institutions, finding my way back into them felt almost impossible.

"Dear," Dr. Doyle chuckled, "the question is, can *they* handle *you*? You are a force to be reckoned with. Compassionate, pragmatic, and hardworking. A lethal combination for a doctor."

He got up, rounding the desk between us, and offered me his hand. I took it, rising to my feet. Dr. Doyle engulfed me in a hug. The deep, bone-crushing kind that rearranged your entire being in just the right way.

When I stepped out of the clinic for the last time in my life, I found myself looking behind at the building's door with a soft smile but without longing.

Doing what I did never truly fulfilled me.

It dulled my pain.

I was ready for the next chapter in my life.

To stitch people back together, atoning for all the lives my future husband would no doubt rip apart.

I forgive you, mon cheri. You were just a kid. Besides, maybe, just maybe I put you in an impossible situation, too, I heard Ms. B's voice in my head and knew, with a decent amount of both disappointment and relief, that I wasn't going to hear her voice very often from now on. Her job was truly done now.

I took out my phone, striding absentmindedly to the Prius.

I had a lot of missed calls from Cillian, Hunter, and Devon. Gosh, they really couldn't handle how yesterday went down with Sam and me. They needed to get over themselves.

The texts, however, gave me pause.

Cillian: Answer.

Hunter: Please just pick up the phone. We are not trying to yell at you for the engagement.

Cillian: Sam is in the hospital. Brigham. He's been shot twice. He's in critical condition.

Hunter: You have to come see him. He is asking for you.

Devon: Aisling, darling, your brothers are quite disoriented, too much to pay attention to the finer details. But as a solicitor, one

must wonder, if you are currently at work, and your workplace is the hospital we're in, how come we can't seem to reach you?

I jumped into the car, flooring it all the way to the hospital, my heart in my throat.

My worst fear had materialized.

Sam's sins finally caught up with him.

Aisling

I blasted through the ER doors, running toward the waiting area, where Hunter, Cillian, Devon, and Troy were standing with a frantic-looking Sparrow.

The latter paced from side to side, seeming to be deep in conversation on the phone with her daughter, urging her not to come.

"No, honey, someone needs to take care of the kids. Please don't leave them with Persy. She has her hands full as it is. I'll keep you abreast."

It was the first time I'd seen my future in-laws since Sam proposed, and it was in less than positive circumstances. I threw myself at Hunter, grabbing onto the lapels of his pea coat.

"Where is he?"

"Hey," Hunter said gravely, his voice lower and more concerned than I'd ever heard before. Cillian would not look at me. Did they know something I didn't? The thought made me want to kneel right there and throw up on the floor. "He's in surgery right now. I guess you can't go inside, but surely you can ask the staff how he is doing? You work here and everything. You must know some of the doctors."

Still in a daze, I mumbled something about it being a huge hospital and not wanting to take advantage of my position, although I could tell Hunter looked at me funny. The walls were closing in on me. My family was becoming suspicious. Why had it taken me so long to get here if I worked in the premises?

Because I never actually worked here. I just couldn't tell you what it was that I did.

The great irony of getting caught in the lie on the day I quit my job with Dr. Doyle didn't escape me, but my mind was occupied with all things Sam. I stared longingly at the door Hunter gestured toward. Behind it doctors were fighting for Sam's life.

"Tell me what happened again," Troy insisted, badgering Cillian and Hunter, and they recited the entire scene. How they came to talk to Sam about my engagement to him (at this point they stared at me pointedly), how they discussed it at length. How they didn't hear anything when the Russians put bullets in Johnny and Grayson's heads because they used a silencer. How the Bratva burst through Sam's office door, aiming their weapon at him.

"He's a strong fucker." Hunter sniffled. "On our way here he was half-conscious. He even asked us to call you, Aisling."

All eyes lifted and rested on me, burning a hole through my face. Wrapping my arms around myself, I ignored them, waltzing over to a nearby window and staring out of it.

The world kept on spinning, and it felt like losing Ms. B all over again, only much worse. Cars honked, cluttered together in neat lines on the road. Clouds sailed. Women cooed at each other's strollers on the streets.

Suddenly, I felt bloated and swollen with resentment.

At my parents for depriving me from having Sam until it was

too late. At myself for listening to them, for waiting around, for denying myself of what I wanted. And at Sam, who ruthlessly devoured Boston—to the point where Boston had no choice but to devour him right back.

"Hunter," I called out, still staring out the window, my eyes glued to the street. He approached me, stopping right next to me.

"Call Mother. I want her here. For once in this lifetime, I want her to comfort me."

"Are you sure?" He frowned. "I don't want this to have the opposite effect. What if she ends up nagging you about her psoriasis or tries to drag you to a shopping spree at the mall?"

"She won't," I said with conviction.

The women with the strollers on the street hugged each other goodbye and went their separate ways. I was filled with nausea when I realized it was possible I would never have babies with Sam. That this could be it for us. "I won't let her."

Hunter nodded curtly, stepping aside to call my mother.

Then, alone, with my face tilted in the opposite direction of everyone, I allowed the tears to fall. One by one, they slid down my cheeks, hot and salty.

I needed to let them go or else I'd drown.

Nineteen

Aisling

AN HOUR LATER, MY MOTHER WALKED INTO THE WAITING room. There was still no word from the doctors inside the operating room. Several times, Sparrow, Troy, and Cillian tried to nudge me to check in with the reception, pull some strings as a doctor at this hospital. I noticed Devon and Hunter were surprisingly quiet and solemn. They knew.

Mother flung her arms over my shoulders, burying her face in my neck.

"Oh, Aisling, how terrible. Poor Sam. I hope he'll be okay. Although, I suppose, he got what was coming for him, doing what he does and all."

My blood froze in my veins. I peeled her away from my body. No one else had heard what she said, but it didn't matter. I was done being understanding of her, of her condition. Her loose tongue and looser morals had consequences, and it was time she knew it. I took a step back.

"I'm engaged to him," I announced robotically.

Her mouth fell open. My brothers must have kept it a secret from her. No doubt thinking the engagement might be short-lived. Well, it wasn't. There was only one way out of this engagement right now, and that was if Sam died.

"Aisling, you can't …" She grabbed her gold necklace, rearranging it over her neck nervously. She was clad in a black velvet suit and a vintage Chanel bag, and I realized, a few moments too late, that it wasn't only her words that bothered me but also the fact she took her time getting ready to come to the hospital when I called for her.

She lowered her voice, grabbing onto my wrist and tugging me to the corner of the room to make sure no one could hear us. "Honey, he is not for you."

I yanked my arm away, scowling at her. "You don't know what's good for me. All you want is for me to stay in the house and cater to you."

"Honey! That is ridiculous. If anything, I—"

"Don't finish that sentence," I warned, lifting a finger. "I called you here today because I wanted your support, not to hear you nagging. This is how it's going to be from now on, Mother. You'll be giving support, not just getting it. You will not pass judgment on me. You will be a *mother*. No longer my responsibility. Am I clear?"

She stared at me, blinking, and my heart clenched when I realized we were like a filtered mirror. I looked just like her. Same dainty build, delicate bones, and coiffed hair. Same lips and nose and naturally curled eyelashes.

But I was different. Strong. Resilient.

She touched her fingers to her cheek, sighing.

"You're right. I did abuse your kind heart, Aisling. I didn't want to believe it, but of course I did. You were so good, and I was so weak. I wasn't used to people being good under my roof. Your father and Cillian are cold as ice. Hunter has the best intentions, but I never quite could worm my way into his heart. You were my rock. My everything. And losing you … I couldn't imagine such a scenario. I'm sorry. I'm so sorry. I—" she stopped, bowing her head as her shoulders began to rock to the rhythm of her sobs. "I was the one who suggested your father should pay Sam extra not to get near you."

An icicle pierced through my heart, and I took a deep, sudden breath, reaching for a nearby wall to try to right myself.

My mother continued, her eyes carefully staring at the floor.

"I saw the way you looked at him the first time you saw him. You must believe this wasn't always about me, Aisling. I was thinking about you, too. He was too old, too dangerous, and too rough around the edges for a gentle-bred girl like you. But yes, in the spirit of honesty, I knew a man like that could scoop you with the same frightening ease you'd take Shelly out from her cage when you gave her baths. You were going to leave me all alone with your father in this big mansion, and I wasn't ready for that. With each year that passed, I tried mustering the courage to tell you. To come clean. Selfishly, I couldn't."

I was fully aware that somewhere in my periphery, our friends and family were watching us, so I refrained from causing a scene. As it was, Hunter and Cillian looked on high alert, ready to pounce on Mother and take her away from me, knowing she had a talent for stealing the limelight, no matter the situation.

Despite the initial shock and deep sense of betrayal, Dr. Doyle was right. There was nothing to be done about our pasts. The only way was forward. I could let what my mother did define our relationship or reinvent it.

And standing there, while Sam was in the operating room, hanging in the balance between life and death, everything was crystal clear to me.

If you loved somehow, you had to give them a second chance.

Not for them.

For *you*.

I took a step toward her, tilting my head up regally.

"I forgive you, Jane, not because you deserve it, but because I don't deserve to live the rest of my life motherless because of your mistakes. You are going to make it up to me, though. Big time. You can start by bringing all of us coffees and pastries. The Brennans haven't eaten all day, and I'm famished."

She nodded, wiping her face quickly, sniffling.

"Will do. Right away. Oh, Aisling, thank you so much." She

grabbed my hands and squeezed them. "I will not let you down, love. You will see."

She ran toward the elevators on her high heels, ignoring the disturbed glares of onlookers.

I was choosing me now.

Me ... and the man I loved.

It had been six hours since I'd arrived at the hospital, and there was still no word from the operating room. I knew no news wasn't necessarily bad news. It meant they were still working hard to save his life. I *also* knew that it didn't matter.

I was dangerously close to a massive heart attack.

Nurses and doctors rushed in and out of the room, wearing bloodied uniforms and grave frowns. I shamelessly pounced on them, demanding answers, but they shook me off every time.

The waiting room thickened with people. At first, I failed to notice it, too wrapped up in running all possible scenarios and outcomes to Sam's condition in my head, but now, lifting my gaze from my lap, I saw it.

Troy, Sparrow, Cillian, Hunter, Devon, my parents, and Sailor were here now, together but alone, each of us shaken to the core.

The distress for Sam's well-being was thick in the air, hanging like fog above our heads.

Troy was on the phone, barking orders, demanding action, no doubt trying to find more information about the attack, planning how to strike back at the Bratva. Sparrow looked so frail, I was afraid if I reached out and touched her she would break.

I moved over to her. "It'll be okay," I whispered, trying to convince myself the same in the process.

Hunter had told me the bullets pierced Sam's shoulder and chest. It was hard to estimate the damage when I had no concrete information.

Finally—*finally*—a middle-aged doctor in stained scrubs with sweaty temples came out of the operating room. I was the first to dart in his direction, with Sparrow following closely behind me.

"Hello, I'm Dr. McKinnley. Are you the wife?" He turned to me.

"I will be soon." I jerked Sparrow close to me. "This is his mother. Please tell us how he is doing."

He ran his gaze over me skeptically. He wasn't supposed to hand out information to those who weren't Sam's kin.

"Aisling is a doctor here, too. An OB-GYN," Sparrow explained, putting a protective hand over my shoulder. "You can tell her."

The doctor shot me another look and turned his focus back to Sparrow.

"It was a close call. He is still not out of the woods yet. The main issue isn't the shoulder wound. We removed the bullet, and although it's still early to tell, it is my belief that the bullet did not tear through more than muscle tissue and did not touch any of the nerves. Our main concern was the chest wound. It hit too close to home, to put it bluntly. In close proximity to the heart. It took us three hours to remove the bullet alone. He lost a lot of blood. The next twenty-four hours will be critical. We're moving him to the recovery room as we speak. He needs a good rest. I cannot stress that enough. For that reason, we would prefer if he sees one visitor at a time."

Sparrow and I exchanged glances. I didn't dare hope. She was his mom, after all. She deserved to see him first. My future mother-in-law squeezed my hand in hers.

"Over two decades ago I told Sam that one day a woman would walk into his life and prove to him that he doesn't hate all women. He put up a good fight, I'll give him that, but I think you finally broke him. It's you he'll want to see when he opens his eyes. In fact, I am told by Troy that he specifically asked for you when he was rushed here. You should go."

"Are you sure?" I bit my lower lip.

She smiled, pain marring her expression. "Absolutely positive, dear."

I followed Dr. McKinnley along the narrow linoleum hallway like a punished kid, not sure what was waiting for me at the end of the journey. When the surgeon pushed the door open, he said, "Remember, he is frail right now, even if he doesn't look it."

I nodded, closing the door after me and staring at Sam from a safe distant. I was a doctor. I'd seen blood and gore in my life. But there was something about Sam's pain that was too intimate and real to me. He lay there with his eyes closed, this beast of a man, so imposing, so imperial, and yet so quiet and boyish right now.

"Oh, Sam." I cupped my mouth, rushing to the foot of the bed, sinking down to the floor and burying my face next to his arm. "What have they done to you? Please make it through this. Please."

Tears coated every inch of my face. I moaned loudly, howling, making noises I had no idea I was capable of. He was finally mine, and I was losing him.

It was the sort of cruelty I couldn't fathom.

"There is so much I have to tell you. So much news. You can't die on me now. It's a highly inconvenient time, Sam. What kind of gentleman are you?" I huffed.

I thought I felt him move slightly next to me, but he didn't say anything, didn't even groan, so obviously I was just imagining it.

"I quit my job. I'll be on the lookout for residencies. I need you to help me sort through them. And what about kids? I want a lot of them, and we need to start practicing. Then there's the Cillian and Hunter matter. Who will annoy them, if you die?"

Another small movement. I jerked my head upright, studying Sam's face closely. His eyes were still shut, his breathing labored. I stared at him as I opened my mouth, cautiously speaking again.

"Of course, if you die on me now, at some point in the future— very far in the future—I'll be able to get over you and move on. But for now, I just want you to—"

Sam's hand moved slightly. He grabbed my wrist and tugged me to him, his eyes snapping open. He groaned in pain at the sudden movement and flashed me a canine scowl.

"No one is going to get over fucking anyone, Fitzpatrick. Now shut up and let me rest."

Surprised, I stared at him with open delight. My ploy had worked. I pouted, leaning backward and giving him some space. His hold on my wrist tightened, but he was still so very weak.

"Let me rephrase … let me rest where I can see you, feel you, and smell you."

"You asshole," I hissed under my breath. "I thought you were going to die."

"Yeah, I heard about the Grand Prix dick tour once I'm in a coffin. It'll have to wait another few decades or so. Sorry."

"I was just teasing to see if you were conscious. I thought I felt you move," I explained, watching as his eyes shut again, his throat bobbing with a hard swallow.

"I know, sweetheart." His tone turned soft, scratchy.

"Can I do anything for you?" I asked.

"Can you climb on top of me and ride me?"

"No."

"Then you can't do anything for me, Nix."

"Everyone is waiting outside. They are worried sick." I rubbed his uninjured arm. "I should go out and tell them you're okay."

He nodded then grunted again, realizing his mistake. Everything must've hurt, and I made a mental note to ask the nurses to up his morphine dose.

"But I'm not going to go out there until you promise me something," I warned.

His eyes were still closed when he asked, "Yes?"

"You asked me to quit my job, and I did, even though I did so with a heavy heart, knowing I won't be able to help so many people who are in pain. Now I'm asking you to bow out of the battle with the Bratva, Sam. No more bloodshed. No more. I don't deserve to become a widow because of your pride. Give up Brookline. Turn your back on this side of the city. Troy never took it over for a reason. Promise me."

"It is not in my nature to lose."

"Yet sometimes—not often—you will. You have to lose Brookline or you'll be losing me. This is an ultimatum, Sam. I will not be made a widow at twenty-eight."

He opened his eyes, looking at me, surprised.

His voice dropped low. "Are you threatening me?"

"Yes," I said simply.

I had to do this. For him. For myself. For his family and our future children. If he cared more about a piece of Boston than he did about me, marrying him was going to be a mistake. I felt oddly reassured by that simple logic. We held each other's gaze, silent for a moment. His jaw ticked with annoyance.

"I can make this work," he said. "I'll talk to Vasily."

"Give up Brookline."

"I'll get more security."

I shook my head, standing up from the floor, wiping my cheeks clean of tears.

"I'm sorry, Sam, but it's not enough. I'm not putting my heart in the hands of a man who won't take care of it."

"Goddammit, woman." He turned his head sideways, closing his eyes, swallowing hard. "Fine. Fine."

I knew how difficult it was for him to say this, to make this sacrifice. I leaned down and kissed his cheek softly.

"Thank you. I'll go tell the others you are awake."

Stepping backward and getting ready to leave, I turned around and heard his voice, sharp and cutting like glass.

"That's what it feels like, doesn't it?" he wondered, half in awe. "Love. I can't believe I caught feelings like some fucking amateur. So many of them, too. This is deplorable."

I grinned, glancing at him from behind my shoulder. He shook his head, scowling at the wall.

"Say that again," I said.

"I'm a fucking amateur."

"The love part." I laughed.

He turned to glare at me.

"I love you, you little fool. I insisted on no prenup because I didn't want you to run away, not because I cared about the money. It was never about the money. Even when I took the job with Gerald and Cillian, there was one thing I cared about, and it had nothing to do with power. I had that before I set foot in your house. I wanted to be close to you, even if I hated not being able to have you. I visited your father on a weekly basis. This thing was bigger than both of us, but we had a lot to lose."

The idea that I wasn't the only one who waited to catch glimpses of him made my heart stutter. I walked back to him, gently placing my hand on his cheek. He curled his fingers over my arm, looking up at me.

"I was close to blowing it all to shit, wasn't I? You and me. The night you ran away into the woods. I could feel it."

I shook my head.

"I never stopped loving you, Sam. Even—and especially—when you least deserved my love."

"Kiss me, Nix." He tugged me down to him. Our lips met. His were cold and dry and chapped, and I quivered, wanting to cry with what he'd been through. I pressed feathery kisses around his mouth, chin, and neck, smiling down at him, kissing his forehead one last time.

"I love you," I whispered.

"I fucking live for you," Sam retorted. "*Literally*. I'm about to give up a lot to have you."

"So you should." I walked away, taking one last glance at him, knowing we were going to have a million more goodbyes.

And a million more hellos, too.

I ran to the waiting room, breaking the good news with a rush of stuttering words. Sparrow squealed and darted toward the room. My parents let out a relieved breath, though I wasn't entirely sure what my father was doing here in the first place. Was it the guilt of keeping us apart for all these years?

Cillian and Hunter were the only ones who didn't look visibly delighted by the news. They glared at me hard as I rehashed the moment in which Sam woke up, obviously omitting the lovey-dovey stuff that would make them gag.

"Hey, Ash, can we speak to you?" Hunter cleared his throat, throwing a glance at my parents. "*Alone.*"

He turned around before I could answer, marching down the hallway. Cillian followed him wordlessly. Frowning, I went after them, something cold and stony settling in my chest. This didn't sound good.

They stopped when we reached the junction between the elevators and the emergency exit, a good length away from our parents. They both turned to look at me. All I needed was one look to figure out that they knew everything.

"What have you been playing at, Aisling?" Cillian demanded, his voice like icicles dripping down my skin, causing goose bumps to rise in its wake. "We went to the front desk and asked for you when we first arrived here. We couldn't reach you on your cell, so we thought to go downstairs and check. The receptionists told us there was no Dr. Fitzpatrick in the hospital. Ran through the database. In fact, we went as far as going to the gynecology department *ourselves* to look for you—maybe you weren't registered yet because you are still doing your residency—but I'm sure you know we came back empty-handed."

"You are working somewhere," Hunter pointed out. "The long hours, the hospital scrubs, your disappearing acts during dinners. What the hell is it you've been doing?"

I must have turned pale because even though they still looked at me like they wanted to kill me, they schooled their faces and stopped showering me with questions. I knew I had two options. Come clean and own up to what I did for almost a year or let them live with a half-assed lie. A lie wouldn't be so harmful. After all, I quit.

Still, I couldn't lie to them. Not again. My lies were piling up neatly on my conscience. Besides, I could no longer pretend to be someone I wasn't. Someone tailor-made for my family to ensure they were happy and fulfilled and proud of me.

My parents.

My brothers.

My professors.

Even the late Ms. B molded me into the woman she wanted me to become.

No more.

So I told them. I opened my mouth, and the truth came out. About Dr. Doyle. How we'd met. About Ms. B's death and how it affected me. About the first time I saw Sam. How it wasn't the day the Fitzpatricks had invited him over along with the Brennans, but months before that. I told them I had quit. That I couldn't put myself at risk anymore to help others. That Sam bent my arm and wouldn't budge.

"It's the first and last thing that fucker did right," Hunter mumbled, pulling me into a hug, pressing me close to his heart. "Fuck, Ash, I'm so sorry. We were so wrapped up in our own shit, we never really stopped to consider what you were going through after your governess died. It didn't help that you always looked like you knew what you were doing. The perfect daughter."

"He is right," Cillian said pithily. "We neglected you for far too long. We'll be rectifying that in the future."

"So…" I looked between them "…you're not judging me? For what I did?"

"Judging you?" Cillian lifted a brow. "You just proved to be a true Fitzpatrick. Darkly complex and terribly pragmatic. I'm proud to call you my sister."

Twenty

Sam

TEN DAYS LATER, I GOT OUT OF THE HOSPITAL. AISLING AND Sparrow doted on my ass like I was a baby, fussing over me and checking on me every single hour, dropping my masculinity levels to new lows I was pretty sure only poodles with designer haircuts had suffered.

The first two days, I humored them, mostly because I was trying to play nice with my fiancée. By day three, however, I made the executive decision to throw all the fucks the doctors had asked I give about my health out the window.

"Nix, stop." I caught her hand. It rested on my chest in our apartment—yes, *our* apartment—as she patted my forehead with a hot, wet cloth. "No more of this bullshit. I'm going back to the streets tonight."

Her peacock eyes widened in horror, her rosebud mouth pouting. "You're still recovering."

"I'm bored out of my ass, and I have a job to do."

"You can do it when you're feeling better."

"I'm feeling pretty fucking great. Would you like me to demonstrate?" I raised an eyebrow, my eyes dropping to the impressive bulge in my pants. No matter my physical state, whenever Aisling was in the room so was my need to fuck her through the mattress, floor, and earth.

"We had a deal, remember?" She withdrew her hand from mine, stepping back, standing in front of me in our bedroom.

"Yes, my love. I was right fucking there when we had it." I smiled impatiently.

It was one thing to give up half my kingdom for her. It was quite a-fucking-nother to be happy about it. "Yet another reason why I need to get my ass out of bed and take care of business. Give me my phone." I snapped my fingers toward the nightstand.

She quirked an eyebrow, knotting her arms over her chest.

She was my fiancée, not my soldier. I had a long way to go when it came to treating her like the princess that she was. Mostly because I'd never had to treat anyone well my entire life.

"Please. And thank you." I grinned wolfishly, and she picked my phone up, handing it over to me.

"Who are you calling?"

I already had the phone pressed to my ear. "Troy."

"Where are you two going?"

"You'll find out soon enough."

"You're always going to keep me on my toes, aren't you?" She sighed but looked happy about it. I grabbed the hem of her dress and pulled her down for a filthy, deep kiss.

"Not at all. Sometimes I'll keep you on your back, too. And on all fours. But whatever your position, I promise you'll fucking enjoy it."

The following evening, Troy parked in front of Vasily Mikhailov's Russian deli in Brookline. He tossed me a doubtful look.

"You sure you wanna do this? You can tell her you did it, and she'll be none the wiser. I know you've worked hard to conquer Brookline."

"Whatever happened to chewing more than I could swallow?"

"Just playing devil's advocate before you make a move."

"You don't have to play devil's advocate with me. I know what goes on inside the devil's head." I pushed the passenger door open, sliding out and cocking my gun as I did. I heard Troy doing the same behind me. We rounded his car, popping the trunk open. Vasily's daughter, Masha, blinked at the sudden light coming from behind our shoulders, her mouth gagged, her hands and feet tied together behind her back.

I smiled cordially. "Miss Mikhailov, thank you for contributing to our cause."

She murmured something hysterical around the fabric covering her mouth, but I couldn't distinguish it.

"What's that?" I asked. "Never mind. You were never captured for your conversational skills. Only as a pawn to ensure your daddy knows I will slaughter you if he doesn't bend to my will."

I hoisted her up over my shoulder, marching toward the deli.

The bell above the deli's door chimed as we stepped inside. I aimed my gun toward the shop owner with my free hand, an elderly Russian man with a weather-beaten face marred with red and blue from years of braving the cold. Masha was still draped over my shoulder, like a pig on its way to slaughter, still dressed in the same expensive coat and designer heels she wore on her shopping spree this morning.

"Where's Vasily?" I clipped.

The man's eyes flared at the sight in front of him. Masha thrashed desperately, trying to wriggle out of my hands.

"I ... I ..." he started, knowing full well he was not allowed to let people into the back office. That was where his boss was situated.

I turned my aim from his head to Masha's spine, digging the gun into her bones. "Better fucking hurry or you'll have to explain to your boss why his daughter's guts are spilled all over your floor. I'm guessing it'll be a bitch to clean up, too. Though, I doubt he'll spare your life after letting it happen."

"Come with me!" the man blurted out, jumping from his place behind the counter, rounding it and pushing an old wooden door open.

The place smelled of pickles, dried meat, and smoke. I followed the man's back, Troy at my heels. After passing through a narrow, dusty corridor we reached another door. He opened it.

Vasily was at his desk, surrounded by three of his high-ranked men. He had the pointy, fox-look of a comic book villain, which he highlighted with good suits and bad manners. But not even a fucking ball gown could hide the fact that his face was riddled with knife scars. My initials—S.A.B.—were carved into his forehead, jagged and white.

His bodyguards were on alert, two on each side, all of them possessing the peculiar look of semitrailers and similar IQs. The middle-aged man with silver hair and pale blue eyes looked up at me, putting his cigar down in an ashtray, sending smoke whirling to the ceiling.

"Brennan. You're alive."

"And you're surprised." I rearranged Masha on my shoulder. Even though I used my healthy shoulder to carry her and not the one his men put a bullet through, I still wasn't my usual self. Normally, carrying a woman of Masha's slight weight was akin to wearing a goddamn scarf.

"And I see you brought your daddy." Vasily's eyes slid from me to Troy, who stood beside me.

"Seemed fair," Troy clipped dryly, "seeing as you have an entire army surrounding you. Not used to doing the dirty work anymore, are you, Vasily?"

"And it shows. Two bullets, and not one pierced my heart," I *tsked*, shaking my head. "My toddler nephew has better aim in the toilet while potty training."

Masha twisted in my arms, responding to her father's words and tenor. I drugged her a little—enough to keep her silent and easy to manage—and I knew these animals were wondering if I used the opportunity to shove my dick in her, and maybe even arranged it so a Brennan bastard was inside her to ensure the Bratva could never touch me again.

"What do you want?" Vasily demanded, darting up from his leather seat. "You obviously came here for retaliation, so just spit it out. And no, my daughter cannot be a part of the deal. She is an innocent. We have a code," he growled.

"*You* have a code," I corrected. "I lack morals and fucks. So it is either my way or the highway, and considering you were very close to sending me to an early grave, you better take my terms, no stipulations and no negotiations."

"Speak!" Vasily slapped a hand over his desk, seething. "And put her down, for God's sake!"

"I'll give you back Brookline, but you will hand me monthly protection money. A percentage of all your businesses," I said flatly.

Vasily's eyes narrowed.

"Protection from what? We are the Bratva! We protect ourselves."

"Hey, I never promised to make sense." I shrugged, and Masha moaned against my shoulder, weeping through the cloth covering her mouth. "But right now, I have soldiers everywhere in your territory. I am making more money than you ever did here. If you want me to retreat, you need to make it worth my while."

Vasily stroked his chin, considering my proposition. His men were ready for battle—I could tell by the way their muscles bunched under their shirts.

"Have you touched her?" he asked, his Russian accent thickly coating each word with worry.

"No," I said honestly. "I require my women to be willing and conscious."

I also prefer them to be just one woman—Aisling. I still couldn't believe she made me go through with this. Give up such a strategic part of Boston. Love was a bitch, but it was something I had to endure in order to keep Nix.

"Put her down," Vasily repeated, his voice shaking slightly. In all the time I'd known him, Vasily Mikhailov's voice had never wavered. He was scared.

"Concede," I hissed.

He lowered his head, so close to defeat the despair was tangible in the air.

"What's your protection rate?"

"Eight percent of all your businesses' clean profit."

"Six," he clipped, jotting down something on a piece of paper resting on his desk, already making the calculation.

"Eight. Love is priceless, Mikhailov," I reminded him.

He looked up. "Fine. Now put her down."

I put Masha on the floor. She flailed, her eyes erratically looking for her father among the shadows of people in the room. Vasily ran to her, crouching down and removing a knife from his Italian loafers. He began tearing the ropes that tied her together, whispering Russian endearments in her ear, his face contorted with emotion.

Troy put a hand on my shoulder.

"Time to go, son."

"All right, Dad."

It was the first time I called him Dad, but I knew it was not going to be the last.

I turned around and followed him, feeling him smiling, even with his back to me.

For the first time since I was born, I felt something foreign and addictive.

I belonged.

Epilogue

Aisling

"Just for the record, I will never forgive you." My mother scooped her Hermes bag from the chapel's floor, her heels clicking provocatively as she sashayed outside.

My father stood behind her, shrugging helplessly, a what-can-you-do expression on his face. Troy and Sparrow were behind them, gathering their belongings.

"She can and will forgive you. Dinner is at eight. Please don't be late." He kissed both my cheeks, giving Sam, who stood by my side, a firm handshake.

Belle was the next person to slide out of her pew.

"I can't believe you." She bristled in delight, clutching my arms, shaking me a little. "You actually went ahead with it."

"A Vegas wedding." Persephone slid from the same pew, Cillian standing right next to her. Persy held her tummy, in which my next nephew or niece was cooking quite nicely. "Who would have thought?"

"I would," Sam cut harshly through everyone's coos and murmurs. "Seeing as Aisling wasn't the only person to get married today. Besides, it was a classy Vegas wedding."

"That's an oxymoron," Cillian pointed out.

"No, he is right. It was totally classy." Sailor's face popped out of nowhere. Hunter stood close to her. "Nothing says elegance quite like being married by Elvis himself while a bunch of aging men dressed like *NSync sing a botched karaoke version of 'It's Gonna Be Me' in the background. Isn't that what Prince William and Kate did for their wedding?" Sailor frowned, curling her fingers under her chin thoughtfully.

"I do believe Wills and Kate had Take That wannabes singing 'Relight my Fire' at the reception," Devon interrupted, clearing his throat. The British man seemed so out of place at the cheesy chapel, I let out a giggle.

"We couldn't afford to wait." I bit down on my lip. "My residency is starting in a couple of weeks, and I wouldn't have time to plan my lunch breaks, let alone a wedding, not to mention—"

"I knocked her up." Sam delivered the news flatly, no hint of emotions in his voice. I whipped my head toward him, shocked that he let our secret out and grateful that my parents weren't in our vicinity anymore.

Sam kept his eyes on our friends, not me, while I very possibly blushed myself into an early grave inside my respectable white dress.

"Aisling wanted to wait until her residency was over, but my sperm had other ideas."

"What do you mean?" Persy frowned, her hand moving in circles around her belly.

"Did the condom break?" Belle interfered, keeping it blunt. "Do you buy cheap-ass johnnies, Samuel? Or did you poke holes in it with a needle? I heard a rock star autobiography where something like that happened to him. Okay, fine, watched a movie."

"Phew," Hunter laughed, "for a second there I thought you started reading."

"I'm sorry, isn't the illiterate idiot convention next door?" Cillian inquired tersely. "I believe Samuel and Aisling are trying to break the news of a new pregnancy in the family."

"Hell, bro," Hunter snorted. "I'm just trying to take your mind off the fact that Brennan sexed our baby sister up."

"Hunter!" Everyone shrieked in unison, other than Emmabelle, who laughed, enjoying herself, and Devon, who was too busy staring at Belle to care what everyone was saying.

"Anyway, no." I shook my head. "I was on the pill and was very good about it. There's always a very slight chance the pill won't work. And I guess it happened to me." I grinned, looking up at Sam while he pressed a proud kiss to my forehead.

Two months after Sam told Vasily Mikhailov he could have Brookline back, we went out to celebrate the fact I got accepted to a nearby hospital to begin my residency. It was my favorite Thai place, and even though we had a wonderful time, I went to bed feeling ill. When I woke up the next morning, I puked my guts out and figured something must have upset my stomach.

But then it happened the morning after.

And after.

And after.

"When's the last time you had your period?" Sam had questioned when I closed in on a week of throwing up each morning and feeling miraculously better during the rest of the day. "Because we've been having sex every day for at least nine weeks in a row now."

I'd scrunched my nose, thinking about it.

My cycles were pretty regular, and besides, I was on the pill.

"I can't be pregnant," I'd said finally.

"Can't or don't want to be?" Sam had raised an eyebrow.

"Both?" I'd winced, but deep down I knew there wouldn't be one part of me that would be upset if I found out I was pregnant.

"I'll go get us a pregnancy test right now."

"Thank you."

And here we were a week later, married in Vegas in front of our closest friends and family. I'd always imagined having a grand, fancy wedding, but as soon as I realized I was pregnant, I knew a massive wedding wasn't what I wanted. It was simply what was expected of me. What I really wanted was to be married to the man of my dreams as soon as humanly possible.

The man who had given me a new ferret for my last birthday and didn't even look surprised or put off by the fact I had named it Shelly, after my previous ferret.

Besides, as Sam had pointed out, he won our marriage in a card game. It was only fitting we would get married in the gambling capital of the world. The symmetry of the narrative pleased me.

Two monsters, promising their lives to one another in Sin City.

"I bet Sam managed to knock you up somehow when he realized the kind of wedding your parents wanted you to have would take half a century to plan." Sailor laughed, side-eyeing her brother knowingly.

I looked up to my husband and noticed the sly smile on his face.

He couldn't have.

He wouldn't … would he?

Cocking my head slightly, I narrowed my eyes at him.

"Sam?" I asked.

My husband pressed a kiss to my mouth.

"I'm the fixer," was all he said, keeping it at that.

I had never told anyone what the last thing Ms. B told me right after she demanded I stop visiting to help her.

"I can't handle you anymore, but one day you'll find a man who can. And when you find him, mon cheri, you hold onto him, no matter what, for he will bend to your will, even though he'll put up a fight."

I opened my eyes, looked up at my husband of ten minutes, and smiled.

I feared no evil.

But I did fall in love with one.

Sam

Four months later.

CILLIAN DROPPED HIS CARDS ON THE TABLE IN BADLAND'S card room, glancing at his phone with a frown. "I'm out."

"You're out?" Hunter echoed, eyeing his older brother with apparent shock. "You're never out."

"I am when my wife's water breaks." Cillian tossed his cards onto Hunter's lap, his shoulder brushing mine as I leaned over the table to grab another card. Cillian stopped to raise his finger toward me in warning.

"Your smug smirk is unwarranted, Brennan. Not only are you next, but knowing my sister, she'll have four children at the very least. Good luck getting some sleep in the next decade or so."

He made a quick exit before I could respond that nothing could persuade me a pregnant Aisling was a bad idea. Nix had never been hornier in her entire fucking life. I was on-call three times a day for dick duty, even though she was still working long hours at the hospital most days.

She also turned out to have a sweet tooth, which meant I had to feed her candy and chocolate whenever her heart desired.

At night, I'd slip under the covers next to her and press my hand to her swollen stomach, feeling my son kicking up a storm. He was so alive and happy inside her, I couldn't wait to meet him.

"As it happens, my revenge for the smirk-fest just walked

through the door in the shape of your very pregnant wife. Hello, sis," I heard Cillian drawl behind my back. I turned around to find Nix standing there just as Cillian bent to kiss her on the cheek, her belly poking out in her scrubs, a tired smile on her face.

"Five games of blackjack, Brennan?" She offered me a hand, drawing curious glances from all the men around us.

I very rarely stayed at Badlands after dark these days, and when I did, it was mostly to keep my brothers-in-law in check.

"What's the stakes?" I eyed her skeptically. "Make it worth my while, Mrs. Brennan. I already have everything I need."

She sauntered toward me, a taunting smirk on her face, and bent toward my ear. The whole room held its breath.

"You'll get to rip off the red satin lingerie I'm wearing right now if you win," she whispered.

Nix leaned backward, straightening her back.

"And if you win?" I asked nonchalantly.

She wasn't going to win.

I always won.

"I want us to buy a house. I like our apartment fine, don't get me wrong, but I want somewhere big and spacious."

"Somewhere to fit all the kids you are planning on giving him," Hunter coughed into his fist in the background, drawing laughter.

Aisling offered me her hand again, staring at me under her soot-black eyelashes. "What do you say?"

I took her hand and shook it.

She didn't have to know I'd already purchased the land right next to her parents' house and that I was going to build the house of her dreams there.

Just like she didn't know about that night at the carnival, when I had locked myself in the portable restroom after kissing her because for the first time since I was nine, facing the world was too much.

Lust lingers, love stays.

Lust is impatient, love waits.

Lust burns, love warms.
Lust destroys, but love? Love kills.
S.A.B.
I was wrong. Love didn't kill me. Love saved me.
Aisling was going to find out about both my surprises soon.
But not yet.
Not until I tore the satin lingerie off of her.
And showed her that everyone could love.
But monsters? We loved a little harder.

The End

Acknowledgements

Thank you so much for taking the time to read this book. I loved telling the story of Sam and Aisling, and the moment I wrote The End was bittersweet, since this series means so much to me.

I couldn't have done this without my amazing team of editors: Tamara Mataya, Paige Maroney Smith, and Angela Marshall Smith. Special thanks to Tijuana Turner, Vanessa Villegas, Lana Kart, Chelsea Humphrey and Amy Halter for reading this book beforehand.

Kimberly Brower, Jenn Watson, Catherine Anderson—thank you so much for all you do.

Stacey Ryan Blake and Letitia Hasser—your work is beyond amazing, I am so grateful to have you.

And to you, the readers, bloggers and supporters. I couldn't have done this without you.

Please consider leaving a brief, honest review before you move on to your next book adventure.

Love,

L.J. Shen.

Stay connected

Join my Newsletter
http://eepurl.com/b8pSuP

Follow me on Instagram
www.instagram.com/authorljshen

Add me on Facebook
www.facebook.com/authorljshen

Also by

L.J. SHEN

Sinners of Saint:
Defy (#0.5)
Vicious (#1)
Ruckus (#2)
Scandalous (#3)
Bane (#4)

All Saints High:
Pretty Reckless (#1)
Broken Knight (#2)
Angry God (#3)

Boston Belles:
The Hunter (#1)
The Villain (#2)
The Monster (#3)
The Take (#4, TBA 2022)

Standalones:
Tyed
Sparrow
Blood to Dust
Midnight Blue
Dirty Headlines
In the Unlikely Event
The Kiss Thief
Playing with Fire
The Devil Wears Black

Before you go, here's a small excerpt of Pretty Reckless. If you enjoy the world of Boston Belles, you will love All Saints High…

Prologue

It started with a lemonade
And ended with my heart
This, my pretty reckless rival, is how our screwed-up story starts

Age Fourteen.

Daria

T HE TILES UNDER MY FEET SHAKE AS A HERD OF BALLERINAS blazes past me, their feet pounding like artillery in the distance.

Brown hair. Black hair. Straight hair. Red hair. Curly hair. They blur into a rainbow of trims and scrunchies. My eyes are searching for the blond head I'd like to bash against the well-worn floor.

Feel free not to be here today, Queen Bitch.

I stand frozen on the threshold of my mother's ballet studio, my pale pink leotard sticking to my ribs. My white duffel bag dangles from my shoulder. My tight bun makes my scalp burn. Whenever I let my hair down, my golden locks fall off in chunks on the bathroom floor. I tell Mom it's from messing with my hair too much, but that's BS. And if she gave a damn—*really* gave one, not just pretended to—she'd know this, too.

I wiggle my banged-up toes in my pointe shoes, swallowing the ball of anxiety in my throat. Via isn't here. *Thank you, Marx.*

Girls torpedo past me, bumping into my shoulders. I feel their giggles in my empty stomach. My duffel bag falls with a thud. My classmates are leaner, longer, and more flexible with rod-straight backs like an exclamation mark. Me? I'm small and muscular like a question mark. Always unsure and on the verge of snapping. My face is not stoic and regal; it's traitorous and unpredictable. Some wear their hearts on their sleeves—I wear mine on my mouth. I smile with my teeth when I'm happy, and when my mom looks at me, I'm always happy.

"You should really take gymnastics or cheer, Lovebug. It suits you so much better than ballet."

But Mom sometimes says things that dig at my self-esteem. There's a rounded dent on its surface now, the shape of her words, and that's where I keep my anger.

Melody Green-Followhill is a former ballerina who broke her leg during her first week at Juilliard when she was eighteen. Ballet has been expected of me since the day I was born. And—just my luck—I happen to be exceptionally bad at it.

Enter Via Scully.

Also fourteen, Via is everything I strive to be. Taller, blonder, and skinnier. Worst of all, her natural talent makes my dancing look like an insult to leotards all over the world.

Three months ago, Via received a letter from the Royal Ballet Academy asking her to audition. Four weeks ago—she did. Her hot-shot parents couldn't get the time off work, so my mom jumped at the chance to fly her on a weeklong trip to London. Now the entire class is waiting to hear if Via is going to study at the Royal Ballet Academy. Word around the studio is she has it in the bag. Even the Ukrainian danseur Alexei Petrov—a sixteen-year-old prodigy who is like the Justin Bieber of ballet—posted an IG story with her after the audition.

Looking forward to creating magic together.

It wouldn't surprise me to learn Via can do magic. She's always been a witch.

"Lovebug, stop fretting by the door. You're blocking everyone's way," my mother singsongs with her back to me. I can see her reflection through the floor-to-ceiling mirror. She's frowning at the attendance sheet and glancing at the door, hoping to see Via.

Sorry, Mom. Just your spawn over here.

Via is always late, and my mother, who never tolerates tardiness, lets her get away with it.

I bend down to pick up my duffel bag and pad into the studio. A shiny barre frames the room, and a floor-to-ceiling window displays downtown Todos Santos in all its photogenic, upper-crust glory. Peach-colored benches grace tree-lined streets, and crystal blue towers sparkle like the thin line where the ocean kisses the sky.

I hear the door squeaking open and squeeze my eyes shut.

Please don't be here.

"Via! We've been waiting for you," Mom's chirp is like a BB gun shooting me in the back, and I tumble over my own feet from the shockwave. Snorts explode all over the room. I manage to grip the barre, pulling myself up a second before my knees hit the floor. Flushed, I grasp it in one hand and slide into a sloppy plié.

"Lovebug, be a darling and make some room for Via," Mom purrs.

Symbolically, Mother, I'd love for Via to make my ass some room, too.

Of course, her precious prodigy isn't wearing her ballet gear today even though she owns Italian-imported leotards other girls can only dream of. Via clearly comes from money because even rich people don't like shelling out two hundred bucks for a basic leotard. Other than Mom—who probably figures I'll never be a true ballerina so the least she can do is dress me up like one.

Today, Via is wearing a cropped yellow Tweety Bird shirt and ripped leggings. Her eyes are red, and her hair is a mess. Does she even make an effort?

She throws me a patronizing smirk. "*Lovebug.*"

"*Puppy,*" I retort.

"Puppy?" She snorts.

"I'd call you a bitch, but let's admit it, your bite doesn't really have teeth."

I readjust my shoes, pretending that I'm over her. I'm *not* over her. She monopolizes my mother's time, and she's been on my case way before I started talking back. Via attends another school in San Diego. She claims it's because her parents think the kids in Todos Santos are too sheltered and spoiled. Her parents want her to grow up with *real* people.

Know what else is fake? Pretending to be something you're not. I own up to the fact I'm a prissy princess. Sue me (Please do. I can afford really good legal defense).

"Meet me after class, Vi," Mom quips, then turns back around to the stereo. Vi *(Vi!)* uses the opportunity to stretch her leg, stomping on my toes in the process.

"Oops. Looks like you're not the only clumsy person around here, Daria."

"I would tell you to drop dead, but I'm afraid my mom would force me to go to your funeral, and you legit aren't worth my time."

"I would tell you to kiss my ass, but your mom already does that. If she only liked you half as much as she likes me. It's cool, though; at least you have money for therapy. And a nose job." She pats my back with a smirk, and I hate, *hate*, **hate** that she is prettier.

I can't concentrate for the rest of the hour. I'm not stupid. Even though I know my mother loves me more than Via, I also know it's because she's genetically programmed to do so.

Centuries tick by, but the class is finally dismissed. All the girls sashay to the elevator in pairs.

"Daria darling, do me a favor and get us drinks from Starbucks. I'm going to the little girls' room, then wrapping something up real quick with Vi." Mom pats my shoulder, then saunters out of the studio, leaving a trail of her perfume like fairy dust. My mom would donate all her organs to save one of her students' fingernails. She smothers her ballerinas with love, leaving me saddled me with jealousy.

I grab Mom's bag and turn around before I have a chance to exchange what Daddy calls "unpleasantries" with Via.

"You should've seen her face when I auditioned." Via stretches in front of the mirror behind me. She's as agile as a contortionist. Sometimes I think she could wrap herself around my neck and choke me to death.

"We had a blast. She told me that by the looks of it, not only am I in, but I'm also going to be their star student. It felt kind of..." She snaps her fingers, looking for the word. I see her in the reflection of the mirror but don't turn around. Tears are hanging on my lower lashes for their dear lives. "A redemption, or something. Like you can't be a ballerina because you're so, you know, *you*. But then there's *me*. So at least she'll get to see someone she loves make it."

Daddy says a green Hulk lives inside me, and he gets bigger and bigger when I get jealous, and sometimes, the Hulk blasts through my skin and does things the Daria he knows and loves would never do. He says jealousy is the tribute mediocrity pays to genius, and I'm no mediocre girl.

Let's just say I disagree.

I've always been popular, and I've always fought hard for a place in the food chain where I can enjoy the view. But I think I'm ordinary. Via is extraordinary and glows so bright, she burns everything in her vicinity. I'm the dust beneath her feet, and I'm crushed, and bitter, and *Hulky*.

Nobody *wants* to be a bad person. But some people—like me—just can't help themselves. A tear rolls down my cheek, and I'm thankful we're alone. I turn around to face her.

"What the hell is your problem?"

"What isn't?" She sighs. "You are a spoiled princess, a shallow idiot, and a terrible dancer. How can someone so untalented be born to *the* Melody Green-Followhill?"

I don't know! I want to scream. *No one wants to be born to a genius. Marx, bless Sean Lennon for surviving his own existence.*

I eye her pricey pointe shoes and arch a mocking eyebrow. "Don't pretend I'm the only princess here."

"You're an airhead, Daria." She shakes her head.

"At least I'm not a spaz." I pretend to be blasé, but my whole body is shaking.

"You can't even get into a decent first position." She throws her hands in the air. She isn't wrong, and that enrages me.

"Again—why. Do. You. Care!" I roar.

"Because you're a waste of fucking space, that's why! While I'm busting my ass, you get a place in this class just because your mother is the teacher,."

This is my chance to tell her the truth.

That I'm busting mine even harder, precisely because I wasn't born a ballerina. Instead, my heart shatters like glass. I spin on my heel and dart down the fire escape, taking the stairs two at a time. I pour myself out into the blazing California heat. Any other girl would take a left and disappear inside Liberty Park, but I take a right and enter Starbucks because I can't—*won't*—disappoint my mom more than I already have. I look left and right to make sure the coast is clear, then release the sob that has weighed on my chest for the past hour. I get into line, tugging open Mom's purse from her bag as I wipe my tears away with my sleeve. Something falls to the floor, so I pick it up.

It's a crisp letter with my home address on it, but the name gives me pause.

Sylvia Scully.

Sniffing, I rip the letter open. I don't stop to think that it isn't mine to open. Seeing Via's mere name above my address makes me want to scream until the walls in this place fall. The first thing that registers is the symbol at the top.

The Royal Ballet Academy.

My eyes are like a wonky mixed tape. They keep rewinding to the same words.

Acceptance Letter.

Acceptance Letter.

Acceptance Letter.

Via got accepted. I should be thrilled she'll be out of my hair in a few months, but instead, the acidic taste of envy bursts inside my mouth.

She has everything.

The parents. The money. The fame. The talent. Most of all—my mother's undivided attention.

She has everything, and I have nothing, and the Hulk inside me grows larger. His body so huge it presses against my diaphragm.

A whole new life in one envelope. *Via's* life hanging by a paper. A paper that's in my hand.

"Sweetie? Honey?" The barista snaps me out of my trance with a tone that suggests I'm not a sweetie nor a honey. "What would you like?"

For Via to die.

I place my order and shuffle to the corner of the room so I can read the letter for the thousandth time. As if the words will change by some miracle.

Five minutes later, I take both drinks and exit on to the sidewalk. I dart to the nearest trash can to dispose of my iced tea lemonade so I can hold the letter without dampening it. Mom probably wanted to open it with Via, and I just took away their little moment.

Sorry to interrupt your bonding sesh.

"Put the drink down, and nobody gets hurt," booms a voice behind me, like liquid honey, as my hand hovers over the trash can. It's male, but he's young. I spin in place, not sure I heard him right. His chin dipped low, I can't see his face clearly because of a Raiders ball cap that's been worn to death. He's tall and scrawny—almost scarily so—but he glides toward me like a Bengal tiger. As if he's found a way to walk on air and can't be bothered with mundane things like muscle tone.

"Are we throwing this away?" He points at the lemonade.

We? Bitch, at this point, there's not even a you to me.

I motion to him with the drink. He can have the stupid iced tea lemonade. Gosh. He is interrupting my meltdown for a lemonade.

"Nothing's free in this world, Skull Eyes."

I blink, willing him to evaporate from my vision. Did this jackass really just call me Skull Eyes? At least I don't look like a skeleton. My mind is upstairs with Via. Why does Mom receive letters on her behalf? Why couldn't they send it directly to Via's house? Is Mom adopting her ass now?

I think about my sister, Bailey. At only nine, she already shows promise as a gifted dancer. Via moving to London might encourage Mom to put Bailey in the Royal Ballet Academy, too. Mom had talked about me applying there before it became clear that I could be a Panera bagel before I'd become a professional ballerina. I begin to glue the pieces of my screwed-up reality together.

What if I had to migrate to London to watch both girls make it big while I swam in my pool of mediocrity?

Bailey and Via would become BFFs.

I'd have to live somewhere rainy and gray.

We'd leave Vaughn and Knight and even Luna behind. All my childhood friends.

Via would officially take my place in Mom's heart.

Hmm, no thanks.

Not today, Satan.

When I don't answer, the boy takes a step toward me. I'm not scared although…maybe I should be? He's wearing dirty jeans—I'm talking mud and dust, not, like, purposely haphazard—and a worn blue shirt that looks two sizes too big with a hole the size of a small fist where his heart is. Someone wrote around it in a black Sharpie and girlie handwriting, *Is it a sign?—Adriana, xoxo* and I want to know if Adriana is prettier than me.

"Why are you calling me Skull Eyes?" I clench the letter in my fist.

"Because." He slopes his head so low all I can see are his lips, and they look petal-soft and pink. Feminine, almost. His voice is smooth to a point it hurts a little in my chest. I don't know why. Guys my age are revolting to me. They smell like pizza that has sat in the sun for days. "You have skulls in your eyes, Silly Billy. Know what you need?"

For Mom to stop telling me that I suck?

For Via to disappear?

Take your pick, dude.

I shove my free hand into my mom's wallet and pluck out a ten-dollar bill. He looks as if he could use a meal. I pray he'll take it before Mom comes down and starts asking questions. I'm not supposed to talk to strangers, much less strangers who look like they are dumpster diving for their next meal.

"Sea glass." He thrusts his hand in my direction, ignoring the money and the drink.

"Like the stuff you get on Etsy?" I huff.

Great. You're a weirdo, too.

"Huh? Nah, that shit's trash. Orange sea glass. The real stuff. Found it on the beach last week and Googled it. It's the rarest thing in the world, you know?"

"Why would you give a total stranger something so precious?" I roll my eyes.

"Why not?"

"Um, hello, attention span much? Weren't you the one who just said nothing in this world is free?"

"Who said it's free? Did you get all your annual periods today at once or something?"

"Don't talk about my period!"

"Fine. No period talk. But you need a real friend right now, and I'm officially applying for the position. I even dressed the part. Look." He motions to his hobo clothes with an apologetic smile.

And just like that, heat pours into my chest like hot wax. Anger, I find, has the tendency to be crisp. I really want to throat punch him. He pities me? *Pities.* The guy with the hole in his shirt.

"You want to be my friend?" I bark out a laugh. "Pathetic much? Like, who even says that?"

"Me. I say that. And I never claimed not to be pathetic." He tugs at his ripped shirt and raises his head slowly, unveiling more of his face. A nose my mom would call Roman and a jaw that's too square for someone my age. He's all sharp angles, and maybe one day he will be handsome, but right now, he looks like an anime cartoon character. Mighty Max.

"Look, do you want the lemonade and money or not? My mom should be here any minute."

"And?"

"And she can't see us together."

"Because of how I look?"

Duh.

"No, because you're a boy." I don't want to be mean to him even though, usually, I am. Especially to boys. Especially to boys with beautiful faces and honey voices.

Boys can smell heartbreak from across a continent. Even at fourteen. Even in the middle of an innocent summer afternoon. We girls have an invisible string behind our belly button, and only certain guys can tug at it.

This boy...he will snap it if I let him.

"Take the sea glass. Owe me something." He motions to me with an open palm. I stare at the ugly little rock. My fist clenches around the letter. The paper hisses.

The boy lifts his head completely, and our eyes meet. He studies me with quiet interest as though I'm a painting, not a person. My heart is rioting all over, and the dumbest thought crosses my mind. Ever notice how the heart is *literally* caged by the ribs? That's insane. As if our body knows it can break so easily, it needs to be protected. White dots fill my vision, and he's swimming somewhere behind them, against the stream.

"What's in the letter?" he asks.

"My worst nightmare."

"Give it to me," he orders, so I do. I don't know why. Most likely because I want to get rid of it. Because I want Via to hurt as much as I do. Because I want Mom to be upset. *Marx, what's wrong with me?* I'm a horrible person.

His eyes are still on mine as he tears the letter to shreds and lets the pieces float like confetti into the trash can between us. His eyes are dark green and bottomless like a thickly fogged forest. I want to step inside and run until I'm in the depth of the woods. Something occurs to me just then.

"You're not from here," I say. He is too pure. Too good. Too real.

He shakes his head slowly. "Mississippi. Well, my dad's family. Anyway. Owe me something," he repeats, almost begging.

Why does he want me to owe him something?

So he could ask for something back.

I don't relent, frozen to my spot. Instead, I hand him the lemonade. He takes it, closes the distance between us, pops the lid open, and pours the contents all over the ruined letter. His body brushes against mine. We're stomach to stomach. Legs to legs. Heart to heart.

"Close your eyes."

His voice is gruff and thick and different. This time, I surrender.

I know what's about to happen, and I'm letting it happen anyway. My first kiss.

I always thought it would happen with a football player or a pop star or a European exchange student. Someone outside of the small borders of my sheltered, Instagram-filtered world. Not with a kid who has a hole in his shirt. But I need this. Need to feel desired and pretty and wanted.

His lips flutter over mine, and it tickles, so I snort. I can feel his warm breath skating across my lips, his baseball cap grazing my forehead and the way his mouth slides against mine, lips locking with uncertainty. I forget to breathe for a second, my hands on his shoulders, but then something inside me begs me to dart my tongue out and really taste him. We're sucking air from each other's mouths. We're doing it all wrong. My lips open for him. His open, too. My heart is pounding so hard I can feel the blood whooshing in my veins when he says, "Not yet. I'll take that, too, but not yet."

A groan escapes my lips.

"What would you have asked of me if I took the sea glass?"

"To save me all your firsts," he whispers somewhere between my ear and mouth as his body brushes away from mine.

I don't want to open my eyes and let the moment end. But he makes the choice for both of us. The warmth of his body leaves mine as he takes a step back.

I still don't have the guts to open my mouth and ask for his name.

Ten, fifteen, twenty seconds pass.

My eyelids flutter open on their own accord as my body begins to sway.

He's gone.

Disoriented, I lean against the trash can, fiddling with the strap of my mother's bag. Five seconds pass before Mom loops her arm around mine out of nowhere and leads me to the Range Rover. My legs fly across the pavement. My head twists back.

Blue shirt? Ball cap? Petal lips? Did I imagine the whole thing?

"There you are. Thanks for the coffee. What, no iced tea lemonade today?"

After I fail to answer, we climb into her vehicle and buckle up. Mom sifts through her Prada bag resting on the center console.

"Huh. I swear I took four letters from the mailbox today, not three."

And that's when it hits me—*she doesn't know.* Via got in, and she has no idea the letter came today. Then this guy tore it apart because it upset me…

Kismet. Kiss-met. Fate.

Dad decided two years ago that he was tired of hearing all three girls in the household moaning, "Oh, my God," so now we have to replace the word *God* with the word *Marx*, after Karl Marx, a dude who was apparently into atheism or whatever. I feel like God or Marx—*someone*—sent this boy to help me. If he were even real. Maybe I made him up in my head to come to terms with what I did.

I open a compact mirror and apply some lip gloss, my heart racing.

"You're always distracted, Mom. If you dropped a letter, you'd have seen it."

Mom pouts, then nods. In the minute it takes her to start the engine, I realize two things:

One—she was expecting this letter like her next breath.

Two—she is devastated.

"Before I forget, Lovebug, I bought you the diary you wanted." Mom produces a thick black-cased leather notebook from her Prada bag and hands it to me. I noticed it before, but I never assume things are for me anymore. She's always distracted, buying Via all types of gifts.

As we ride in silence, I have an epiphany.

This is where I'll write my sins.

This is where I'll bury my tragedies.

I snap the mirror shut and tuck my hands into the pockets of my white hoodie, where I find something small and hard. I take it out and stare at it, amazed.

The orange sea glass.

He gave me the sea glass even though I never accepted it.

Save me all your firsts.

I close my eyes and let a fat tear roll down my cheek.

He was real.

Penn

Question: Who gives their most precious belonging to a girl they don't know?

Answer: This motherfucker right here. Print me an "I'm with stupid" shirt with an arrow pointing straight to my dick.

Could've sold the damn thing and topped off Via's cell phone credit. Now that ship's sailed. I can spot it in the distance, sinking quickly.

The worst part is that I knew nothing would come out of it. At fourteen, I've only kissed two girls. They both had enormous tongues and too much saliva. This girl looked like her tongue would be small, so I couldn't pass up trying.

But the minute my lips touched hers, I just couldn't do it. She looked kind of manic. Sad. Clingy? I don't fucking know. Maybe I just didn't have the balls. Maybe watching her three times a week from afar paralyzed me.

Hey, how do you turn off your own mind? It needs to shut up. Now.

My friend Kannon passes me the joint on my front porch. That's the one perk of having your mom live with her drug-dealing boyfriend. Free pot. And since food is scarce these days, I'll take whatever is on the table.

A bunch of wannabe gangsters in red bandanas cross our side of the street with their pit bulls and a boom box playing angry Spanish rap. The dogs bark, yanking on their chains. Kannon barks right back at them. He's so high his head might hit a fucking plane. I take a hit, then hand Camilo the joint.

"I'll lend you fifty so you can make the call." Camilo coughs. He is huge and tan and already has impressive facial hair. He looks like someone's Mexican dad.

"We don't need to call anyone!" my twin sister yells from the grass next to us. She is lying face down, sobbing into the yellow lawn. I think she is hoping the sun will burn her into the ground.

"Are y'all deaf or something?! I didn't get in!"

"We'll take the money." I ignore her. We have to call the ballet place. Via can't stay here. It ain't safe.

"I love you, Penn, but you're a pain in the ass." She hiccups, plucking blades of grass and throwing them in our direction without lifting her head. She'll thank me later. When she is famous and rich—do ballerinas get rich?—and I'm still sitting here with my dumb friends smoking pot and salivating over lemon-haired Todos Santos girls. Maybe I won't have to stand on street corners and deal. I'm good at shit. Sports and fighting mainly. Coach says I need to eat more protein for muscle and more carbs to get some body fat, but that's not happening anytime soon because most of my money is spent buying Via's bus tickets to her ballet classes.

I tag along because I'm hella worried about her riding on that bus alone. Especially in winter when it gets dark early.

"I thought you said your sister's good? How come she didn't get in?" Kannon yawns, moving his hand over his long dreads. The sides of his head are shaved, creating a black man-bun. I punch his arm so hard he collapses back on the rocking chair with a silent scream, clutching his bicep, still hardy-har-harring.

"I think a demonstration is in order. Chop-chop, Via. Show us your moves." Cam puts "Milkshake" by Kelis on his phone, balling a gum wrapper in his hand and throwing it at the back of her head.

Her sobs stop, replaced with catatonic silence. I turn around, scrubbing my chin before twisting back to Camilo and swinging a fist at his jaw. I hear it unlock from its usual place and him *harrumphing*.

Darting up from the grass, Via runs into the house and slams the door behind her. I'm not sure what business she has sitting in the living room when Rhett is home, griping about being tired and hungry. She will probably get into a screaming match with him and return to the porch with her tail between her legs. My mom is too high to interfere, but even when she does, she chooses her boyfriend's side. Even when he uses Via's leotards, which her teacher buys for her, to shine his shoes. He does that often to get a rise out of her. On days she shows up to class in her torn leggings and hand-me-down shirts, she spends the bus ride sobbing. Those are usually the days when I rub his briefs on the public toilet seats in Liberty Park.

It's incredibly therapeutic.

"Hand me the fifty." I open my palm and turn to Cam, who slaps the bill into my hand obediently. I'm going to buy myself and Via burgers the size of my face, then top the credit on her phone so she can call Mrs. Followhill.

I charge down my street to In-N-Out, Camilo and Kannon trailing me like the wind. Cracked concrete and murals of dead teenagers wearing halos line the street. Our palm trees seem to hunch down from the burden of poverty, leaning over buildings that are short and yellow like bad teeth.

But twenty minutes later, the satisfaction of clutching a paper bag filled with greasy burgers and fries is overwhelming. Via's gonna forget all about her meltdown when she sees it. I push the door to my house open, and the first thing I see makes me drop the food to the floor.

My mother's boyfriend is straddling my sister on the couch, his jiggling belly pouring out on her chest. He pummels her face, his sweaty, hairy chest glistening and his arm flexing every time he does. His ripped jeans are unbuttoned, and his zipper is all the way down. She is wheezing and coughing, trying to breathe. Without thinking, I dash toward them and unplaster him from her. Her face is bloody, and she's croaking out weak protests, telling him that he's a cheap bastard, and he keeps yelling that she is a thieving whore. I grab Rhett by the collar of his shirt and pull him from her. He swings with the momentum, falling on the floor. I punch his face so hard, the sound of his jaw cracking echoes around the room. He whips his head back, hitting the floor. I spin back to Via, and all I see is her back as she slides through her own blood, tripping to the door. I grab her wrist, but she wiggles free. Something falls between us with a soft click. I pick it up, and it looks like a tooth. Jesus fucking Christ. He knocked her tooth out.

"I'm sorry," she says, her voice muffled from the blood in her mouth. "I'm sorry. I can't, Penn."

"Via!" I cry out.

"Please," she yells. "Let me go."

I try to chase her, slipping in the trail of blood she leaves behind. My hands are covered in it now. I stand and start for the still-open door. A hand snatches me back and throws me on the couch.

"Not so quick, little asshole. Now's your turn."

I close my eyes and let it happen, knowing why Via has to run.

Geography is destiny.

It's been three days since Via ran away.

Two and a half since I've last managed to stomach anything without throwing it up (Pabst counts, right?).

After Rhett beat her up for stealing his phone and trying to call London, I'm not surprised she ain't back. I know better than to fuck with Rhett. Via is usually even more cautious with him because she's a girl. It was a moment of weakness on her part, and it cost her more than she was willing to pay.

On Friday afternoon, I find myself loitering outside her ballet class, hoping she'll appear. Maybe she's crashing at her teacher's house. They seem close, but it's hard to tell since Via puts on a mask every time the bus we board slides into the city limits of Todos Santos. The fact she hasn't touched base yet makes me heave when I think about it. I'm telling myself she has her reasons.

At six, pink-wearing girls start pouring out of the building. I dawdle by the shiny black Range Rover with my hands in my pockets, waiting for the teacher. She comes out last, waving and laughing with a bunch of students. Another girl walks beside her. The girl I kissed, to be exact. The girl I've been obsessing over for a year, to be super-exact. She is beautiful like the shit hanging in the museums. In a really sad, distant, look-but-don't-touch way. I trek toward them, and they meet me halfway. The girl's eyes widen, and she looks sideways to see if anyone else is here to witness us talking. She thinks I'm here for her.

"Hi." She tucks hair behind her ears, her gaze traveling to Mrs. Followhill in a silent I-swear-I-don't-know-this-guy plea.

"Hey." I kill the butterflies in my stomach because now's not the place and definitely not the time, then turn to the teacher. "Ma'am, my sister, Via, is in your class. I haven't seen her in three days."

The teacher's eyebrows pinch together as though I just announced I'll be taking a shit on the hood of her vehicle. She tells the blonde to wait inside the giant Range Rover, then tugs at my arm, heading toward an alleyway. Sandwiched between two buildings, she sort of forces me to sit down on a tall step (dafuq?) and starts talking.

"I've been calling her five times a day and leaving messages," she whispers hotly in my face. "I wanted to let her know she'd been accepted to the Royal Academy. When the letter never arrived, I called them to check. Everything is in motion now. As I said before, you needn't worry about the tuition. I'll be paying the fee."

My nostrils flare. All this in her future, and she could be lying in a ditch right now. Goddamn Via. Goddamn all pretty, volatile fourteen-year-old girls.

"Well, ma'am, thank you for the gift she'll never be able to cash in on since *we* can't find her," I respectfully mock her. But *we* is just me. Mom is out of it—she never really bothered bouncing out of her first drug binge some years ago—and Rhett is probably happy he has one less mouth to feed. When the truancy officer called from school earlier, I told him Via went to my aunt's, something my mother later confirmed when he showed up on our doorstep. Mom, wild-haired and sucking on a cigarette as if it were an oxygen mask, never once asked if it was true. If I call the police, they'll dump both our asses in foster care. Maybe together, but probably not. I can't let that happen. I can't be separated from Via.

Mrs. Followhill stares at me with an expression as if she just realized she caught a stomach bug. She is probably wondering how I dare speak to her like that. Usually, I'm a bit more user-friendly. Then again, I don't usually have to deal with a missing sister. I clean my mother's puke from the walls and close the bathroom door on Rhett when he falls asleep on the toilet seat. I don't look at grown-ups with the same air of reverence her daughter does.

"Whoa." That's all Mrs. Followhill says.

"Thanks for the insight. Have a nice life." I stand and swagger toward the street. She catches my arm and yanks me back. I twist around to face her.

"My daughter…" She licks her lips, then looks down, looks *guilty*. The girl is leaning against the Rover, staring at us, chewing on her thumbnail. "My daughter and Via haven't been getting along. I tried to encourage them to communicate, but the more I pushed them together, the more they seemed to dislike one another. I *think* I had a letter go missing last week. A letter that could have been…important. I don't even know why I'm telling you this." She lets out a breath, shaking her head. "I guess I just…I don't want to know, you know? I hate the fact that my mind is even going there."

But maybe it should.

The flashback crashes into my memory.

The paper that hissed in her little fist.

Me taking it from her.

Tearing it apart.

Throwing it into the trash can, watching her face blossom into bliss.

Pouring the lemonade on the remains for good measure when her blue eyes twinkled the request.

Setting my sister's dreams on fire.

Kicking this entire nightmare into motion.

My jaw flexes, and I take a step back. I throw one last glance at the chick, filing her into memory.

Archive under: Shit List.

Revisit document: When I'm able to ruin her.

"So Via's not with you?" My voice hardens around the words. Like tin. I'm desperate. I have no lead. I want to rip the world apart to find her, but the world is not mine to destroy. The world just continues turning at the same pace, because kids like Via and me? We disappear all the time, and no one notices.

Mrs. Followhill shakes her head. She hesitates, touching my arm. "Hey, why don't you come with me? I'll drop Daria off at home, and we can look for her."

Daria.

I turn around and stalk toward the bus stop, feeling stupid and hateful and alive. More alive than I've ever felt. Because I want to kill Daria. Daria made everything fade into the background the first time I saw her, and while I was busy admiring, everything around us burned.

You look like you could use a friend, I told her. Stupid boyish faith. I mentally throw it onto the ground and stomp on it on my way to the bus as it slides to the curb.

Daria was right. I was pathetic. Stupid. Blinded by her hair and lips and sweet melancholy.

Making a beeline to the bus stop, I hear Mrs. Followhill yelling my name behind me in the distance. She knows my name. She knows me. Us. I don't know why it disturbs me. I don't know why I still give a fuck that this girl knows I'm poor.

I hop on the first available bus, not sure where it will take me.

As far away from the girl, but not far enough from myself.

The burn in my chest intensifies, the hole around my heart growing bigger, and my grandmother whispers in the back of my mind.

Skull Eyes.

Pretty Reckless is available now